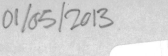

Pra

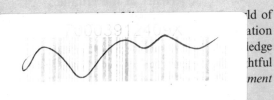

Deon Meyer lives and works in Melkbosstrand on the South African West Coast with his wife and four children. Other than his family, Deon's big passions are motor-cycling, music, reading, cooking and rugby. He has recently retired from his day job as a consultant on brand strategy for BMW Motorrad, and is now a full time author.

Deon Meyer's books have attracted worldwide critical acclaim and a growing international fanbase. Originally written in Afrikaans, they have now been translated into several languages, including English, French, Italian, Spanish, German, Dutch, Bulgarian, Czech, Danish and Norwegian.

Devil's Peak won South Africa's ATKV Prose Prize in 2004.

Devil's Peak

Deon Meyer

Translated by K L Seegers

HODDER

First published in Great Britain in 2007 by Hodder & Stoughton
An Hachette Livre UK company

First published in paperback in 2008

5

A CIP catalogue record for this title is available from the British Library.

ISBN 978 0 340 82266 1

Typeset in Plantin Light by Hewer Text UK Ltd, Edinburgh
Printed and bound by Clays Ltd, St Ives plc

Hodder & Stoughton policy is to use papers that are natural,
renewable and recyclable products and made from wood grown in
sustainable forests. The logging and manufacturing processes are expected
to conform to the environmental regulations of the country of origin.

Hodder & Stoughton Ltd
338 Euston Road
London NW1 3BH

www.hodder.co.uk

PART ONE

Christine

I

The moment before the clergyman folded back the carton flaps the world stood still and she saw everything with a greater clarity. The robust man in his middle years had a diamond-shaped birthmark on his cheek that looked like a distorted pale rose teardrop. His face was angular and strong, his thinning hair combed back, his hands massive and rough, like those of a boxer. The books behind him covered the whole wall in a mosaic of alternating colours. The late afternoon Free State sun threw a shaft of light onto the desktop, a magic sunbeam across the box.

She pressed her hands lightly against the coolness of her bare knees. Her hands were perspiring, her eyes searching for clues in the slightest shift of his expression, but she saw only calm, perhaps some suppressed, benign curiosity about the content of the carton. In the moment before he lifted the flaps, she tried to see herself as he saw her – evaluate the impression she was trying to create. The shops in town had been no help; she had to use what she had. Her hair was long, straight and clean, the multicoloured blouse sleeve-less; a shade too tight, perhaps, for this occasion, for him? A white skirt that had shifted up to just above her knees as she sat down. Her legs were smooth and lovely. White sandals. Little gold buckles. Her toenails unpainted, of that she had made sure. Just a single ring, a thin gold band on her right hand. Her make-up was light, delicately downplaying the fullness of her mouth.

Nothing to betray her. Apart from her eyes and her voice.

He lifted the flaps, one after the other, and she realised she was sitting on the edge of the armchair, leaning forward. She wanted to lean back, but not now, she must wait for his reaction.

The last flap was folded back, the box open.

'*Liewe Genade*,' he said in Afrikaans and half rose to his feet. *Sweet Mercy.*

He looked at her, but he seemed not to see her and his attention returned to the contents of the box. He thrust one of his big hands in, took something out and held it up to the sun.

'Sweet mercy,' he repeated with his hands in front of him. His fingers felt for authenticity.

She sat motionless. She knew his reaction would determine everything. Her heart thumped, she could even hear it.

He replaced the object in the carton, retracted his hands, leaving the flaps open. He sat again, taking a deep breath as if he wanted to compose himself and then looked up at her. What was he thinking? What?

Then he pushed the carton to one side, as if he didn't want it to come between them.

'I saw you yesterday. In church.'

She nodded. She had been there – to take his measure. To see if she would be recognised. But it was impossible, since she had attracted so much attention anyway – strange young woman in a small town church. He preached well, with compassion, with love in his voice, not so dramatic and formal as the ministers of her youth. When she walked out of the church she was certain it was right to come here. But now she wasn't so sure . . . He seemed upset.

'I . . .' she said, her thoughts scrambling for the right words.

He leaned towards her. He needed an explanation; that she well understood. His arms and hands made a straight line on the edge of the desk, from elbow to interlinked fingers flat on the desk. He was wearing a formal shirt unbuttoned at the neck, light blue with a faint red stripe. His sleeves were rolled up, forearms hairy where the sun caught them. From outside came the sounds of a weekday afternoon in a small town – the Sotho people greeting one another across the breadth of the street, the municipal tractor accelerating duh-duh-duh up to the garage, the cicadas, the clanging beat of a hammer alternating with the mindless barking of two dogs.

'There's a lot I have to tell you,' she said, and her voice sounded small and lost.

At last he moved, his hands folded open.

'I hardly know where to start.'

'Begin at the beginning,' he said softly, and she was grateful for the empathy.

'The beginning,' she approved, voice gaining strength. Her fingers gathered the long blonde hair from where it hung over her shoulder and tossed it back with a rhythmic, practised motion.

2

It began for Thobela Mpayipheli late on a Saturday afternoon at a filling station in Cathcart.

Pakamile was seated beside him, eight years old, bored and tired. The long road from Amersfoort lay behind them, seven dreary hours of driving. When they turned in at the garage the child sighed. 'Still sixty kilometres?'

'Only sixty kilometres,' he said consolingly. 'Do you want a cold drink?'

'No thanks,' said the boy and lifted up the 500-ml Coca Cola bottle that had been lying at his feet. It was not yet empty.

Thobela stopped at the pumps and climbed out of the pick-up. There was no attendant in sight. He stretched his limbs, a big black man in jeans, red shirt and running shoes. He walked around his vehicle, checked that the motorbikes on the load bed were still firmly strapped down – Pakamile's little KX 65 and his big BMW. They had been learning to ride off-road that weekend, an official course through sand and gravel, water, hills, humps, gullies and valleys. He had seen the boy's self-confidence grow with every hour, the enthusiasm that glowed within him like an ember with every 'Look, Thobela, watch me!'

His son . . .

Where were the petrol attendants?

There was another car at the pumps, a white Polo – the engine idled, but there was no one in the car. Strange. He called out, 'Hello!' and saw movement in the building. They must be coming now.

He turned around to unlatch the pick-up bonnet, glancing at the western horizon where the sun was going down . . . soon it would be dark. Then he heard the first shot. It reverberated through the quiet of the early evening and he jumped in fright and dropped instinctively to his haunches. 'Pakamile!' he screamed. 'Get down!' But his last words were deafened by another shot, and another, and he saw them coming out of the door – two of them, pistols in hand, one carrying a white plastic bag, eyes wild. They spotted him, shot. Bullets slammed against the pump, against the pick-up.

He shouted, a guttural roar, leapt up, jerked open the pick-up door and dived in, trying to shield the boy from the bullets. He felt the little body shiver. 'Okay,' he said, and heard the shots and the lead whining over them. He heard one car door slam, then another and screeching tyres. He looked up – the Polo was moving towards the road. Another shot. The glass of an advertising display above him shattered and rained down on the pick-up. Then they were in the road, the Volkswagen's engine revving too high and he said, 'It's okay, okay,' and felt the wet on his hand and Pakamile had stopped shivering and he saw the blood on the child's body and he said: 'No, God, no.'

That is where it began for Thobela Mpayipheli.

He sat in the boy's room, on his bed. The document in his hand was his last remaining proof.

The house was as quiet as the grave, for the first time since he could remember. Two years ago Pakamile and he had pushed open the door and looked at the dusty interior, the empty rooms. Some of the light fittings were hanging askew from the ceiling, kitchen cupboard doors were broken or just ajar, but all they saw was potential, the possibilities of their new house overlooking the Cata River and the green fields of the farm in high summer. The boy had run through the house leaving footprints in the dust. 'This is my room, Thobela,' he had called down the passage. When he reached the master bedroom he had expressed his awe at the vast space in a long whistle. Because all he knew was a cramped four-room house in the Cape Flats.

That first night they slept on the big veranda. First they had watched the sun disappear behind the storm clouds and the twilight deepen over the yard, watched the shadows of the big trees near the gate blend with the darkness, and the stars magically open their silver eyes in the firmament. He and the boy, squeezed up against each other with their backs against the wall.

'This is a wonderful place, Thobela.'

There was a deep sense of comfort in Pakamile's sigh and Thobela was eternally relieved, because it was only a month since the boy's mother had died and he had not known how they would adjust to the change of environment and circumstance.

They spoke of the cattle they would buy, a milk cow or two, a few fowls ('. . . and a dog, Thobela, please, a big old dog'). A vegetable garden at the back door. A patch of lucerne down by the riverbank. They had dreamed their dreams that night until Pakamile's head had dropped against his shoulder and he had laid the boy down softly on the bedding on the floor. He had kissed him on the forehead and said, 'Good night, my son.'

Pakamile was not of his own blood. The son of the woman he had loved, the boy had become his own. Very quickly he had come to love the boy like his own flesh and blood, and in the months since they had moved here he had begun the long process of making it official – writing letters, filling in forms and being interviewed. Slow bureaucrats with strange agendas had to decide whether he was suitable to be a parent, when the whole world could see that the bond between them had become unbreakable. But, at last, after fourteen months, the registered documents had arrived; in the long-winded, clumsy language of state officialdom, these put the seal on his adoption.

And now these pages of yellow-white paper were all he had. These, and a heap of new ground under the pepper trees by the river. And the minister's words, meant to comfort: 'God has a purpose with everything.'

Lord, he missed the boy.

He could not accept that he would never hear that chuckling laugh again. Or the footsteps down the passage. Never slow, always in a rush, as if life were too short for walking. Or the boy calling his name from the front door, voice loaded with excitement over some new discovery. Impossible to accept that he would never feel Pakamile's arms around him again. That, more than anything – the contact, the absolute acceptance, the unconditional love.

It was his fault.

There was never an hour of the day or night that he did not relive the events at the garage with the fine-tooth comb of self-reproach. He should have realised, when he saw the empty Polo idling at the pumps. He should have reacted more swiftly when he heard the first shot, he should have thrown himself over the child then, he should have been a shield, he should have taken the bullet. He should. It was his fault.

The loss was like a heavy stone in him, an unbearable burden. What would he do now? How would he live? He could not even see tomorrow, neither the sense nor the possibility. The phone rang in the sitting room, but he did not want to get up – he wanted to stay here with Pakamile's things.

He moved sluggishly, feeling the emotion pressing against him. Why could he not weep? The telephone rang. Why would the grief not break out?

Inexplicably, he was standing with the instrument in his hand and the voice said: 'Mr Mpayipheli?' and he said: 'Yes.'

'We've got them, Mr Mpayipheli. We've caught them. We want you to come and identify them.'

Later he unlocked the safe and placed the document carefully on the topmost shelf. Then he reached for his firearms, three of them: Pakamile's airgun, the .22 and the hunting rifle. He took the longest one and walked to the kitchen.

As he cleaned it with methodical concentration he slowly became aware that guilt and loss were not all that lay within him.

'I wonder if he believed,' she said, the minister's full attention on her now. His eyes no longer strayed to the box.

'Unlike me.' The reference to herself was unplanned and she wondered for a moment why she said it. 'Maybe he didn't go to church or such, but he might have believed. And perhaps he could not understand why the Lord gave to him and then took away. First his wife, and then his child on the farm. He thought he was being punished. I wonder why that is? Why we all think that when something bad happens? I do too. It's weird. I just could never work out what I was being punished for.'

'As an unbeliever?' asked the minister.

She shrugged. 'Yes. Isn't it strange? It's like the guilt is here inside us. Sometimes I wonder if we are being punished for the things we are going to do in the future. Because my sins only came later, after I was punished.'

The minister shook his head and took a breath as if to answer, but she didn't want to be sidetracked now; didn't want to break the rhythm of her story.

They were out of reach. There were eight men behind the one-way glass, but he could only focus on the two for whom his hate burned. They were young and devil-may-care, their mouths stretched in the same 'so-what' smirks, their eyes staring a challenge at the window. For a moment he considered the possibility of saying he recognised none of them and then waiting outside the police station with the hunting rifle . . . But he wasn't prepared, hadn't studied the exits and streets outside. He lifted his finger like a rifle barrel and said to the superintendent: 'There they are, numbers three and five.' He did not recognise the sound of his own voice; they were the words of a stranger.

'You are sure?'

'Dead sure,' he said.

'Three and five?'

'Three and five.'

'That's what we thought.'

They asked him to sign a statement. Then there was nothing more he could do. He walked to his pick-up, unlocked the door and got in, conscious of the rifle behind the seat and the two men somewhere inside the building. He sat and wondered what the superintendent would do if he asked for a few moments alone with them, because he felt the compulsion to thrust a long blade into their hearts. His eyes lingered a moment on the front door of the police station and then he turned the key and drove slowly away.

3

The public prosecutor was a Xhosa woman and her office was filled with the pale yellow dossiers of her daily work. They were everywhere. The desk was overloaded and the heaps overflowed to the two tables and the floor, so they had to pick their way to the two chairs. She had a sombre quality and a vague absence, as if her attention was divided between the countless documents, as if the responsibility of her work was sometimes too heavy to bear.

She explained. She was the one who would lead the state prosecution. She had to prepare him as a witness. Together they must convince the judge that the accused were guilty.

That would be easy, he said.

It is never easy, she replied, and adjusted her large gold-rimmed spectacles with the tips of her thumb and index finger, as if they could never be wholly comfortable. She questioned him about the day of Pakamile's death, over and over, until she could see the event through his eyes. When they had finished, he asked her how the judge would punish them.

'If they are found guilty?'

'When they are found guilty,' he replied with assurance.

She adjusted her spectacles and said one could never predict these things. One of them, Khoza, had a previous conviction. But it was Ramphele's first offence. And he must remember that it was not their intent to murder the child.

'Not their intent?'

'They will attest that they never even saw the child. Only you.'

'What sentence will they get?'

'Ten years. Fifteen? I can't say for sure.'

For a long moment he just stared at her.

'That is the system,' she said with an exonerating shrug.

A day before the court case was to begin he drove his pick-up to Umtata because he needed to buy a couple of ties, a jacket and black shoes.

He stood in his new clothes before the long mirror. The shop assistant said, 'That looks *sharp*,' but he did not recognise himself in the reflection – the face was unfamiliar and the beard which had appeared on his cheeks since the boy's death grew thick and grey on the chin and cheeks. It made him look harmless, and wise, like a stalwart.

The eyes mesmerised him. Were they his? They reflected no light, as if they were empty and dead inside.

From the late afternoon he lay on his hotel bed, arms behind his head, motionless.

He remembered: Pakamile in the shed above the house milking a cow for the first time, all thumbs, in too much of a hurry. Frustrated that the teats would not respond to the manipulation of his small fingers. And then, at last, the thin white stream shooting off at an angle to spray the shed floor and the triumphant cry from the boy: 'Thobela! Look!'

The small figure in school uniform that waited every afternoon for him, socks at half-mast, shirt-tails hanging, the backpack disproportionately big. The joy every day when he drew up. If he came on the motorbike, Pakamile would first look around to see which of his friends was witness to this exotic event, this unique machine that only he had the right to ride home on.

Sometimes his friends slept over; four, five, six boys tailing Pakamile around the farmyard. 'My father and I planted all these vegetables.' 'This is my father's motorbike and this is mine.' 'My father planted all this lucerne himself, hey.' A Friday night . . . everyone in a Christmas bed in the sitting room, jammed in like sardines in a flat tin. The house had vibrated with life. The house was full. Full.

The emptiness of the room overwhelmed him. The silence, the contrast. A part of him asked the question: what now? He tried to banish it with memories, but still it echoed. He thought long about it, but he knew in an unformulated way that Miriam and Pakamile had been his life. And now there was nothing.

He got up once to relieve himself and drink water and went back to lie down. The air conditioner hissed and blew under the window. He stared at the ceiling, waited for the night to pass so the trial could begin.

The accused sat alongside each other: Khoza and Ramphele. They looked him in the eyes. Beside them the advocate for the defence stood up: an Indian, tall and athletically lean, flamboyant in a smart black suit and purple tie.

'Mr Mpayipheli, when the state prosecutor asked you what your profession was, you said you were a farmer.'

He did not answer, because it was not a question.

'Is that correct?' The Indian had a soothing voice, as intimate as if they were old friends.

'It is.'

'But that is not the whole truth, is it?'

'I don't know what . . .'

'How long have you been a so-called farmer, Mr Mpayipheli?'

'Two years.'

'And what was your profession before you began farming?'

The state prosecutor, the serious woman with the gold-rimmed spectacles, stood up. 'Objection, Your Honour. Mr Mpayipheli's work history is irrelevant to the case before the court.'

'Your Honour, the background of the witness is not only relevant to his reliability as a witness, but also to his behaviour at the filling station. The defence has serious doubts about Mr Mpayipheli's version of the events.'

'I shall allow you to continue,' said the judge, a middle-aged white man with a double chin and a red complexion. 'Answer the question, Mr Mpayipheli.'

'What was your profession before you went farming?' repeated the advocate.

'I was a gofer at a motorbike retailer.'

'For how long?'

'Two years.'

'And before that?'

His heart began to race. He knew he must not hesitate, nor look unsure.

'I was a bodyguard.'

'A bodyguard.'

'Yes.'

'Let us go one step further back, Mr Mpayipheli, before we return to your answer. What did you do before you, as you say, became a bodyguard?'

Where had the man obtained this information? 'I was a soldier.'

'A soldier.'

He did not answer. He felt hot in his suit and tie. He felt sweat trickle down his back.

The Indian shuffled documents on the table before him and came up with a few sheets of paper. He walked to the state prosecutor and gave her a copy. He repeated the process with the judge and placed one before Thobela.

'Mr Mpayipheli, would it be accurate to say you tend towards euphemism?'

'Objection, Your Honour, the defence is intimidating the witness and the direction of questioning is irrelevant.' She had glanced at the document and began to look uncomfortable. Her voice had reached a higher note.

'Overruled. Proceed.'

'Mr Mpayipheli, you and I can play evasion games all day but I have too much respect for this court to allow that. Let me help you. I have here a newspaper report' – he waved the document in the air – 'that states, and I quote: "Mpayipheli, a former Umkhonto We Sizwe soldier who received specialist training in Russia and the former East Germany, was connected until recently to a drugs syndicate on the Cape Flats . . ." End of quote. The article refers to a certain Thobela Mpayipheli who was wanted by the authorities two years ago in connection with the disappearance of, and I quote once more, "government intelligence of a sensitive nature".'

Just before the prosecutor leapt up, she glanced fiercely at Thobela, as if he had betrayed her. 'Your Honour, I must protest. The witness is not on trial here . . .'

'Mr Singh, are you going somewhere with this argument?'

'Absolutely, Your Honour. I ask for just a moment of the court's patience.'

'Proceed.'

'Is that what this newspaper article is referring to, Mr Mpayipheli?'

'Yes.'

'Excuse me, I can't hear you.'

'Yes.' Louder.

'Mr Mpayipheli, I put it to you that your version of the events at the filling station is just as evasive and euphemistic as your description of your background.'

'That is . . .'

'You are a highly trained military man, schooled in the military arts, urban terrorism and guerrilla warfare . . .'

'I object, Your Honour – that is not a question.'

'Overruled. Let the man finish, madam.'

She sat down, shaking her head, with a deep frown behind the gold-rimmed spectacles. 'As it pleases the court,' she said, but her tone said otherwise.

'And a "bodyguard" for the drug syndicate in the Cape for two years. A *bodyguard*. That is not what the newspapers say . . .'

The state prosecutor stood up, but the judge pre-empted her: 'Mr Singh, you are testing the patience of the court. If you wish to lead evidence, please await your turn.'

'My sincere apologies, Your Honour, but it is an affront to the principles of justice for a witness under oath to fabricate a story—'

'Mr Singh, spare me. What is your question?'

'As it pleases the court, Your Honour. Mr Mpayipheli, what was the specific purpose of your military training?'

'That was twenty years ago.'

'Answer the question, please.'

'I was trained in counter-espionage activities.'

'Did this include the use of firearms and explosives?'

'Yes.'

'Hand-to-hand combat?'

'Yes.'

'The handling of high-pressure situations?'

'Yes.'

'Elimination and escape.'

'Yes.'

'And at the filling station you say, and I quote: "I ducked behind the petrol pump," when you heard the shots?'

'The war was over ten years ago. I was not there to fight, I was there to fill up . . .'

'The war was not over for you ten years ago, Mr Mpayipheli. You took the war to the Cape Flats with your training in death and injury. Let us discuss your role as bodyguard . . .'

The prosecutor's voice was high and plaintive. 'Your Honour, I object in the strongest—'

At that moment Thobela saw the faces of the accused; they were laughing at him.

'Objection sustained. Mr Singh, that is enough. You have made your point. Do you have any specific questions about the events at the filling station?'

Singh's shoulders sagged, as if wounded. 'As it pleases the court, Your Honour, I have.'

'Then get on with it.'

'Mr Mpayipheli, did you forget that it was *you* who attacked the accused when they left the filling station?'

'I did not.'

'You did not forget?'

'Your Honour, the defence . . .'

'Mr Singh!'

'Your Honour, the accused . . . excuse me, the witness is evading the question.'

'No, Mr Singh, it is you who are leading the witness.'

'Very well. Mr Mpayipheli, you say you did not charge at the accused in a threatening manner?'

'I did not.'

'You did not have a wheel spanner or some tool . . .'

'I object, Your Honour, the witness has already answered the question.'

'Mr Singh . . .'

'I have no further questions for this liar, Your Honour . . .'

4

'I think he believed he could make things right. Anything,' she said in the twilit room. The sun had dropped behind the hills of the town and the light entering the room was softer. It made the telling easier, she thought, and wondered why.

'That is the thing that I admired most. That somebody stood up and did something that the rest of us were too afraid to do, even if we wanted to. I never had the guts. I was too scared to fight back. And then I read about him in the papers and I began to wonder: maybe I could also . . .'

She hesitated a fraction and then asked with bated breath: 'Do you know about Artemis, Reverend?'

He did not react at first, sitting motionless, tipped slightly forward, engrossed in the story she was telling. Then he blinked, his attention refocused.

'Artemis? Er, yes . . .' he said tentatively.

'The one the papers wrote about.'

'The papers . . .' He seemed embarrassed. 'Some things pass me by. Something new every week. I don't always keep up.'

She was relieved about that. There was an imperceptible shift in their roles – he the small-town minister, she the wordly-wise one, the one in the know. She slipped her foot out of its sandal and folded it under her, shifting to a more comfortable position in the chair. 'Let me tell you,' she said with more self-assurance.

He nodded.

'I was in trouble when I read about him for the first time. I was in the Cape. I was . . .' For a fraction of a second she hesitated and wondered if it would upset him. 'I was a call girl.'

*　　*　　*

At half-past eleven that night he was still awake on his hotel bed when someone knocked softly on his door, apologetically.

It was the public prosecutor, her eyes magnified behind the spectacles.

'Sorry,' she said, but she just looked tired.

'Come in.'

She hesitated a moment and he knew why: he was just in his shorts, his body glistening with perspiration. He turned around and picked up his T-shirt, motioning her to take the single arm-chair. He perched on the end of the bed.

She sat primly on the chair; her hands folded the dark material of her skirt over her plump legs. She had an officious air, as if she had come to speak of weighty things.

'What happened today in court?' he asked.

She shrugged.

'He wanted to blame *me*. The Indian.'

'He was doing his job. That's all.'

'His job?'

'He has to defend them.'

'With lies?'

'In law there are no lies, Mr Mpayipheli. Just different versions of the truth.'

He shook his head. 'There is only one truth.'

'You think so? And what one truth is there about you? The one where you are a farmer? A father? A freedom fighter? Or a drug dealer? A fugitive from the state?'

'That has nothing to do with Pakamile's death,' he said, anger creeping into his words.

'The moment Singh brought it up in court, it became part of his death, Mr Mpayipheli.'

Rage flooded over him, reliving the day of frustration: 'All that Mister, Mister, so polite, and objections and playing little legal games . . . And those two sitting there and laughing.'

'That is why I have come,' she said. 'To tell you: they have escaped.'

He did not know how long he sat there, just staring at her.

'One of them overpowered a policeman. In the cells, when he brought him food. He had a weapon, a knife.'

'Overpowered,' he said, as if tasting the word.

'The police . . . They are short of manpower. Not everyone turned up on shift.'

'They both got away.'

'There are roadblocks. The station commander said they won't get far.'

The rage inside him took on another face that he did not wish her to see. 'Where would they go?'

She shrugged once more, as if she was beyond caring. 'Who knows?'

When he did not respond, she leaned forward in the chair. 'I wanted to tell you. You have the right to know.'

She stood up. He waited for her to pass him, then stood up and followed her to the door.

There was doubt in the minister's face. He had shifted his large body back and cocked his head sideways, as if waiting for her to qualify her statement, to complete the sentence with a punch line.

'You don't believe me.'

'I find it . . . unlikely.'

Somewhere she felt emotion. Gratitude? Relief? She did not mean to show it but her voice betrayed her. 'My professional name was Bibi.'

His voice was patient as he responded. 'I believe you. But I look at you and I listen to you and I can't help wondering why. Why was that necessary for you?'

This was the second time she had been asked that. Usually they asked 'How?' For them she had a story to fit expectations. She wanted to use it now – it lay on her tongue, rehearsed, ready.

She drew a breath to steady herself. 'I could tell you I was always a sex addict, a nymphomaniac,' she said with deliberation.

'But that is not the truth,' he said.

'No, Reverend, it is not.'

He nodded as if he approved of her answer. 'It's getting dark,' he said, standing up and switching on the standard lamp in the corner. 'Can I offer you something to drink? Coffee? Tea?'

'Tea would be lovely, thank you.' Did he need time to recover, she wondered?

'Excuse me a moment,' he said, and opened the door diagonally behind her.

She remained behind, alone, wondering what was the worst thing he had heard in this study. What small-town scandals? Teenage pregnancies? Affairs? Friday night domestics?

What made someone like him stay here? Perhaps he liked the status, because doctors and ministers were important people in the rural areas, she knew. Or was he running away like she was? As he had run off just now; as if there was a certain level of reality that became too much for him.

He came back, shutting the door behind him. 'My wife will bring the tea soon,' he said and sat down.

She did not know how to begin. 'Did I upset you?'

He pondered a while before he answered, as if he had to gather the words together. 'What upsets me is a world – a society – that allows someone like you to lose the way.'

'We all lose our way sometimes.'

'We don't all become sex workers,' he motioned towards her in a broad gesture, to include everything. 'Why was that necessary?'

'You are the second person to ask that in the past month or so.'

'Oh?'

'The other one was a detective in Cape Town.' She smiled as she recalled. 'Griessel. He had tousled hair. And soft eyes, but they looked right through you.'

'Did you tell him the truth?'

'I almost did.'

'Was he a . . . what do you call it?'

'A client?' She smiled.

'Yes.'

'No. He was . . . just . . . I don't know . . . lost?'

'I see,' said the minister.

There was a soft tap on the door and he had to get up to take the tea tray.

5

Detective Inspector Benny Griessel opened his eyes to his wife standing before him, shaking his shoulder with one hand and urgently whispering, 'Benny,' she said. 'Benny, please.'

He was lying on the sitting-room couch, that much he knew. He must have fallen asleep here. He smelt coffee; his head was thick and throbbing. One arm squashed under him was numb, circulation cut off by the weight of his body.

'Benny, we have to talk.'

He groaned and struggled to sit up.

'I brought you some coffee.'

He looked at her, at the deep lines on her face. She was still stooped over him.

'What time is it?' His words battled to connect with his vocal chords.

'It's five o'clock, Benny.' She sat next to him on the couch. 'Drink the coffee.'

He had to take it with his left hand. The mug was hot against his palm.

'It's early,' he said.

'I need to talk to you before the children wake up.'

The message borne on her tone penetrated his consciousness. He sat up straight and spilled the coffee on his clothes – he was still wearing yesterday's. 'What have I done?'

She pointed an index finger across the open-plan room. The bottle of Jack Daniels stood on the dining-room table beside his plate of untouched dinner. The ashtray was overflowing and a smashed glass lay in shards beside the overturned bar stools at the breakfast counter.

He took a gulp of coffee. It burned his mouth, but could not take the sick taste of the night away. 'I'm sorry,' he said.

'Sorry isn't good enough any more,' she said.

'Anna . . .'

'No, Benny, no more. I can't do this any more.' Her voice was without inflection.

'Jissis, Anna.' He reached a hand out to her, saw how it shook, the drunkenness still not expelled from his body. When he tried to put his hand on her shoulder, she moved away from his touch, and that's when he noticed the small swelling on her lip, already beginning to turn the colour of wine.

'It's over. Seventeen years. That's enough. It's more than anyone could ask.'

'Anna, I . . . it was the drink, you know I didn't mean it. Please, Anna, you know that's not *me*.'

'Your son helped you off that chair last night, Benny. Do you remember? Do you know what you said to him? Do you remember how you cursed and swore, until your eyes rolled back in your head? No, Benny, you can't – you can never remember. Do you know what he said to you, your son? When you were lying there with your mouth open and your stinking breath? Do you know?' Tears were close, but she suppressed them.

'What did he say?'

'He said he hates you.'

He absorbed that. 'And Carla?'

'Carla locked herself in her room.'

'I'll talk to them, Anna, I'll make it right. They know it's the work. They know I am not like that . . .'

'No, Benny.'

He heard the finality in her voice and his heart contracted. 'Anna, no.'

She would not look at him. Her finger traced the swelling on her lip and she walked away from him. 'That is what I tell them every time: it's the work. He's a good father, it's just his work, you must understand. But I don't believe it any more. *They* don't believe it any more . . . Because it *is* you, Benny. It is you. There are other policemen who go through the same things every day, but they don't get drunk. They don't curse and shout and break their stuff and hit their wives. It's finished now. Completely finished.'

'Anna, I will stop, you know I have before. I can. You know I can.'

'For six weeks? That is your record. Six weeks. My children need more than that. They deserve more than that. *I* deserve better than that.'

'*Our* children . . .'

'A drunk can't be a father.'

Self-pity washed over him. The fear. 'I can't help it, Anna. I can't help it, I am weak, I need you. Please, I need you all – I can't go on without you.'

'We don't need you any more, Benny.' She stood up and he saw the two suitcases on the floor behind her.

'You can't do that. This is my house.' Begging.

'Do you want us on the street? Because it is either you or us. You can choose, because we will no longer live under the same roof. You have six months, Benny – that is what we are giving you. Six months to choose between us and the booze. If you can stay dry you can come back, but this is your last chance. You can see the children on Sundays, if you want. You can knock on the door and if you smell of drink I will slam it in your face. If you are drunk you needn't bother to come back.'

'Anna . . .' He felt the tears welling up in him. She could not do this to him; she did not know how dreadfully hard it was.

'Spare me, Benny, I know all of your tricks. Shall I carry your suitcases outside, or will you take them yourself?'

'I need to shower, I must wash, I can't go out like this.'

'Then I will carry them myself,' she said, and took a suitcase in each hand.

There was an atmosphere of faint despair in the detective's office. Files lay about in untidy heaps, the meagre furniture was worn out and the outdated posters on the walls made hollow claims about crime prevention. A portrait of Mbeki in a narrow, cheap frame hung askew. The floor tiles were a colourless grey. A dysfunctional fan stood in one corner, dust accumulated on the metal grille in front of the blades.

The air was thick with the oppressive scent of failure.

Thobela sat on a steel chair with grey-blue upholstery and the foam protruding from one corner. The detective stood with his back to the wall. He was looking sideways out of the grimy window at the parking area. He had narrow, stooped shoulders and grey patches in his goatee.

'I pass it on to Criminal Intelligence at Provincial Headquarters. They put it on the national database. That's how it works.'

'A database for escapees?'

'You could say so.'

'How big would this database be?'

'Big.'

'And their names just sit there on a computer?'

The detective sighed. 'No, Mr Mpayipheli – the photos, criminal records, the names and addresses of families and contacts are part of the file. It is all sent along and distributed. We follow up what we can. Khoza has family in the Cape. Ramphele's mother lives here in Umtata. Someone will call on them . . .'

'Are you going to Cape Town?

'No. The police in the Cape will make enquiries.'

'What does that mean, "make enquiries"?'

'Someone will go and ask, Mr Mpayipheli, if Khoza's family has heard anything from him.'

'And they say "no" and then nothing happens?'

Another sigh, deeper this time. 'There are realities you and I cannot change.'

'That is what black people used to say about apartheid.'

'I think there is a difference here.'

'Just tell me, what are the chances? That you will catch them?'

The detective pushed away from the wall, slowly. He dragged out a chair in front of him and sat with his hands clasped. He talked slowly, like someone with a great weariness. 'I could tell you the chances are good, but you must understand me correctly. Khoza has a previous conviction – he has done time: eighteen months for burglary. Then the armed robbery at the garage, the shooting . . . and now the escape. There is a pattern. A spiral. People like him don't stop; their crimes just become more serious. And that's why chances are good. I can't tell you we will catch them *now*. I can't tell you *when* we will catch them. But we *will*, because they won't stay out of trouble.'

'How long, do you think?'

'I couldn't say.'

'Guess.'

The detective shook his head. 'I don't know. Nine months? A year?'

'I can't wait that long.'

'I am sorry for your loss, Mr Mpayipheli. I understand how you feel. But you must remember, you are only one victim of many. Look at all these files here. There is a victim in every one. And even if you go and talk to the PC, it will make no difference.'

'The PC?'

'Provincial commissioner.'

'I don't want to talk to the provincial commissioner. I am talking to *you*.'

'I have told you how it is.'

He gestured towards the document on the table and said softly: 'I want a copy of the file.'

The detective did not react immediately. A frown began to crease his forehead, possibilities considered.

'It's not allowed.'

Thobela nodded his head in comprehension. 'How much?'

The eyes measured him, estimating an amount. The detective straightened his shoulders. 'Five thousand.'

'That is too much,' he said, and he stood up and started for the door.

'Three.'

'Five hundred.'

'It's my job on the line. Not for five hundred.'

'No one will ever know. Your job is safe. Seven-fifty.'

'A thousand,' he said hopefully.

Thobela turned around. 'A thousand. How long will it take to copy?'

'I will have to do it tonight. Come tomorrow.'

'No. Tonight.'

The detective looked at him, his eyes not quite so weary now. 'Why such a hurry?'

'Where can I meet you?'

The poverty here was dreadful. Shacks of planks and corrugated iron, a pervasive stink of decay and uncollected rubbish. Paralysing heat beat upwards from the dust.

Mrs Ramphele chased four children – two teenagers, two toddlers – out of the shack and invited him to sit down. It was tidy inside, clean but hot, so that the sweat stained his shirt in great circles. There were schoolbooks on a table and photos of children on the rickety cupboard.

She thought he was from the police and he did not disillusion her as she apologised for her son, saying he wasn't always like that; he was a good boy, misled by Khoza and how easily that could happen here, where no one had anything and there was no hope. Andrew had looked for work, had gone down to the Cape, he had finished standard eight and then he said he couldn't let his mother struggle like this, he would finish school later. There was no work. Nothing: East London, Uitenhage, Port Elizabeth, Jeffreys Bay, Knysna, George, Mossel Bay, Cape Town . . . Too many people, too little work. Occasionally he sent a little money; she didn't know where it came from, but she hoped it wasn't stolen.

Did she know where Andrew would go now? Did he know people in the Cape?

Not that she knew.

Had he been here?

She looked him in the eye and said no, and he wondered how much of what she had said was the truth.

★ ★ ★

They had erected the gravestone. *Pakamile Nzululwazi. Son of Miriam Nzululwazi. Son of Thobela Mpayipheli. 1996–2004. Rest in Peace.*

A simple stone of granite and marble set in the green grass by the river. He leaned against the pepper tree and reflected that this was the child's favourite place. He used to watch him through the kitchen window and see the small body etched here, on his haunches, sometimes just staring at the brown water flowing slowly past. Sometimes he had a stick in his hand, scratching patterns and letters in the sand – and he would wonder what Pakamile was thinking about. The possibility that he was thinking of his mother gave him great pain, because it was not something he could fix, not a pain he could heal.

Occasionally he would try to talk about it, but carefully, because he did not want to open the old wound. So he would ask: 'How are things with you, Pakamile?', 'Is something worrying you?' or 'Are you happy?' And the boy would answer with his natural cheerfulness that things were good, he was so very happy, because he had him, Thobela, and the farm and the cattle and everything. But there was always the suspicion that that was not the whole truth, that the child kept a secret place in his head where he would visit his loss alone.

Eight years, during which a father had abandoned him, and he had lost a caring mother.

Surely that could not be the sum total of a person's life? Surely that could not be right? There must be a heaven, somewhere . . . He looked up at the blue sky and wondered. Was Miriam there among green rolling hills to welcome Pakamile? Would there be a place for Pakamile to play and friends and love? All races together, a great multitude, all with the same sense of justice? Waters beside which to rest. And God, a mighty black figure, kingly, with a full grey beard and wise eyes, who welcomed everyone to the Great Kraal with an embrace and gentle words, but who looked with great pain over the undulating landscape of green sweet veld at the broken Earth. Who shook his head, because no one did anything about it because they were all blind to His Purpose. He had not made them like *that*.

Slowly he walked up the slope to the homestead and stood again to look.

His land, as far as he could see.

He realised that he no longer wanted it. The farm had become useless to him. He had bought it for Miriam and Pakamile. It had been a symbol then, a dream and a new life – and now it was nothing but a millstone, a reminder of all the potential that no longer existed. What use was it to own ground, but have nothing?

6

From the second-storey flat in Mouille Point you could see the sea if you got the angle from the window right. The woman lay in the bedroom and Detective Inspector Benny Griessel stood in the living room looking at the photos on the piano when the man from Forensics and the scene photographer came in.

Forensics said: 'Jesus, Benny, you look like shit,' and he answered: 'Flattery will get you nowhere.'

'What have we got?'

'Woman in her forties. Strangled with the kettle cord. No forced entry.'

'That sounds familiar.'

Griessel nodded. 'Same MO.'

'The third one.'

'The third one,' Griessel confirmed.

'Fuck.' Because that meant there would be no fingerprints. The place would be wiped clean.

'But this one is not ripe yet,' said the photographer.

'That's because her char comes in on Saturdays. We only found the others on Monday.'

'So he's a Friday-night boy.'

'Looks like it.'

As they squeezed past him to the bedroom, Forensics sniffed theatrically and said, 'But something smells bad.' Then he said in a lower voice, familiarly, 'You ought to take a shower, Benny.'

'Do your fucking job.'

'I'm just saying,' he said, and went into the bedroom. Griessel heard the clips of their cases open and Forensics say to the photographer: 'These are the only girls I see naked nowadays. Corpses.'

'At least they don't talk back,' came the response.

A shower was not what Griessel needed. He needed a drink. Where could he go? Where would he sleep tonight? Where could he stash his bottle? When would he see his children again? How could he concentrate on this thing? There was a bottle store in Sea Point that opened in an hour.

Six months to choose between us and the booze.

How did she think he would manage it? By throwing him out? By putting yet more pressure on him? By rejecting him?

If you can stay dry you can come back, but this is your last chance.

He couldn't lose them, but he couldn't stay dry. He was fucked, totally fucked. Because if he didn't have them, he wouldn't be able to stop drinking – couldn't she understand that?

His cell phone rang.

'Griessel.'

'Another one, Benny?' Senior Superintendent Matt Joubert. His boss.

'It's the same MO,' he said.

'Any good news?'

'Not so far. He's clever, the fucker.'

'Keep me informed.'

'I will.'

'Benny?'

'Yes, Matt?'

'Are you okay?'

Silence. He could not lie to Joubert – they had too much history.

'Come and talk to me, Benny.'

'Later. Let me finish up here first.'

It dawned on him that Joubert knew something. Had Anna . . . She was serious. This time she had even phoned Matt Joubert.

He rode the motorbike to Alice, to see the man who made weapons by hand. Like their ancestors used to.

The interior of the little building was gloomy; when his eyes had adjusted to the poor light, he looked through the assegais that were bundled in tins, shafts down, shiny blades pointing up.

'What do you do with all of these?'

'They are for the people with tradition,' said the greybeard, his hands busy shaping a shaft from a long sapling. The sandpaper rasped rhythmically up and down, up and down.

'Tradition,' he echoed.

'They are not many now. Not many.'

'Why do you make the long spears too?'

'They are also part of our history.'

He turned to the bundle with shorter shafts. His finger stroked the blades – he was looking for a certain form, a specific balance. He drew one out, tested it, replaced it and took another.

'What do you want to do with an assegai?' asked the old man.

He did not immediately reply, because his fingers had found the right one. It lay comfortable in his palm.

'I am going hunting,' he said. When he looked up there was great satisfaction in the eyes of the greybeard.

'When I was nine, my mother gave me a set of records for my birthday. A box of ten seven-inch singles and a book with pictures of princesses and good fairies. There were stories on them and every story had more than one ending – three or four each. I don't know exactly how it worked, but every time you listened to them, the needle would jump to one of the endings. A woman told the stories. In English. If the ending was unhappy I would play it again until it ended right.'

She wasn't sure why she had brought this up and the minister said: 'But life doesn't work that way?'

'No,' she said, 'life doesn't.'

He stirred his tea. She sat with her cup on her lap, both feet on the floor now, and the scene was like a play she was watching: the woman and the clergyman in his study, drinking tea out of fine white porcelain. So normal. She could have been one of his congregation: innocent, seeking guidance for her life. About a relationship perhaps? With some young farmer? He looked at her in a paternal way and she knew: he likes me, he thinks I'm okay.

'My father was in the army,' she said.

He sipped his tea to gauge the temperature.

'He was an officer. I was born in Upington; he was a captain then. My mother was a housewife at first. Later on she worked at the attorneys' office. Sometimes he was away on the Border for long stretches, but I only remember that vaguely, because I was still small. I am the oldest; my brother was born two years after me. Gerhard. Christine and Gerhard van Rooyen, the children of Captain *Rooies* and Mrs Martie van Rooyen of Upington. The *Rooies* was just because of his surname. It's an army thing; every other guy had a nickname. My father was good looking, with black hair and green eyes – I got my eyes from him. And my hair from my mother, so I expect to go grey early – blonde hair does that. There are photos from when they were married, when she also wore her hair long. But later she cut it in a bob. She said it was because of the heat, but I think it was because of my father.'

His eyes were on her face, her mouth. Was he listening, really hearing her? Did he see her as she was? Would he remember later, when she revealed her great fraud? She was quiet for a moment, lifting the cup to her lips, sipping, saying self-consciously: 'It will take a long time to tell you everything.'

'That is one thing we have lots of here,' he said calmly. 'There is lots of time.'

She gestured at the door. 'You have a family and I—'

'They know I am here and they know it's my work.'

'Perhaps I should come back tomorrow.'

'Tell your story, Christine,' he said softly. 'Get it off your chest.'

'Sure?'

'Absolutely.'

She looked down at her cup. It was half full. She lifted it, swallowed the lot in one go, replaced it on the saucer and put it down on the tray on the desk. She drew her leg under her again and folded her arms. 'I don't know where it went wrong,' she said. 'We were like everyone else. Maybe not quite, because my father was a soldier, and at school we were always the army kids. When the *Flossies* flew out, those aeroplanes to the border, the whole town knew about it – our fathers were going to fight the Communists. Then we were special. I liked that. But most of the time we were like all the others. Gerhard and I went to school and in the afternoon our mother was there and we did homework and played. Weekends we went shopping and barbequed and visited and went to church and every December we went down to Hartenbos and there was nothing odd about us. Nothing that I was aware of when I was six or eight or ten. My father was my hero. I remember his smell when he came home in the afternoon and hugged me. He called me his big girl. He had a uniform with shiny stars on the shoulders. And my mother . . .'

'Are they still living?' the minister asked suddenly.

'My father died,' she said. With finality, as if she would not elaborate further.

'And your mother?'

'It's a long time since I have seen her.'

'Oh?'

'She lives in Mossel Bay.'

He said nothing.

'She knows now. What kind of work I was doing.'

'But she didn't always know?'

'No.'

'How did she find out?'

She sighed. 'That is part of the story.'

'And you think she will reject you? Because now she knows?'

'Yes. No . . . I think she is on a guilt trip.'

'Because you became a prostitute?'

'Yes.'

'And is she to blame?'

She couldn't sit still any more. She stood up in a hurry, and walked over to the wall behind her to get more distance between them. Then she approached the back of the chair and gripped it.

'Maybe.'

'Oh?'

She dropped her head, letting her long hair cover her face. She stood like that, very still.

'She was beautiful,' she said at last, looking up and taking her hands off the chair-back. She moved to the right, towards the bookshelf, her eyes on the books, but she was not seeing them.

'They were in Durban on honeymoon. And the photos . . . She could have had any man. She had a figure. Her face . . . she was so lovely, so delicate. And she was laughing, on all the photos. Sometimes I believe that was the last time she laughed.'

She turned to the minister, leaning her shoulder against the bookshelf, one hand brushing the books, caressingly. 'It must have been hard for my mother when my father was away. She never complained. When she knew he was coming home, she would get the house in order, from one end to the other. Spring-cleaning, she called it. But never herself. Tidy, yes. Clean, but she used less and less make-up. Her clothes became looser, and more dull. She cut her hair short. You know how it is when you live with someone every day – you don't notice the gradual changes.'

She folded her arms again, embracing herself.

'The thing with the church . . . that must be where it started. He came back from the Border and said we were going to another church. Not the Dutch Reformed Church on the base any more; we would be going to a church in town, one that met in the primary school hall on Sundays. Clapping hands and falling down and conversions . . . Gerhard and I would have enjoyed it if our father hadn't been so serious about it. Suddenly we had family devotions at home every day and he prayed long prayers about the demons that were in us. He began to talk of leaving the army, so that he could go and do missionary work, and he walked around with the Bible all day, not the little soldier's Bible, a big one. It was a vicious circle, because the army was probably understanding at first, but later he began praying for God to drive the demons out of the colonel and the brigadier and said that God would open doors for him.'

She shook her head. 'It must have been hard for my mother, but she did nothing.'

She walked back to her chair. 'Not even when he started with me.'

7

He drove the pick-up to Cape Town, because the motorbike would be too conspicuous. His suitcase was beside him on the passenger seat. From Port Elizabeth to Knysna. He saw the mountains and the forests and wondered, as always, how it had looked a thousand years ago, when there were only Khoi and San and the elephants trumpeted in the dense bush. Beyond George the houses of the wealthy sat like fat ticks against the dunes, silently competing for a better sea view. Big houses, empty all year, to be filled perhaps for a month in December. He thought of Mrs Ramphele's corrugated iron shack on the sunburnt flats outside Umtata, five people in two rooms, and he knew the contrasts in this country were too great.

But they could never be great enough to justify the death of a child. He wondered if Khoza or Ramphele had passed this way; if they had driven this road.

Mossel Bay, past Swellendam and over the Breede river, then Caledon and eventually late in the afternoon he came over Sir Lowry's Pass. The Cape lay spread out far below and the sun shone in his eyes as it hung low over Table Mountain. He felt no joy of homecoming, because the memories this place brought lay heavy on him.

He drove as far as Parow. There was a little hotel on Voortrekker Road that he remembered, the New President, where people stayed who wanted to remain anonymous, regardless of colour or creed.

That is where he would begin.

Griessel stood in front of the Serious and Violent Crimes Unit building in Bishop Lavis and considered his options.

He could take the suitcase out of the boot and drag it past Mavis in Reception, around the corner and down the passage to one of the big bathrooms that remained after the old Police College became the new SVC offices. Then he could shower and brush his teeth and scrape off his stubble in the bleached mirror and put on clean clothes. But every fucking policeman in the Peninsula would know within half an hour that Benny Griessel had been turfed out of the house by his wife. That is the way it worked on the Force.

Or he could walk to his office just as he was, smelly and crumpled, and say he had worked through the night, but that story would only maintain the façade temporarily.

There was a bottle of Jack in his desk drawer and three packets of Clorets – two slugs for the nerves, two Clorets for the breath and he was as good as new. Jissis, to feel the thick brown liquid sliding down his throat, all the way to heaven. He slammed the boot shut. Fuck the shower; he knew what he needed.

He walked fast, suddenly light-hearted. Fuck you, Anna. She couldn't do this; he would see a fucking lawyer, one like Kemp who didn't take shit from man or beast. He was the fucking bread-winner, drunkard and all; how could she throw him out? He'd paid for that house, every table and chair. He greeted Mavis, turned the corner, up the stairs, feeling in his pocket for the key. His hand was shaking. He got the door open, closed it behind him, walked around the desk, opened the bottom drawer, lifted the criminal procedure handbook and felt the cold glass of the bottle under-neath. He took it out and unscrewed the cap. Time for a lubrica-tion, his oil light was burning red. He grinned at his own wit as the door opened and Matt Joubert stood there with an expression of disgust on his face.

'Benny.'

He stood transfixed, with the neck of the bottle fifteen centi-metres away from relief.

'Fuck it, Matt.'

Matt closed the door behind him. 'Put that shit down, Benny.'

He did not move, could not believe his bad luck. So fucking close.

'Benny!'

The bottle shook, like his whole body. 'I can't help it,' he said quietly. He could not look Joubert in the eyes. The senior superintendent came and stood next to him, took the bottle out of his hand. He let it go reluctantly.

'Give me the cap.'

Solemnly he handed it over.

'Sit, Benny.'

He sat down and Joubert banged the bottle down. He leaned his large body against the desk, legs straight and arms folded.

'What is going on with you?'

What was the use of answering?

'Now you are an abuser of women and a breakfast drinker?'

She had phoned Joubert. To kick him out was not enough – Anna had to humiliate him professionally too.

'Jissis,' he said with feeling.

'Jissis what, Benny?'

'Ah fuck, Matt, what is the use of talking? How does that help? I am a fuck-up. You know it and Anna knows it and I know it. What is there left to say? I'm sorry I'm alive?' He waited for some reaction, but none came. The silence hung in the room, until he had to know whether he would find some sympathy. He looked up carefully to see his commander's expressionless face. Slowly Joubert narrowed his eyes and a red glow suffused his face. Griessel knew his boss was the hell-in and he retreated. Joubert grabbed him without speaking, jerked him out of the chair by his neck and arm and shoved him towards the door.

'Matt,' he said, 'jissis, what now?' He felt the considerable power of the grip.

'Shut up, Benny,' hissed Joubert, and steered him down the stairs, the footfalls loud on the bare surface. Past Mavis and through the entrance hall, Joubert's hand hard between his shoulders. Then they were outside in the bright sunlight. Never had Joubert been rough with him before. Their shoes crunched over the parking area gravel to the senior superintendent's car. He said 'Matt' again because he could feel pressure in his guts. This mood had never been directed at him before. Joubert did not respond. He jerked open the car door, his big hand pressing the back of Griessel's neck, shoved him in and slammed the door.

Joubert climbed in at the driver's side and turned the key. They shot off with screeching tyres and this noise seemed to release a flood of anger inside Joubert. 'A martyr,' he spat out with total disgust. 'I catch you with a fucking bottle in your hand and that is the best you can do? Act the martyr? You drink and hit women and all I see is self-pity. Benny, Jesus Christ, that's not good enough. In fourteen years, the fourteen fucking years I have worked with you, I have never seen a person so completely fuck-up his life without any help from outside. You should have been a bloody director, but where are you now, Benny? Forty-three and you're an inspector – with a thirst as big as the Sahara. And you hit your wife and shrug your shoulders and say, "I can't help it, Matt." You fucking hit your wife? Where does that come from? Since when?' Joubert's hands were communicating too and spit sprayed against the windscreen while the engine screamed at high revolutions. 'You're sorry you're alive?'

They drove towards Voortrekker Road. Griessel stared ahead. He felt the Jack in his hand again, the desire inside.

When it was quiet he said: 'It was the first time, last night.'

'The first time? What kind of a fucking excuse is that? Does that make it all right? You are a policeman, Benny. You know that's no fucking argument. And you're lying. She says it has been threatening for months. Three weeks ago you shoved her around, but you were too drunk to do it properly. And the children, Benny? What are you doing to them? Your two children who have to see their drunkard of a father come home pissed out of his skull and assault their mother? I should lock you up with the scum, she should lay a fucking charge against you, but all that will achieve is more damage to your children. And what do you do? She throws you out and you run to a bottle. Just booze, Benny, that's all you think about. And yourself. What the fuck is going on inside your head? What has happened to your brains?'

For an instant he wanted to respond, to scream: 'I don't know, I don't know, I don't want to be like this, I don't know how I got here, leave me alone!' Because he was familiar with these questions, and he knew the answers – it was all pointless, it made no difference. He said nothing.

In Voortrekker Road the traffic was heavy, the traffic lights red. Joubert gave the steering wheel a slap of frustration. Griessel wondered where they were going. To the Sanatorium? It wouldn't be the first time Joubert had dropped him off there.

The senior superintendent blew out a long breath. 'Do you know what I think about, Benny? The whole time.' His voice had mellowed now. 'Of the man who was my friend. The little sergeant who came here from Parow, green and full of go. The one who showed the whole bunch of arrogant detectives at Murder and Robbery how to do police work. The little guy from Parow – where is he, where did he go? The one who laughed and had a clever answer for everything. Who was a legend. Fuck, Benny, you were good; you had everything. You had instinct and respect. You had a future. But you killed it. Drank it up and pissed it away.'

Silence.

'Forty-three,' said Joubert, and he seemed to grow angry all over again. He wove through the cars ahead. Another red light. 'And still you are a bloody child.'

Then only silence reigned in the car. Griessel no longer looked where they were going; he was thinking of the bottle that had been so close to his mouth. Nobody would understand; you had to have been there where he was. You had to know the need. In the old days Joubert had also been a drinker, partied hard, but he had never been to *this* place. He didn't know and that's why he didn't understand. When he looked up again they were in Bellville, Carl Cronjé Street.

Joubert turned off. He was driving more calmly now. There was a park, trees and grass and a few benches. He pulled up. 'Come, Benny,' he said and got out.

What were they doing here? Slowly he opened the door.

Joubert was striding ahead. Where were they going – was he going to beat him up behind the trees? How would that help? The traffic on the N1 above droned and hissed, but no one would see a thing. Reluctantly he followed.

Joubert stopped between the trees and pointed a finger. When Griessel reached him he saw the figure on the ground.

'Do you know who that is, Benny?'

Under a heap of newspapers and cartons and an unbelievably grimy blanket a figure moved when it heard the voice. The dirty face turned upward, a lot of beard and hair and two little blue eyes, sunken in their sockets.

'Do you know him?'

'It's Swart Piet,' said Griessel.

'Hey,' said Swart Piet.

'No,' said Joubert. 'Meet Benny Griessel.'

'You gonna hit me?' the man asked. A Shoprite supermarket trolley stood parked behind his nest. There was a broken vacuum cleaner in it.

'No,' said Joubert.

Swart Piet looked askance at the big man in front of him. 'Do I know you?'

'This is you, Benny. In six months. In a year.'

The man extended a cupped hand to them. 'Have you got ten rand?'

'For what?'

'Bread.'

'The liquid version,' said Joubert.

'You must be psychic,' said the man, and laughed with a toothless cackle.

'Where are your wife and children, Swart Piet?'

'Long time ago. Just a rand? Or five?'

'Tell him, Piet. Tell him what work you used to do.'

'Brain surgeon. What does it matter?'

'Is this what you want?' Joubert looked at Griessel. 'Is this what you want to be?'

Griessel had nothing to say. He only saw Swart Piet's hand, a dirty claw.

Joubert turned around and headed for the car.

'Hey,' said the man. 'What's his case?'

Griessel looked at Joubert's back as he walked away. He wasn't going to hit him. All the way out here for a childish lesson in morality. For a moment he loved the big man. Then he grasped something else, turned back and asked: 'Were you a policeman?'

'Do I look like a fool to you?'

'What were you?'

'A health inspector in Milnerton.'

'A health inspector?'

'Help a hungry man, pal. Two rand.'

'A health inspector,' said Griessel. He felt anger ignite inside him.

'Oh hell,' said Swart Piet. 'Are you the guy from Saddles steakhouse?'

Griessel spun around and set off after Joubert. 'He was a health inspector,' he shouted.

'Okay, one rand, my friend. A rand between friends?'

The senior superintendent was already behind the steering wheel.

Griessel was running now. 'You can't do that,' he shouted. Right up to the window. 'You want to compare me with a fucking health inspector?'

'No. I'm comparing you with a fuck-up who can't stop drinking.'

'Did you ask him why he drinks, Matt? Did you ask him?'

'It makes no difference to him any more.'

'Fuck you,' said Griessel, the weariness and the thirst and the humiliation working together. 'I won't be compared with the cockroach patrol. How many bodies has he had to turn over? How many? Tell me. How many child victims? How many women and old ladies beaten to death for a cell phone or a twenty-rand ring? You want the old Benny? Are you looking for the fucker from Parow who was scared of nothing? I'm looking for him too. Every day, every morning when I get up, I look for him. Because at least he knew he was on the right side. He thought he could make a difference. He believed that if he worked long enough and hard enough, we would win, some time or other, to hell with rank and to hell with promotion; justice would triumph and that is all that mattered because we are the white hats. The guy from Parow is dead, Matt. Dead as a doornail. And why? What happened? What's happening now? We are outnumbered. We aren't winning; we are losing. There are more and more of them and there are less of us. What's the use? What help is all the overtime and the hardship? Are we rewarded? Are we thanked? The harder we work, the more we get shat upon. Look here. This is a white skin. What does it mean? Twenty-six years in the Force and it means fuck-all. It's not the booze – I'm not stuck in the rank of inspector because of the booze. You know that. It's affirmative action. Gave my whole fucking life, took all that shit and along came affirmative action. Ten years now. Did I quit, like De Kok and Rens and Jan Broekman? Look at them now, security companies and making money hand over fist and driving BMWs and going home every day at five o'clock. And where am I? A hundred open cases and my wife kicks me out and I am an alcoholic . . . But I am still fucking *here*, Matt. I didn't fucking quit.'

Then all his fuel was burnt and he leaned against the car, his head on his chest.

'I am still fucking here.'

'Hey!' shouted Swart Piet from the trees.

'Benny,' said Joubert softly.

He looked up slowly. 'What?'

'Let's go.'

'Hey!'

As he walked around to the other door, the man's voice carried clear and shrill: 'Hey, you! Fuck you!'

8

'Your father abused you,' said the minister with certainty.

'No,' she said. 'Lots of call girls say that. The stepfather messed with me. Or the mother's boyfriend. Or the father. I can't say that. That was not his problem.'

She checked for disappointment in his face but there was none to see.

'Do you know what I would wish for if I had only one wish? To know what happened to him. I wonder about that a lot. What did he see to make him change? I know it happened on the Border. I know more or less which year, I worked it out. Somewhere in South West Africa or Angola. But what?

'If only I could remember more of how he was before. But I can't. I only remember the bad times. I think he was always a serious man. And quiet. He must have . . . They didn't all come back from the Border like that, so he must have been a certain kind of person. He must have had the . . . what is the word?'

'Tendency?'

'Yes. He must have had the tendency.'

She searched for something for her hands to do. She leaned forward and took the sugar spoon out of the white porcelain pot. It had a municipal coat of arms on the end of the curved handle. She rubbed the metal with the cushion of her thumb, feeling the indentations.

'The school held a fête every year. On a Friday in October. In the afternoon there were *Boeresport* games and in the evening there were stalls. Tombola and target shooting. *Braaivleis*. Everyone would go, the whole town. After the games you would go home and dress up nicely – for the evening. I was fourteen. I borrowed some make-up from Lenie Heysteck and I bought my first pair of jeans with my savings. I had a sky-blue blouse on and my hair was long and I think I looked pretty. I sat in front of the mirror in my room that evening, putting on mascara and eyeshadow to match my blouse, and my lips were red. Maybe I used too much make-up, because I was still stupid, but I felt so pretty. That is something men don't understand. Feeling pretty.

'What if I had taken my black handbag, walked into the sitting room and he had said, "You look beautiful, Christine." What if he had stood up, taken my hand and said, "May I have this dance, Princess?" '

She pressed the curve of the sugar spoon against her mouth. She felt the old and familiar emotion.

'That is not what happened,' said the minister.

'No,' she said. 'That is not what happened.'

Thobela had memorised the address of Khoza's brother in Khaye-litsha, but he didn't drive there directly. On the spur of the moment he left his original route two off ramps west of the airport and drove into Guguletu. He went looking for the little house he had lived in with Miriam and Pakamile. He parked across the street and switched off the engine.

The little garden that he and the boy had nurtured with so much care and effort and water in the sand of the Cape Flats was faded in the late summer. There were different curtains in the windows of the front room.

He and Miriam had slept in that room.

Down the street, childish voices shrieked. He looked and saw boys playing soccer, shirt-tails hanging out, socks around their ankles. Again, he remembered how Pakamile used to wait for him every afternoon on that street corner from about half-past five. Thobela used to ride a Honda Benly, one of those indestructible little motorbikes that made him look like a daddy-long-legs on it, and the boy's face would light up when he came around the corner and then he would run, racing the motorbike the last hundred metres to their gate.

Always so happy to see him, so hungry to talk and keen to work in the front garden with its sunflowers, in the back vegetable garden full of runner beans, white pumpkins and plump red tomatoes.

He reached a hand out slowly to turn the key, reluctant to let go of the memories.

Why had everything been taken from him?

Then he drove away, back to the N2, and past the airport. He took the off ramp and turned right and Khayelitsha surrounded him – traffic and people, small buildings, houses, sand and smells and sounds, huge adverts for Castle and Coke and Toyota, hand-painted signboards for home industries, hairdressers and panel beaters, fresh vegetable stalls alongside the road, dogs and cows. A city apart from the city, spread out across the dune lands.

He chose his route with care, referring to the map he had studied, because it was easy to get lost here: the road signs few, the streets sometimes broad, sometimes impossibly narrow. He stopped in front of a house, a brick building in the centre of the plot. Building materials lay about, an extra room had been erected to window height, an old Mazda 323 stood on blocks, half covered by a tarpaulin.

He got out, approached the front door and knocked. Music was playing inside, American rap. He knocked again, harder, and the door opened. A young girl, seventeen or eighteen, in T-shirt and jeans. 'Yes?'

'Is this the home of Lukas Khoza?'

'He's not here.'

'I have a message for John.'

Her eyes narrowed. 'What sort of message?'

'Work.'

'John is not here.'

'That's a pity,' he said, 'he would have liked the job.' He turned to go, then stopped. 'Will you let him know?'

'If I see him. Who are you?'

'Tell him the guy who gives good work tips was here. He will know.' He turned away again, as if he had lost interest.

'John hasn't been here for ages. I don't even know where he is.'

He sauntered towards the pick-up and said with a shrug, 'Then I will give the job to someone else.'

'Wait. Maybe my father will know.'

'Luke? Is he here?'

'He's at work. In Maitland. At the abattoir.'

'Maybe I will go past there. Thank you.'

She did not say goodbye. She stood in the doorway, hip against the doorframe, and watched him. As he slipped in behind the wheel he wondered whether she spoke the truth.

She told the minister about the evening her father called her a whore. How he stood over her in the bathroom and made her scrub off the make-up with a face cloth and soap and water. She wept as he lectured her and said not in *his* house. There would be no whoring in *his* house. That was the night it began. When the thing happened inside her. As she recalled the tirade, she was aware of what was going on between her and the minister, because it was familiar territory. She was explaining The Reason and he wanted to hear it. They. Men looked at her, after she had done her job, after she had opened her body to them with gentle hands and caressing words and they wanted to hear her story, her tragic tale. It was a primitive thing. They wanted her really to be good. The whore with the golden heart. The whore who was so nearly an ordinary girl. The minister had it too – he stared intently at her, so ready to empathise with her. But at least with him, the other thing was absent. Her clients, almost without exception, wanted to know if it was also a sex thing – really good, but also horny. Their fantasy of the nympho myth. She was aware of all these things as she sketched her story.

'I've thought about it so much, because that is where it all began. That night. Even now, when I think about it, there is all this anger. I just wanted to look nice. For myself. For my father. For my friends. He didn't want to see that, just all this other stuff, this evil. And then the religion thing just got worse. He forbade us to dance or go to movies and sleep over at friends and visit. He smothered us.'

The minister shook his head as if to say: 'The things parents do.'

'I can't get a grip on it. Gerhard, my brother, did nothing. We had the same parents and the same house and everything, but he did nothing. He just grew quiet and read books in his room, escaped into his stories and into his head. And me? I went looking for trouble. I wanted to become exactly what my father was afraid of. Why? Why was I built like that? Why was I made like this?'

The minister watched while she talked, watched her hands and eyes, the expressions that flitted in rapid succession across her face. He observed her mannerisms, the hair she used with such expertise, the fingers that punctuated her words with tiny movements and the limbs that spoke in an unbroken and sometimes deliberate body language. He placed it alongside the words and the content, the hurt and the sincerity and the obvious intelligence, and he learned something about her: she was enjoying this. On some level, probably unconscious, she enjoyed the limelight. As if, regardless of the trash that had been dumped on it, somewhere her psyche sheltered unscathed.

At twelve o'clock, hunger pangs drew Griessel's attention away from the murder file he had been buried in. That was when he remembered that today there would be no sandwich, no lunch parcel neatly wrapped in clingfilm.

He looked up from the paperwork and the room loomed suddenly large around him. What was he going to do? How would he manage?

Thobela made an error of judgement with Lukas Khoza. He found him at the abattoir, in a blood-spattered plastic apron, busy spraying away the blood from the off-white floor tiles of the slaughterhouse floor with a fat red hosepipe. They walked outside so Khoza could have a smoke break.

Thobela said he was looking for his brother, John, because he had a job for him.

'What sort of work?'

'You know, work.'

Khoza eyed him in distaste. 'No, I don't know and I don't want to know. My brother is trash and if you are his kind, so are you.' He stood, legs apart in a challenging stance, cigarette in hand, between the abattoir building and the stock pens. Large pink pigs milled restlessly behind the steel gates, as if they sensed danger.

'You don't even know what kind of job I am talking about,' said Thobela, aware that he had chosen the wrong approach, that he had been guilty of a generalisation.

'Probably the usual work he does. Robbery. Theft. He will break our mother's heart.'

'Not this time.'

'You lie.'

'No lie. I swear. I don't want him for a criminal purpose,' he said with spirit.

'I don't know where he is.' Khoza crushed the butt angrily under the thick sole of his white gumboots and headed for the door behind him.

'Is there someone else who might know?'

Khoza halted, less antagonistic. 'Maybe.'

Thobela waited.

For a long time Khoza hesitated. 'The Yellow Rose,' he said, and opened the door. A high scream, almost human, rang out from inside. Behind Thobela the pigs surged urgently and pressed against the bars.

9

Thobela drove to the Waterfront, deliberately choosing the road that ran along the mountain so that he had a view of the sea and the harbour. He needed that – space and beauty. The role he had played had disturbed him and he couldn't understand why. Impersonation was nothing new to him. In his days in Europe it had been part of his life. The East Germans had coached him in it down to the finest detail. Living the Lie was his way of life for nearly a decade; the means justified by the goal of Liberty, of Struggle.

Had he changed this much?

He came around the bulging thigh of the mountain and a vista opened up below: ships and cranes, wide blue water, city buildings and freeways, and the coastline curving gracefully away to Blouberg. He wanted to turn to Pakamile and say: 'Look at that, that is the most beautiful city in the world,' and see his son gaze in wonder at all this.

That is the difference, he thought. It felt as though the child was still with him, all around him.

Before Pakamile, before Miriam, he had been alone; he was the only judge of his actions and the only one affected by them. But the boy had moved his boundaries and widened his world so that everything he said and did had other implications. Lying to Lukas Khoza now made him as uncomfortable as if he had been explaining himself to Pakamile. Like the day they went walking in the hills of the farm and he wanted to teach his son to use the rifle with greater responsibility, a piece of equipment to treat with care.

The rifle had awakened the hunter in the boy. As they walked he pointed the unloaded rifle at birds, stones and trees, made shooting noises with his mouth. His thoughts went full circle until he asked: 'You were a soldier, Thobela?'

'Yes.'

'Did you shoot people?' Asked without any macabre fascination: that is how boys are.

How did you answer that? How did you explain to a child how you lay in ambush with a sniper's rifle in Munich, aiming at the enemy of your ally; how you pulled the trigger and saw the blood and brains spatter against the bright blue wall; how you slunk away like a thief in the night, like a coward. That was *your* war, *your* heroic deed.

How did you describe to a child the strange, lost world you lived in – explain about apartheid and oppression and revolution and unrest? About East and West, walls and strange alliances?

He sat down with his back to a rock and he tried. At the end he said you must only take up a weapon against injustice; you must only point it at people as a very last resort. When all other forms of defence and persuasion were exhausted.

As now.

That is what he would like to tell Pakamile now. The end justifies the means. He could not allow the injustice of his murder to go unpunished; he could not meekly accept it. In a country where the System had failed them, it was now the last resort, even if this world was just as hard to explain, just as complicated to understand. Somebody had to take a stand. Somebody had to say, 'This far, and no further.'

That is what he had tried to teach the boy. That is what he owed his son.

He knocked on doors the whole afternoon, and by four o'clock Detective Inspector Benny Griessel knew the victim was forty-six-year-old Josephine Mary McAllister, divorced in 1994, dependable, unremarkable administrative assistant at Benson Exports in Waterkant Street. She was a member of the New Gospel Church in Sea Point, a lonely woman whose former husband lived in Pietermaritzburg and whose two children worked in London. He knew she was a member of the public library, favouring the books of Barbara Cartland and Wilbur Smith, owned a 1999 Toyota Corolla, had R18,762.80 in a current account at Nedbank, owed R6,456.70 on her credit card, and on the day of her death had booked a plane ticket to Heathrow, apparently planning to visit her children.

He also had, as with the previous two murders, not a single significant clue.

When he dragged his cases across the threshold of her apartment he understood the risk in what he was doing, but he told himself he had no choice. Where the hell should he go? To a hotel, where alcohol was one finger on the telephone away? Forensics had already been through here and there was no other key but the one in his pocket.

Josephine Mary McAllister's flat had no shower, only a bath. He ran it half full and lay in the steaming water, watching his heart sending delicate ripples across the surface with each rhythmic beat.

The broad connection between McAllister, Jansen and Rosen was elementary. All middle-aged, living alone in Green Point, Mouille Point. No forced entry. Each strangled with an electric cord from the victim's kitchen. How did the perpetrator pick his victims? On the street? Did he sit in a car and watch until he spotted a potential victim? And then just knock on the door?

Impossible. McAllister and Rosen's apartment blocks had security gates and intercom systems. Women didn't open up for strange men – not any more. Jansen's house had a steel gate at the front door.

No, somehow he befriended them. Then made a date for a Friday night and picked them up or brought them home. And used the electric cord, which he found in the kitchen. Did he take it into the sitting room or the bedroom? How did he manage to surprise them? Because there was not much sign of struggle – no tissue under fingernails, no other bruising.

He must be strong. Fast, and methodical.

The forensic psychologist in Pretoria said the fucker would have a record, possibly for minor offences: assault, theft, trespassing, even arson. Most likely for sexual offences, rape perhaps. 'They don't start with murder, they climb the ladder. If you catch him, you will find him in possession of pornography, sadomasochistic stuff. One thing I can tell you: he won't stop. He's getting more skilful and more and more self-confidence.'

Griessel took the soap and washed his body, wondering if she had sat in here before he fetched her. Had she prepared herself for the date, unknowing, a lamb to the slaughter?

He would get him.

Friday nights. Why Fridays?

He rinsed off the soap.

Was Friday the only night he was free of responsibilities? What professions were off on Friday nights? Or rather what professions worked on Friday nights? Only bloody policemen, that's all – the rest of the world partied. And murdered.

He climbed out of the bath, walked dripping over to his cases and took out a towel. Anna had placed one neatly on top of the clothes. She had packed carefully for him, as if she cared. But now he rummaged around in the suitcases. He would have to hang the clothes up, or they would be wrinkled.

He had to find a place to stay. For six months.

He listened to the silence in the flat, suddenly aware that he was alone. That he was sober. He chose some clothes and dressed.

Despite her anger, Anna had packed his clothes with care. She would be in the kitchen now, still in her work clothes, clattering pots and pans, radio playing on the table. Carla would be sitting at the dining-room table with her homework books, twisting the point of the pencil in her hair. Fritz would be in front of the television, remote in hand, skipping channels continuously, searching, impatient. Always on the go. He was like that too – things must happen.

Jesus, what had happened to his life?

Pissed away. With the help of Klipdrift and Coke and Jack Daniels.

Alcoholics Anonymous, Step Ten: Continue to take personal inventory and when you are wrong, promptly admit to it.

He sighed deeply. Desire pressed against his ribcage from inside. He did not want to be here. He wanted to go home. He wanted his family back, his wife and his children. He wanted his life back. He would have to start over. He wanted to be like he was before – the policeman from the Parow station who laughed at life. Could one begin again? Now. At forty-three?

Where would you begin, to start over?

You don't have to be a genius to work that one out. He wasn't sure whether he had said that out loud.

He must buy a newspaper and look for a place in the classified ads, because this fucking flat gave him the heebie-jeebies. But first he must phone. He found Mrs McAllister's phone directory in a drawer of the cupboard by the phone. He opened it near the front, and slid his finger down the list, turned a page, looked again until he found the number.

He would try one more time. One last fucking time.

He rang the number. It did not ring for long.

'Alcoholics Anonymous, good afternoon,' said a woman's voice.

By chance Thobela bought the *Argus*. It was something to do while he ate fish and chips from a cardboard carton, the seagulls waiting like beggars on the railing for alms. He spread the paper open on the table before him. First he read the main article without much interest – more political undercurrents in the Western Cape, allegations of corruption and the usual denials. He dipped the chips in the seafood sauce. That was when he spotted the small column in the right bottom corner.

COPS CALLED 'INCOMPETENT' –
BABY RAPIST CASE DISMISSED

He read. When he had finished, he pushed the remains to one side. He gazed out over the quiet water of the harbour. Pleasure boats with sunburned tourists on board cruised out in a line to serve cocktails off Llandudno and Clifton when the sun went down. But he was blind to the scene. He sat there staring and motionless for a long time with his big hands framing the article. Then he read it again.

There was a knock on the study door and the minister said, 'Come in.'

The woman who put her head around the door was in her middle years, her black hair cut short against her head and her nose long and elegant. 'Sorry to disturb you. I have made some snacks.'

The two women summed each other up with a glance. Christine saw false self-assurance, subservience, a slim body hidden by a sensible frock. A busy woman with able hands that only laboured in the kitchen. The sort of woman who had sex in order to have children, not for pleasure. A woman who would turn away stiffly if her husband's mouth and tongue slid lower than the small, worn breasts. Christine knew her type, but she didn't want to let on and tried to seem inconspicuous.

The minister stood up and crossed to his wife to take the tray from her. 'Thank you, Mamma,' he said.

'It's a pleasure,' she said, smiling tight-lipped at Christine. Her eyes said, for the tiniest moment, 'I know your kind,' before she softly closed the door.

In a detached way the minister placed the tray on the desk – sandwiches, chicken drumsticks, gherkins and serviettes.

'How did you meet?' she asked. He had gone back to his chair.

'Rita and I? At university. Her car broke down. She had an old Mini Minor. I was passing on my bicycle and stopped.'

'Was it love at first sight?'

He chuckled. 'It was for me. She had a boyfriend in the army.'

Why, she would have liked to ask. What did you see in her? What made you choose her? Did she look like the ideal rectory wife? A virgin? Pure. She imagined the romance, the propriety, and she knew it would have bored her to death at that age.

'So you stole her away from him?' she asked, but wasn't really interested any more. She felt an old jealousy rising.

'Eventually.' He smiled in a self-satisfied way. 'Please, have something to eat.'

She wasn't hungry. She took a sandwich, noting the lettuce and tomato filling, the way the bread was cut in a perfect triangle. She placed it on a plate and put it on her lap. She wanted to ask how he had managed to wait, how he had suppressed his urges until after the wedding. Did student ministers masturbate, or was that a sin too in their world?

She waited until he began to eat a drumstick, holding the leg bone in his fingers. He leaned forward so that he ate above the plate. His lips glistened with fat.

'I had sex the first time when I was fifteen,' she said. 'Proper sex.'

She wanted him to choke on his food, but his jaw only stalled a moment.

'I chose the boy. I picked him out. The cleverest one in the class. I could have had anyone, I knew that.'

He was helpless with the chicken half eaten in his hand and his mouth full of meat.

'The more my father prayed about the demons in me, the more I wanted to see them. Every night. Every night we had to sit in the lounge and he would read from the Bible and pray long prayers and ask God to cast the Devil out of Christine. The sins of the flesh. The temptations. While we held hands and he sweated and talked till the windows rattled and the hair on my neck stood up. I would wonder, what demons? What did they look like? What did they do? How would it feel if they came out? Why did he focus on me? Was it something I couldn't help? At first I didn't have a clue. But then boys at school began to look at me. At my body.'

She didn't want the plate on her lap any more. She plonked it down on the desk and folded her hands under her breasts. She must calm down; she needed him, perfect wife and all.

Her father would inspect her every morning like one of his men. He would not let her out of the door until he had approved the length of her skirt. Sometimes he would send her back to tie up her hair or to wash off some barely visible mascara, until she learned to leave a little earlier and apply her make-up in the mirror of the school toilets. She did not want to forgo the newly discovered attention of boys. It was a strange thing. At thirteen she had been just one of the crowd: flat-chested, pale and giggly. Then every-thing began to grow – breasts, hips, legs, lips – a metamorphosis that made her father rabid and had an odd effect on all the men around her. Matric boys began to greet her, teachers began to linger at her desk, Standard Sixes began to look at her sideways and whisper to each other behind cupped hands. Eventually she twigged. It was during this time that her mother began to work and Christine became part of a group who went to a parentless house after school to smoke and occasionally to drink. And Colin Engelbrecht had said to her from behind the blue cloud of a Chesterfield that she had the sexiest body in school, it was now officially accepted. And if she would be willing to show him her breasts, just once, he would do anything.

The other girls in the room had thrown cushions at him and screamed that he was a pig. She had stood up, unbuttoned her shirt, unhooked her bra and exposed her breasts to the three boys in the room. She had stood there with her big boobs and for the first time in her life felt the power, saw the enthralment in their eyes, the jaw-dropping weakness of lust. How different from her father's terrible disgust.

That is how she came to know the demons.

After that, nothing was the same again. Her display of her breasts was talked about, she realised later, because the level of interest increased and the style of their approach changed. This act had created the possibility of wildness, the chance of getting lucky. So she began to use it. It was a weapon, a shield and a game. The ones she favoured were occasionally rewarded with admission to her room and a long sweaty petting session in the midday heat of Upington, the privilege of stroking and licking her breasts while she watched their faces with absolute concentration and cherished the incredibly deep pleasure – that she was responsible for this ecstasy, the panting, the thundering heartbeat.

But when their hands began to drift downwards, she returned them softly but firmly to above the waist, because she wanted to control when that would happen, and with whom.

The way *she* wanted it, exactly as she fantasised when she lay in her bed late at night and masturbated, slowly teasing the devil with her fingers until she drove him out with a shuddering orgasm. Only to find the next night that he was back inside, lurking, waiting for her hand.

It was at the school sports day of her Standard-Eight year that she seduced the handsome, good and clever, but shy Johan Erasmus with his gold-rimmed glasses and fine hands. It happened in the long grass behind the bus shed. He was the one who was too afraid to look at her, who blushed blood red if she said hello. He was soft – his eyes, his voice, his heart. She wanted to give her gift to him because he never asked for it.

And she had.

10

'My name is Benny Griessel and I am an alcoholic.'

'Hello, Benny,' said thirty-two voices in a happy chorus.

'Last night I drank a whole bottle of Jack Daniels and I hit my wife. This morning she kicked me out the house. I have gone one day without drinking. I am here because I can't control my drinking. I am here because I want my wife and children and my life back.' While he was listening to the desperation in his voice, someone began to clap, and then the dingy little church hall resounded with applause.

He lingered in the dark outside the long, unimaginative building, instinctively taking an inventory of exits, windows and the distance to his pick-up. The Yellow Rose must have been a farmhouse once, a smallholder's home in the 1950s before the high tide of Khayelitsha pushed past.

Below the roof ridge was a neon sign with the name and a bright yellow rose. Rap music thumped inside. There were no curtains in the windows. Light shone through and made long tracks across the parking lot, joyful lighthouses on a treacherous black reef.

Inside they sat densely bunched around cheap tables. He spotted a few European tourists with the forced bonhomie of nervous people, like missionaries in a village of cannibals. He threaded his way through and saw two or three seats vacant at the pinewood bar. Two young black barmen busied themselves filling orders behind it. Waitresses slipped expertly up to them, each wearing a yellow plastic rose flapping from the thin T-shirt fabric above their chests.

'What's your pleasure, big dog?' the barman asked him in a vaguely American accent. *Biehg dawg.*

'Do you have Windhoek?' he asked in his mother tongue.

'Lager or Light, my friend?'

'Are you a Xhosa?'

'Yes.'

He would have liked to say, 'Then speak Xhosa to me,' but he refrained, because he needed information.

'Lager, please.'

The beer and a glass appeared before him. 'Eleven rand eighty.'

Eleven rand eighty? Alchemists Inc. He gave him fifteen. 'Keep the change.'

He raised the glass and drank.

'I hope you will still feel like applauding when I have finished,' said Griessel when the ovation died down. 'Because tonight I will say what I should have said in nineteen ninety-six. And you won't necessarily like what you hear.' He glanced at Vera, the coloured woman with the sympathetic smile who was chairing the meeting. A sea of heads was turned towards him, every face an echo of Vera's unconditional support. He felt extremely uncomfortable.

'I have two problems with the AA.' His voice filled the hall as if he were there alone. 'One is that I don't feel I fit in here. I am a policeman. Murder is my speciality. Every day.' He gripped the back of the blue plastic chair in front of him. He saw his knuckles were white with tension and he looked up at Vera, not knowing where else to look. 'And I drink to make the voices stop.'

Vera nodded as if she understood. He looked for another focal point. There were posters on the wall.

'We scream when we die,' he said, soft and slow, because he had to express it right. 'We all cling on to life. We hang on very tight, and when someone pries our fingers loose, we fall.' He saw his hands were demonstrating this in front of him; two fierce claws opening up. 'That is when we scream. When we realise it won't help to grab any more because we are falling too fast.'

The foghorn at Mouille Point mourned far and deep. It was deathly quiet in the church hall. He took a deep breath and looked at them. There was discomfort; the cheerfulness had frozen.

'I hear it. I can't help it. I hear it when I walk in on a scene while they are lying there. The scream hangs there – waiting for someone to hear it. And when you hear it, it gets in your head and it stays there.'

Someone coughed nervously to his left.

'It is the most dreadful sound,' he said, and looked at them, because now he did want their support. They avoided his eyes.

'I never talked about it,' he said. Vera shifted as if she wanted to say something. But she mustn't speak now. 'People will think I'm not right in the head. That's what *you* think. Right now. But I'm not crazy. If I were, alcohol would not help. It would make it worse. Alcohol helps. It helps when I walk in on a murder scene. It helps me get through the day. It helps when I go home and see my wife and children and I hear them laughing, but I know that scream lies waiting inside them as well. I know it is waiting there and one day it will come out and I am scared that I am the one who will hear it.'

He shook his head. 'That would be too much to bear.'

He looked down at the floor and whispered: 'And the thing that frightens me most is that I know that scream is inside *me*.'

He looked up into Vera's eyes. 'I drink because it takes away that fear too.'

'When last was John Khoza here?' Thobela asked the barman.

'Who?'

'John Khoza.'

'Yo, man, there are so many dawgs coming in here.'

He sighed and took out a fifty-rand note, pushing it with his palm over the bar counter.

'Try to remember.'

The note disappeared. 'Sort of a thin dude with bad skin?'

'That's him.'

'He mostly talks to the Boss Man – you'll have to ask him.'

'When last did he come to talk to the Boss Man?'

'I work shifts, man, I'm not here all the time. Haven't seen John-dawg for ages.' He moved off to serve someone else.

Thobela swallowed more beer. The bitter taste was familiar, the music was too loud and the bass notes vibrated in his chest. Across the room near the window was a table of seven. Raucous laughter. A muscular coloured man with complex tattoos on his arms balanced on a stool. He downed a big jug of beer, shouted something, although the words were lost, and held the empty jug aloft.

It was all too hollow, too contrived for Thobela, this joviality. It always had been, since Kazakhstan, although that was a long time ago. A hundred and twenty black brothers in a Soviet training camp who drank and sang and laughed at night. And longed for home, bone-tired. Comrades and warriors.

The barman came past again.

'Where can I find the Boss Man?'

'It can be arranged.' He stood there expectant, without batting an eyelid.

He took out another fifty. The barman did not move. Another one. A palm swept the money away.

'Give me one minute.'

'The second problem is with the Twelve Steps. I know them off by heart and I can understand them working for other people. Step One is easy, because I fu . . ., I know my life is out of control, alcohol has taken over. Step Two says a Power greater than ourselves can heal us. Step Three says just turn over our will and our lives to Him.'

'Amen,' said a couple of them.

'The problem is,' he said with as much apology as he could put into his voice, 'I don't believe there is such a Power. Not in this city.'

Even Vera avoided his gaze. For a moment longer he stood in the silence. Then he sighed. 'That is all I can say.' He sat down.

By the end of his second beer he saw the Boss Man approaching him from across the room, a fat black man with a shaven head and a gold ring on every finger. He would stop at a table here and there, almost shouting as he spoke to the guests – from the bar his words were drowned in the racket – until he reached Thobela. There were tiny drops of perspiration on his face as if he had exerted himself. Jewellery glittered as he offered his right hand.

'Do I know you?'

His voice was remarkably high and feminine and his eyes small and alert. 'Madison Madikiza; they call me the Boss Man.'

'Tiny.' He used a nickname from the past.

'Tiny? Then my name is Skinny,' said the Boss Man. He had an infectious giggle that screwed up his eyes and shook his entire body as he hoisted it onto a bar stool. A tall glass materialised in front of him, the contents clear as water.

'Cheers.' He drank deeply and wiped his mouth with his sleeve, waving an index finger up and down in Thobela's direction. 'I know you.'

'Ah . . .' His pulse accelerated as he focused more sharply on the man's features. He did not want to be caught unawares. Recognition meant trouble. There would be connotations, a track with a start and an end.

'No, don't tell me, it will come to me. Give me a minute.' The little eyes danced over him, a frown creased the bald head. 'Tiny . . . Tiny . . . Weren't you . . .? No, that was another fellow.'

'I don't think—'

'No, wait, I must place you. Hell, I never forget a face . . . Just tell me, what is your line?'

'This and that,' he said cautiously.

The fingers snapped. 'Orlando Arendse,' said the Boss Man. 'You rode shotgun for Orlando.'

Relief. 'That was a long time ago.'

'Memory like an elephant, my friend. Ninety-eight, ninety-seven, thereabouts, I still worked for Shakes Senzeni, God rest his soul. He had a chop shop in Gugs and I was his foreman. Orlando asked for a sit-down over division of territory, d'you remember? Big meeting in Stikland and you sat next to Orlando. Afterwards Shakes said that was clever, we couldn't speak Xhosa among ourselves. Fuck, my friend, small world. I hear Orlando has retired, the Nigerians have taken over the drug trade.'

'I last saw Orlando two or three years ago.' He could remember the meeting, but not the man in front of him. There was something else, a realisation of alternatives – if he had remained with Orlando, where would that have left him now?

'So, what do you do now?'

He could keep to his cover with more conviction now. 'I am freelance. I put jobs together . . .' What would he have done when Orlando retired? Operated a nightclub? Run something on the periphery of the law. How close to a potential truth was the story he was fabricating now?

'A broker?'

'A broker.' There was a time when it was possible, when it could have been true. But that lay in the past. What lay ahead? Where was he going?

'And you have something for Johnny Khoza?'

'Maybe.'

Shouts rang out above the music and they looked around. The strong coloured man was dancing on the table now with his shirt off. A dragon tattoo spat faded red fire across his chest while bystanders urged him on.

Boss Man Madikiza shook his head. 'Trouble brewing,' he said, and turned back to Thobela. 'I don't think Johnny is available, my friend. I hear he's on the run. They got him in Ciskei for AR and manslaughter. He did a service station – Johnny never thinks big. So when the court case went wrong, it cost him big money to buy a key, you know what I'm saying. I don't know where he is, but he is definitively not in the Cape. He would have come creeping in here long ago if he was. In any case, I have better talent on my books – just tell me what you need.'

For the first time the possibility occurred to him that he might not get them. The possibility that his search could be fruitless, that they had crept into a hole somewhere where he could not get at them. The frustration pressed heavily down on him, making him feel sluggish and impotent. 'The thing is,' he said, although he already knew it would not work, 'Khoza has information on the potential job. A contact on the inside. Is there no one who would know where he is?'

'He has a brother . . . I don't know where.'

'No one else?' Where to now? If he couldn't find Khoza and Ramphele? What then? With an effort he shook off the feeling and concentrated on what the Boss Man was saying.

'I don't know too much about him. Johnny is small time, one of many who try to impress me. They are all the same – come in here with big attitude, throw their money around in front of the girls like they were big gangstas, but they do service stations. No class. If Johnny has told you he has a contact on the inside for a serious score, you should be careful.'

'I will.' The farm was not an option. He could not go back. With this frustration in him it would drive him insane. What was he going to do?

'Where can I get hold of you? If I hear something?'

'I will come back.'

The Boss Man's little eyes narrowed. 'You don't trust me?'

'I trust nobody.'

The little laugh bubbled up, champagne from a barrel, and a marshmallow hand patted him on the shoulder. 'Well said, my friend . . .'

There was a crash louder than the music. The dancing dragon's table had broken beneath him and he fell spectacularly, to the great enjoyment of the onlookers. He lay on the floor holding his beer glass triumphantly above him.

'Fuck,' said the Boss Man and got up from the stool. 'I knew things would get out of hand.'

The coloured man stood up slowly and gestured an apology in Madikiza's direction. He nodded back with a forced smile.

'He will pay for the table, the shit.' He turned to Thobela. 'Do you know who that is?'

'No idea.'

'Enver Davids. Yesterday he walked away from a baby rape charge. On a technicality. Fucking police misplaced his file, can you believe it – a genuine administrative fuck-up; you don't buy your way out of that one. He's more bad news than the *Financial Mail*. General of the Twenty-Sevens. He got Aids in jail from a *wyfie*. More cell time than Vodacom, and they parole him and he goes and rapes a baby, supposed to cure his Aids . . . Now he comes and drinks here, because his own people will string him up, the fucking filthy shit.'

'Enver Davids,' said Thobela slowly.

'Fucking filthy shit,' said the Boss Man again, but Thobela was beyond hearing. Something was beginning to make sense. He could see a way forward.

His hands trembled on the steering wheel. They had a life of their own. He felt cold in the warm summer night and he knew it was withdrawal. He knew it was beginning – it was going to be a terrible night in the flat of Josephine Mary McAllister.

He reached out to the radio, locating the knob with difficulty, and pressed it. Music. He kept the volume low. At this time of night Sea Point's streets were alive with cars and pedestrians, people going somewhere with purpose. Except for him.

They had made a circle around him once everyone was finished. They gathered around him, touched him as if to transfer something to him through their hands. Strength. Or belief? Faces, too many faces. Some faces told a story in the rings around their eyes and mouths, like the rings of a tree. Heartbreaking stories. Others were masks hiding secrets. But the eyes, all the eyes were the same – piercing, glowing with willpower, like someone in floodwaters hanging on to a thin green branch. He will see, they said. He will see. What he did see was that he was part of The Last Chance Club. He felt the same desperation, the same dragging floodwaters.

The tremor ran through him like a fever. He could hear their voices and he turned the music up. Rhythm filled the car. Louder. Rock, Afrikaans, he tried to follow the words.

Ek wil huis toe gaan na Mamma toe,
Ek wil huis toe gaan na Mamma toe.

Too much synthesizer, he thought, not quite right, but good.
Die rivier is vol, my trane rol.

He parked in front of the block of flats, but didn't get out. He allowed his fingers to run down the imaginary neck of a base guitar – that's what the song needed, more base. Lord, it would be good to hold a base guitar again. The trembling limb jerked to a rhythm all of its own and made him want to laugh out loud.

'n Bokkie wat vanaand by my wil lê. . .

Nostalgia. Where were the days, where was the twenty-year-old little fucker who throttled a base guitar in the police dance band until the very walls shook?

Sy kan maar lê, ek is 'n loslappie.

Emotion. His eyes burned. Fuck, no, he wasn't a crybaby. He banged the radio off, opened the door and got out fast, so he could get away from this place.

I I

The minister wondered if she was telling the whole truth – he searched between her words and in her body language. He could see the anger, old and new, the involuntary physical self-consciousness. The continuous, practised offering of mouth, breasts and hair. Her eyes had a strange shape, almost oriental. And they were small. Her features were not delicate, but had an attractive regularity. Her neck was not thin, but strong. Her gaze sometimes skittered away as though she might betray something: a thirst for acceptance? Or was there something rotten? Or spoilt, like a child still wanting her own way, craving attention and respect, an ego feeding on alternating current – now brave, now incredibly fragile.

Fascinating.

He phoned his wife just after ten, when he knew she would have had her bath and would be sitting on their bed with her dressing gown pulled above her knees smoothing cream on her legs, and then turning to the mirror and doing the same to her face with delicate movements of her fingertips. He wanted to be there now to watch her do it, because his memories of that were not recent.

'I am sober,' was the first thing he said.

'That's good,' she said, but without enthusiasm, so that he didn't know how to continue.

'Anna . . .'

She did not speak.

'I'm sorry,' he said with feeling.

'So am I, Benny.' Without inflection.

'Don't you want to know where I am?'

'No.'

He nodded as if he had been expecting it.

'I'll say goodnight then.'

'Goodnight, Benny.' She put the phone down and he held his cell phone to his ear for a little longer and he knew she did not believe he would make it.

Perhaps she was right.

She saw that she had entranced him and said: 'In Standard Nine I slept with a teacher. And with a buddy of my father.' But he did not react.

'What do you think?' she asked. Suddenly she had to know.

He hesitated for so long that she became anxious. Had he heard, was he listening? Or was he revolted by her?

'I think you are deliberately trying to shock me,' he said, but he was smiling at her and his tone was as soft as water.

For a moment she was embarrassed. Unconsciously, her hand flew up to her hair, the fingers twisting the ends.

'What interests me is why you would want to do that. Do you still think I will judge you?'

It was only part of the truth, but she nodded fractionally.

'I can hardly blame you for that, as I suspect experience has taught you that that is what people do.'

'Yes,' she said.

'Let me tell you that counselling from a Christian point of view distinguishes between the person and the deed. What we do is sometimes unacceptable to God, but we are never unacceptable to Him. And He expects the same from me, if I am to do His work.'

'My father also thought he was doing God's work.' The words were out in reflex, an old anger.

He grimaced as if in pain, as if she had no right to make this comparison.

'The Bible has been used for many agendas. Fear too.'

'So why does God allow that?' She knew the question was lying in wait and she had not seen it.

'You must remember . . .'

Her hands seemed to lose their grip, she seemed to have lost her footing. 'No, tell me. Why? Why did He write the Bible like that so that everyone could use it as they please?' She could hear her own voice, the way it spiralled, how it carried the emotion with it. 'If He loves us so much? What did I do to Him? Why didn't He give me an easy road too? Like you and your wife? Why did He give me Viljoen and then allow him to blow his brains out? What was my sin? He gave me my father – what chance did I have after that? If He wanted me to be stronger, why didn't He make me stronger? Or cleverer? I was a child. How was I supposed to know? How was I supposed to know grown-ups were fucked up?' The sound of the swearword was sharp and cutting and she heard it as he would and it made her stop. Angrily, she wiped the wet off her cheeks with the back of her hand.

When he did react, he surprised her again. 'You are in trouble,' he said nearly inaudibly.

She nodded. And sniffed.

He opened a drawer, took out a box of tissues and pushed it over the desk towards her. Somehow this gesture disappointed her. History – she was not the first.

'Big trouble,' he said.

She ignored the tissues. 'Yes.'

He put a big, freckled hand on the cardboard box. 'And it has to do with this?'

'Yes,' she said, 'it has to do with that.'

'And you are afraid,' he said.

She nodded.

He pressed a hand over the man's mouth and the assegai blade against his throat and waited for him to wake. It came with a jerk of the body and eyes opening wide and wild. He put his head close to the small ear and whispered, 'If you keep quiet, I will give you a chance.' He felt the power of Davids' body straining against the pressure. He cut him with the tip of the blade against the throat, but lightly, just so that he could feel the sting. 'Lie still.'

Davids subsided, but his mouth moved under the hand.

'Quiet,' he whispered again, the stink of drink in his nostrils. He wondered how sober Davids was, but he could wait no longer – it was nearly four o'clock.

'Let's go outside, you and me. Understand?'

The shaven head nodded.

'If you make a noise before we are outside, I will cut you.'

Nod.

'Come.' He allowed him to get up, got behind him with the assegai under Davids' chin, arm around his throat. They shuffled through the dark house to the front door. He felt the tension in the man's muscles and he knew the adrenaline was flowing in him too. They were outside, on the pavement, and he took a quick step back. He waited for Davids to turn to him, saw the dragon's raging red eyes, and took the knife from his pocket, a long butcher's knife he had found in a kitchen drawer.

He passed it to the coloured man.

'Here,' he said. 'This is your chance.'

At quarter-past seven when Griessel entered the parade room of the Serious and Violent Crimes building in Bishop Lavis, he did not feel the buzz.

He sat with his head down, paging aimlessly through the dossier on his lap, searching for a starting point on which to build his oral report. He was light-headed – thoughts darting like silver fish, diving aimlessly into a green sea, this way, that way, evasive, always out of reach. His hands were sweating. He couldn't say he had nothing to report. They would laugh at him. Joubert would crap him out. He would have to say he was waiting for Forensics. Jissis, if he could just keep his hands still. He felt nauseous, an urge to throw up, vomit out all the shit.

Senior Superintendent Matt Joubert clapped his hands twice and the sharp sound echoed through him. The voices of the detectives quieted.

'You have probably all heard,' said Joubert, and a reaction ran through his audience: 'Tell them, Bushy.' There was contentment in his voice and Griessel read the mood. Something was going on.

Bezuidenhout stood against the opposite wall and Griessel tried to focus on him, his eyes flickering, blink-blink-blink-blink. He heard Bushy's gravelly voice: 'Last night Enver Davids was stabbed to death in Kraaifontein.'

A joyful riot broke out in the parade room. Griessel was perplexed. Who was Davids?

The noise droned through Griessel, the sickness growing inside. Christ, he was sick, sick as a dog.

'His pals say they went drinking at a shebeen in Khayelitsha and came home to the house in Kraaifontein about one a.m., when they went to sleep. This morning, just after five, someone knocked on the door to say there was a man lying dead in the street.'

Griessel knew he would hear the sound.

'Nobody heard or saw anything,' said Inspector Bushy Bezuidenhout. 'It looks like a knife fight. Davids has slash wounds to the hands and one on the neck, but at this stage the fatal wound seems to be a stab through the heart.'

Griessel saw Davids fall backwards, mouth stretched wide, the fillings in his teeth rusty brown. The scream, at first as thick as molasses, a tongue slowly sticking out, and the scream growing thin, thinner than blood. And it came to him.

'They should have cut off his balls,' said Vaughn Cupido.

The policemen laughed and that made the sound accelerate, the long thin trail scorched through the ether. Griessel jerked his head away, but the sound found him.

Then he vomited, dry and retching and he heard the laughter and heard someone say his name. Joubert? 'Benny, are you alright? Benny?' But he was not fucking alright, the noise was in his head, and it would never get out.

He drove first to the hotel room in Parow. Davids' blood was on his arms and clothes. Boss Man's words repeated in his head: *He got Aids in jail from a* wyfie.

He washed his big body with great concentration, scrubbed down with soap and water, washed his clothes afterwards in the bath, put on a clean set and walked out to his pick-up.

It was past five when he came outside – the east was beginning to change colour. He took the N1 and then the N7 and the Table View off ramp near the smoking, burning refinery where a thousand lights still shone. Minibus taxis were already busy. He drove as far as Blouberg, thinking of nothing. He got out at the sea. It was a cloudless morning. An unsettled breeze still looking for direction blew softly against his skin. He looked up to the mountain where the first rays of the sun made deep shadows on the cliffs, like the wrinkles of an old man. Then he breathed, slowly in and out.

Only when his pulse had slowed to normal did he take from the cubbyhole, where he had stowed it yesterday, the *Argus* article, neatly torn out.

'Does someone want to harm you?' asked the minister.

She blew her nose loudly and looked at him apologetically, rolling up the tissue in her hand. She took another and blew again.

'Yes.'

'Who?' He reached under his desk and brought out a white plastic wastepaper basket. She tossed the tissues into it, took another and wiped her eyes and cheeks.

'There is more than one,' she said, and the emotions threatened again. She waited a moment for them to subside. 'More than one.'

12

'Are you sure he is guilty?' he had asked Boss Man Madikiza, because ideas had materialised in his head out of nowhere and his blood was boiling.

The fat man snorted and said Davids had been in his office before the drinking began. Boastful and smug. The police had his cum, in their hands, the dee-en-ay evidence, they could have nailed him right there with a life sentence with their test tubes and their microscopes and then they *moered* the bottle away, thick as bricks, and so the prosecutor came up to the judge dragging his feet and said dyor onner, we fucked up a little, no more dee-en-ay, no more rape charge. Did that judge *kak* them out, my bro', like you won't believe. 'What kind of person?' the Boss Man asked Thobela with total revulsion, 'what kind of person rapes a baby, I ask you?'

He had nothing to say.

'And they've gone and abolished the death penalty,' the Boss Man said as he got up.

Thobela said goodbye and left and went and sat in his pick-up. He put his hand behind the seat and felt the polished shaft of the assegai. He stroked the wood with his fingers, back and forth, back and forth.

Someone had to say, 'This far, and no further.'

Back and forth.

So he waited for them.

When the minister moved away from her and sat on the edge of the desk, she knew something had altered between them, a gap had been bridged. Maybe it was just on her side that a certain anxiety had subsided, a fear allayed, but she could see a change in his body language – more ease.

If he would be patient, she said, she would like to tell the whole story, everything. So that he could understand. Perhaps so she could also understand, because it was hard. For so long she had believed she was doing what she had to, following the only course available. But now . . . she wasn't so sure.

Take your time, he said, and his smile was different. Paternal.

The last thing Griessel could remember, before they took him to Casualty at Tygerberg Hospital and injected him with some or other shit that made his head soft and easy, was Matt Joubert holding his hand. The senior superintendent, who said to him all the way in the ambulance, over and over: 'It's just the DTs, Benny, don't worry. It's just the DTs.' His voice bore more worry than comfort.

She went to university to study physiotherapy. The whole family accompanied her on a scorching hot Free State day in January. Her father had made them all kneel in her hostel room and had prayed for her, a long dramatic prayer that made the sweat pop out on his frowning forehead and exposed the wickedness of Bloemfontein in detail.

She remained standing on the pavement when the white Toyota Cressida eventually drove away. She felt wonderful: intensely liberated, a floating, euphoric sensation. 'I felt as though I could fly,' were the words she used. Until she saw her mother look back. For the first time she could really see her family from the outside, and her mother's expression upset her. In that short-lived moment, the second or two before the mask was replaced, she read in her mother's face longing, envy and desire – as if she would have liked to stay behind, escape as her daughter had. It was Christine's first insight, her first knowledge that she was not the only victim.

She had meant to write to her mother after initiation, a letter of solidarity, love and appreciation. She wanted to say something when her mother phoned the hostel for the first time to find out how things were going. But she never could find the right words. Maybe it was guilt – she had escaped and her mother had not. Maybe it was the new world that never left time or space for melancholy thoughts. She was swept up in student life. She enjoyed it immensely, the total experience. Serenades, Rag, hostel meetings, social coffee-breaks, the lovely old buildings, dances, Intervarsity, men, the open spaces of the campus's lawns and streams and avenues of trees. It was a sweet cup and she drank deeply, as if she could never have enough of it.

'You won't believe me, but for ten months I didn't have sex. I was one hundred per cent celibate. Heavy petting, yes, there were four, five, six guys I played around with. Once I slept the whole night with a medical student in his flat in Park Street, but he had to stay above the belt. Sometimes I would drink, but I tried to only do that on a girls' night out, for safety.'

Her father's letters had nothing to do with her celibacy – long, disjointed sermons and biblical references that she would later not even open and deliberately toss in the rubbish bin. It was a contract with the new life: 'I would do nothing to make a ba . . . a mess of it.'

She would not tempt fate or challenge the gods. She vaguely realised it was not rational, since she did not perform academically, she was constantly on the edge of failing, but she kept her part of the deal and the gods continued to smile on her.

Then she met Viljoen.

In sharp criticism of the state's handling of the case, Judge Rosenstein quoted recent newspaper reports on the dramatic increase in crimes against children.

'In this country 5,800 cases of rape of children younger than 12 years old were investigated last year, and some 10,000 cases where children between 11 and 17 years old were involved. In the Peninsula alone, more than 1,000 cases of child molestation were reported last year and the number is rising.

'What makes these statistics even more shocking is the fact that only an estimated 15 per cent of all crimes against children are actually reported. And then there is the matter of children as

murder victims. Not only are they being caught in the crossfire of gangland shootings, or become the innocent prey of paedophiles, now they are being killed in this senseless belief that they can cure Aids,' he said.

'The facts and figures clearly indicate that society is already failing our children. And now the machinery of the state is proving inadequate to bring the perpetrators of these heinous crimes to justice. If children can't depend on the justice system to protect them, to whom can they turn?'

Thobela folded the article up again and put it in his shirt pocket. He walked down to the beach, feeling the sand soft beneath his shoes. Just beyond reach of the white foaming arcs spilling across the sand he stood, hands in pockets. He could see Pakamile and his two friends running in step along the beach. He could hear their shouts, see their bare torsos and the sand grains clinging to their skins like stars in a chocolate firmament, arms aloft like wings as their squadron flew in formation just above the waterline. He had taken them to Haga Haga on the Transkei coast for the Easter weekend. They camped in tents and cooked over a fire, the boys swam and caught fish with hand lines in the rock pools and played war games in the dunes. He heard their voices till late at night in the other tent, muffled giggling and chatting.

He blinked and the beach was empty and he was overwhelmed. Too little sleep and the after-effects of excess adrenaline.

He began to walk north along the beach. He was looking for the absolute conviction he had felt in the Yellow Rose, that this is what he must do; as if the universe was pointing the way with a thousand index fingers. It was like twenty years ago when he could feel the absolute rightness of the Struggle – that his origins, his instincts, his very nature had been honed for that moment, the total recognition of his vocation.

Someone had to say, 'This far.' *If children can't depend on the justice system to protect them, to whom can they turn?* He was a warrior and there was still a war in this land.

Why did it all sound so hollow now?

He must get some sleep; that would clear his perspective. But he did not want to, did not feel attracted to the four walls of the hotel room – he needed open space, sun, wind and a horizon. He did not want to be alone in his head.

He had always been a man of action, he could never stand by and watch. That is what he was and what he would be – a soldier, who faced the child rapist and felt all the juices of war flood his body. It was right, regardless how he might feel now. Regardless that this morning his convictions did not have the same impregnability.

They would start to leave the children of this land alone, the dogs, he would make sure of that. Somewhere Khoza and Ramphele were hiding, fugitives for the moment, invisible. But some time or other they would reappear, make contact or do something, and he would pick up their trail and hunt them down, corner them and let the assegai do the talking. Some time or other. If you wanted to get the prey, you had to be patient.

In the meantime there was work to do.

'I was clueless about money. There was just never enough. My father put a hundred rand a month in my account. A hundred rand. No matter how hard I tried, it would only last two weeks. Maybe three if I didn't buy magazines or if I smoked less or if I pretended I was busy when they went to movies or to eat out or chill . . . but it was never enough and I didn't want to ask for more because he would want to know what I was doing with it and I would have to listen to his nagging. I heard they were looking for students at a catering business in Westdene. They did weddings and functions and paid ninety rand for a Saturday night if you would waitress or serve, and they gave you an advance for the clothes. You had to wear black pantyhose and a black pencil skirt with a white blouse. I went to ask and they gave me a job, two sweet middle-aged gays who would have a huge falling out every fortnight and then make up just in time for the next function.

'The work was okay, once you got used to being on your feet for so long, and I looked stunning in the pencil skirt, even if I say so

myself. But most of all I liked the money. The freedom. The, the
. . . I don't know, to walk down Mimosa Mall and look at the
Diesel jeans and decide I wanted them and buy them. Just that
feeling, always knowing your purse was not empty – that was cool.

'At first I just did Saturdays, and then Fridays too and the
occasional Wednesday. Just for the money. Just for the . . . power,
you could say.

'Then in October we did the Schoemans Park golf-day party. I
went outside for a smoke after the main course, and Viljoen was
standing on the eighteenth green with a bottle in his hand and such
a knowing look on his face. He asked me if I wanted a slug.'

They must have injected him with something, because it was
morning when he woke, slowly and with difficulty, and he just
lay with his face to the hospital wall. It was a while before he
realised there was a needle and a thin tube attached to his arm. He
was not shaking.

A nurse came in and asked him questions and his voice was hoarse
when he answered. He might have been speaking too loudly,
because she sounded far away. She took his wrist and in her other
hand held a watch that was pinned to her chest. He thought it was
odd to wear it there. She put a thermometer into his dry mouth and
spoke in a soft voice. She was a black woman with scars on her
cheeks, fossil remnants of acne. Her eyes rested softly on him and she
wrote something on a snow-white card and then she was gone.

Two coloured women brought him breakfast, shifting the trolley
over the bed. They were excitable, chittering birds. They put a
steaming tray on the trolley and said: 'You must eat, Sarge, you
need the nourishment.' Then they disappeared. When the doctor
arrived it was still there, cold and uneaten, and Griessel lay like a
foetus, hands between his legs and his head feeling thick. Unwilling
to think, because all his head had to offer was trouble.

The doctor was an elderly man, short and stooped, bald and
bespectacled. The hair that remained around his head grew long
and grey down his back. He read the chart first and then came to sit
beside the bed.

'I pumped you full of thiamine and Valium. It will help with the withdrawal. But you have to eat too,' he said quietly.

Griessel just lay there.

'You are a brave man to give up alcohol.' Matt Joubert must have talked to him.

'Did they tell you my wife left me?'

'They did not. Was it because of the drink?'

Griessel shifted partially upright. 'I hit her when I was drunk.'

'How long have you been dependent?'

'Fourteen fucking years.'

'Then it is good that you stopped. The liver has its limits.'

'I don't know if I can.'

'I also felt like that and I have been dry for twenty-four years.'

Griessel sat up. 'You were an alky?'

The doctor's eyes blinked behind the thick lenses. 'That's why they sent for me this morning. You could say I am a specialist. For eleven years I drank like a fish. Drank away my practice, my family, my Mercedes Benz. Three times I swore I would stop, but I couldn't keep my balance on the wagon. Eventually I had nothing left except pancreatitis.'

'Did she take you back?'

'She did,' said the doctor and smiled. 'We had two more children, just to celebrate. The trouble is, they look like their father.'

'How did you do it?'

'Sex played an important role.'

'No, I mean . . .'

The doctor took Griessel's hand and he laughed with closed eyes. 'I know what you mean.'

'Oh.' For the first time Griessel smiled.

'One day at a time. And the AA. And the fact that I had hit rock bottom. There was no more medication to help, except disulfiram, the stuff that makes you throw up if you drink. But I knew from the literature it is rubbish – if you really want to drink, you just stop taking the pills.'

'Are there drugs now that can make you stop drinking?'

'No drug can make you stop drinking. Only you can.'

Griessel nodded in disappointment.

'But they can make withdrawal easier.'

'Take away the DTs.'

'You have not yet experienced delirium tremens, my friend. That only comes three to five days after withdrawal begins. Yesterday you experienced reasonably normal convulsions and, I imagine, the hallucinations of a heavy drinker who stops. Did you smell strange scents?'

'Yes.'

'Hear strange things?'

'Yes.' With emphasis.

'Acute withdrawal, but not yet the DTs, and for that you should be thankful. DTs is hell and we haven't found a way to stop it. If it gets really bad, you could get *grand mal* seizures, cardiac infarction or stroke, and any one of the three could kill you.'

'Jesus.'

'Do you really want to stop, Griessel?'

'I do.'

'Then today is your lucky day.'

13

She was a coloured woman with three children, and a husband in jail. She was the receptionist at the Quay Delta workshop in Paarden Island and it was never her intention to send the whole thing off at a tangent.

The *Argus* came at 12.30 every day, four papers for the waiting room so that clients could read while they waited for their cars to be finished. It was her habit to quickly scan the main news headlines of the day. Today she did this with more purpose because she had expectations.

She found it on the front page just below the fold in the newspaper. The headline already told her that all was not right.

POLICE LINKED TO KILLING OF
ALLEGED CHILD RAPIST

Quickly she read through the article and clicked her tongue.

The South African Police Services (SAPS) might have been responsible for the vigilante-style murder of alleged child rapist Enver Davids last night.

A spokesperson for the Cape Human Rights Forum, Mr David Rosenthal, said his organisation had received 'sensitive information from a very reliable source inside the police services' in this regard. The source indicated that the Serious and Violent Crimes Unit (SVC) was involved in the killing.

HIV-positive Davids, who was freed on charges of murder and child rape three days after the SVC had misplaced DNA evidence pertinent to the case, was found stabbed to death on a Kraaifontein street early this morning.

Senior Superintendent Matt Joubert, head of the SVC, vigorously denied the allegation, calling the claim that two of his detectives tracked down Davids and killed him 'malicious, spurious and devoid of all truth'. He admits that the unit was upset and frustrated after a judge sharply criticised their management of the case and then dismissed it . . .

The woman shook her head.

She would have to do something. This morning when she went into her dark kitchen to get the bottle of Vicks for her child's chest she could see the movement from her window. She had been a witness to the awful dance on the pavement. She had recognised Davids' face in the streetlight. Of one thing she was absolutely sure. The man with the short assegai was not a policeman. She knew the police; she could spot a policeman a mile away. She had had plenty of them on her doorstep. Like this morning when they had come to ask if she had seen anything and she had denied any knowledge.

She looked up the telephone number of the *Argus* on their front page and dialled it. She asked for the journalist who had written the article.

'It wasn't the police who killed Enver Davids,' she said without introduction.

'To whom am I speaking?'

'It doesn't matter.'

'And how do you know this, madam?'

She had been expecting the question. But she could not say or they would get her. They would track her down if she gave too much information.

'You might say I have first-hand knowledge.'

'Are you saying you were involved in this killing, madam?'

'All I want to say is that it wasn't the police. Definitely not.'

'Are you a member of Pagad?'

'No, I'm not. It wasn't a group. It was one person.'

'Are you that person?'

'I am going to put the phone down now.'

'Wait, please. How can I believe you, madam? How do I know you are not a crank?'

She thought for a moment. Then she said: 'It was a spear that killed him. An assegai. You can go and check that.'

She put the phone down.

That is how the Artemis story began.

Joubert and his English wife came to visit him that evening. All he could see was the way they kept touching each other, the big senior superintendent and his red-headed wife with the gentle eyes. Married four years and still touching like a honeymoon couple.

Joubert told him about the allegation that the unit was responsible for Davids' death. Margaret Joubert brought him magazines. They talked about everything but his problem. When they left Joubert gripped his shoulder with a big hand and said, 'Hang in there, Benny.' After they had gone he wondered how long it had been since he and Anna had touched each other. Like that.

He could not recall.

Fuck, when last had they had sex? When last did he even want to? Sometimes, in the semi-drunken state of his day, something would prompt him to think about it, but by the time he got home the alcohol would long since have melted the lead in his pencil.

And what of Anna? Did she feel the need? She didn't drink. She had been keen in the days before he began drinking seriously. Always game when he was, sometimes twice a week, folding her delicate fingers around his erection and playing their ritual game that had begun spontaneously and they had never dropped. 'Where did you get this thing, Benny?'

'Sale at Checkers, so I took four.'

Or: 'I traded with a Jew for nine inches of boere sausages. Don't be afraid, he's bald.' He would think of something new every time and even when he was less ingenious and more banal she would laugh. Every time. Their sex was always joyous, cheerful, until her orgasm made her serious. Afterwards they would hold each other and she would say, 'I love you, Benny.'

Pissed away, systematically, like everything.

He yearned. Where were the days, Lord, could he ever get them back? He wondered what she did when the desire was on her? What had she done the past two or three years? Did she see to herself? Or was there. . . ?

Panic. What if there was someone? Jissis, he would fucking shoot him. Nobody touched his Anna.

He looked at his hands, clenched fists, white knuckles. Slowly, slowly, the doctor had said he would make emotional leaps, anxiety . . . He must slow down.

He unclenched his fists and drew the magazines closer.

Car. Margaret Joubert had brought him men's magazines but cars were not his scene. Nor was *Popular Mechanics.* There was a sketch of a futuristic aeroplane on the cover. The cover story read, *New York to London in 30 Minutes?*

'Who cares,' he said.

His scene was drinking, but they don't publish magazines for that.

He switched off the light. It would be a long night.

The woman at the Internet café in Long Street had a row of earrings all down the edge of her ear and a shiny object through her nostril. Thobela thought she would have been prettier without it.

'I don't know how to use these things,' he said.

'It's twenty rand an hour,' she said, as if that would disqualify him straight away.

'I need someone to teach me,' he said patiently, refreshed after his afternoon nap.

'What do you want to do?'

'I heard you can read newspapers. And see what they wrote last year too.'

'Archives. They call them Internet archives.'

'Aaah . . .' he said. 'Would you show me?'

'We don't really do training.'

'I will pay.'

He could see the synapses fire behind her pale green eyes: the potential to make good money out of a dumb black, but also the possibility that it could be slow, frustrating work.

'Two hundred rand an hour, but you will have to wait until my shift is over.'

'Fifty,' he said. 'I will wait.'

He had taken her unawares, but she recovered well. 'A hundred, take it or leave it.'

'A hundred and you buy the coffee.'

She put out a hand and smiled. 'Deal. My name is Simone.'

He saw there was another shiny object on her tongue.

Viljoen. He was not tall, barely half a head taller than she was. He was not very handsome, and wore a copper bracelet on his wrist and a thin gold chain around his neck that she never much liked. It was not that he was poor – he just had no interest in money. The Free State sun had bleached his eight-year-old 4×4 pick-up until you would be hard pressed to name the original colour. Day after day it stood in the parking lot of the Schoemans Park Golf Club while he coached golf, or sold golf balls in the pro shop or played a round or two with the more important members.

He was a professional golfer. In theory. He had only lasted three months on the Sunshine Tour before his money ran out because he could not putt under pressure. He got the shakes, 'the yips', he called them. He would set up the putt and walk away and line up and set himself up again but always putted too short. Nerves had destroyed him.

'He became the resident pro at Schoemans Park. I found him that night on the eighteenth green with a bottle in his hand. It was weird. It was like we recognised each other. We were the same kind. Sort of on the sidelines. When you are in a hostel, you feel it quickly – that you don't quite belong. Nobody says anything, everyone is nice to each other and you socialise and laugh and worry together about exams, but you are not really "in".

'But Viljoen saw it. He knew it, because he was like that too.

'We began to talk. It was just so . . . natural, from the beginning. When I had to go in, he asked me what I was doing afterwards, and

I said I had to catch a lift back to the hostel, so I couldn't do anything and he said he would take me.

'So when everyone had gone, he asked me if I would caddy for him, because he wanted to play a bit of golf. I think he was a little drunk. I said you can't play golf in the dark, and he said that's what everyone thinks, but he would show me.'

The Bloemfontein summer night . . . She could smell the mown grass, hear the night sounds, and see the half moon. She could remember the way the light from the clubhouse veranda reflected off Viljoen's tanned skin. She could see his broad shoulders and his odd smile and the expression in his eyes and that aura about him, that terrible solitariness he carried around with him. The noise of the golf club striking the ball and the way it flew into the darkness and him saying: 'Come, caddy, don't let the roar of the crowd distract you.' His voice was gentle, self-mocking. Before every shot they would drink from the bottle of semi-sweet white wine still cold from the fridge. 'I don't get the yips at night,' he said, and he made his putts, long and short. In the dark he made the ball roll on perfect lines, over the humps in the greens, till it fell clattering into the hole. On the fairway of the sixth hole he kissed her, but by then she already knew she liked him too much and it was okay, absolutely okay.

'He played nine holes in the dark and in that time I fell in love,' was all she told the minister. She seemed to want to preserve the memories of that night, as if they would fade if she took them out of the dark and held them up to the light.

In the sand bunker beside the ninth hole they sat and he filled in his scorecard and announced he had a 33.

So much – she teased him.

So little – he laughed. A muted sound, sort of feminine. He kissed her again. Slowly and carefully, like he was taking care to do it right. With the same care he stretched her out and undressed her, folding each piece of clothing and putting it down on the grass above. He had knelt over her and kissed her, from her neck to her ankles, with an expression on his face of absolute wonder: that he had been granted this privilege, this magical opportunity. Eventually he went into her and there was intensity in his eyes of huge emotion and his rhythm increased, his urgency grew and grew and he lost himself in her.

She had to drag herself back to this present, where the minister waited with apparent patience for her to break the silence.

She wondered why memories were so closely linked to scent, because she could smell him now, here – deodorant and sweat and semen and grass and sand.

'At the ninth hole he made me pregnant,' she said, and reached out a hand for the tissues.

14

Barkhuizen, the doctor with the thick spectacles, his long hair in a cheeky plait this time, came around again the next morning after Griessel had swallowed his breakfast without enthusiasm or appetite.

'I'm glad you're eating,' he said. 'How do you feel?'

Griessel made a gesture that said it didn't matter.

'Finding it hard to eat?'

He nodded.

'Are you nauseous?'

'A bit.'

The doctor shone a light in his eyes.

'Headache?'

'Yes.'

He put a stethoscope to his chest and listened, finger on Griessel's pulse.

'I have found you a place to stay.'

Griessel said nothing.

'You have a heart like a horse, my friend.' He took the stethoscope away, put it in the pocket of his white coat and sat down. 'It's not much. Bachelor flat in Gardens, kitchen and living room below, wooden stairs up to a bedroom. Shower, basin and toilet. One two per month. The building is old but clean.'

Griessel looked away to the opposite wall.

'Do you want it?'

'I don't know.'

'How's that, Benny?'

'Just now I was angry, Doc. Now I don't give a fuck.'

'Angry with whom?'

'Everyone. My wife. Myself. You.'

'Don't forget it's a process of mourning you are going through because your friend the bottle is dead. The first reaction is anger at someone because of that. There are people who get stuck in the anger stage for years. You can hear them at the AA, going off at everyone and everything, shouting and swearing. But it doesn't help. Then there is the depression. That goes hand in hand with withdrawal. And the listlessness and fatigue. You have to get through it; you have to come out the other side of withdrawal, past the rage to resignation and acceptance. You must go on with your life.'

'What fucking life?'

'The one you must make for yourself. You have to find something to replace drink. You need leisure, a hobby, exercise. But first one day at a time, Benny. And we have just been talking about tomorrow.'

'I have fuck-all. I've got suitcases of clothes, that's all.'

'Your wife is having a bed delivered to the flat, if you want the place.'

'Did you talk to her?'

'I did. She wants to help, Benny.'

'Why hasn't she been here?'

'She said she believed too easily last time. She said this time she must stick to her decision. She will only see you when you are completely dry. I think that is the right thing.'

'You have all worked this out fucking beautifully, haven't you?'

'The *Rooi Komplot*, the great conspiracy. Everyone is against you. Against you and your bottle. It's hard, I know, but you're a tough guy, Benny. You can take it.'

Griessel just stared at him.

'Let's talk about your medication,' said Barkhuizen. 'The stuff I want to prescribe . . .'

'Why do you do it, Doc?'

'Because the drugs will help you.'

'No, Doc, why do you get involved? How old are you?'

'Sixty-nine.'

'Fuck, Doc, that's retirement age.'

Barkhuizen smiled and the eyes screwed up behind the thick lenses. 'I have a beach house at Witsand. We were retired there for three months. By then the garden was lovely and the house was right and the neighbours met. Then I began to want the bottle. I realised that was not what I should do.'

'So you came back.'

'To make life difficult for people like you.'

Griessel watched him for a long time. Then he said: 'The medication, Doc.'

'Naltrexone. The trade name is ReVia, don't ask me why. It works. It makes withdrawal easier and there are no serious contra-indications, as long as you stick to the prescription. But there is a condition. You must see me once a week for the first three months and you must go to the AA regularly. That is not negotiable. It's an all-or-nothing proposition.'

'I'll take it.' He had no hesitation.

'Are you certain?'

'Yes, Doc, I am certain. But I want to tell you something, so you know what you are letting yourself in for,' he said, and he tapped an index finger on his temple.

'Tell me, then.'

'It's about the screaming, Doc. I want to know if the medication will help for the screaming.'

The minister's children came to say goodnight. They knocked softly on the door and he hesitated at first. 'Excuse me, please,' he said to her and then called, 'Come in.' Two teenage boys disguised their curiosity about her with great difficulty. The older one was maybe seventeen. He was tall, like his father, and his youthful body was strong. His lightning glance assessed her chest measurement and her legs as she sat there. He spotted the tissue in her hand and there was an attentiveness about him that she recognised.

'G'night, Dad,' they said one after another and kissed him.

'Night, boys. Sleep well.'

'G'night, ma'am,' said the younger one.

'G'night,' said the other, and when his back was turned to his father, he looked into her eyes with undisguised interest. She knew he saw her hurt instinctively and the opportunities that offered, like a dog on a blood spoor.

She was annoyed. 'Goodnight,' she said and turned her eyes away, unavailable.

They closed the door behind them.

'Richard will be head boy next year,' said the minister with a certain pride.

'You have these two boys?' A mechanical question.

'They are a handful,' he said.

'I can imagine.'

'Do you need anything? More tea?'

'I should go and powder my nose.'

'Of course. Down the passage, second door on the left.'

She stood up. Smoothed down her skirt, front and back. 'Excuse me,' she said as she opened the door and walked down the passage. She found the toilet, switched on the light and sat down to urinate.

She was still annoyed with the boy. She was always aware that she gave off a scent that said to men, 'Try me'. Some combination of her appearance and her personality, as if they knew . . . But even here? This little twerp. A minister's son?

She became conscious of the loud noise of her urine stream in the stillness of the house.

Didn't these people play music? Watch television?

She was sick of it. She didn't want to smell like that any more. She wanted to smell like the woman of this house, the faithful wife: an I-want-to-love-you woman. She had always wanted to.

She finished, wiped, flushed, opened the door and put off the light. She walked back to the study. The minister was not there. She stood in front of the bookshelf, looking at the bookends packed thick and thin beside each other – some old and hardbacked and others new and bright; all about God or the Bible.

So many books. Why did they have to write so much about God? Why was it necessary? Why couldn't He just come down and say, 'Here I am, don't worry.'

Then He could explain to her why He had given her this scent. Not just the scent, but the weakness and the trouble. And why He had never tested Missus Fucking Prude here with her sensible frock and able hands? Why was she spared? Why did she get a dependable carthorse for a husband? What would she do if the elders of the church came sniffing around her with those hungry eyes that said, 'My brain is in my penis'?

Probably catch her breath in righteous indignation and hand out tracts all round. The scene playing out in her head made her laugh out loud, just one short, unladylike laugh. She put her hand over her mouth, but too late. The minister was standing behind her.

'Are you okay?' he asked.

She nodded and kept her back turned until she had control.

The extent of it nearly overwhelmed Thobela.

The girl with the earrings first gave him a basic lesson on the workings of the Internet, and then she let him click the mouse on the screen. He battled because the coordination between his hand and the mouse and the little arrow on the screen was clumsy. He improved steadily, however. She showed him connections and web addresses, boxes he could type words in and the big 'Back' arrow if he got lost.

When at last she was satisfied he could manage on his own and he had solemnly handed over the agreed amount, he began his search.

'*Die Burger* and IOL have the best online archives,' she said, and wrote down the www-references for him. He typed in his key words and systematically refined his search. Then came the flood.

At least 40 per cent of all cases of child rape can be ascribed to the myth that it cures Aids.

People who exploit children for sex in many parts of the world are more likely to be local residents looking for a 'good-luck charm' or a cure for Aids than a paedophile or sexual tourist, rights activists told a UN conference on Thursday.

Thousands of schoolgirls in South Africa and the Western Cape are daily exposed to sexual violence and harassment at schools.

From April 1997 to March this year, 1,124 children who had been physically and sexually abused were treated by the TygerBear Social Welfare Unit for Traumatised Children at Tygerberg Hospital. This is only children who were brought to the hospital: the actual number is much greater.

Sexual molestation and the abuse of young children is reaching epidemic proportions in Valhalla Park, Bonteheuwel and Mitchells Plain. A spokesperson reports that 945 cases of sexual molestation and child abuse have been reported to their office.

Children as young as three years old watch social workers at the TygerBear Unit of the Tygerberg Hospital with wary eyes. Barely out of nappies, these victims of sexual assault have already learned that adults are not to be trusted.

The two domestic violence units on the Peninsula are working on more than 3,200 cases, of which the majority are complaints of serious sexual and other crimes against children.

Of every 100 cases of child abuse in the Western Cape, only 15 are reported to the police, and in 83 per cent of these cases the offender is known to the child.

Once an offender has been diagnosed as a 'confirmed paedophile', there will always be a chance that he will express his paedophilic tendencies again, said Professor David Ackerman, clinical psychologist at the University of Cape Town.

One report after another, a never-ending stream of crimes against children. Murder, rape, maltreatment, harassment, assault, abuse. After an hour he had had enough, but he forced himself to continue.

A three-year-old girl was locked in a cage while her grandparents allegedly sexually assaulted her and failed to provide for even her most basic needs, Mpumalanga police said on Wednesday. Sergeant Anelda Fischer said police recently received a tip-off from a travelling pastor that a child was being incarcerated in a compound outside White River.

Fischer said that when police went to investigate they found the girl had already been removed from the cage. However, she said there was evidence the child had been battered with sticks or other weapons and had been sexually assaulted. It also seemed the child had no clothes of her own and had to beg naked for food. She slept on bits of plastic in the cage.

Colin Pretorius, the owner and head of a crèche in Parow, is being charged on the grounds that he sexually assaulted eleven boys between the ages of six and nine years over a period of four years. He was released on bail of R10,000.

At last he stood and walked unsteadily to the desk to pay for his use of the Internet.

Viljoen and she had three months together before he blew his brains out.

'At first I was just angry with him. Not heartbroken – that came later, because I truly loved him. And I was scared. He left me with the pregnancy and I didn't know what to do or where to go. But I was dreadfully angry because he was such a coward. It happened a week after I told him I was pregnant, on a Monday night. I took him to the Spur and told him there was something I had to tell him and then I told him and he just sat there and said nothing. So then I said to him he didn't have to marry me, just help me, because I didn't know what to do.

'Then he said: "Jissis, Christine, I'm no good as a father – I am a fuck-up, a drunken golfer with the yips."

'I said he didn't have to be a father, I didn't want to be a mother yet, I just didn't know what to do. I was a student. I had a crazy father. If he had to find out about the baby, he would go off the deep end. He would lock me up or something.

'Then he said let him think about it, make a plan, and the whole week he didn't phone, and Friday night, just before I had to go to work, I decided I would phone him one last time and if he still tried to avoid me, well, then, fuck him, excuse me, but it was a very difficult time. And then they said there had been an accident, he was dead, but it wasn't an accident. He had locked the pro shop and sat down at a little table and put a revolver against his head.

'It took me two years to stop being angry and remember that those three months with Viljoen were good. It was when I began to wonder what I would tell my child about her father. Some time she would want to know and—'

'You have a child?' asked the minister; for the first time he was taken aback.

'. . . and I would have to decide what to tell her. He didn't even leave a note. Didn't even write anything for her. He didn't even say he was sorry, it was depression, or he didn't have the guts or anything. So I decided I would tell her about those three months, because they were the best of my life.'

She was quiet then and sighed deeply. After a pause the minister asked, 'What is her name?'

'Sonia.'

'Where is she?

'That is what my story is about,' she said.

15

Griessel almost missed it. Two nurses came around early in the morning with the meal trolley, when he was already dressed and packed and ready to be discharged. His mind was elsewhere and he was not listening to their chatter as they approached his hospital room.

'. . . so then when she found out it was an old trick of his, he confessed. She says he had worked out that all the middle-aged girls go and buy comfort food at the Pick and Pay on Friday nights because they will be sitting in front of the TV all evening and that's when he pushes his trolley down the aisles and picks the prettiest one to chat up. That's how he got Emmarentia. Oh, hallo, Sarge, up already? Cheese omelette this morning, everyone's favourite.'

'No thank you,' he said, taking his suitcase and heading for the door. But he stopped and asked, 'Friday nights?'

'Sarge?'

'Say that again about Emmarentia and Pick and Pay?'

'Hey, Sarge, you don't have to be so desperate, you're not bad looking,' said one.

'There's something of the Russian noble in you,' said the other. 'Such sexy Slavic features.'

'No, that's not—'

'Maybe sometimes a bad hair day, but that can be fixed.'

'Anyway, that's a wedding band I see, isn't it?'

'Wait, wait, wait,' he held up his hands. 'I'm not interested in women . . .'

'Sarge! We could have sworn you were hetero.'

He was starting to get cross, but he looked hard at their faces and saw their deliberate mischief. He laughed helplessly with them, from his belly. The door opened and his daughter Carla stood there in her school uniform. She was momentarily confused by the scene – then relieved. She embraced her father.

'I hope that's his child,' one nurse said.

'Can't be, he's queer as a three-rand note.'

'Or his boyfriend in drag?'

They had Carla laughing with her head on his chest and eventually she said, 'Hallo, Pa.'

'You will be late for school.'

'I wanted to know if you were alright.'

'I'm alright, my child.'

The nurses were leaving and he asked them to explain again about Emmarentia.

'Why do you want to know, Sarge?'

'I'm working on this case. We can't work out how the victims are selected.'

'So the sarge wants to consult us?'

'I do.'

They sketched a verbal picture as an alternating duet. Jimmy Fortuin picked up an occasional score at the Pick and Pay on a Friday afternoon, because by then it was crawling with single women.

'But middle-aged. The young ones still have the guts to fly solo in the clubs, or they gang up, strength in numbers.'

'They buy food for Friday night and the weekend: treats, you know, to spoil themselves a bit. Comfort food.'

'Between five and seven, that's hunting season for Jimmy, 'cause they're all on the way home from work. Easy pickings, because Jimmy is a motor mouth, a charmer.'

'Just at Pick and Pay?'

'That's just *his* convenience store, but Checkers would also work.'

'There's something about a supermarket . . .'

'Kind of hopeless . . .'

'Desperation . . .'

'The Lonely Hearts Shopping Club.'

'Last stand at the OK Bazaars.'

'Sleepless in the Seven Eleven.'

'You know?'

Laughing he said he understood, thanked them and left.

He dropped Carla off at school with the car that Joubert had left for him.

'We miss you, Daddy,' she said as they stopped at the school gates.

'Not as much as I miss all of you.'

'Mommy told us about the flat.'

'It's just temporary, my child.' He took her hand and pressed it. 'This is my third sober day today,' he said.

'You know I love you, Daddy.'

'And I love you.'

'Fritz too.'

'Did he say that?'

'He didn't have to say it.' She hurriedly opened her case. 'I brought you this, Daddy.'

She took out an envelope and gave it to him. 'You could pick us up at school sometimes. We won't tell Mommy.' She grabbed him around the neck and hugged him. Then she opened her door.

' 'Bye, Daddy,' she said with a serious face.

' 'Bye, my child.'

He watched her hurry up the steps. His daughter with the dark hair and strange eyes that she had inherited from him.

He opened the envelope. There were photographs in it, the family picture they had taken two years ago at the school bazaar. Anna's smile was forced. His was lopsided – not quite sober that night. But there were all four of them, together.

He turned the picture over. *I love you, Daddy.* In Carla's pretty, curving handwriting, followed by a tiny heart.

'That December I worked, pregnant or not. I phoned home and said I would be staying. I wasn't going home to Upington, or with them to Hartenbos. My father was not happy. He drove through to Bloemfontein to come and pray for me. I was petrified he would see that I was pregnant, but he didn't; he was too busy with other things in his head. I told him I would stay in an outside room at Kallie and Colin's place, as I was helping them with all the year-end functions, weddings and company do's for employees and there weren't so many students to help. I wanted to make good money, so that I would be more financially independent.

'That was the last time I saw him. He kissed me on the cheek before he left and that was the closest he ever came to his grand-daughter.

'Kallie caught me throwing up one morning in January. He had brought my breakfast to the outside room and he stood and watched me vomiting in the toilet. Then he said: "You're preggies, sweet-heart," and when I didn't reply he said, "What are you going to do?"

'I told him I was going to have the baby. It was the first time that I really knew it myself. I know it's weird, but with Viljoen and my father and everything . . . Until that moment only I knew. It was kind of unreal. Like a dream, and maybe I thought I would wake up, or the baby would just go away on its own or something. I didn't want to think about it, I just wanted to go on.

'Then he asked if I would put the baby up for adoption, and I said I don't know but I said I was going to Cape Town at the end of the month, so would they please give me all the shifts they could? So he asked me if I knew what I was doing and I said no, I didn't know what I was doing, because it was all rather new to me.

'They saw me off at Hoffman Square, with a present for the baby, a little blue babygro and booties and little shoes and bibs and an envelope for me – a Christmas bonus, they said. And they gave me a few names of gay friends they had in Cape Town in case I needed help.

'I cried that day, all the way to Colesberg. That was when I felt Sonia kick for the first time, as if to say, that's enough, we must pull ourselves together, we would be okay. Then I knew that I would not give her up.'

Griessel found what he was searching for in the three lab reports. He walked over to Matt Joubert's office and waited for the senior superintendent to finish on the telephone.

'The forensic report does not exclude an assegai,' Joubert was saying into the instrument, 'but they are doing more tests, and it will take time. You will have to call back in a day or two. Right. You're welcome. Thanks. 'Bye.'

He looked up at Griessel. 'It's good to have you back, Benny. How are you feeling?'

'Frighteningly sober. What was that about an assegai?'

'That Enver Davids thing. Suddenly the *Argus* has all these questions. I can see trouble coming.'

Griessel put the lab reports down in front of Joubert and said, 'The bastard is picking them up at Woolworths. Friday afternoons. Look here, I missed it because I didn't know what I was looking for, but Forensics analysed the trash cans of all three victims and in two of them there are Woolies bags and till slips and in the third one just a till slip, but all three were there, at the one on the Waterfront on the Friday of the murders between . . . er . . . half-past four and seven o'clock.'

Joubert examined the reports. 'It's thin, Benny.'

'I know, but this morning I heard expert witnesses, Matt. Seems to me only old married people like us think a supermarket is a place to buy groceries.'

'Explain,' said Joubert, wondering how long this light would keep burning in Griessel's eyes.

Thobela found a public phone in the Church Street Mall that worked with coins and thumbed through the tattered phone book for the number of the University of Cape Town Psychology Department. He called and asked for Professor David Ackerman.

'He is on ward rounds. In what connection is this?'

'I am researching an article on crimes against children. I have just a few questions.'

'With which publication are you?'

'I am freelance.'

'Professor Ackerman is very busy . . .'

'I only need a few minutes.'

'I will have to phone you back, sir.'
'I'm going to be in and out – can I call tomorrow?'
'To whom am I speaking?'
'Pakamile,' he said. 'Pakamile Nzuluwazi.'

16

At first the Cape was not good to her.

For one, the wind blew for days on end, a storm-strength southeaster. Then they stole her only suitcase at Backpackers in Kloof Nek, where for a hundred rand a night she was sharing a room with five grumbling, superior young German tourists. Flats were scarce and expensive, public transport complicated and unreliable. Once she walked all the way to Sea Point to check out a possible place, but it was a disappointing dump with a broken windowpane and graffiti on the walls.

She stayed in Backpackers for two weeks before she found the attic room in an old block of flats in Belle Ombre Street in Tamboers Kloof. What had once been a boxroom had been converted into a small, livable space – the bath and toilet were against one wall, the sink and kitchen cupboard against the other; there was a bed and table and an old rickety wardrobe. Another door opened onto the roof, from where she could see the city crescent, the mountain and the sea. At least neat and clean for R680 per month.

Her biggest problem was inside her because she was afraid. Afraid of the birth that drew nearer every day, the care of the baby afterwards, the responsibility; afraid of the anger of her father when she made the call or wrote the letter – which, she had not yet decided. Above all, afraid of the money running out. Every day she checked her balance at the autobank and compared the balance against the list of the most essential items she would need: cot, baby clothes, nappies, bottles, milk formula, blankets, pan, pot, two-plate stove, mug, plate, knife, fork and spoon, kettle, portable FM-radio. The list continued to grow and her bank balance continued to shrink until she found work as a waitress at a large coffee shop in Long Street. She worked every possible shift that she could, while she could still hide the bump under her breasts.

The numbers on the statements ruled her life. They became an obsession. Six eight zero was the first target of every month, the non-negotiable amount of her rent. It was the low-water mark of her book-keeping and the source of unrest in her dreams at night. She discovered the flea market at Green Point Stadium and haggled over the price of every item. At the second-hand shops in Gardens and in Kloof Street she bought a cot, a bicycle and a red and blue carpet. She painted the cot on the roof with white, lead-free enamel paint, and when she found there was paint left over she gave the old yellowish-green racing bike with narrow tyres and dropped handlebars a couple of coats as well.

In a *Cape Ads* that someone left in the coffee shop she found an advertisement for a backpack baby carrier. And she phoned, argued the price down, and had it delivered. It would allow her to ride the bicycle with the baby on her back along the mountain and next to the sea at Mouille Point, where there were swings and climbing frames and a kiddies' train.

Every Saturday she took twenty rand to play the Lotto and she would sit by the radio and wait for the winning numbers that she had marked on the card with a ballpoint pen. She fantasized about what she would do with the jackpot money. A house was top of the list – one of those modern rebuilt castles on the slopes of the mountain, with automatic garage doors, Persian carpets on the floor and kelims and art on the walls. A huge baby room with seabirds and clouds painted on the ceiling and a heap of bright, multicoloured toys on the floor. A Land Rover Discovery with a baby seat. A walk-in wardrobe filled with designer labels and shoes in tidy rows on the floor. An Espresso machine. A double-door fridge in stainless steel.

One afternoon, about three o'clock, she was sitting on the roof with a cup of instant coffee when she heard the sounds of sex drifting up from the block of flats below. A woman's voice, uh-uh-

uh-uh, gradually climbing the scales of ecstasy, every one a little higher, a little louder. In the first minutes the sound was meaningless, just another noise of the city, but she recognised it and was amused at the odd hour. She wondered if she were the only listener, or whether the sound reached other ears. She felt a small sexual stimulus ripple through her body. Followed by envy as the sounds accelerated, faster, louder, higher. The envy grew along with it for all that she did not have, until the shrill orgasm made her get up and bend her arm with the nearly-empty mug back in order to throw it at everything that conspired against her. She didn't aim at any specific target, her rage was too general. Rage against the loneliness, the circumstances, the wasted opportunities.

She did not throw it. She lowered her arm slowly, unwilling to pay for a new mug.

Early in March she could postpone the call no longer. She rode all the way to the Waterfront for a public phone, in case they traced the call. She phoned her mother at the attorneys' office where she worked. It was a short conversation.

'My God, Christine, where are you?'

'I dropped out, Mom. I'm okay. I've got a job. I just want to—'

'Where are you?' Her voice was tinged with hysteria. 'The police are looking for you too now. Your father will have a stroke, he phones them in Bloemfontein every day.'

'Mom, tell him to drop it. Tell him I am sick and tired of his preaching and his religion. I am not in Bloemfontein and he won't find me. I am fine. I am happy. Just leave me alone. I am not a child any more.' She couldn't tell where the anger came from. Had fear unleashed it?

'Christine, you can't do this. You know your father. He is furious. We are terribly worried about you. You are our child. Where are you?'

'Mom, I'm going to put the phone down now. Don't worry about me, Mom, I am fine. I will phone you to let you know I am okay.' Afterwards she thought she should have said something like, 'I love you, Mom.' But she had just slammed the phone down, got on her bike and ridden away.

She only phoned again when Sonia was a week old, early in June, because then she had a great need to hear her mother's voice.

Thobela was drinking a Coke at the Wimpy outside tables in St Georges. He read the front-page article of the *Argus* that speculated about the death of Enver Davids. Sensationalised by an anonymous woman's phone call.

Someone had seen him with the assegai. But had not reported him.

He had been too focused. No, he hadn't been thorough enough, not entirely calculated. There had been a witness. He should have known there would be publicity. Media interest. Screaming headlines and speculation and accusations.

Could the killing of child rapist Enver Davids be the work of a female vigilante – and not the South African Police Services, as was previously suspected?

Strange consequences.

Would the police be able to trace the female caller? Would she be able to give them a description of him?

It didn't really matter.

He turned the page. On page three there was an article on a radio station's phone-in opinion poll. Should the death penalty be reinstated? Eighty-seven per cent of listeners had voted 'yes'.

On page two were short reports of the day's criminal activity. Three murders in Khayelitsha. A gang-related shooting took a woman's life in Blue Downs. A man was wounded in Constantia during a car hijacking. A cash in-transit robbery in Montague Gardens: two security guards in intensive care. A seventy-two-year-old woman raped, assaulted and robbed in her home in Rosebank. A farmer in Limpopo Province gunned down in his shed.

No children today.

A waitress brought his bill. He folded the paper and leaned back in his chair. He watched the people walking down the mall, some purposefully, some strolling. There were stalls, clothes and art-works. The sky was blue above, a dove came down to land on the pavement with its tail and wings spread wide.

It was déjà vu, all this, this existence. A hotel room somewhere with his suitcase half unpacked, long days to struggle through, time to wait out before the next assignment. Paris was his place of waiting, another city, another architecture, other languages; but the feeling was the same. The only difference was that in those days his targets had been picked for him in a sombre office in East Berlin, and the little stack of documents with photographs and pages of single-spaced typing was delivered to him by courier. His war. His Struggle.

A lifetime ago. The world was a different place, but how easy it was to slip into the old routines again – the state of alertness, the patience, the preparation, planning, the anticipation of the next intense burst of adrenaline.

Here he was again. Back in harness. The circle was complete. It felt as if the intervening period had never existed, as if Miriam and Pakamile were a fantasy, like an advertisement in the middle of a television drama, a disturbing view of aspirations of domestic bliss.

He paid for his cold drink and walked south to the pay phones and called the number again. 'Is Professor Ackerman available now?'

'Just a moment.'

She put him through. He used the other name again and the cover of freelance journalism. He said he had read an article in the archives of *Die Burger* where the professor stated that a fixated paedophile always reoffended. He wanted to understand what that meant.

The professor sighed and paused a while before he answered. 'Well, it sort of means what it says, Mr Nulwazi.'

'Nzuluwazi.'

'I'm sorry, I'm terrible with names. It means the official line is that, statistically, rehabilitation fails to a substantial degree. In other words, even after an extended prison sentence, there is no guarantee that they won't commit the same crime again.' There was weariness of life in the man's voice.

'The official line.'

'Yes.'

'Does that differ from reality?'

'No.'

'I get the idea you don't support the official line.'

'It is not a matter of support. It is a matter of semantics.'

'Oh?'

'Can we go off the record here, Mr Nulwazi?'

This time he ignored the pronunciation. 'Of course.'

'And you won't quote me?'

'You have my word.'

The professor paused again before he answered, as if weighing the worth of it. 'The fact of the matter is that I don't believe they *can* be rehabilitated.'

'Not at all?'

'It's a terrible disease. And we have yet to find the cure. The problem is that, no matter how much we would like to believe we are getting closer to a solution, there doesn't seem to be one.' Still the desperate, despairing weariness. 'They come out of prison and sooner or later they relapse, and we have more damaged children. And the damage is huge. It is immeasurable. It destroys lives, utterly and completely. It causes trauma you wouldn't believe. And there seem to be more of them every year. God knows, it is either a matter of our society creating more, or that the lawlessness in this country is encouraging them to come out of the woodwork. I don't know . . .'

'So what you are saying is that they shouldn't be released?'

'Look, I know it is inhuman to keep them in prison for ever. Paedophiles have a tough time in penitentiaries. They are considered the scum of the earth in that world. They are raped and beaten and humiliated. But they serve their sentences and go through the programmes and then they come out and they relapse. Some right away, others a year or two or three down the line. I don't know what the answer is, but we will have to find one.'

'Yes,' said Thobela, 'we will have to find one.'

How tedious the clergyman's day-to-day existence must be, because he was still sitting there with the same interest. He was still listening attentively to her story, his expression neutrally sympathetic, his arms relaxed on the desk. It was quiet in the house, outside as well, just the noise of insects. It was strange to her, accustomed as she was to the eternal sound of traffic, people on the move in a city. Always on the go.

Here there was nowhere to go to.

'I had no more money. If you don't have money, you must have time, to stand in long queues with your child on your hip for vaccinations or cough medicine or something to stop diarrhoea. If you have a child and you have to work, then you have to pay for daycare. If you are waitressing then you have to pay extra for someone to look after it at night. Then you have to walk back to your flat with your baby at one in the morning in winter, or you have to pay for a taxi. If you won't work at night, you miss the best shifts with the biggest tips. So you buy nothing for yourself, and this week you try this and next week you try that until you know you just can't win.'

'I couldn't cope any more – there were just too many things. Every Monday I read the *Times Job Supplement* and handed in my CV for every possible job: secretarial, medical rep, clerk. Then, if you were lucky they would invite you for an interview. But it is always the same. No experience? Oh, you have a child. Are you divorced? Oh. Sorry, we want experience. We want someone with a car. We need someone with book-keeping.

'Sorry, it's an affirmative action position. I left the coffee shop because the tips were too small and it was still winter too and that's off-season. I worked at Trawlers, a seafood place that opened up on Kloof Street, and one night a guy said, "Do you want to make real money?" So I said, "Yes". Then he asked me "How much?" and I didn't click and I said, "As much as I can." Then he said, "Three hundred rand", and I asked, "Three hundred rand what – per day?" Then he got this smile on his face and said, "Per night, actually." He was just an average guy, about forty, with spectacles and a little paunch and I said, "What must I do?" and he said, "You know", and I still didn't click. Then he said, "Bring me a pen and I will write down my hotel room for you", and at last I clicked and I just stood staring at him. I wanted to scream at him, what did he think I was, and I stood there so angry, but what could I do, he was a customer. So I went to fetch his bill, and when I looked again he was gone. He had left a hundred-rand tip and a note with his hotel number and he had written 'Five hundred? For an hour.' And I put it in my pocket, because I was afraid someone might see it.

'Five hundred rand. When your rent is six hundred and eighty, then five hundred is a lot of money. If you have to pay four-fifty for daycare and extra on weekends, because that's where the tips are, five hundred fills a big gap. If you need three thousand to get through the month and you never know if you will make it and you have to save for a car, because when you have to pick up your child and it's raining . . . then you take that bit of paper out of your pocket and you look at it again. But who understands that? What white person understands that?

'Then you think, what difference does it make? You see it every day. A couple come in and he wines and dines her and for what? To get her into bed. What is the difference? Three hundred rand for dinner or five hundred for sex.

'They hit on me in any case, the men. Even when I was pregnant, in the coffee shop, and afterwards, at Trawlers, even worse. The whole time. Some just give you these looks, some say things like "nice rack" or "cute butt, sweetie"; some ask you straight out what you are doing on Friday night, or "are you attached, sweetness?" The vain ones leave their cell phone numbers on the bill, as if they are God's gift. Some chat you up with pretty little questions. "Where are you from?" "How long have you been in Cape Town?" "What are you studying?" But you know what they really want, because soon they ask you, "Do you have your own place?" or, "Jissie, we are chatting so *lekker*, when do you finish work, so we can chat some more?" At first you think you are very special, because some of them are cute and witty, but you hear them doing it with everyone, even the ugly waitresses. All the time, all of them, like those rabbits with the long-life batteries, never stopping; never mind if they are sixteen or sixty, married or single, they are on the lookout and it never stops.

'Then you get back to your room and think about everything and you think of what you don't have and you think there really is no difference, you think five hundred rand and you lie and wonder what it would be like, how bad could it be to be with the guy for an hour?'

17

All day Griessel had been looking for a decoy, a middle-aged policewoman to push a trolley up and down Woolworths at the Waterfront on Friday night. Hopefully the bastard would choose her. Someone eventually suggested a Sergeant Marais at Claremont, late thirties, who might fit the bill. He phoned her and made an appointment to talk to her.

He took the M5, because it was faster, and turned off at Lansdowne in order to drive up to Main Road. At the off ramp, just left of the road, was an advertising board, very wide and high. Castle Lager. Beer. Fuck it, he hadn't drunk beer in years, but the advert depicted a glass with drops of moisture running down the sides, a head of white foam and contents the colour of piss. He had to stop at the traffic lights and stare at that damn glass of beer. He could taste it. That dry, bitter taste. He could feel it sliding down his throat, but above all he could feel the warmth spreading through his body from the medicine in his belly.

When he came to his senses, someone was hooting behind him, a single, impatient toot. He jumped and drove away, realising only then what had happened and scared by the intensity of the enchantment.

He thought: what the fuck am I going to do? How do you fight something like this, pills or no pills? Jissis, he hadn't drunk beer in years.

He realised he was squeezing the steering wheel and he tried to breathe, tried to get his breath back as he drove.

Before she even stood up from behind the desk, he knew the sergeant was perfect. She had that washed-out look, more lean miles on the clock than her year model indicated; her hair was dyed blonde. She said her name was André. Her smile showed a slightly skew front tooth. She looked as if she expected him to comment on her name.

He sat down opposite her and told her about the case and his suspicions. He said she would be ideal, but he could not force her to be part of the operation.

'I'm in,' she said.

'It could be dangerous. We would have to wait until he tried something.'

'I'm in.'

'Talk to your husband tonight. Sleep on it. You can phone me tomorrow.'

'That won't be necessary. I'll do it.'

He spoke to the station commander, to ask permission, although he did not have to. The big coloured captain complained he didn't have people to spare, they were undermanned as it was and Marais was a key person: who would do her work when she wasn't there? Griessel said it was just Friday nights from five o'clock and her overtime would not appear on the station's budget. The captain nodded. 'Okay, then.'

He drove to Gardens late in the afternoon with the address to his flat on a slip of paper on the seat beside him.

Friend Street . . . what fucking kind of name was that? Mount Nelson's Mansions. Number one two eight.

He had never lived in this area. All his life he had been in the northern suburbs, since school a Parow Arrow, apart from the year in Pretoria at the Police College and three years in Durban as a constable. Jissis, he never wanted to go back there, to the heat and humidity and the stink. Curry and dagga and everything in English. In those days he had an accent you could cut with a cudgel and the *Souties* and Indians teased or taunted him, depending on whether they were colleagues or people he had arrested. *Fuckin' rock spider. Fuckin' hairyback pig. Fuckin' dumb Dutchman policeman.*

Mount Nelson's Mansions. There was a steel fence around it and a large security gate. He would have to park in the street at first and press a button on a sign that said Caretaker to get in and collect his keys and the remote control for the gate. A red brick building that had never been a mansion, maybe thirty or forty years old. Not beautiful, not ugly, it just stood there between two white-plastered apartment blocks.

The caretaker was an old Xhosa. 'You a policeman?' he asked.
'I am.'
'That is good. We need a policeman here.'

He fetched his suitcases from the car and dragged them up one flight of stairs. One two eight. The door needed varnish. It had a peephole in the centre and two locks. He found the right keys and pushed the door open. Brown parquet floor, fuck-all furniture, except for the breakfast counter with no stools, a few bleached melamine kitchen cupboards and an old Defy stove with three plates and an oven. A wooden staircase. He left the cases and climbed the stairs. There was a bed up there, a single bed, the one that had been stored in the garage, his garage. His former garage. Just the wooden bedstead and foam mattress with the faded blue floral pattern. The bedding lay in a pile on the foot of the bed. Pillow and slip, sheets, blankets. There was a built-in wardrobe. A door led to the small bathroom.

He went down to fetch his suitcases.

Not even a bloody chair. If he wanted to sit down, it would have to be on the bed.

Nothing to eat off or drink from or to boil water. He had fuck-all. He had less than when he went to police college.

Jissis.

In his hotel room, Thobela searched under 'P' in the telephone directory. There was the name, *Colin Pretorius*, written just like that, and the address, *122 Chantelle Street, Parow*. He drove to the Sanlam Centre in Voortrekker Road and bought a street guide to Cape Town in CNA.

As the sun disappeared behind Table Mountain, he drove down Hannes Louw Drive and left into Fairfield, right into Simone and, after a long curve, left into Chantelle. The even numbers were on the right. Number 122 was an inconspicuous house with burglar bars and a security gate. The neat garden had two ornamental cypress trees, a few shrubs and a green, mowed lawn, all enclosed by a concrete wall around the back and sides. No signs of life. On the garage wall above the door was a blue and silver sign: *Cobra Security. Armed Rapid Response.*

He had a problem. He was a black man in a white suburb. He knew the fact that he was driving a pick-up would help, keep him colour-free and anonymous in the dusk. But not for ever. If he hung around too long or drove past one time too many, someone would notice his skin colour and begin to wonder.

He drove once around the block and past 122 again, this time observing the neighbouring houses and the long strip of park that curved around with Simone Street. Then he had to leave, back to the shopping centre. There were things he needed.

Griessel sat on the still unmade bed and stared at the wardrobe. His clothes could not fill a third of the space. It was the empty space that fascinated him.

At home his wardrobe was full of clothes he hadn't worn in years – garments too small or so badly out of fashion that Anna forbade him to wear them.

But here he could count on one hand each type of garment she had packed for him, excepting the underpants – there were probably eight or nine, which he had piled in a heap in the middle rack.

Laundry. How would he manage? There were already two days' worth of dirty clothes in a bundle at the bottom of the cupboard, beside the single pair of shoes. And ironing – hell, it was years since he had picked up an iron. Cooking, washing dishes. Vacuuming! The bedroom did have a dirty brown wall-to-wall carpet.

'Fuck,' he said, rising to his feet.

He thought of the beer advertisement again.

God, no, that was the sort of thing that had got him into this situation. He must not. He would have to find something to do. There were the files in his briefcase. But where would he work? On the bed? He needed a stool for the breakfast bar. It was too late to look for one now. He wanted coffee. Maybe the Pick and Pay in Gardens was still open. He took his wallet, cell phone and the keys to his new flat and descended the stairs to the bare living room below.

Thobela bought a small pocket torch, batteries, binoculars and a set of screwdrivers and sat down in a restaurant to study the map.

His first problem would be to get into the suburb. He could not park near the house as the pick-up was registered in his name. Someone might write down the number. Or remember it. He would have to park somewhere else and walk in, but it was still risky. Every second house had a private security company's sign on the wall. There would be patrol vehicles, there would be wary eyes ready to call an emergency number. 'There's a black man in our street.'

Chances were better by day – he might be a gardener on his way to work – but at night the risks multiplied.

He studied the map. His finger traced Hannes Louw Drive where it crossed the N1. If he parked north of the freeway, using the narrow strip of veld and parkland . . . That was the long, slow option, but it could be done.

In the case in which Colin Pretorius stands accused of child molestation and rape, an eleven-year-old boy yesterday testified how the accused called him to his office three years ago and showed him material of a pornographic nature. The accused locked the door and later began to fondle himself and encouraged the boy to do the same.

His next problem would be getting into the house. The front was too visible, he would have to get in the back where the concrete wall hid him from the neighbours. There were the burglar bars. The security contract meant an alarm. And a panic button.

The woman, whose name may not be made public, testified that her five-year-old son's symptoms of stress, which included acute aggression, bedwetting and lack of concentration, obliged his parents to consult a child psychologist. In therapy the boy revealed the molestation over a period of three months by Pretorius, owner of a crèche.

There were two alternatives. Wait for Pretorius to come home. Or try to gain entry. The first option was too unpredictable, too hard to control. The second was difficult, but not impossible.

He paid for his cold drink. He was not hungry. He felt too much anticipation, a vague tension, a sharpening of his senses. He fetched his pick-up from the parking area and left.

During his arrest, police seized Pretorius's computer, CD-ROM material and videos. Inspector Dries Luyt of the Domestic Violence Unit told the court the quantity and nature of the child pornography found was the 'worst this unit has yet seen'.

He flowed with the traffic.

He thought of being with Pakamile, the week before his death, in the mountain landscape of Mpumalanga beyond Amersfoort. On their motorbikes together with the six other students in the bright morning sun, between the pretty wooden houses, his son's eyes fixed on the instructor who spoke to them with such fervour.

'The greatest enemy of the motorbike rider is target fixation. It's in our blood. The connection between eyes and brain unfortunately works this way: if you look at a pothole or a rock, you will ride into it. Make sure you never look directly at the obstruction. Fighter pilots are trained to look ninety degrees away from the target the moment they press the missile-firing buttons. Once you have spotted an obstacle in the road, you know it's there. Search for the way around it; keep your eyes on the line to safety. You and your motorbike will follow automatically.'

He had sat there thinking this was not just a lesson in motorbike riding – life worked like that too. Even if you only realised it late or nearly too late. Sometimes you never did see the rocks. Like when he came back after the war. Battle ready, cocked, primed for the New South Africa. Ready to use his training, his skills and experience. An alumnus of the KGB university, graduate of the Stasi sniper school, veteran of seventeen eliminations in the cities of Europe.

Nobody wanted him.

Except for Orlando Arendse, that is. For six years he protected drug routes and collected drug debts, until he began to notice the rocks and potholes, until he needed to choose a safer line in order not to smash himself on the rocks.

And now?

He parked beside Hendrik Verwoerd Drive, high up against the bump of the Tygerberg, where you can see the Cape stretched out in front of you as far as Table Mountain, glittering in the night.

He sat for a moment, but did not see the view.

Perhaps the motorcycle instructor was wrong: avoiding the obstacles of life was not enough. How does a child choose a line through all the sickness, all the terrible traps? Maybe life needed someone to clear away the obstacles.

When Griessel returned to the flat with both hands full of Pick and Pay bags, Dr Barkhuizen was standing at his door, hand raised to knock.

'I came to see if you were okay.'

Later they sat cross-legged on the kitchen floor, drinking instant coffee from brand new floral mugs, and Griessel told him about the beer advertisement. The doctor said that was just the beginning. He would begin seeing what had been invisible before. The whole world would conspire to taunt him, the universe encourage him to have just one little swallow, just one glass. 'The brain is a fantastic organ, Benny. It seems to have a life of its own, one that we are unaware of. When you drink long enough, it begins to like that chemical balance. So when you stop, it makes plans to restore the balance. It's like a factory of cunning thoughts lodged somewhere, which pumps the best ones through to your conscious state. "Ach, it's just a beer." "What harm can one little drink do?" Another very effective one is the, "I deserve it, I have suffered for a week now and I deserve a small one." Or, even worse, the, "I have to have a drink now, or I will lose all control." '

'How the fuck do you fight it?'

'You phone me.'

'I can't do that every time . . .'

'Yes, you can. Any time, night or day.'

'It can't go on like this for ever, can it?'

'It won't, Benny. I will teach you the techniques to tame the beast.'

'Oh.'

'The other thing I wanted to talk about was those voices.'

He sat in the deep night-shadows of neglected shrubs, in the park that bordered on Simone Street. The binoculars were directed at Pretorius's home, three hundred metres down Chantelle Street.

A white suburb at night. Fort Blanc. No children playing outside. Locked doors, garages and security gates that opened with electronic remote controls, the blue flicker of television screens in living rooms. The streets were silent, apart from the white Toyota Tazz of Cobra Security that patrolled at random, or an occupant coming home late.

Despite these precautions, the walls and towers and moats, the children were not even safe here – it only took one intruder like Pretorius to nullify all the barriers.

There was life in the paedophile's house, lights going on and off.

He weighed up his options, considered a route that would take him away from the streetlights through back gardens up to the wall of Pretorius's house. Eventually he decided the fastest option was the one with the biggest chance of success: down the street.

He stood up, put the binoculars in his pocket and stretched his limbs. He pricked his ears for cars, left the shadows and began to walk with purpose.

'Doc, they are not voices. It's not like I hear a babble. It's . . . like someone screaming. But not outside, it's here inside, here in the back of my head. "Hear" is not even the right word, because there are colours too. Some are black, some are red; fuck, it makes me sound crazy, but it's true. I get to a murder scene. Let's say the case I am working on now. The woman is lying on the floor, strangled with the kettle cord. You can see from the marks on her neck that she has been strangled from behind. You begin to reconstruct how it happened – that's your job, you have to put it all together. You know she let him in, because there is no forced entry. You know they were together in the room because there is a bottle of wine and two glasses, or the coffee things. You know they must have talked, she was at ease, suspecting nothing, she was standing there and he was behind her saying something and suddenly there was this thing around her neck and she was frightened, what the fuck, she tried to get her fingers under the cord. Perhaps he turned her around, because he is sick, he wanted to see her eyes, he wanted to watch her face, because he's a control freak and now she sees him and she knows . . .'

He had to make a quick decision. He walked around the house and past the back door and saw that it was the best point of entry, no security gate, just an ordinary lock. He had to get in fast: the longer he remained outside, the greater the chance of being spotted.

He had the assegai at his back, under his shirt, the shaft just below his neck and the blade under his belt. He lifted his hand and pulled out the weapon. He raised a booted foot and, aiming for the lock, kicked open the door with all his strength.

The verdict in the case against crèche owner Colin Pretorius on various charges of child rape and molestation and the possession of child pornography is expected tomorrow. Pretorius did not testify.

The kitchen was dark. He ran through it towards the lights. Down the passage, left turn, to what he assumed was the living room. Television noise. He ran in, assegai in hand. Living room, couch, chairs, a sitcom's canned noise. Nobody. He spun around, spotted movement in the passage. The man was there, frozen in the light of a doorway, mouth half agape.

For a moment they stood facing each other at opposite ends of the passage and then the prey moved away and he attacked. The alarm must be in the bedroom. He had to stop him. The door swung shut. He dropped his shoulder, six, five, four paces, the door slammed, three, two, one, the snick of a key turning in the lock and he hit the door with a noise like a cannon shot, pain racking his body.

The door withstood him.

He was not going to make it. He stepped back, preparing to kick the door in, but it would be too late. Pretorius was going to activate the alarm.

'The picture in my head, Doc . . . It's like she's hanging from a cliff and clinging to life. As he strangles her, as the strength drains out of her, she feels her grip loosen. She knows she must not fall, she doesn't want to, she wants to live, she wants to climb to the top, but he squeezes the life out of her and she begins to slip. There is a terrible fear, because of the dark below; it's either black or red or brown down below and she just can't hold on any more and she falls.'

He felt a moment of panic: the locked door, the sharp pain in his shoulder, knowledge that the alarm would sound. But he drew a deep breath, made his choices and kicked the door with his heel. Adrenaline coursed thickly. Wood splintered. The door was open now. The alarm began to wail somewhere in the roof. Pretorius was at the wardrobe, reaching up, feeling for a weapon. He bumped him against the cupboard, the tall, lean figure, bespectacled with a sloppy fringe. He fell. Thobela was on him, knee to chest and assegai against his throat.

'I am here for the children,' he said loudly over the racket of the alarm, calm now.

Eyes blinked at the assegai. There was no fear. Something else. Expectation. A certain fatalism.

'Yes,' said Pretorius.

He jammed the long blade through the man's breastbone.

'It's when they fall that they scream. Death is down there and life is up here and the scream comes up, it always comes up to the top, it stays here. It moves fast, looks like a . . . like water you throw out of a bucket. That is all that is left. It is full of horrible terror. And loss . . .'

Griessel was quiet for a while; when he continued, it was in a quieter voice. 'The thing that scares me most is that I know it's not real, Doc. If I rationalise it, I know it's my imagination. But where does it come from? Why does my head do this? Why is the scream so shrill and clear and so loud? And so bloody despairing? I am not crazy. Not really – I mean, isn't there a saying that if you know you are a little bit mad you are okay, because the really insane have no idea?

Barkhuizen chuckled. It caught Griessel by surprise, but it was a sympathetic chuckle and he grinned back.

He sprinted through the house as the alarm wailed monotonously. Out the back door, around the corner of the house to the lighted street. He swerved right. He could see the park over the way, the security of the dark and the shadows. He felt a thousand eyes on him. Legs pumped rhythmically, breath raced; instinctively he pulled his head into his shoulders and tensed his back muscles for the bullet that would come, his ears pricked for a shout or the noise of the patrol car as his feet pounded on the tar.

When he reached the shrubbery, he slackened his pace as his night vision was spoiled by the streetlights. He had to plot his course carefully and not fall over anything. He could not afford a twist or sprain.

'You know where it really comes from,' said Barkhuizen.

'Doc?'

'You know, Benny. Think about it. There are contributing factors. Your job. I think you all suffer from post-traumatic stress syndrome – with all the murder and death. But that is not the actual source. It's something else. The thing that makes you drink, too, that made me drink as well.'

Griessel stared at him for a long time and then his head bowed. 'I know,' he said.

'Say it, Benny.'

'Doc . . .'

'Say it.'

'I am afraid to die, Doc. I am so afraid to die.'

He sat behind the wheel. He was still breathing hard, sweat dripped, his heart pounded. Jesus, he was forty – too old for this shit.

He pressed the key into the ignition.

There was one difference. His seventeen targets for the KGB
. . . mostly he was detached, mechanical, even reluctant if it was
some pallid pen-pusher with stooping shoulders and colourless
eyes.

But not this time. This was different. When the assegai pierced
the man's heart, he had a feeling of euphoria. Of absolute rightness.

Perhaps he had, at last, found his true vocation.

18

It was the following morning before she phoned him in his hotel room. From a public phone booth with Sonia on her shoulder.

'Five hundred rand,' was how she identified herself in an even voice that did not betray her anxiety.

It took only a few seconds for him to work it out and he said: 'Can you be here at six o'clock?'

'Yes.'

'Room 1036, in the Holiday Inn opposite the entrance to the Waterfront.'

'Six o'clock,' she repeated.

'What is your name?'

Her brain seemed to stop working. She didn't want to give her own name, but she couldn't think of any other one. She must not hesitate too long or he would know it was a fabrication – she said the first word that came to her lips.

'Bibi.'

Later she would wonder why that? Did it mean anything, have any psychological connotation, some clue by which to understand herself better? From Christine to Bibi. A leap, a new identity, a new creation. It was a birth, in some sense. It was also a wall. At first thin, like paper, transparent and fragile. At first.

'I have thought about it a lot,' she said, because she wanted to get the story right this time.

'The money was a big thing. Like when you play the Lotto and think of what you would do with the jackpot. In your imagination you spend on yourself and your child. Sensible things: you aren't going to squander your fortune. You are not going to be like the nouveau riche. That is why you will win. Because it's owed to you. You deserve it.

'But the money wasn't the main thing. There was another aspect, something I had since my school days. When I had sex with my father's friend. And the teacher. How I felt. I controlled them, but I didn't control myself. How can I explain it? I wasn't *in* myself. Yet I *was*.'

She knew those were not the right words to describe it and made a gesture of irritation with her hands. The minister did not respond, but just waited expectantly, or maybe he was nailed to his seat.

She shut her eyes in frustration and said: 'The easy one is the power. Uncle Sarel, my father's buddy, gave me a lift one day when I was walking home in the afternoon. When I opened the car door and saw the look on his face, I knew he wanted me. I wondered what he would say, what he would do. He held the steering wheel with both his hands because he was trembling and he didn't want me to see. That's when I felt how strong I was. I toyed with him. He said he wanted to talk with me, just for a short while, and could we take a drive? He was scared to look at me and I saw how freaked out he was but I was cool so I said: "Okay, that would be nice." I acted like I was innocent, that's what he wanted. He talked, you know, silly stuff, just talking, and he stopped by the river and I kept on acting and he told me how he had been watching me for so long and how sexy I was, but he respected me and then I put my hand on his cock and watched his face and the look in his eyes and his mouth went all funny and it . . . it excited me.

'It was a good feeling to know he wanted me, it was good to see how much he wanted me, it made me *feel* wanted. Your father thinks you are nothing, but they don't think so. Some grown-ups think you are great.

'But when he had sex with me, it was like I wasn't in my body. It was someone else and I was on one side. I could feel everything, I could feel his cock and his body and all, but I was outside. I looked at the man and the girl and I thought: What is she doing? She will be damaged. But that was also okay.

'That was the weirdest part of all, that the damage was also okay.'

She found someone to stand in for her at Trawlers. She spent the day with Sonia, rode her bike along the seafront as far as the swimming pool in Sea Point and slowly back again. She thought about what she would wear and she felt anticipation and that old feeling of being outside yourself, that vague consciousness of harm and the strange satisfaction it brought.

At four o'clock she left her daughter with the childcare lady and took a slow bath, washed and blow-dried her long hair. She put on a G-string, the floral halterneck, her jeans and sandals. At half-past five she took her bike and rode slowly so as not to arrive at the hotel out of breath and sweaty. This feels almost like a date, she thought. As she wove through the peak-hour traffic in Kloof Street, she saw men in cars turn their heads. She smiled a secret smile, because not one of them knew what she was and where she was going. *Here comes the whore on her bicycle.*

It wasn't so bad.

He was just a regular guy. He had no weird requests. He received her with rather exaggerated courtesy and spoke to her in whispers. He wanted her to stroke him, touch him and lie beside him. But first she had to undress and he shivered and said, 'God, what a body you've got,' and trailed his fingers slowly over her calves and thighs and belly. He kissed her breasts and sucked the nipples. And then the sex. He reached orgasm quickly and groaning and with eyes screwed shut. He lay on top of her and asked: 'How was it for you?' She said it was wonderful, because that was what he wanted to hear.

When she rode her bicycle home up the long gradient, she thought with a measure of compassion that what he had really wanted was to talk. About his work, his marriage, his children. What he really wanted was to expel the loneliness of the four hotel room walls. What he really wanted was a sympathetic ear.

When it became her full-time profession later, she realised most of them were like that. They paid to be someone again for an hour.

That night she just felt she was lucky, because he might have been a beast. In her little flat, while Sonia slept, she took the five new hundred-rand notes from her purse and spread them out in front of her. Nearly a week's work at Trawlers. If she could do just one man a day, for only five days a week, that was ten thousand rand a month. Once all the bills were paid, there would be seven thousand over to spend. Seven thousand rand.

Three days later she bought the cell phone and placed an ad in *Die Burger's Snuffelgids*. She carefully studied the other ads in the 'adult services' section first before deciding on the wording: *Bibi. Fresh and new. 22-year-old blonde with a dream body. Pleasure guaranteed, top businessmen only.* And the number.

It appeared on a Monday for the first time. The phone rang just after nine in the morning. She purposefully did not answer at once. Then in a cool voice: 'Hello.'

He didn't have a hotel room. He wanted to come to her. She said no, she only did travelling. He seemed disappointed. Before the phone rang again, she thought: why not? But there were too many reasons. This was her and Sonia's place – here she was Christine. Safe, only she knew the address. She would keep it that way.

A pattern was established. If they phoned in the morning, it was local men who wanted to come to her. In the late afternoon and evening it was hotel business. The first week she made two thousand rand, as she would take one call per evening and then switch off the phone. Thursday her daughter had not been well and she decided not to work. In the second week she decided to do two per day, one late afternoon and one early evening. It couldn't be too bad and it would give her time to have a good bath, put on fresh perfume . . . It would double her income and compensate for evenings when there were no clients.

Clients. That wasn't her word. One afternoon she had a call, a woman's voice. Vanessa. 'We're in the same trade. I saw your advert. Do you want to go out for coffee?'

That was her initiation into what Vanessa, real name Truida, called the AECW: the Association of Expensive Cape Whores. 'Oh it's like the Woman's Institute, only we don't open with scripture reading and prayer.' Vanessa was *Young student redhead, northern suburbs. Come and show me how. Upmarket and exclusive.*

She recited her life story in a coffee shop in the Church Street Mall. A sharp-featured woman with a flawless complexion, a scar on her chin and red hair from a very expensive bottle. She came from Ermelo. She had so wanted to escape the oppression of her hometown and parents' middle-class existence. She had done one year of secretarial at technical college in Johannesburg and worked in Midrand for a company that maintained compressors. She fell in love with a young Swede whom she met at a dance club in Sandton. Karl. His libido had no limits. Sometimes they spent entire weekends in bed. She became addicted to him, to the intense and multiple orgasms, to the constant stimulus and the tremendous energy. Above all she wanted to continue to satisfy him, even though every week it took a little more, a step further into unknown territory. Like a frog in water that was getting gradually warmer. She was hypnotised by his body, his penis, his worldly wisdom. Alcohol, toys, Ecstasy, role playing. One afternoon he called in a prostitute so they could make a threesome. A month later he took her to a 'club': a lovely big house on a smallholding near Bryanston. He was not unknown at the place, a fact she registered only vaguely. The first week she had to watch while he had sex with two of them, the second week she had to take part – four bodies writhing like snakes – and eventually he wanted to watch while she had sex with two male clients in a huge bedroom with a four poster bed.

When she heard for the first time what the girls at the Bryanston place earned, she laughed in disbelief. Six weeks after Karl dumped her, she drove to the club and asked for a job. She hoped she might see him there; she wanted the money, because she had lost all direction. But she was not so lost that she was blind to the inner workings. Too many of the girls were supporting men, men who beat them, men who took their money from them every Sunday to buy drink or drugs. Too many were dependent on the perks of cocaine, sometimes heroin, which was freely available. The club kept half of their earnings. Once she had got Karl out of her system, she came to Cape Town, alone, experienced and with a purpose.

'The trick is to save, so you don't end up in ten years' time like the fifty-rand whores on the street, hoping someone wants a quick blow job. Keep off the drugs and save. Retire when you are thirty.'

And: 'Do you know about asking names?'

'No.'

'When they phone, ask who is speaking. Ask for his name.'

'What's the point of that? Most of them lie.'

'If they lie, that's good news. Only the married ones lie. I have never had trouble with a married one. It's the ones who can't get a wife that you have to watch. The secret is to use the name he gives you when you speak to him. Over and over. That's how you sell yourself over the phone. Remember, he's still window shopping and there are a lot of adverts and options and he can't claim his five hundred rand from the medical aid. Say his name, even if it is a false one. It says you believe and trust him. It says you think he's important. You massage his ego, make him feel special. That is why he is phoning. So someone will make him feel special.'

'Why are you giving me all these tips?'

'Why not?'

'Aren't we in competition?'

'Sweetheart, it's all about supply and demand. The demand from needy men in this place is unlimited, but the supply of whores who really are worth five hundred rand an hour is . . . Jesus, you should see some of them. And the men get wise.'

And: 'Get yourself a separate place to work. You don't want clients bothering you at home. They do that, turning up drunk on a Saturday night without an appointment and standing on your doorstep weeping: "I love you, I love you."'

And: 'I had a fifty-five thousand rand month once; shit, I never closed my legs, it was a bit rough. But if you can do a steady three guys a day, it's easily thirty thousand in a good month, tax free. Make hay while the sun shines, because some months are slow. December is fantastic. Advertise in the *Argus* as well, that's where the tourists will find you. And on *Sextrader* on the Internet. If he has an accent, ask for six hundred.'

And: 'It's their wives' fault. They all say the same thing. Mamma doesn't want to do it any more. Mamma won't suck me. Mamma won't try new stuff. We're therapists, I'm telling you, I see how they come in and how they go.'

Vanessa told her about the other members of the AECW – Afrikaans and English, white, brown, black and a tiny delicate woman from Thailand. Christine only met three or four of them and spoke to a few more over the phone, but she was reluctant to become involved – she wanted to keep her distance and ano-nymity. But she did take their advice. She found a room at the Gardens Centre and set her sights higher. The money followed.

The days and weeks formed a pattern. Mornings were Sonia's, and weekends, except for the occasional one when she was booked for a hunting weekend, but the money made that worthwhile. She worked from 12:00 to 21:00 and then collected her daughter from the daycare where they thought she was a nurse.

Every third month she phoned her mother.

She bought a car for cash, a blue 1998 Volkswagen City Golf. They moved into a bigger flat, a spacious two-bedroom in the same building. She furnished it piece by piece like a jigsaw puzzle. Satellite television, an automatic washing machine and a micro-wave. A mountain bike for six thousand rand just because the salesman had looked her up and down and showed her the seven-ninety-nine models.

A year after she had placed the first advertisement, she and Sonia went to Knysna for a two-week holiday. On the way back she stopped at the traffic lights in the town and looked at the sign board showing Cape Town to the left and Port Elizabeth to the right. At that moment she wanted to go right, anywhere else, a new city, a new life.

An ordinary life.

Her regular clients had missed her. There were a lot of messages on her cell phone when she turned it back on.

She had been nearly two years in Cape Town when she phoned

home once more. Her mother cried when she heard her daughter's voice. 'Your father died three weeks ago.'

She could hear her mother's tears were not for the loss alone: they also expressed reproach. Implying that Christine had contributed to the heart attack. Reproach that her mother had had to bear it all alone. That she had no one to lean on. Nevertheless, the emotion Christine experienced was surprisingly sharp and deep, so that she responded with a cry of pain.

'What was that noise all about?' her mother asked.

She didn't really know. There was loss and guilt and self-pity and grief, but it was the loss that dumbfounded her. Because she had hated him so much. She began to weep and only later analysed all the reasons: what she had done, her absence, her part in his death. Her mother's loneliness and her sudden release. The permanent loss of her father's approval. The first realisation that death awaited her too.

But she could not explain why the next thing she said was about Sonia. 'I have a child, Ma.'

It just came out, like an animal that had been watching the door of its cage for months.

It took a long time for her mother to answer, long enough to wish she had never said it. But her mother's reaction was not what she expected: 'What is his name?'

'Her name, Ma. Her name is Sonia.'

'Is she two years old?' Her mother was not stupid.

'Yes.'

'My poor, poor child.' And they cried together, about everything. But when her mother later asked: 'When can I see my grandchild? At Christmas?' she was evasive. 'I'm working over Christmas, Ma. Perhaps in the New Year.'

'I can come down. I can look after her while you work.' She heard the desperation in her mother's voice, a woman who needed something good and pretty in her life after years of trouble. In that instant Christine wanted to give it to her. She was so eager to repay her debt, but she still had one secret she could not share.

'We will come and visit, Ma. In January, I promise.'

She didn't work that evening.

That night, after Sonia had gone to sleep, she cut herself for the first time. She had no idea why she did it. It might have been about her father. She rummaged around in the bathroom and found nothing. So she tried the kitchen. In one drawer she saw the knife that she used to pare vegetables. She carried it to the sitting room and sat and looked at herself and knew she couldn't cut where it would show – not in her profession. That's why she chose her foot, the soft underside between heel and ball. She pressed the knife in and drew it along. The blood began to flow and frightened her. She hobbled to the bathroom and held her foot over the bath. Felt the pain. She watched the drops slide down the side of the bath.

Later she cleaned up the blood spoor. Felt the pain. Refused to think about it. Knew she would do it again.

She didn't work the next day either. It was the beginning of December, bonanza month. She didn't want to go on. She wanted the kind of life where she could tell Sonia: 'Granny Martie is coming to visit.' She was weary of lying to the daycare or other mothers at the crèche. She was weary of her clients and their pathetic requests, their neediness. She wanted to say 'yes' the next time a polite, good-looking man came up to her table in McDonald's and asked if he could buy them ice cream. Just once.

But it was holiday season, big-money month.

She negotiated an agreement with herself. She would work as much as she could in December. So that they could afford to spend January with her mother in Upington. And when they came back she would find other work.

She kept to the deal. Martie van Rooyen absorbed herself in her granddaughter in those two weeks in Upington. She also sensed something about her daughter's existence. 'You have changed, Christine. You have become hard.'

She lied to her mother about her work, said she did this and that, worked here and there. She cut her other foot in her mother's bathroom. This time the blood told her she must stop. Stop all of it.

The next day she told her mother she hoped to get a permanent job. And she did.

She was appointed as sales rep for a small company that manufactured medicinal face creams from extract of sea-bamboo. She had to call on chemist shops in the city centre and southern suburbs. It lasted two months. The first setback was when she walked into a Link pharmacy in Noordhoek and recognised the pharmacist as one of her former clients. The second was when her new boss put his hand on her leg while they were travelling in his car. The final straw was her pay slip at the end of the month. Gross income: nine thousand and something. Nett income: six thousand four hundred rand, sales commission included, after tax and unemployment insurance and who knows what had been subtracted.

She rethought her plans. She was twenty-one years old. As an escort she had earned more than thirty thousand rand a month and she had saved twenty thousand of it. After buying the car and a few other large expenses she still had nearly two hundred thousand in the bank. If she could just work another four years . . . until Sonia went to school. Just four years. Save two, two-fifty a year, perhaps more. Then she could afford a normal job. Just four years.

It nearly worked out. Except one day she answered the phone and Carlos Sangrenegra said: 'Conchita?'

19

He checked out of the Parow hotel. His requirements had changed. He wanted to be more anonymous, have fewer witnesses of his coming and going. He drove into the city centre where he could pass the time without attracting attention. From a public phone in the Golden Acre he called the detective in Umtata to ask for news of Khoza and Ramphele.

'I thought you were going to catch them.'

'I'm not getting anywhere.'

'It's not so easy, hey?'

'No, it's not.'

'Yes,' said the detective, mollified by the capitulation. 'We haven't really got anything from our side either.'

'Not really?'

'Nothing.'

In Adderley Street he bought *Die Burger* and went into the Spur on Strand Street for breakfast. He placed his order and shook the paper open. The main news was the 2010 Soccer World Cup bid. At the bottom of page one was an article headed, *Gay couple arrest over child's death*. He read that one. A woman had been arrested on suspicion of the murder of her partner's five-year-old daughter. The child was hit over the head with a billiard cue, apparently in a fit of rage.

His coffee arrived. He tore open a paper tube of sugar, poured it into his cup and stirred.

What was he trying to do?

If children can't depend on the justice system to protect them, to whom can they turn?

How would he achieve it? How would he be able to protect the children by his actions? How would people know: you cannot lay a finger on a child. There must be no doubt – the sentence of death had been reinstated.

He tested the temperature of the coffee with a careful sip.

He was in too much of a hurry. It would happen. It would take a little time for the message to get across, but it would happen. He must just not lose focus.

'It's not going to happen,' said Woolworth's head of corporate communication, a white woman in her early forties. She sat beside André Marais, the female police sergeant, in a meeting room of the chain store head office in Longmarket Street. The contrast between the two women was marked. It's only money, thought Griessel, and environment. Take this manicured woman in her tight grey suit and leave her at the charge desk in Claremont for three months on a police salary and then let's take another look.

There were six around the circular table: January, the Waterfront store manager, Kleyn – the communications woman, Marais, Griessel and his shift partner for the month, Inspector Cliffy Mketsu.

'Oh yes it is,' said Griessel derisively enjoying himself. 'Because you won't like the alternative, Mrs Kleyn.' He and Mketsu had decided that he would play the bad cop and Cliffy would be the peace-loving, good cop Xhosa detective.

'What alternative?' The woman's extremely red mouth was small and dissatisfied under the straight nose and over made-up eyes. Before Griessel could reply she added: 'And it's *Ms* Kleyn.'

'McClean?' asked Cliffy, slightly puzzled, and slid her business card closer across the table. 'But here it says . . .'

'*Ms*,' she said. 'As in neither Mrs or Miss. It's a modern form of address which probably hasn't yet penetrated the police.'

'Let me tell you what has penetrated the police, *Ms* Kleyn,' said Griessel, suspecting it would not be difficult to act mean with this particular woman. 'It has penetrated us that this afternoon we are going to hold a press conference and we are going to tell the media there is a serial killer on the loose in the shopping aisles of Woollies. We are going to ask them to please warn the unsuspecting public to stay away before another innocent, middle-aged Woollies custo- mer is strangled with a kettle cord. This modus operandi has penetrated the police, *Ms* Kleyn. So don't you tell me "it's not going to happen", as if I came to ask if we could hold trolley races up and down your aisles.'

Even through all that foundation he could see she had turned a deep shade of red.

'Benny, Benny,' said Cliffy in a soothing tone. 'I don't think we have to make threats. We must understand Ms Kleyn's point of view too. She is only considering the interests of her customers.'

'She is only considering the interests of her company. I say we talk to the press.'

'That's blackmail,' said Kleyn, losing confidence.

'It's unnecessary,' said Cliffy. 'I am sure we can come to some arrangement, Mrs Kleyn.'

'We will have to,' said January, the manager of the Waterfront branch.

'Did I say *Mrs*? Oh, I am sorry,' said Cliffy.

'We can't afford that kind of publicity,' said January.

'It's strength of habit,' said Cliffy.

'I will not be blackmailed,' said Kleyn.

'Of course not, *Ms* Kleyn.'

'I'm going,' said Griessel, standing up.

'Could I say something?' asked Sergeant Marais in a gentle voice.

'Naturally, *Ms* Marais,' said Cliffy jovially.

'You are afraid something might happen to customers in the shop?' she asked Kleyn.

'Of course I am. Can you imagine what that publicity would mean?'

'I can,' said Marais. 'But there is a way to remove the risk altogether.'

'Oh?' said Kleyn.

Griessel sat down again.

'All we want to do is to get the suspect to make contact with me. We hope he will initiate a conversation and get himself invited to a woman's home. We can't confront him in the shop or try to arrest him: there are no grounds. So really there is no risk of a confrontation.'

'I don't know . . .' said Kleyn, and looked dubiously at her long red fingernails.

'Would it help if I was the only policeman in the supermarket?'

'Steady on, Sergeant,' said Griessel.

'Inspector, I will be carrying a radio and we know the supermarket is a safe environment. You can be outside, all over.'

'I think that's a good idea,' said Cliffy.

'I don't see why we should change good police procedure just because the Gestapo don't like it,' said Griessel and got to his feet again.

Kleyn sucked in her breath sharply, as if to react, but he didn't give her the chance. 'I'm leaving. If you want to sell out, do it without me.'

'I like your proposals,' said Kleyn to André Marais quickly, so that Griessel could hear it before he was out the door.

Thobela was standing at the reception desk of the Waterfront City Lodge when the *Argus* arrived. The deliveryman dropped the bundle of newspapers beside him on the wooden counter with a dull thump. The headline was right under his nose, but he was still filling in the registration card and his attention was not on the big letters:

VIGILANTE KILLER TARGETS 'CHILD MOLESTERS'

His pen stalled over the paper. What was written there – what did they know? The clerk behind the desk was busy at the keyboard of the computer. He forced himself to finish writing and hand the card over. The clerk gave him the room's electronic card key and explained to him how to find it.

'May I take a newspaper?'

'Of course, I'll just charge it to your account.'

He took a paper, and his bag, and headed for the stairs. He read.

One day before crèche owner Colin Pretorius (34) was to receive judgement on several charges of rape and molestation, he apparently became the second victim of what could be an assegai-wielding vigilante killer bent on avenging crimes against children.

He realised he was standing still and his heart was bumping hard in his chest. He glanced up, took the stairs to the first floor and waited until he was there before reading more.

The investigating officer, Inspector Bushy Bezuidenhout of the Serious and Violent Crimes Unit (SVC), did not rule out the possibility that the bladed weapon was the same one used in the Enver Davids stabbing three days ago.

In an exclusive report, following an anonymous phone call to our offices, The Argus *yesterday revealed that the 'bladed weapon' was an assegai . . .*

How much did they know? His eyes searched the columns.

Inspector Bezuidenhout admitted that the police had no suspects at this time. Asked whether the killer might be a woman, he said that he could not comment on the possibility (see page 16: The Artemis Factor).

He opened his room door, put the bag on the floor and spread the newspaper open on the bed. He turned to page 16.

Greek mythology had its female protector of children, a ruthless huntress of the gods called Artemis, who could punish injustice with ferocious and deadly accuracy – and silver arrows. But just how likely is a female avenger of crimes against children?

'It is possible that this vigilante is a woman,' says criminologist Dr Rita Payne. 'We are ruthless when it comes to protecting our kids, and there are several appropriate case studies of mothers committing serious crimes, even murder, to avenge acts against their children.'

But there is one reason why the suspected modern-day Artemis might not be female: 'An assegai isn't a likely weapon for a woman. In instances where women did use a blade to stab or cut a victim, it was a weapon of opportunity, not premeditation,' Dr Payne said.

However, this does not completely rule out a female vigilante . . .

He felt uncomfortable about this publicity. He pushed the newspaper to one side and got up to open the curtain. He had a view over the canal and the access road to the Waterfront. He stood and stared at the incessant stream of cars and pedestrians and wondered what was bothering him, what was the cause of this new tension. The fact that the police were investigating as if he were a common criminal? He had known that would happen, he had no illusions about that. Was it because the paper made it all sound so shallow? What did it matter if it was a woman or a man? Why not focus on the root of the matter?

Somebody was doing something. Someone was fighting back.

'Artemis.'

He spat out the word, but it left an unpleasant aftertaste.

Since she had told him about Sonia, the minister seemed to have grown weary. His thinning hair lay flatter on his scalp, smoothed by the big hand that touched it every now and then. His beard began to shadow his jaw in the light of the desk lamp, the light blue shirt was rumpled and the rolled-up sleeves hung down unevenly. His eyes were still on her with the same focus, the same undivided attention, but touched now with something else. She thought she saw a suspicion there, a premonition of tragedy.

'You were very convincing today, Benny,' said Cliffy Mketsu as they followed André Marais to the car.

'She pisses me off, that fucking *Ms*,' he said, and he saw Sergeant Marais's back stiffen ahead of him.

'Now you think I have a thing against women, Sergeant,' he said. He knew what was wrong with him. He knew he was walking on the edge. Jissis, the pills were doing fuck-all – he wanted a drink, his entire body was a parched throat.

'No, Inspector,' said Marais with a meekness that irritated.

'Because you would be wrong. I only have a thing about women like *her*.' He said in a falsetto voice: '*It's a modern form of address which probably hasn't yet penetrated the police*. Why must they always have something to say about the fucking police? Why?'

Two coloured men came walking towards them down the pavement. They looked at Griessel.

'Benny . . .' said Cliffy, laying a hand on his arm.

'Okay,' said Griessel, and took the keys out of his jacket pocket when they reached the police car. He unlocked it, got in and stretched across to unlock the other doors. Mketsu and Marais got in. He put the key in the ignition.

'What does she want to be a *Ms* for? What for? What is wrong with Mrs? Or Miss. It was good enough for six thousand years and now she wants to be a fucking *Ms*.'

'Benny.'

'What for, Cliffy?' He couldn't do this. He had to have a drink. He felt for the slip of paper in his pocket, not sure where he had put it.

'I don't know, Benny,' said Cliffy. 'Let's go.'

'Just wait a minute,' he said.

'If I was her, I would also want to be Ms,' said André Marais quietly from the back seat.

He found the paper, unclipped his seat belt and said: 'Excuse me,' and got out of the car. He read the number on the paper and phoned it on his cell phone.

'Barkhuizen,' said the voice on the other side.

He walked down the pavement away from the car. 'Doc, those pills of yours are not doing a damn thing for me. I can't go on. I can't do my work. I am a complete bastard. I want to hit everyone. I can't go on like this, Doc, I'm going to buy myself a fucking litre of brandy and I'm going to drink it, Doc, you hear?'

'I hear you, Benny.'

'Right, Doc, I just wanted to tell you.'

'Thank you, Benny.'

'Thank you, Benny?'

'It's your choice. But just do me one favour, before you pour the first one.'

'What's that, Doc?'

'Phone your wife. And your children. Tell them the same story.'

20

She sat looking at Sonia. The child lay on the big bed, one hand folded under her, the other a little dumpling next to her open mouth. Her hair was fine and glossy in the late-afternoon sun shining through the window. She sat very still and stared at her child. She was not looking for features that reminded her of Viljoen, she was not revelling in the perfection of her limbs.

Her child's body. Unmarked. Untouched. Holy, stainless, clean.

She would teach her that her body was wonderful. That she was beautiful. That she was allowed to be beautiful. She could be attractive and desirable – it was not a sin, nor a curse, it was a blessing. Something she could enjoy and be proud of. She would teach Sonia that she could put on make-up and pretty clothes and walk down the street and draw the attention of men and that was fine. Natural. That they would storm her battlements like soldiers in endless lines of war. But she had a weapon to ensure that only the one she chose would conquer her – love for herself.

That was the gift she would give to her daughter.

She got up and fetched the new knife that she had bought from @Home. She took it to the bathroom and locked the door behind her. She stood in front of the mirror and lightly and slowly drew the blade over her face, from her brow to her chin.

How she longed to press the blade in. How she longed to cleave the skin and feel the burn.

She took off her T-shirt, unsnapped the bra behind her back and let it fall to the floor. She held the knifepoint against her breast. She drew a circle around her nipple. In her mind's eyes she saw the blade flash as she carved long stripes across her breast. She saw the marks criss-crossed.

Just another two years.

She sat on the rim of the bath and swung her feet over. She placed her left foot on her right knee. She held the knife next to the cushion beside her big toe. She cut, fast and deep, right down to her heel.

When she felt the sudden pain and saw the blood collecting in the bottom of the bath, she thought: You are sick, Christine. You are sick, sick, sick.

'In the beginning Carlos was quite refreshing. Different. With me. I think it is more okay in Colombia to visit a sex worker than it is here. He never had that attitude of "what if someone saw me" like most of my clients. He was a small, wiry man without an ounce of fat on him. He was always laughing. Always glad to see me. He said I was the most beautiful conchita in the world. "You are Carlos's blonde bombshell." He talked about himself like that. He never said "I". "Carlos wants to clone you, and export you to Colombia. You are very beautiful to Carlos."

'He had nice hands, that's one of the things I remember about him. Delicate hands like a woman's. He made a lot of noise when we had sex, sounds and Spanish words. He shouted so loud once that someone knocked on the door and asked if everything was okay.

'The first time he gave me extra money, two hundred rand. "Because you are the best." A few days later he phoned again. "You remember Carlos? Well, now he cannot live without you."

'He made me laugh, at first. When he came to my place in the Gardens Centre. Before I started going to him, before I knew what he did. Before he became jealous.'

Before Carlos she wrote the letter.

You were a good mother. Pa was the one who messed up. And me. That is why I am leaving Sonia with you. She wanted to add something, words to say that her mother deserved a second chance with a daughter, but every time she scratched out the lines, crumpled up the paper and started over.

Late at night she would sit on the rim of the bath and stroke the knife over her wrists. Between one and three, alone, Sonia asleep in her cheerful bedroom with the seagulls on the ceiling and Mickey Mouse on the wall. She knew she could not let the knife cut in, because she could not abandon her child like that. She would have to make another plan with more limited damage.

She wondered how much blood could flow in the bath.

How great would the relief be when all the bad was out?

Carlos Sangrenegra, with his Spanish accent and his odd English, his tight jeans and the moustache that he cultivated with such care. The little gold crucifix on a fine chain around his neck, the one thing he kept on in bed, although they weren't actually in the bed much. 'Doggie, conchita, Carlos likes doggie.' He would stand with feet planted wide apart on the floor; she would be bent over the edge of the bed. From the start he was different. He was like a child. Everything excited him. Her breasts, her hair colour, her eyes, her body, her shaven pubic hair.

He would come in and undress, ready and erect, and he wouldn't want to chat first. He was never uncomfortable.

'Don't you want to talk first?'

'Carlos does not pay five hundred rand for talking. That he can get free anywhere.'

She liked him, those first few times, perhaps because he enjoyed her so intensely, and was so verbal about it. Also, he brought flowers, sometimes a small gift, and left a little extra when he went. It was her perception that it was a South-American custom, this generosity, since she had never had a Latin-American client before. Germans and Englishmen, Irishmen (usually drunk), Americans, Hollanders (always found something to complain about) and Scandinavians (possibly the best lovers overall). But Carlos was a first. A Colombian.

That origin meant nothing to her, just a vaguely remembered orange patch on a school atlas.

'What do you do?' After his theatrical orgasm, he was lying with his head between her breasts.

'What does Carlos do? You don't know?'

'No.'

'Everybody knows what Carlos do.'

'Oh.'

'Carlos is a professional lover. World heavyweight love champion. Every fuck is a knockout. You should know that, conchita.'

She could only laugh.

He showered and dressed and took extra notes from his wallet and put them on the bedside cupboard saying: 'Carlos gives you a little extra.' In that rising tone, as if it were a question, but she was used to that. Then he put his hand back in his jeans pocket and said: 'You don't know what Carlos does?'

'No.'

'You don't know what the number one export of Colombia is?'

'No.'

'Ah, conchita, you are so innocent,' he said, and he brought out a little transparent plastic packet in his hand, filled with fine white powder. 'Do you know what this is?'

She made a gesture with her hand to show she was guessing. 'Cocaine?'

'Yes, it is cocaine, of course it is cocaine. Colombia is the biggest cocaine producer in the world, conchita.'

'Oh!'

'You want?' He held the packet up towards her.

'No, thanks.'

That made him laugh uproariously. 'You don't want A-grade, super special number one uncut Colombian snow?'

'I don't take drugs,' she said, a bit embarrassed, as if it were an insult to his national pride.

Suddenly he was serious. 'Yes, Carlos's conchita is clean.'

She ascribed the early signs to his Latin blood, just another characteristic that was refreshingly different.

He would ring and say: 'Carlos is coming over.'

'Now?'

'Of course *now*. Carlos misses his conchita.'

'I miss you, too, but I can only see you at three o'clock.'

'*Tree* o'clock?'

'I have other clients too, you know.'

He said a word in Spanish, two cutting syllables.

'Carlo-o-o-o-s,' she stretched it out soothingly.

'How much they paying you?'

'The same.'

'They bring you flowers?'

'No, Carlos . . .'

'They give you extra?'

'No.'

'So why see them?'

'I have to make a living.'

He was silent until she said his name.

'Carlos will come tomorrow. Carlos wants to be first, you unnerstand? First love of the day.'

'He phoned one day and he said he was going to send someone to pick me up. These two guys that I didn't know came in a big BMW, one of those with a road map on a television up front, and they took me to Camps Bay. We got out, but you couldn't see the house, it was up on the slope. You go up in a lift. Everything is glass and the view is out of this world, but there wasn't really furniture in it. Carlos said he had just bought it and I must help him, as he wasn't very good with decorating and stuff.

'Maybe that was the night I clicked for the first time. I had been there for half an hour when I looked at my watch, but Carlos was angry and said: "Don't look at your watch."

'When I wanted to protest, he said: "Carlos will take care of you, hokay?"

'We ate on the balcony, on a blanket, and Carlos chatted as if we were boyfriend and girlfriend. The other two who fetched me were around somewhere, and he told me they were bodyguards and there was nothing to be scared of.

'Then he asked me: "How much do you get in a month, conchita?" I didn't like to say. Lots of them ask, but I never say – it's not their business. So I told him: "That's private."

'Then he came out with it. "Carlos do not want his girlfriend to see other guys. But he knows you must make a living, so he will pay what you make. More. Double."

'So I said: "No, Carlos, I can't," and that made him angry, for the first time. He smacked all the food around on the blanket and screamed at me in Spanish, and I thought he would hit me. So I took my handbag and said I had better go. I was scared; he was another person, his face . . . The bodyguards came walking out and talked to him and suddenly he calmed down and he just said: "Sorry, conchita, Carlos is so sorry." But I asked him, please, could they just take me home, and he said he would do it himself and all the way he was sorry and he made jokes and when I got out he gave me two thousand. I took it, because I thought if I tried to give it back he would be angry again.

'The next morning I phoned Vanessa and asked her what I should do, this guy thinks I am his girlfriend and he wants to pay me to be with just him and she said that is bad news, I must get rid of him, that sort of thing could ruin my whole business. So I said thanks and bye, because I didn't want to tell her this guy is in drugs and he has a terrible temper and I haven't a clue how to get rid of him.

'So I phoned Carlos and he said he was terribly sorry, it was his work that made him like that, and he sent flowers and I started to think it would be okay. But then they assaulted one of my clients, just outside the door of my room in the Gardens Centre.

The master bedroom of the Camps Bay house had a four-poster bed now. He had retained an expensive, well-known interior decorator who had begun with the bedroom and everything was in white: curtains, bedding, drapes on the bed like the sails of a ship. He showed off like a little boy, keeping his hands over her eyes all the way down the passage and then: 'Ta-daaa!' and watched her reaction. He asked her four or five times, 'You like the master's bedroom?' and she said, 'It's beautiful,' because it was.

He dived onto the bed and said, 'Come to Carlos,' and he was exuberant, even more boisterous than usual, and she tried to forget about the bodyguards somewhere in the house.

Later he lay beside her and softly traced little circles around her nipple with the tip of the little gold crucifix. 'Where do you live, conchita?'

'You know . . .'

'No, where do you *live*?'

'Gardens Centre,' she replied, hoping he would drop the subject.

'You think Carlos is stupid because he looks stupid? You work there, but where is your home, where is the place with your pictures on the fridge?'

'I can't afford another place, you pay me too little.'

'Carlos pay you too little? Carlos pay you too much. All the time the moneyman is saying: "Carlos, we are here to make a profit, remember."'

'You have a bookkeeper?'

'Of course. You think Carlos is small fish? Cocaine is big business, conchita, very big business.'

'Oh.'

'So you will take Carlos to your house?'

Never, she thought, never ever, but said, 'One day . . .'

'You don't trust Carlos?'

'Can I ask you a question?'

'Conchita, you can ask Carlos anything.'

'Did you have my client beaten up?'

'What client?' But he couldn't carry off the lie and his eyes turned crafty. He is a child, she thought, and it frightened her.

'Just a client. Fifty-three years old.'

'Why do you think Carlos beat him?'

'Not you. But maybe the bodyguards?'

'Did he buy drugs?'

'No.'

'They only beat up people who do not pay for drugs, hokay?'

'Okay.' She knew what she wanted to know. But it helped not at all.

21

Griessel and Cliffy sat in the fish restaurant a hundred metres beyond the entrance to Woolworths, each with a small earphone. They heard André Marais saying, 'Testing, testing' for the umpteenth time, but this time with a tinny voice in the background calling, 'Next customer, please.'

Cliffy Mketsu nodded, as he did every time. It irritated Griessel immensely. Marais couldn't fucking see them nod, she was in the food section of Woolworths and they were here. She was only wearing a microphone, not earphones. One-way communication only, but Cliffy had to nod.

At a table opposite, a man and a woman were drinking red wine. The woman was middle-aged, but pretty, like Farrah Fawcett, with big, round, golden earrings and lots of rings on her fingers. The man looked young enough to be her son, but took her hand every now and again. They bothered Griessel. Because they were drinking wine. Because he could taste the dark flavour in his mouth. Because they were rich. Because they were together. Because they could drink and be together and what of him? He could sit here with Nodding Cliffy Mketsu, clever Cliffy, busy with his Masters in Police Science, a good policeman, but confused, hopelessly absent-minded, as if his head was in his books all the time.

Would he and Anna ever be able to sit and enjoy themselves like that? Sit holding hands and sipping wine and gazing into each other's eyes? How did people do that? How do you regain the romance after twenty years of married life? Actually, it was fucking irrelevant, because he would never be able to sip wine again. Not if you were an alcoholic. You couldn't drink a thing. Nothing. Not a fucking drop. Couldn't even smell the red wine.

He had told Doc Barkhuizen he was going to get drunk, but the Doc had said: 'Phone your wife and children and tell them,' because he knew Griessel could not do that. He wanted to smash his cell phone on the bloody pavement, he wanted to break something but he just screamed, he didn't know what, not words. When he turned around, Cliffy and André Marais were sitting rigidly in the car pretending nothing had happened.

'Vaughn, are you receiving properly?' Cliffy asked the other team over the microphone. They were looking at Woolworths clothes on the second floor, the one above the food department.

'Ten-four, good buddy,' said Inspector Vaughn Cupido, as if it were a game. He and Jamie Keyter were the back-up team. Not *Yaymie* as the locals would say it, he called himself *Jaa-mie*. Nowadays everyone had foreign names. What was wrong with good, basic Afrikaner names? The men weren't Griessel's first choice either, as Cupido was careless and Keyter was a braggart, recently transferred from Table View Station after he had made the newspapers with one of those stories where facts do not necessarily interfere with sensation. 'Detective breaks car-theft syndicate single-handed.' With his bulging Virgin Active biceps and the kind of face to make schoolgirls swoon, he was one of the few white additions to the Serious and Violent Crimes Unit. This was the team that had to protect André Marais and catch a fucking serial killer: an alcoholic, a braggart and a sloppy one.

There was another matter on his mind; two, three things that came suddenly together: were the older woman and the young man opposite married? To each other? What if Anna had a young man who held her hand on Friday nights? He couldn't believe that she no longer wanted it, of that he was convinced. You didn't just switch off her sort of warmth like a stove plate just because her husband was a fucking alky. She met men at work – what would she do if there was a young man who was interested and sober? She was still attractive, despite the crow's feet at the corners of her eyes – due to her husband's drinking habit. There was nothing wrong with her body. He knew what men were like; he knew they would try. How long would she keep saying 'no'? How long?

He took out his cell phone, needing to know where she was on a Friday night. He rang, holding the phone to the ear without the earphone.

It rang.

He looked across at Farrah Fawcett and her toy boy.

They were gazing into each other's eyes with desire. He swore they were just plain horny.

'I thi . . . it's tha . . . . . . t,' said André Marais in the earphone.

'What?' said Griessel, looking at Cliffy, who merely shrugged and tapped his radio receiver with the tip of his index finger.

'Hello,' said his son.

'Hello, Fritz.'

'Hi, Dad.' There was no joy in his son's voice.

'How are you?'

But he couldn't hear the answer as the earphone buzzed in his ear and he only caught a fraction of what Sergeant André Marais was saying: '. . . can't afford . . .'

'What are you doing, Fritz?'

'Nothing. It's just Carla and me.' His son sounded depressed, and there was a dull tone to his voice.

'How's your reception, Vaughn?' Cupido asked. 'Her mike isn't good.'

'Just Carla and you?'

'Mom's out.'

'I usually just buy instant,' said André Marais clearly and distinctly.

'She's talking to someone,' said Cliffy.

Then they heard a man's voice over the ether, faintly: 'I can't do without a good cup of filter in the morning.'

'Dad? Are you there?'

'I'll have to call later, Fritz, I'm at work.'

'Okay.' Like he expected it.

'What . . . name?'

'. . . dré.'

'Fuck,' said Cupido, 'her fucking mike.'

'Bye, Fritz.'

'Bye, Dad.'

'We might be too far away,' said Jamie Keyter.

'Stay where you are,' said Griessel.

'Pleased to meet you,' said the policewoman below in Woolworths food hall.

'A fish on the hook,' said Cupido.

Cliffy nodded.

Mom's out.

'Just keep calm,' said Griessel, but he meant it for himself.

Thobela made a noise of frustration in his deep voice as he rose from the hotel bed in one sudden movement. He had lain down at about three o'clock with the curtains drawn to shut out the sun, closed his eyes and lay listening to the beat of his heart. His head buzzed from too little sleep and his limbs felt like lead. Weary. With deliberate breathing he tried to drain the tension from his body. He sent his thoughts away from the present, sent them to the peaceful waters of the Cata River, to the mist that rolled like wraiths over the round hills of the farm . . . to realise only moments later that his thoughts had jumped away and were pumping other information through his consciousnesses to the rhythm of the pulse in his temples.

Pretorius reaching for the weapon in his wardrobe.

Eternity in the moments before he reached the man, and the alarm wailing, wailing, to the rhythm of his heartbeat.

A heavy woman towering above a little girl and the billiard cue rising and falling, rising and falling with demonic purpose and the blood spattering from the child's head and he knew that was his problem – the woman, the woman. He had never executed a woman. His war was against men, always had been. In the name of the Struggle, seventeen times. Sixteen in the cities of Europe, one in Chicago: men, traitors, assassins, enemies, condemned to death in the committee rooms of the Cold War, and he was the one sent to carry out the sentence. Now two in the name of the New War. Animals. But male.

Was there honour in the execution of a woman?

The more he forced his thoughts elsewhere, the more they scurried back, until he rose up with that deep sound and plucked aside the curtains. There was movement outside, bright sunlight and colour. He looked over the canal and the entrance to the Waterfront. Labourers streamed on foot towards the city centre, to the taxi ranks in Adderley Street. Black and coloured, in the brightly coloured overalls of manual labourers. They moved with purpose, hasty to start the weekend, somewhere at a home or a shebeen. With family. Or friends.

His family was dead. He wanted to jerk open the window and scream: Fuck you all, my family is dead!

He drew a deep breath, placed his palms on the cool windowsill and let his head hang. He must get some sleep; he could not go on like this.

He turned back to the room. The bedspread was rumpled. He pulled it straight, smoothing it with his big hands, pulling and stretching it till it was level. He puffed up the pillows and laid them tidily down, one beside the other. Then he sat on the bed and picked up the telephone directory from the bedside drawer, found the number and rang Boss Man Madikiza at the Yellow Rose.

'This is Tiny. The one who was looking for John Khoza, you remember?'

'I remember, my brother.' The uproar of the nightclub was already audible in the background this late afternoon.

'Heard anything?'

'Haiziko. Nothing.'

'Keep your ear to the ground.'

'It is there all the time.'

He got up and opened the wardrobe. The stack of clean clothes on the top shelf was very low, the piles of folded dirty laundry were high – socks, underwear, trousers and shirts, each in their own separate pile.

He took the two small plastic holders of detergent and softener from his case, and sorted the washing into small bundles. The ritual was twenty years old, from the time in Europe when he had learned to live out of a suitcase. To be in control, orderly and organised. Because the call could come at any time. In those days he had made a game of it, the sorting of clothes according to colour had made him smile, because that was apartheid – the whites here, the blacks there, the mixed colours in their own pile; each group afraid that another group's colour would stain them. He had always washed the black bundle first, because 'here blacks come first'.

He did that now, just from habit. Pressed and rubbed the material in the soapy water – rinse once, then again, twist the clothes in long worms to squeeze out the water – until his muscles bulged. Hung them out. Next the coloured clothes, and the whites could wait till last.

Next morning he would ring reception and ask for an ironing board and iron and do the part he enjoyed the most – ironing the shirts and trousers with a hissing, hot iron till they could be hung on hangers in the wardrobe with perfect flat surfaces and sharp creases.

He draped the last white shirt over the chair and then stood indecisively in the centre of the room.

He could not stay here.

He needed to pass the time until he could attempt sleep again. And he must think through this matter of the woman.

He picked up his wallet, pushed it in his trouser pocket, took the key card for his room and went out the door, down the stairs and outside. He walked around the corner to Dock Road, where the people were still walking to their weekend. He fell in behind a group of five coloured men and kept pace with them up Coen Steytler. He eavesdropped on their conversation, following the easy, directionless talk with close attention all the way to Adderley.

It was not André Marais's fault that Operation Woollies descended into total chaos. She acted out her role as a lonely, middle-aged woman skilfully and with vague, careful interest as the man began to chat with her between the wine racks and the snack displays.

Later she would think that she had expected an older man. This one was barely thirty: tallish, slightly plump, with a dark, five o'clock shadow. His choice of clothes was strange – the style of his checked jacket was out of date, the green shirt just a shade too bright, brown shoes unpolished. 'Harmless' was the word on her tongue, but she knew appearance counted for nothing when it came to crime.

He asked her, in English with an Afrikaans accent, if she knew where the filter coffee was, and she replied that she thought it was that way.

With a shy smile he told her he was addicted to filter coffee and she replied that usually she bought instant as she could not afford expensive coffee. He said he couldn't manage without a good cup of filter coffee in the morning, charmingly apologetic, as if it were sinful. 'Italian Blend,' he said.

Oddly, she explained to Griessel later, at that moment she quite liked him. There was a vulnerability to him, a humanity that found an echo in herself.

Their trolleys were side by side, hers with ten or twelve items, his empty. 'Oh?' she said, fairly certain he was not the one they were looking for. She wanted to get rid of him.

'Yes, it's very strong,' he said. 'It keeps me alert when I am on the Flying Squad.'

She felt her guts contract, because she knew he was lying. She knew policemen, she could spot them a mile away and he was not one, she knew.

'Are you a policeman?' she asked, trying to sound impressed.

'Captain Johan Reyneke,' he said, putting out a rather feminine hand and smiling through prominent front teeth. 'What is your name?'

'André,' she said, and felt her heart beat faster. Captains did not do Flying Squad – he must have a reason for lying.

'André,' he repeated, as if to memorise it.

'My mother wanted to use her father's name, and then she only had daughters.' She used her standard explanation, although there was no question in his voice. With difficulty she kept her voice level.

'Oh, I like that. It's different. What work do you do, André?'

'Oh, admin, nothing exciting.'

'And your husband?'

She looked into his eyes and lied. 'I am divorced,' she said, and looked down, as if she were ashamed.

'Never mind,' he said, 'I'm divorced too. My children live in Johannesburg.'

She was going to say her children were out of the house already, part of the fabrication she and Griessel had discussed, but there was a voice from behind, a woman's voice, quite shrill. 'André?'

She glanced over her shoulder and recognised the woman, Molly, couldn't recall her surname. She was the mother of one of her son's school friends, one of those over-eager, terribly involved parents. Oh God, she thought, not now.

'Hi,' said André Marais, glancing at the man and seeing his eyes narrow, and she pulled a face, trying to communicate to him that she would rather not have this interruption.

'How are you, André? What are you doing here? What a coincidence.' Molly came up to her, basket in hand, before she realised that the two trolleys so close together meant something. She read the body language of the man and the woman and put two and two together. 'Oh, sorry, I hope I didn't interrupt something.'

André knew she had to get rid of the woman, because she could see in the clenching of Reyneke's hands that he was tense. The whole affair was on a knifepoint and she wanted to say: 'Yes, you are interrupting something' or 'Just go away'. But before she could find the right words, Molly's face cleared and she said: 'Oh, you must be working together – are you also in the police?' and she held out her hand to Reyneke. 'I'm Molly Green. Are you on an operation or something?'

Time stood still for André Marais. She could see the outstretched hand, which Reyneke ignored, his eyes moving from one woman to the other in slow motion; she could actually see the gears working in his brain. Then he bumped his trolley forward in her direction and he shouted something at her as the trolley collided with her and she lost her balance.

Molly screamed incoherently.

André staggered against the wine rack, bottles fell and smashed on the floor. She fell on her bottom, arms windmilling for balance, then she grabbed at her handbag, got her fingers on it and searched for her service pistol while her head told her she must warn Griessel. Her other hand was on the little microphone that she held to her mouth and said, 'It's him, it's him!'

Reyneke was beside her and jerked the pistol from her hand. She tried to rise, but her sandals slipped in the wine and she fell back with her elbow on a glass shard. She felt a sharp pain. Twisting her body sideways she saw which way he ran. 'Main entrance!' she shouted, but realising her head was turned away from the microphone, she grabbed it again. 'Main entrance, stop him!' she screamed. 'He has my firearm!' Then she saw the blood pouring from her arm in a thick stream. When she lifted up her arm to inspect it she saw it was cut to the bone.

Griessel and Cliffy leapt up and ran when they heard Molly Green scream over the radio. Cliffy missed the turn, bumping against a table where two men were eating sushi. 'Sorry, sorry,' he said and saw Griessel ahead, Z88 in hand, saw the faces of bystanders and heard cries here and there. They raced, shoes slapping on the floor. He heard Marais's voice on the microphone: 'Main entrance, stop him!'

Griessel arrived at the wide door of Woolworths, service pistol gripped in both hands and aimed at something inside the store, but Cliffy was trying to brake and he slipped on the smooth floor. Just before he collided with Griessel, he spotted the suspect, jacket flapping, big pistol in his hand, who stopped ten paces away from them, also battling not to slip.

But Cliffy and Griessel were in a pile on the ground. A shot went off and a bullet whined away somewhere.

Cliffy heard Griessel curse, heard high, shrill screams around them. 'Sorry, Benny, sorry,' he said, looking around and seeing the suspect had turned around and headed for the escalator. Cupido and Keyter, pistols in hand, were coming down the other one, but it was in fact the ascending escalator. For an instant it was extremely funny, like a scene from an old Charlie Chaplin film: the two policemen leaping furiously down the steps, but not making much progress. On their faces, the oddest expressions of frustration, seriousness, purposefulness – and the sure knowledge that they were making complete idiots of themselves.

Griessel had sprung up and set off after the suspect. Cliffy got to his feet and followed, up the escalator with big leaps to the top. Griessel had turned right and spotted the fugitive on the way to the exit on the second level. He heard Griessel shout, glanced back. Griessel could see the fear on the man's face and then he stopped and aimed his pistol at Griessel. The shot rang out and something plucked at Cliffy, knocked him off his feet and threw him against Men's Suits: Formal. He knew he was hit somewhere in the chest, he was entangled in trousers and jackets, looking down at the hole near his heart. He was going to die, thought Cliffy Mketsu, he was shot in the heart. He couldn't die now. Griessel must help. He rolled over. He felt heavy. But light-headed. He moved garments with his right arm; the left was without feeling. He saw Griessel tackle the fugitive. A male mannequin in beachwear tottered and fell. A garish sunhat flew through the air in an elegant arch, a display of T-shirts collapsed. He saw Griessel's right hand rise and fall. Griessel was beating him with his pistol. He could see the blood spray from here. Up and down went Griessel's hand. It would make Benny feel better; he needed to release that rage. Hit him, Benny, hit him – he's the bastard who shot me.

Thobela Mpayipheli was waiting for the traffic lights on the corner of Adderley and Riebeeck Street when he heard a voice at his elbow.

'Why djoo look so se-ed?'

A street child stood there, hands on lean, boyish hips. Ten, eleven years old?

'Do I look sad?'

'Djy lyk like the ket stole the dairy. Gimme sum money for bred.'

'What's your name?'

'What's *djor* name?'

'Thobela.'

'Gimme sum money for bred, Thobela.'

'First tell me your name.'

'Moses.'

'What are you going to do with the money?'

'What did I say it was for?'

Then there was another one, smaller, thinner, in outsize clothes, nose running. Without thinking Thobela took out his handkerchief.

'Five rand,' said the little one, holding out his hand.

'Fokkof, Randall, I saw him first.'

He wanted to wipe Randall's nose but the boy jumped back. 'Don' touch me,' said the child.

'I want to wipe your nose.'

'What for?'

It was a good question.

'Djy gonna give us money?' asked Moses.

'When did you last eat?'

'Less see, what month is this?'

In the dusk of the late afternoon another skinny figure appeared, a girl with a bush of frizzy tangled hair. She said nothing, just stood with outstretched hand, the other holding the edges of a large, tattered man's jacket together.

'Agh, fock,' said Moses. 'I had this under control.'

'Are you related?' asked Thobela.

'How would *we* know?' said Moses, and the other two giggled.

'Do you want to eat?'

'Jee-zas,' said Moses. 'Just my luck. A fokken' stupid darkie.'

'You swear a lot.'

'I'm a street kid, for fuck's sake.'

He looked at the trio. Grimy, barefoot. Bright, living eyes. 'I'm going to the Spur. Do you want to come?'

Dumbstruck.

'Well?'

'Are you a pervert?' asked Moses with narrowed eyes.

'No, I'm hungry.'

The girl jabbed an elbow in Moses' ribs and made big eyes at him.

'The Spur will throw us out,' said Randall.

'I'll say you are my children.'

For a moment all three were quiet and then Moses laughed, a chuckling sound rising through the scales. 'Our daddy.'

Thobela began to walk. 'Are you coming?'

It was ten or twelve paces further on that the girl's small hand clasped a finger of his right hand and stayed there, all the way to the Spur Steak Ranch in Strand Street.

22

She sat staring at the window without seeing.

'I thought I was cutting myself because of my father, at first,' she said softly, and sighed, deeply, remembering. 'Or because of Viljoen. I thought I was handling the work and that I was okay with it.'

She turned and looked at him, back in the present. 'I never clicked it was the work that made me like that. Not then. I had to get out of it first.'

He nodded, slowly, but did not respond.

'And then things changed, with Carlos,' she said.

Carlos phoned early, just after nine, to say he wanted to book her for the whole night. 'Carlos does not want money fight. Three thousand, hokay? But you must look sexy, conchita. Very sexy, we are having a formal party. Black dress, but show your tits. Carlos wants to brag. My guys will pick you up. Seven o'clock.' He put the phone down.

She waited for her anger to rise and fade. She sat on the edge of the bed, with the cell phone still to her ear. She felt the futility, knew that her anger was useless.

Sonia came up to her, doll in hand. 'Are we going to ride bicycle, Mamma?'

'No, my love, we are going shopping.' The child skipped off towards her room as if shopping was her favourite activity.

'Hey, you.'

Sonia halted in the doorway and peeped over her shoulder mischievously.

'Me?' She knew her part in this ritual.

'Yes, you. Come here.'

She ran across the carpet, still in her green pyjamas, into her mother's arms.

'You're my love,' Christine began their rhyme and kissed her neck.

'You're my life,' giggled Sonia.

'And your beauty makes me shiver.'

'You're my heaven, you're my house.' Her head was on Christine's bosom.

'You're my only paradise,' she said and hugged the child tight. 'Go and get dressed. It's time to shop till we drop.'

'Shoptill hedrop?'

'Shoptill hedrop. That's right.'

Three years and four months. Just another two years, then school. Just another two years and her mother would be done with whoring.

She phoned Carlton Hair and Mac for late-afternoon appointments and took Sonia along to Hip Hop across Cavendish Square. The sales people paid more attention to the pretty child with blonde ringlets than they did to her.

She stood in front of the mirror in a black dress. The neckline was low, the hem high, bare back.

'That is very sexy,' said the coloured shop assistant.

'Isn't,' said Sonia. 'Mamma looks pretty.'

They laughed. 'I'll take it.'

They were too early for her hair and make-up. She took her daughter to Naartjie in the Cavendish Centre. 'Now you can choose a dress for yourself.'

'I also want a black one.'

'They don't have black ones.'

'I also want a black one.'

'Black ones are just for grown-ups, girl.'

'I also want to be grown-up.'

'No you don't. Trust me.'

*   *   *

The carer looked in disapproval at her outfit when she dropped Sonia off.

'I don't know how late the function will finish. It's best if she sleeps over.'

'In that dress it will finish very late.'

She ignored the comment, hugged her daughter tight. 'Be good. Mamma will see you in the morning.'

'Tatta, Mamma.'

Just before the door closed behind her, she heard Sonia say: 'My mamma looks very pretty.'

'Do you think so?' said the carer in a sour voice.

It was a weird evening. In the entertainment area of the house in Camps Bay, inside and outside beside the pool, were about sixty people, mostly men in evening suits. Here and there was a blonde with breasts on display or long legs showing through split dresses and ending in high heels. Like décor, she thought, pretty furniture. They hung on a man's arm, smiled, said nothing.

Quickly she grasped that that was what Carlos expected of her. He was ecstatic over her appearance. 'Ah, conchita, you look perfect,' he said when she arrived.

It was the United Nations: Spanish-speaking, Chinese, or Oriental at least, small men who followed her with hungry eyes, Arabs in togas – or whatever you called them – who ignored her, each with his moustache. Two Germans. English. One American.

Carlos, the Host. Jovial, smiling, joking, but she felt sure he was tense, nervous even. She followed his example, held a glass, but did not drink.

'You know who these people are?' he asked her later, whispering in her ear.

'No.'

'Carlos will tell you later.'

Food and drink came and went. She could see the men were no longer sober, but only because the conversation and laughter were a bit louder. Ten o'clock, eleven, twelve.

She stood alone at a pillar. Carlos was somewhere in a kitchen organising more food to be sent. She felt a hand slide under her dress between her legs, fingers groping. She froze. The hand was gone. She looked over her shoulder. A Chinese man stood there, small and dapper, sniffing deeply at his fingers. He smiled at her and walked away. All she could think of was that Carlos must not see that.

Two Arabs sat at a glass table arranging cocaine in lines with credit cards and sharing it with a companion whose nipple showed above the neckline of her black dress. One of the men inhaled deeply over the table, leaned back in his chair and slowly opened his eyes. Languidly he stretched out a hand towards her and took the nipple between his fingers. He squeezed. The woman grimaced. He's hurting her, thought Christine. She was transfixed.

Late that night her bladder was full. She went upstairs looking for the privacy of Carlos's en-suite bathroom. The bedroom door was shut and she opened it. A blonde in a blood-red dress was gripping one of the posts of the bed and her dress was rucked up to bare her bottom. Behind her stood one of the Spanish men with his trousers around his ankles.

'You want to watch?'

'No.'

'You want to fuck?'

'I'm with Carlos.'

'Carlos is nothing. You kiss my girl, yes?'

Quietly she closed the door and heard the man laugh inside the room.

Even later. Only a small group of guests remained in the swimming pool – two women, six or seven men. Extremely drunk. She had never seen group sex before and it fascinated her. Four men were with one of the women.

Carlos came and stood behind her. 'What do you think?'

'It's weird,' she lied.

'Carlos not for groups. Carlos is a one conchita man.' He put his arms around her, but they continued to watch. Small, rhythmic waves lapped at the edge of the pool.

'It looks sexy,' he said.

She put her hand on his crotch and felt it was hard. Time to earn her pay.

'First Carlos drinks,' he said, and went to fetch a bottle.

She didn't know whether to blame the drink, but Carlos was different in bed – desperate, urgent, as if he wanted to prove himself.

'I want you to hurt me,' she said.

Maybe he did not hear. Maybe he did not want to. He just went on.

When he had finished and lay wet with his own perspiration beside her, head between her breasts, he asked: 'Carlos was good for you?'

'You were great.'

'Yes. Carlos is a great lover,' he said in all seriousness. Then he was quiet, for so long that she wondered if he was asleep.

Suddenly he rose to his feet, crossed to where he had dropped his trousers on the floor and took out a packet of cigarettes. He lit two and passed one to her before sitting down beside her, with his feet folded under him. His eyes were bloodshot.

'These people . . .' he said with venom and a deep furrow of distaste on his forehead. She knew him well enough to know he was not sober.

She drew on the cigarette.

'They did not even thank Carlos for the party. They come, they drink and snort and eat and fuck and then they leave, no goodbye, no "thank you, Carlos, for your hospitality".'

'It was a good party, Carlos.'

'*Sí*, conchita. Cost a lot of money, famous chef, best *licores*, best *putas*. But they have no respect for Carlos.'

'Carlos is nothing,' the man in his bedroom had said.

'You know who they are, conchita? You know? They are *banditos*. They are shit. They make money with drugs. Mexicans!' He spat out the word. 'They are nothing. They are *burros*, *mulas* for the Yankees. Cubans. What are they? And the Afghans. Peasants, I tell you.'

'Afghans?'

'*Si*. Those arses holes in the dresses. *Conchas!*'

So the Arabs were Afghans. 'Oh.'

'And the China and the Thai, and the Vietnam, what are they? They are *mierda*, Carlos tell you, they have nothing but chickens and bananas and heroin. They fuck their mothers. But they come to Carlos, to this beautiful house and they have no manners. You know who they are, conchita? They are drugs. The Afghans and the Vietnam and the Thai, they bring heroin. They bring here, because here is safe, no police here. They take cocaine back. Then Sangrenegra brothers take heroin to America and to Europe. And the South Americans, they help supply, but little, because Sangrenegra brothers control supply. That is Carlos and Javier. My big brother is Javier. He is biggest man in drugs. Everybody know him. We take heroin, we give cocaine, we give money, we . . . we *distribuya*. We take to whole world. Carlos will tell Javier about the disrespect. They think Carlos is little brother, Javier is not here, so they can shit on me. They cannot shit on me, conchita. I will shit on *them*.' He squashed the cigarette disdainfully in the ashtray.

'Come, conchita, Carlos show you something.' He took her arm and drew her along. He picked up his trousers, took out a bunch of keys, took her hand and led her down the passage, down the stairs, through the kitchen, down more stairs to a pantry. The house was completely deserted by now. He opened a half-concealed door at the back of the pantry. There were three locks, each with its own key.

'Carlos show you. Sangrenegra is not small time.' He pressed a light switch. Another door. A small electronic number pad on the wall. He typed in a number. 'Oh, eight, two, four, four, nine, you know that number, conchita?'

'Yes.' They were the first six numbers of her cell phone number.

'That is how much Carlos love you.'

It was a steel door that opened automatically. A fluorescent light flickered on inside. He pulled her inside. A space as large as a double garage. Shelves up to the ceiling. Plastic bags on the racks, from one end to the other, all filled with white powder.

Then she saw the money.

'You see, conchita? You see?'

'I see,' she said, but her voice was gone and it came out as a whisper.

They were in the pool, just Carlos and her. She sat on the step with her lower body in the water. He was standing in the water with his arms around her and his face against her belly.

'Conchita, will you tell Carlos why you become . . . you know.'

'A whore.'

'You are not a whore,' he said distastefully. 'An escort. Why did you become an escort?'

'You don't want to know the truth, Carlos.'

'No, conchita. I do. The real truth.'

'Sometimes I think you want me to be this good girl. I am not a good girl.'

'You are. You have a good heart.'

'You see, if I tell you the truth you don't want to hear it.'

He straightened his arms so he could look at her. 'You know what? That is not the way Carlos thinks. Look at me, conchita. I am in drugs. I have killed guys. But I am not bad. I have a good heart. You see? You can be good, and you can do things that are not so good. So tell me.'

'Because I like to fuck, Carlos.'

'*Si?*'

'*Si,*' she said. 'That is my drug.'

'How old were you? When you fucked first?'

'I was fifteen.'

'Tell Carlos.'

'I was at school. And this boy, he was sixteen. He was very beautiful. He walked home with me every afternoon. And one day he said I must come home with him. I was very curious. And so I went. And he said I had beautiful breasts. He asked if he could see them. And I showed him. Then he asked if he could touch them. And I said yes. And then he started to kiss me. On my nipples. He started to suck my nipples. And then it happened, Carlos. The drug. It was . . . It was like nothing I had ever felt before. It was *intense*. I liked it so much.'

'And then he fucked you?'

'Yes. But he was not experienced. He came too quickly. He was so excited. I didn't have an orgasm. So afterwards, I wanted more. But not with boys. With men. So I seduced my teacher . . .'

'You fucked your teacher?'

'Yes.'

'And who else?'

'A friend of my father. I went to his home when his wife was away. I said I wanted to talk to him. I said I was very curious about sex, but I cannot talk to my parents about it, because they are so conservative. And I know he is different. He asked if I would like it if he showed me. I said yes. But you know what, Carlos? He was just as excited as the boy. He could not control himself.'

'Who else?'

'I fucked a lot of guys at university. For free. And then one day I thought, why for free? And that is how it happened.'

'Look,' said Carlos and pointed at his erection. 'Carlos likes your story.'

'Then fuck me, Carlos. I love it so much.'

Wasserman, the acclaimed playwright, Professor of Afrikaans and Nederlands. Fifty-three years old, with a soft body, bushy beard and a beautiful, beautiful voice. At the start of every session she would have to lie in the bath so he could urinate on her, or else he could not get an erection. But from there on he was normal, except for the reading glasses – the better to see her breasts. He would come once a fortnight at three in the afternoon, as he had a younger wife who 'might want something too'. He needed time to recharge before the evening. But his young wife would not let herself be pissed on, that was why he came to Christine.

They were waiting for him at precisely four o'clock. When he opened the door to leave her place at the Gardens Centre, they hit him with a pick handle, breaking his teeth and jaw.

She heard the commotion and grabbed a dressing gown. 'No!'

she screamed. They were wearing balaclavas, but she knew they were the bodyguards. One looked her in the eyes and kicked Wasserman where he lay. Then they both kicked him. Seven ribs broken.

'I will call the police!' One of them laughed. Then they dragged him by the feet to the stairs and down two flights and left him there, bleeding and moaning.

She grabbed her cell phone and ran down to him. She bent over him. The damage made her nauseous. She touched his broken face with her fingertips. He opened his eyes and looked at her. There was a question through the agony.

'I'm calling an ambulance,' she said, holding his hand while she spoke.

He made a noise.

'I can't stay here,' she said. 'I can't stay here.' There would be police. Questions. Arrest. She, Sonia could not afford that.

He just moaned, lying on his side in a pool of blood around his face.

She heard doors opening.

'The ambulance is on its way.' She squeezed Wasserman's hand and then ran upstairs to her room and locked the door behind her. Feverishly she dressed herself. Carlos. What was she to do?

When she went out quietly, she went down first. She saw there were security personnel with Wasserman at the foot of the stairs. They did not see her. She walked up one flight of stairs, trying to keep calm. She walked slowly so as not to attract attention. She pressed the button for the lift, waited. Voices below. The lift took an eternity to arrive.

Carlos.

She phoned him once she reached the street. He did not answer his phone.

She went to her flat, sat on a chair in her sitting room with her phone in her hand. What was she going to do?

Later she phoned the ambulance services. They had taken Wasserman to City Park. She phoned the hospital. 'We can't give out information.'

'This is his sister.'

'Hold on.'

She had to listen to synthesised music, sounding tinny in her ear.
Eventually Casualty answered. 'He's in Intensive Care, but he
should be okay.'

Carlos. She phoned again. It just kept on ringing. She wanted to
get in her car and drive to his house. She wanted to hit him, smash
his skull with a pick handle. He didn't have the right. He couldn't
do this. She wanted to go to the police, she wanted to blow him off
the earth. Rage consumed her. She looked for her telephone book
and got the number of the police.

No. Too many complications.

She wept, but from frustration. Hate.

When she had calmed down she went to fetch Sonia. When she
crossed the street holding her daughter's hand, she saw the BMW
on the other side, back window rolled down. He sat there watching,
but not her. His eyes were on the girl and there was a strange
expression on his face. It felt as if someone had their fist around her
heart and were squeezing her to death.

The BMW pulled up alongside her when she was helping Sonia
into her car.

'Now I know everything, conchita.' He looked at Sonia, looked
at her child. If she had had a gun at that moment, she would have
shot him in the face.

PART TWO

Benny

23

Griessel was never uncomfortable with the bosses, mainly because he could drink them under the table singly or as a group. Or outwork them. He maintained a higher case solution rate than any one of them had in their days as detectives, alcoholic or not. But tonight he was not at ease. They stood in the little sitting room outside the Intensive Care Unit of City Park Hospital, although there were chairs available: Senior Superintendents Esau Mtimkulu and Matt Joubert, first and second in command of SVC, Commissioner John Afrika, the provincial head of detection, and Griessel. Cupido and Keyter sat just out of hearing. Their ears were pricked but they could not hear anything. When a member lay in Intensive Care, the big guns spoke in muffled tones.

'Give me that Woolworths man's number, Matt,' said Commissioner Afrika, a coloured veteran who had come up through the ranks in Khayelitsha, the Flats and the old Murder and Robbery Units. 'I hear they are running to the minister, but to hell with them. I'll deal with him. That is the least of our problems . . .' Here it comes, thought Griessel. He should never have hit the bastard, he knew that; never in his life had he carried on like that before. If they were to throw out the case because he had lost control, if a fucking serial murderer were to walk because Benny Griessel was angry at the entire world . . .

'Benny,' said Commissioner Afrika, 'you say it was the tackle that caused his face to be injured like that?'

'Yes, Commissioner.' He looked into the man's eyes and they knew, all four of them in the circle, what was happening now. 'There was this shop mannequin standing just in the wrong place.

Reyneke's face hit the face of the mannequin. That's where the cuts came from.'

'He must have hit it fucking hard,' said Superintendent Mtimkulu.

'When I tackled him, I held his arms down because he had a firearm. So he couldn't shield his face with his hands. That's why he hit it so hard.'

'And then he confessed?'

'He lay there bleeding, and then he cried, "I can't help it, I can't help it", but with Cliffy wounded my attention was . . . er . . . divided. Only later under interrogation did I ask him what he meant. What it is that he can't help.'

'And what did he say then?'

'At first he didn't want to say anything. So . . . I asked Cupido and Keyter to leave, so that I could talk to him alone.'

'And then he confessed?'

'He confessed, Commissioner.'

'Will it stand up in court?'

'The whole sequence in the interrogation room is on video, Commissioner. I just asked to be alone with the suspect and, once they had left, I just looked at him. For a long time. Then I said: "I know you can't help it. I understand." And then he began to talk.'

'Full confession.'

'Yes, Sup. All three of the women. Details that were not in the newspapers. We've got him, whoever he gets as his lawyer. And there's a previous conviction. Rape. Four years ago in Montagu.'

'And the only witness of the mannequin incident is Cliffy Mketsu?'

'That's right, Matt.'

All four looked across at the double doors that led to the ICU.

'Okay,' said the head of Investigation. 'Good work, Benny. Really good work . . .'

The double doors opened. A doctor approached them; such a young man that he looked as if he should still be at university. There were bloodstains on his green theatre overalls.

'He will be alright,' said the doctor.

'Are you sure?' asked Griessel.

The doctor nodded. 'He was very, very lucky. The bullet missed nearly everything, but badly damaged the S4 area of his left lung. That is the tip of the upper lobe, anterior segment. There is a possibility that we will have to remove it, just a small piece, but we will decide once he has stabilised.'

We, thought Griessel. Why did they always talk about *us*, as if they belonged to some secret organisation?

'That's good news,' said the commissioner without conviction. 'Oh, and we have a message for a Benny.'

'That's me.'

'He says the guy fell badly against the cash register.'

All four stared at the doctor with great interest. 'The cash register?' asked Griessel.

'Yes.'

'Do me a favour, Doc. Tell him it was the mannequin.'

'The mannequin.'

'Yes. Tell him the man fell against the mannequin and the mannequin fell on the cash register.'

'I will tell him.'

'Thanks, Doc,' said Griessel, and turned to the commissioner, who nodded and turned away.

He bought a Zinger burger and a can of Fanta Orange at KFC and took them home. He sat on his 'sitting-room' floor eating without pleasure. It was the fatigue, the after-effects of adrenaline. Also, the things waiting in the back of his mind that he did not want to think about. So he concentrated on the food. The Zinger didn't satisfy his hunger. He should have ordered chips, but he didn't like KFC's chips. The children ate them with gusto. The children even ate McDonalds's thin cardboard chips with pleasure, but he could not. Steers's chips, yes. Steers's big fat barbeque-seasoned chips. Steers's burgers were also better than anything else. Decent food. But he didn't know where the nearest Steers was and he wasn't sure if they would still be open at this time. The Zinger was finished and he had sauce on his fingers.

He wanted to toss the plastic bag and empty carton container in the bin, but remembered he didn't have a bin. He sighed. He would have to shower – he still had some of Reyneke's and Cliffy's blood on him.

You have six months, Benny – that is what we are giving you. Six months to choose between us and the booze. Would you buy furniture for just six months? He couldn't eat on the floor for six fucking months. Or come home to such a barren place. Surely he was entitled to a chair or two. A small television. But first, get out of these clothes and shower and then he could sit on his bed and make a list for tomorrow. Saturday. He was off this weekend.

Terrifying. Two whole days. Open. Perhaps he ought to go to the office and get his paperwork up to date.

He washed his hands under the kitchen tap, put the carton and the can and the used paper serviette into the red and white plastic packet and put it in a corner of the kitchen. He climbed the stairs while unbuttoning his shirt. Thank God they didn't have to wear jacket and tie any more. When he started with Murder and Robbery it was suits.

Where was Anna tonight?

The plastic shower curtain was torn in one corner and the water leaked onto the floor. It had a faded pattern of fish. He would have to get a bathmat as well. A new shower curtain too. He washed his hair and soaped his body. Rinsed off in the lovely hot, strong stream of water.

When he turned off the taps he heard his cell phone ringing. He grabbed the towel, rubbed it quickly over his head, took three strides to the bed and snatched it up.

'Griessel.'

'Are you sober, Benny?'

Anna.

'Yes.' He wanted to protest at her question, wanted to be angry, but he knew he had no right.

'Do you want to see the children?'

'Yes, I would very—'

'You can collect them on Sunday. For the day.'

'Okay, thank you. What about you? Can I also—'

'Let's just keep to the children, for now. Ten o'clock? Ten to six?'

'That's fine.'

'Goodbye, Benny.'

'Anna!'

She did not speak, but did not cut him off.

'Where were you this evening?'

'Where were you, Benny?'

'I was working. I caught a serial murderer. Cliffy Mketsu was shot in the lung. That's where I was.' He had the moral high ground, a little heap, a molehill, but better than nothing. 'Where were you?'

'Out.'

'Out?'

'Benny, I sat at home for five years while you were drunk or out and about. Either drunk or not at home. Don't you think I deserve a Friday night out? Don't you think I deserve to watch a movie, for the first time in five years?'

'Yes,' he said, 'you deserve that.'

'Goodbye, Benny.'

Did you watch the movie alone? That's what he wanted to ask, but the moral contours had shifted too quickly and he heard the connection go dead in his ear. He threw the towel to the floor and took a black pair of trousers from the cupboard to put on. He fetched pen and paper from his briefcase and sat down on the bed. He stared at the towel on the floor. Tomorrow morning it would still be lying there and it would be damp and smelly. He got up and hung the towel over the rail in the bathroom, went back to the bed and arranged the pillow so he could lean against it. He began his list.

Laundry.

There was a laundromat at the Gardens Centre. First thing tomorrow.

Rubbish bin.

Iron.

Ironing board.

Fridge?

Could he manage without a fridge? What would he keep in it? Not milk – he drank his coffee black. On Sunday the children would be here and Carla loved her coffee; always had a mug in her hand when she did her homework. Would she be content with powdered milk? The fridge might be necessary, he would see.

Fridge?

Shower curtain.

Bath mat.

Chairs/sofa. For the sitting room.

Bar stools. For the breakfast nook.

How the hell was he going to support two households on a police salary? Had Anna thought of that? But he could already hear her answer: 'You could support a drinking habit on a police salary, Benny. There was always money for drink.'

He would have to buy another coffee mug for the children's visit. More plates and knives, forks and spoons. Cleaning stuff for dishes, dusty surfaces, the bathroom and the toilet.

He made fresh columns on the page, noted all the items, but he could not keep the other things in his head at bay.

Today he had made a discovery. He would have to tell Barkhuizen. This thing about being scared of death was not entirely true. Today, when he charged at Reyneke on the top level of Woolworths with the pistol pointed at him and the shot going off, the bullet that had hit Cliffy Mketsu because Reyneke could not shoot for toffee . . .

That is when he had discovered he was not afraid of dying. That is when he knew he wanted to die.

He woke early, just before five. His thoughts went to Anna. Did she go to the movies alone? But he didn't want to play with those thoughts. Not this early, not today. He got up and dressed in trousers, shirt and trainers only, and went out without washing.

He chose a direction; three hundred metres up the street he saw the morning, felt the languor of the early summer, heard the birds and the unbelievable silence over the city. Colours and textures and light of crystal.

Table Mountain leaned towards him, the crest something between orange and gold, fissures and clefts were pitch-black shadows against the angle of the rising sun.

He went up Upper Orange Street, turned into the park and sat on the high wall of the reservoir to look out. To the left Lion's Head became the curves of Signal Hill, and below a thousand city windows were a mosaic of the sun. The sea was deep blue beyond Robben Island, far off to Melkbos Strand. Left of Devil's Peak lay the suburbs. A 747 came in over the Tyger Berg and its shadow flashed over him in an instant.

Fuck, he thought, when had he last seen this?

How could he have missed it?

On the other hand, he pulled a face, if you are sleeping off your hangover in the morning, you won't see sunrise over the Cape. He must remember this, the unexpected advantage of teetotalism.

A wagtail came and perched near him, tail going up and down, dapper steps like a self-important station sergeant. 'What?' he said to the bird. 'Your wife left you too?' He received no reply. He sat until the bird flew up after some invisible insect, and then he rose and looked up at the mountain again and it gave him a strange pleasure. Only he was seeing it this morning, nobody else.

He walked back to the flat, showered and changed and drove to the hospital. Cliffy was resting, they told him. He was stable, in no danger. He asked them to tell him Benny had been there.

It was just before seven. He drove north with the N1, on a freeway still quiet – the Cape only got going by about ten o'clock on a Saturday. Down Brackenfell Boulevard and the familiar turnoffs to his house. He drove past the house only once, slowly. No sign of life. The lawn was cut, the postbox emptied, the garage door closed. A policeman's inventory. He accelerated away because he did not want his thoughts to penetrate the front door.

He drank only coffee at a Wimpy in Panorama, because he had never been one for breakfast, and waited until the shops opened.

He found a two-seater couch and two armchairs at Mohammed

'Love Lips' Faizal's pawnshop in Maitland. The floral cover was slightly bleached. There were faint coffee stains on the arm of one chair. 'This is too much, L.L.,' he said over the R600 price tag.

'For you, Sarge, five-fifty.'

Faizal had been in Pollsmoor for eighteen months for trafficking in stolen goods and he was reasonably certain three-quarters of the car radios had been brought in by the drug addicts of Observatory.

'Four hundred, L.L. Look at these stains.'

'One steam clean and it's good as new, Sarge. Five hundred and I don't make a cent.'

Faizal knew he was no longer a sergeant, but some things will never change. 'Four-fifty.'

'Jissis, Sarge, I have a wife and kids.'

By chance he saw the bass guitar, just the head protruding from behind a steel cabinet of brand new tools.

'And that bass?'

'You into music, Sarge?'

'I have tickled the neck of a bass in my day.'

'Well bless my soul. It's a Fender, Sarge, pawned by a wannabe rapper from Blackheath, but his ticket expires only next Friday. Comes with a new Dr Bass times two-ten-b cabinet with a three-u built-in rack, two-two-fifty watt Eminence tens, and a LeSon tweeter.'

'I don't know what the fuck you're talking about.'

'It's a bloody big amp, Sarge. It'll blow you away.'

'How much?'

'Are you serious, Sarge?'

'Maybe.'

'It's a genuine pawn, Sarge. Clean.'

'I believe you, L.L. Relax.'

'Do you want to start a band now?' The suspicion was still there. Griessel grinned. 'And call it Violent Crimes?'

'So what then?'

'How much are you asking for the guitar and amp, L.L.?'

'Two thousand, for sure. If the wannabe doesn't return the ticket.'

'Oh.' It was too much for him. He had no idea what these things cost. 'Four-fifty for the sitting-room suite?'

Faizal sighed. 'Four seventy-five and I'll throw in free delivery and a six-piece coaster set with tasteful nudes depicted thereupon.'

He got the three bar stools at the place in Parow that sold only pine furniture and he paid R175 apiece, a scary amount, but he loaded them in the car, two on the back seat and one in front, and took them to his flat, because tomorrow his kids would be here and at least there was something for them to sit on. By eleven he was sitting with a newspaper at the laundromat, waiting for his clothes to be clean and dry so he could pack them in his new plastic laundry basket and iron them on his new ironing board with his new iron.

Then Matt Joubert phoned and he said: 'I know you are off, Benny, but I need you.'

'What's up, Boss?'

'It's the guy with the assegai, but I'll explain when you arrive. We are at Fisantekraal. On a smallholding. Come via Durbanville on Wellington Avenue, right on the R three-one-two and just opposite the railway bridge go left. Phone me when you get there and I will direct you.'

He checked the cycle on the washing machine. 'Give me forty,' he said.

It was an equestrian establishment. *High Grove Riding School. Riding lessons for adults and children. Outrides*. He drove past the stables before he reached the house. Everything was in a state of partial dilapidation, as all these places were, never enough money to fix everything. Police cars, a SAPS van, Forensic's little bus. The ambulance must have left already.

Joubert stood in a circle of four other detectives, just two from their unit, the other two probably from Durbanville station. When he stopped there were dogs, barking, tails wagging, two little ones and two black sheepdogs. He got out to the smell of manure and lucerne hay.

Joubert approached him with outstretched hand. 'How's it going, Benny?'

'Sober, thank you.'

Joubert smiled. 'I can see. Are you suffering?'

'Only when I don't drink.'

The commander laughed. 'I respect your tenacity, Benny. Not that I ever doubted . . .'

'Then you must be the only one.'

'Come, so we can talk first.'

He led him to an empty stable and sat on a bale of hay. The sun projected perfect round dots on the floor through holes in the corrugated iron roof. 'Sit down, Benny, this will take some time.'

He sat.

'The victim is Bernadette Laurens. She was released on Thursday on bail of fifty thousand rand. Charged with the murder of her partner's five-year-old daughter. They lived together as a couple. Partner's name is Elise Bothma. Last weekend the child was hit on the head with a billiard cue, one blow . . .'

'Lesbetarian?'

Joubert nodded. 'Last night the dogs began to bark. Laurens got up to see what was going on. When she did not return to bed, Bothma went to look for her. Fifteen metres from the front door she found the body. One stab wound to the heart. I am waiting for the pathology report, but it could be the assegai man.'

'Because she killed a child.'

'And the stab wound.'

'The papers say it is an assegai woman.'

'The papers are full of shit. There's no way a woman could have murdered the previous two victims. Enver Davids was a jailbird, well built, strong. According to the scene, Colin Pretorius had time to defend himself, but he didn't stand a chance. Laurens was a strong woman, round about one point eight metres tall, eighty kilograms. And women shoot, they don't stab with a blade. In any case, not multiple victims. As you know, the chance that a woman is involved in multiples is one per cent.'

'I agree.'

'One of the sheepdogs is limping this morning. Bothma believes it might have been kicked or hit in the process. But apart from that, not much. The Durbanville people will come and help to question the neighbours.'

Griessel nodded.

'I want you to take charge of the whole investigation, Benny.'

'Me?'

'For many reasons. In the first place, you are the most experienced detective in the unit. In the second, in my opinion, you are the best. Third, the commissioner mentioned your name. He's very pleased with your work yesterday and he knows big trouble when he sees it. We have a circus on our hands, Benny. With the media. An avenging murderer, punishment for crimes against children, death penalty . . . you can imagine.'

'And fourth, I have the time, now that I no longer have a wife and kids.'

'That was not part of my reasoning. But I must say this: I thought it might help – keep you too busy to think of drink.'

'Nothing could keep me that busy.'

'The last thing that made me ask you is that I know you enjoy this kind of thing.'

'That's true.'

'Are you in?'

'Of course I'm fucking in. I was in the moment you said "assegai". You could have saved the rest. You know that "positive feedback" shit never worked with me.'

Joubert stood up. 'I know. But it had to be said. You must know you are appreciated. And, oh, the commissioner says you have all the manpower you need. We must just let him know where we need help. He will do the necessary. For the present, Keyter is your partner. He's on his way . . .'

'Not a fock.'

'Cliffy is in hospital, Benny, and there is no one else available full-time . . .'

'Keyter is an idiot, Matt. He is a little braggart station detective with an attitude and a big head. He knows fuck-all. What happened to the manpower you just promised me?'

'For foot work, Benny. I can't spare men from the unit. You know everyone is snowed under with work. And Keyter is new. He has to learn. You will have to mentor him.'

'Mentor him?'

'Make an investigator of him.'

'It's times like this,' said Griessel, 'that I know why I'm an alcoholic.'

24

Griessel, Keyter and the dogs sat in Elise Bothma's sitting room. Keyter, in a loose white shirt, tight jeans and new bright blue Nike Crosstrainers, asked the questions as if he were the senior investigator. 'What sort of dog is this, ma'am? Looks like a Pomeranian cross, but don't they bark a lot at night? I hear they bark so much, the genuine Pomeranians . . . looks like there is a bit of Dachshund in this one. You say you heard the dogs and then Miss Laurens went out to look?'

She was a fragile woman. Her eyes were red-rimmed and her voice gentle and she hadn't been expecting the question at the tail end of the dog speech. 'Yes,' she said. She sat hunched up and did not raise her head. Her fingers were entangled in a tissue. The room smelt strongly of dogs and rooibos tea.

'Do you know what time that was?' asked Keyter.

She said something, but they couldn't hear it.

'You need to speak louder. We can't hear a word you say.'

'It must have been just before two,' said Elise Bothma, and sank back, as if the effort was too great.

'But you are not sure?'

She just shook her head.

'Do we know what time she phoned the station?' Keyter asked Griessel.

He felt like getting up right there and taking the little shit outside to ask him who the fuck did he think he was, but this was not the time.

'Two thirty-five,' said Griessel.

'Okay,' said Keyter. 'Let us say the dogs began barking just before two and she got up then to look. Did she take something with her? A weapon? Snooker stick or something?'

Bothma shuddered and Griessel decided this was the last one he would stand before taking Keyter outside. 'A revolver.'

'A revolver?'

'Yes.'

'What revolver?'

'I don't know. It was hers.'

'And where is the revolver now?'

'I don't know.'

'Did anyone find a revolver with the body?'

Griessel just shook his head.

'So the revolver is missing now?'

Bothma nodded slightly.

'And then, when did you get up to go and look?'

'I don't know what time it was.'

'But why did you go out? What made you?'

'She was too long. She was gone too long.'

'And you found her lying there?'

'Yes.'

'Just as she was when we came?'

'Yes.'

'And nothing else?'

'No.'

'And then you phoned the station?'

'No.'

'Oh?'

'The emergency number. One zero triple one.'

'Oh. Then you waited in the house until they came?'

'Yes.'

'Okay,' said Keyter. 'Okay. That's the story.' He stood up. 'Thank you very much and sorry for the loss and all that.'

Bothma made the slight nod of her head again, but still no eye contact.

Griessel stood and Keyter moved towards the door. He was taken aback when he saw Griessel sitting down on the sofa next to the woman. He didn't turn back but stood there in the doorway looking impatient.

'How long were you together?' Griessel asked her, gently and sympathetically.

'Seven years,' said Bothma, and pressed the tissue against her cheeks.

'What?' said Keyter from the door. Griessel looked at him meaningfully and held a finger to his lips. Keyter came back and sat down.

'She had a temper.' A statement. Bothma nodded.

'Did she sometimes hurt you?'

Nod.

'And sometimes hurt your child?'

The head said 'yes' and tears ran.

'Why did you stay?'

'Because I have nothing.'

Griessel waited.

'What could I do? Where could I go? I don't have a job. I worked for her. Did the books. She looked after us. Food and clothing. She taught Cheryl to ride. She was good with her most of the time. What could I do?'

'Were you angry with her over what she did to Cheryl?'

The thin shoulders shook.

'But you stayed with her?'

She put her small hands over her face and wept. Griessel put a hand in his pocket and took out a handkerchief. He held it out to her. It was a while before she saw it.

'Thank you.'

'I know it's hard,' he said.

She nodded.

'You were very angry with her.'

'Yes.'

'You thought of doing something to her.'

Bothma paused before she said anything. On the carpet a sheepdog scratched itself. 'Yes.'

'Like stabbing her with a knife?'

Bothma shook her head at that.

'The revolver?'

Nod.

'Why didn't you?'

'She hid it.'

He waited.

'I didn't kill her,' said Elise Bothma and looked up at him. He saw she had green eyes. 'I didn't.'

'I know,' said Griessel. 'She was too strong for you.'

He waited until Keyter was in his car and then he stood at the window and he talked quietly, because there were still other policemen in the yard. 'I want you to understand a few things fucking well,' he said, and Keyter looked up at him in surprise.

'Number one. You will not open your mouth again during questioning, unless I give you permission. Do you understand?'

'Jissis. What did I do?'

'Do you understand?'

'Okay, okay.'

'Number two. I did not ask for you. You were given to me. With the instruction that I must teach you to be a detective. Number three. To learn, you will have to listen. Do you understand?'

'I *am* a fucking detective.'

'You are a fucking detective? Tell me, mister fucking detective, where do you start a murder investigation? Where is the first place you look?'

'Okay,' said Keyter reluctantly.

'Okay what, Jaaa-mie?'

'Okay, I get it.'

'Get what?'

'What you said.'

'Say it, Jaaa-mie.'

'Why do you keep calling me, Jaaa-mie? I get it, okay? First you look near the victim.'

'Did you look there?'

Keyter said nothing, just held his steering wheel in the ten-to-two position.

'You are not a wart on a detective's backside. Two years at Table View Station says nothing. Burglaries and vehicle theft don't count here, Jaaa-mie. You button your lip and listen and learn. Or you can go to Matt Joubert now and tell him you can't work with me.'

'Okay,' said Keyter.

'Okay what?'

'Okay, I won't talk.'

'And learn.'

'And learn.'

'Then you can get out again, because we are not finished here.' He took a step back to make room for the door. Keyter got out, shut the door and folded his arms on his chest. He leaned back against his car.

'Are we sure that she didn't do it?' asked Griessel.

Keyter shrugged. When he saw that was not sufficient, he said 'No', cautiously.

'Did you hear what I said inside there?'

'Yes.'

'Do you think she could have done it?'

'No.'

'But she wanted to?'

'Yes.'

'Now think, Jaaa-mie. Put yourself in her shoes.'

'Huh?'

'Think the way she would think,' said Griessel, and suppressed the impulse to cast his eyes heavenwards.

Keyter unfolded his arms and pressed two fingers to his temples. Griessel waited.

'Okay,' said Keyter.

Griessel waited.

'Okay, she is too small to stab Laurens.' He looked at Griessel for approval. Griessel nodded.

'And she can't get her hands on the revolver.'

'That's right.'

The fingers worked against his temples.

'No, fuck, I don't know,' said Keyter with an angry gesture and straightened up.

'How would *you* feel?' said Griessel, patience dragging at his voice like lead. 'Your child is dead. And it's your lover who did it. How would you feel? You hate, Jamie. You sit here in the house and you hate. She is sitting in the police cells and you know she will get out on bail, some time or other. And you wish you could beat her to death for what she has done. You imagine it in your head, how you shoot her, or stab her. And then on the radio you hear about this man who has his knife in for people who mess with children. Or you read the papers. What do you do, Jamie? You weep and you hope. You wish. Because you are small and weak and you need a superhero. You think: what if he comes with his big assegai? And you like thinking about it. But the week is too long, Jamie. Later you start thinking: what if he doesn't come? Bothma said the revolver was hidden. So ten to one she had looked for it. Why, Jamie? In case the assegai man didn't come. And then, what is the next logical step? You look for the assegai man. And where do you begin to look? Where do you look for someone who has it in for Laurens just as much as you? Because she had a temper. A hard woman. Where do you look?'

'Okay,' said Keyter and kicked at a clump of grass with a Nike Crosstrainer. 'Okay, I get it. You look here, on the plot.'

'There's hope for you, Jamie.'

'The labourers?'

'That's right. Who cleans the stables? Who cuts the feed? Who did Laurens shout and swear at when they came to work late? Who will do a little favour for five hundred rand?'

'I get it.'

'I want you to go and talk, Jamie. Watch the body language, look at the eyes. Don't make accusations. Just talk. Ask if they saw anything. Ask if Laurens was a difficult employer. Be sympathetic. Ask if they have heard of the assegai man. Give them a chance to talk. Sometimes they talk easily and too much. Listen, Jamie. Listen with both your ears and your eyes and your head. The thing with a murder investigation is, first you look at it from a distance, look at everything. Then you come a step closer and look again. Another step. You don't charge in – you stalk.'

'I get it.'

'I'm going in to the office. We need the other case files. I am going to ask the investigating officers to tell me everything about Davids and Pretorius. Phone me when you are finished, then you come in.'

'Okay, Benny.' Grateful.

'Okay,' he said, turning to go to his car and thinking: fuck, I'm starting to talk like him too.

25

He was still in conference with the other two investigating officers when Cloete, the liaison officer, phoned and said the media had heard there was another Artemis murder.

'A what?'

'You know, the assegai thing.'

'Artemis?'

'The *Argus* started that crap, Benny. Some or other Greek god that went around stabbing with a spear or something. Is it true?'

'That a Greek god went around . . .'

'*No, man*, that the Laurens woman who beat the child to death is the latest victim?'

The media. Fuck. 'All I can say now is that Laurens was found dead outside her house this morning. The post mortem is not finished yet.'

'They will want more than that.'

'I don't have more than that.'

'Will you phone me when there is more?'

'I will,' he lied. He was definitely not intending to feed information to the press.

Faizal phoned him just before he went to the mortuary, to ask if he could deliver the sitting-room suite. He drove to the flat to open up and then raced to Salt River where Pagel was waiting for him.

He heard the music as he closed the door of the state mortuary behind him and it made him grin. That is how you could tell Professor Phil Pagel, chief pathologist, was at work. For Pagel played only Beethoven on his ten-thousand rand hi-fi system in his office, as loud as was necessary.

'Ah, Nikita,' said Pagel with genuine pleasure when Griessel looked in his door. He was seated behind a computer and had to get up to turn the music down. 'How are you, my friend?'

Pagel had been calling him 'Nikita' for twelve years. The first time he had met Griessel he had remarked: 'I am sure that is how the young Khruschev would have looked.' Griessel had to think hard who Khrushchev was. He had always had immense respect for highly educated and cultured people, he who had only his matric and police examinations. Once he had said to Pagel: 'Damn, Prof, I wish I were as clever as you.' But Pagel had looked back at him and said: 'I suspect you are the clever one, Nikita, and you have street smarts, too.'

He liked that. Also the fact that Pagel, who featured so often on the social pages, Friends of the Opera, Save the Symphony Orchestra, Aids Action Campaign, treated him as an equal. Always had. Pagel didn't seem to age – tall and lean and impossibly handsome, some people said he looked like the star of some or other television soap that Griessel had never seen.

'Well, thank you, Prof. And you?'

'Splendid, my dear fellow. I have just finished with the unfortunate Miss Laurens.'

'Prof, they have given me the whole show – Davids, Pretorius, the works. Bushy and them tell me you think this is also an assegai.'

'Not think. I am reasonably sure. What is different about you, Nikita? Have you cut your hair? Come, let me show you.' He walked ahead down the passage and opened the swing doors of the post mortem laboratory with a deft thump of his palms. 'It's a long time since we saw an assegai – it's no longer a weapon of choice. Twenty years ago it was more common.'

There was the smell of death and formalin and cheap air freshener in the room and the air conditioning was set quite low. Pagel unzipped the black body bag. Laurens's remains lay there naked, like a cocoon. There was a single wound in the middle of her torso between two small breasts.

'What was not present with Davids,' said Pagel as he snapped on a pair of rubber gloves, 'is the exit wound. Entry wound was wide, about six centimetres, but there was nothing behind. My conclusion was a very broad blade, or two stabs with a single, thinner blade – most unlikely, however. But I didn't think "assegai". With Pretorius we have the exit wound, two point seven centimetres wide, and the entry wound of six point two. That's when the penny dropped.'

He turned Laurens's body on its side. 'Look here, Nikita. Exit wound right behind, just beside the spinal column. I had to cut the entry wound for chemical analysis, so you can no longer see, but it was even wider – six point seven, six point seven five.'

He lowered the body carefully on its back again, and covered it again.

'It tells us a couple of things which you will find interesting, Nikita. The blade is long; I estimate about sixty centimetres. We see a great deal of stab wounds inflicted with butcher's knives – you know, the kind you can buy at Pick and Pay, about a twenty-five centimetre blade. Those wounds display clearly only one cutting edge and sometimes an exit wound, but never wider than a centimetre. Entry wounds usually three, occasionally four centimetres. Here we have two cutting edges, much like a bayonet, but wider and thinner. Considerably wider. A bayonet also does more damage internally – designed for it, did you know? So we have a blade sixty centimetres long, with a narrow piercing point growing steadily wider towards the back where it is just under seven centimetres. Do you follow, Nikita?'

'I'm with you, Prof.'

'It's the classical assegai, nothing else approaches that description. Not even a sword wound. Sword wounds are naturally very rare, I think I have seen two in my life. Swords have a much wider exit wound and the wound widths are much more uniform. But that is not the only difference. The results of the chemical analysis produced a few surprises. Microscopic quantities of ash, animal fats and a few compounds we could not identify at first, but had to go through the tables. It appeared it was Cobra. You know, the polish people use to shine their floors. Animal fats were of bovine origin. You don't find that on swords. I began to look around,

Nikita, as it has been a long time since we had an assegai, one tends to forget. Let's go to my office, the notes are there. Something different about you. Wait, let me guess . . .' Pagel went ahead to his office.

Griessel looked down at his clothes. Everything was as usual, he couldn't see anything different.

'Sit, dear fellow, and let me get my story straight.' He removed a black lever-arch file from the shelf and paged through it.

'The ash. They use it to polish the blade, the blacksmiths. I suppose they are assegai smiths as they only make those. Ancient method, they used it to polish Cape silver in the old days, sometimes you see pieces in the antique shops, the wear is distinctive. This tells us the assegai was made in the traditional way. But we will come back to that. The same applies to the beef lard and the Cobra polish. That is not for the blade but for the shaft. The Zulus use it to treat the wood, to make it smooth and shiny. To preserve the wood and prevent warping.

'All very well, you will say, but that isn't much help in catching the fellow – with Cobra polish? I made some calls, Nikita, I have some friends in the curio business. They say there are three kinds of assegai on the market today. The ones we can ignore are the ones they sell at the flea market on Greenmarket Square. Those come from the north, some from as far away as Malawi and Zambia – poor workmanship, with short, thin blades and metal shafts and lots of African baroque wirework. They are made for the tourists and are replicas of some or other ritual assegais of various African cultures.

'The second kind is the so-called antique or historical spear or assegai – either the short stabbing assegai or the long throwing spear. Both have blades which match our wound profile, but there is one major difference: the antique assegai blade is pitch black from ox-, sheep's or goat's blood, as the Zulus use it for slaughtering. To kill the animal. The ash residue will also be visible under the microscope in much greater quantities. Do you know, Nikita, they sell the old assegais for five or six thousand apiece? Up to ten thousand if there is good evidence of age.

'But none of your victims had traces of animal blood, which means your assegai is either antique but very well cleaned, or it is one of the third kind: exactly the same form and manufacture as the antiques, but recently made. And the rust tells us it is the latter. I asked them to look for oxidation deposits in the wound under the spectrometer and there were practically none. No rust, no age. Your assegai has been made in the last three or four years, more likely in the last eighteen months.

'Oh, and one more thing: I suspect the assegai is not thoroughly cleaned after every murder. We found traces of the first two victims' blood and DNA in Laurens's wound. Which means it is the same weapon and most likely the same murderer.'

There went his theory that Bothma had been involved with the murder of Laurens. He nodded at Pagel.

'The thing is, Nikita, there are not many people making traditional assegais any more. Demand is small. The craft mostly survives in the rural areas of KwaZulu where the traditions are still practised and they still slaughter oxen in the old way. Where they still use beef lard for the shafts and buy Cobra to polish their *stoeps*. I also don't believe we are dealing with the long throwing spear. The entry angle of the wound is not high enough. I think this is a stabbing assegai, made by a blacksmith somewhere on the Makathini plains, in the past year. Naturally the question is, how on earth did it get from there to here, in the hands of a man who has a bone to pick with people who do harm to children? An odd choice of weapon.'

'A man, Prof?'

'I believe so. It's the depth of the wound. To push an assegai through a breastbone is not so hard, but to thrust one right through the body, breaking a rib on the way and protruding four or five centimetres out the back takes a lot of power, Nikita. Or a lot of rage or adrenaline, but if it is a woman, she is an Amazon.'

'It's a good choice of weapon, Prof. Quiet. Efficient. You can't trace it like a firearm.'

'But even the assegai is not small, Nikita. Metre and a half, maybe longer.'

Griessel nodded. 'The question is: why an assegai? Why not a big hunting knife or a bayonet? If you want to stab there is plenty of equipment.'

'Unless you want to make a statement.'

'That's what I'm thinking too, but what fucking statement? What are you saying? I am a Zulu and I love children?'

'Or maybe you want the police to think you are a Zulu while all the time you are a Boer from Brackenfell.'

'Or you want to attract attention to your cause.'

'You can't deny, Nikita, that it's a good cause. My first impulse is to let him go his way.'

'No, fuck, Prof, I can't agree with that.'

'Come on, you must admit his cause has merit.'

'Merit, Prof? Where's the merit?'

'Much as I believe in the justice system, it is not perfect, Nikita. And he fills an interesting gap. Or gaps. Don't you think there are a few people out there who will think twice before they hurt their children?'

'Prof, child abusers are lower than lobster shit. And every one I ever arrested I felt like killing with a blunt instrument. But that's not the point. The point is, where do you draw the line? Do you kill everyone that can't be rehabilitated? Psychopaths? Drug addicts who steal cell phones? A Seven–Eleven owner who grabs his forty-four Magnum because a manic-depressive kleptomaniac steals a tin of sardines? Does his cause have merit too? Shit, Prof, not even the psychiatrists can agree on who can be rehabilitated or not; every one has a different story in court. And now we want every Tom, Dick and Harry with an assegai to make that call? And this whole thing about the death penalty . . . Suddenly everyone wants it back. Between you and me, I am not by definition against the death penalty. I have put fuckers away who more than deserved that. But about one thing I can't argue, it was never a deterrent. They murdered just as much in the old days, when they were hanged or fried in the chair. So, I see no merit in it.'

'Powerful argument.'

'Chaos, Prof. If we allow bush justice. It's just the first step to chaos.'

'You're sober, Benny.'

'Prof?'

'That's what's different about you. You're sober. How long?'

'A few days, Prof.'

'Good heavens, Nikita, it's like a voice from the past.'

26

Before he reached his car, Jamie Keyter phoned to report, and without thinking Griessel said, 'Meet me at the Fireman's.' As he drove down Albert Street in the direction of the city his thoughts were on assegais and murders and the merits of a vigilante.

'Powerful argument,' the prof had said, but where had it all come from? He hadn't stopped to think. Just talked. He could swear a part of him had listened in amazement to his argument and thought, 'What the fuck?'

Suddenly he was this great crime philosopher. Since when?

Since he had given up the booze. Since then.

It was like someone had adjusted the focus so he could see the past five or six years more clearly. Was it possible to have stopped thinking for so long? Stopped analysing things? Had he done his work mechanically, by rote, according to the rules and the dictates of the law? Crime scene, case file, footwork, information, handing over, testimony, done. Alcohol was like a golden haze over everything, his buffer against thought.

What he was now and the way he thought, wasn't how it had been in the beginning. In the beginning he had operated in terms of 'us' and 'them', two opposites, two separate groups on either side of the law, sure in his belief that there was a definite difference, a dividing line. For whatever reason. Genetic, perhaps, or psychological, but that was how it was; some people were criminals and some were not and it was his job to purify society of the former group. Not an impossible task, just a huge one. But straightforward mostly. Identify, arrest and remove.

Now, on this end of the alcohol tunnel, in his rediscovered sobriety, he realised he no longer believed in that.

He now knew everyone had it in them. Crime lay quiescent in everyone, a hibernating serpent in the subconscious. In the heat of avarice, jealousy, hatred, revenge, fear, it reared up and struck. If it never happened to you, consider it luck. Lucky if your path through life detoured around trouble so that when you reached the end and the worst you had done was steal paperclips from work.

That was why he had told Pagel that a collective line must be drawn. There had to be a system. Order, not chaos. You couldn't trust an individual to determine justice and apply it. No one was pure, no one was objective, no one was immune.

Albert Street became New Market became Strand and he wondered when he had begun thinking like that. When had he passed the turning point? Was it a process of disillusionment? Seeing colleagues who had given in to temptation, or pillars of the community that he had led away in handcuffs? Or was it his own fall? Discovery of his own weaknesses. The first time he had realised he was drunk at work and could get away with it? Or when he raised his hand to Anna?

It didn't matter.

How do you catch a vigilante? That mattered.

Murder equals motive. What was the assegai man's? The why?

Was there even a simple motive here? Or was he like a serial killer, motive hidden somewhere in the short circuits of faulty neural wiring? So that there was fuck-all, no spoor leading to a source, no strand you could twiddle with and tug on until a bit came loose and you get hold of it and start unravelling.

With a serial murderer you had to wait. Examine every victim and every murder scene. Build a profile and place every bit of evidence alongside the rest and wait for a picture to form, hoping it would make sense, hoping it would reflect reality. Wait for him to make a mistake. Wait for his self-confidence to bloom and for him to become careless and leave a tyre track or a smear of semen or a fingerprint. Or you were just lucky and overheard two nurses chatting about supermarkets. You took a big gamble and the very first Friday you put out the bait, hit the jackpot.

In the old days they used to talk about Benny's Luck, shaking their heads: 'Jissis, Benny, you're so fuckin' lucky, my friend,' and it would make him fed up. He was never 'lucky' – he had instinct. And the courage to follow it. And in those days he had been given the freedom to do so. 'Carry on, Benny,' his first Murder and Robbery CO, Colonel Willie Theal, had said. 'It's the results that count.' Skinny Willie Theal, of whom the late fat Sergeant Nougat O'Grady had said: 'There but for the grace of God, goes Anorexia.' In those days the Criminal Procedure Act was a vague sort of guideline that they used as it suited them. Now O'Grady was buried and Willie Theal in Prince Albert with lung cancer and a police pension and if you didn't read a scumbag his rights before you arrested him they threw the fucking case out of court.

But it was part of the system and the system created order and that was good; if only he could create order in his life, too. That ought to be easy, as the Criminal Procedure Act of the alcoholic was the Twelve Steps.

Fuck. Why couldn't he just follow it blindly? Why couldn't he become a disciple without thinking, without a feeling of despair in the pit of his stomach when he read the Second Step which said you must believe that a Power greater than yourself is going to heal your drinking madness?

He turned right in Buitengracht, found parking, got out and walked in the early evening to the neon sign: *Fireman's Arms*. The southeaster plucked at his clothes as if trying to hold him back, but he was through the door and the tavern opened up before him, the safe, warm heart, musty with the smell of cigarette smoke and beer that had been spilt drop by drop on the carpet over the years. Camaraderie in the bowed shoulders hunched over glasses, television in the corner showing the Super Sport cricket highlights. He stood still a moment, allowing the atmosphere to settle over him.

Homecoming. He felt the yearning to sit at the wooden bar counter with its multitude of stains. The yearning to order a brandy and Coke. To settle in for the first deep draught and feel the synapses in his brain tingle with pleasure and the warmth glide through him. Just one drink, his head said to him, and then he fled, banged open the door and strode out. A tremor travelled through his body, because he knew that chorus: just one drink. He walked hastily to his car. He had to get in and lock the door and leave. Now.

His phone rang. He gripped it in a hand already shaking. 'Griessel.'

'Benny, it's Matt.'

'Jissis.' Out of breath.

'What?'

'Good timing.'

'Oh?'

'I . . . uh . . . I was just on my way home.'

'I am at the provincial commissioner's office. Could you come by here?' His tone of voice said: Don't ask, I can't talk now.

'Caledon Square?'

'Yes.'

'I'll be there now.'

He phoned Keyter and said something had come up.

'Okay.'

'We'll talk tomorrow.'

'Okay, Benny.'

There were four people in the commissioner's office. Griessel only knew three of them – the provincial commissioner himself, head of investigations, John Afrika, and Matt Joubert.

'Inspector, my name is Lenny le Grange and I am a member of Parliament,' said the fourth with an outstretched hand. Griessel shook it. Le Grange had on a dark blue suit and bright red tie like a thermometer. His grip was cool and bony.

'I am truly sorry to bother you at this time of the evening – I hear you've had a long day. Please sit down; we won't detain you long. How is the investigation proceeding?'

'As well as can be expected,' he said, glancing at Joubert for help.

'Inspector Griessel is still familiarising himself with the case files,' said Joubert as they all found places around the commissioner's round conference table.

'Naturally. Inspector, let me go straight to the point. I have the dubious privilege to be the chairman of the Parliamentary Portfolio Committee of Justice and Political Development. As you may have gathered from the media, we are busy developing a new Sexual Offences Bill.'

Griessel had gleaned nothing from the media. But he nodded.

'Very good. Part of the bill is a proposed Register of Sexual Offenders, a list of names of everyone who has been convicted of a sexual offence – rapists, sex with minors, you name it. Our recommendation is that the register be made available to the public. For instance, we want to prevent parents handing their child over to a paedophile when they enrol the child in a crèche.

'To be honest, this aspect of the new bill is controversial. There are people who say it is a contravention of the constitutional right to privacy. It is one of those cases that create division across party lines. At this stage it looks as if we are going to push the bill through, but our majority is not large. I am sure you're beginning to understand why I'm here.'

'I understand,' said Griessel.

The MP took a white sheet of paper from his jacket pocket.

'Just to make matters more interesting, I would like to read an extract from *Die Burger* of two weeks ago. I gave a press conference and they quoted me thus: *"If there are consequences for the sexual offender, such as vigilante attacks on him or inability to find work, then let it be so. A sexual offender forfeits the right to privacy. The right to privacy is not more important than a woman or child's right to physical integrity," the chairman of Portfolio Committee for Justice and Political Development, Advocate Lenny le Grange, said yesterday.'*

Le Grange looked pointedly at Griessel. 'Me and my big mouth, Inspector. One says these things because one believes with such passion that our women and children must be protected. One says it out of reaction to what one perceives as far-fetched scare stories dreamt up by the Opposition. I mean, a vigilante . . . Perhaps I thought it would never happen. Or if it did happen, it would be an isolated incident where the police would rapidly step in and make an arrest. One never foresees . . . not what is going on at the moment.'

Le Grange leaned over the table. 'They are going to make me eat my words. But that goes with the job. It's the risk I run. I don't care about that. But I do care about the bill. That's why I am asking you to stop this vigilantism. So we can protect our women and children.'

'I understand,' he said again.

'What do you need, Benny?' asked the commissioner, as if they were old friends.

He hesitated before answering. He looked from the politician to the Western Cape chief of police and then he said: 'The one thing that is no longer available, Commissioner. Time.'

'And apart from that?' His tone said that was not the answer he had wanted.

'What Benny is saying is that this sort of case is complicated. The problem is lack of an obvious motive,' said Matt Joubert.

'That's right,' said Griessel. 'We don't know why he is doing it.'

'Why would anyone do it?' asked le Grange. 'Surely it's to protect children. That's obvious.'

'Motive,' said John Afrika, 'is usually an identifier, Mr le Grange. If the assegai man's motive is purely to protect children, that identifies him as one of about ten million concerned men in this country. Everyone wants to protect children, but only one is committing murder to do so. What makes him different? Why did he choose this way? That is what we need to know.'

'There are a few things that would help,' said Griessel.

Everyone looked at him.

'We need to know if Enver Davids was the first one. As far as we know, he is the first in the Western Cape. But crime against children is everywhere. Perhaps he started somewhere else.'

'What would that help?' asked le Grange.

'The first one could be significant. The first one would be personal. Personal vengeance. And then he decides he likes it. Maybe. We must consider it. The second thing that could help is other assegai murders or attacks. It's a unique weapon. The state pathologist says they don't see them any more. You don't buy a new assegai at the Seven–Eleven. Why did he go to the trouble of getting one? Then there is the question of where he got it. Professor Pagel says Zululand. Could our colleagues in Durban help? Do they know who makes and sells them? Could they ask the questions? And the last thing we can do is draw up a list of all the reported crimes against children in the past eighteen months. Particularly those where the suspects have not been apprehended.'

'Do you think he's taking revenge?' asked Advocate le Grange.

'Just another possibility,' said Griessel. 'We must consider them all.'

'There are hundreds of cases,' said the commissioner.

'That is why Benny said time is the one thing he needs,' said Matt Joubert.

'Damn,' said le Grange.

'Amen,' said John Afrika.

The southeaster was blowing so hard they had to run doubled over to their cars.

'You did well in there, Benny,' shouted Joubert above the roar of the wind.

'So did you.' And then: 'You know, if you drank more, you too could have been an inspector now.'

'Instead of a senior superintendent that has to deal with all this political shit?'

'Exactly.'

Joubert laughed. 'That's one way to look at it.'

They reached Griessel's car. 'I'm going to look in on Cliffy quickly,' he said.

'I'm coming too. See you there.'

Gently he pushed open the door of the hospital room and saw them sitting there – the woman and two children around the bed, all bathed in the yellow pool of the bedside lamp. Mketsu's wife holding his hand, the children on either side, their eyes on their wounded father. And Cliffy lying there with a soft smile, busy telling them something.

Griessel stopped, reluctant to intrude. And something else, a consciousness of loss, of envy, but Cliffy saw him and his smile broadened and he said, 'Come in, Benny.'

On the threshold of his flat was a small glass vase with a single, unfamiliar red flower. And a small note under the vase, folded twice.

He picked it up, opened the letter and hope welled up in him. Anna?

Welcome to our building. Pop in for tea when you have the time. At the bottom. *Charmaine. 106.*

Fuck. He looked down the passage in the direction of 106. All was quiet. Somewhere he could hear a television. He unlocked his door quickly and went in, closing it softly. He placed the vase on the breakfast bar. He read the note again, crumpled it up and tossed it in his new rubbish bin. Not the sort of thing he wanted his children to see lying around tomorrow.

His sitting-room suite. He stood back and inspected it. Tried to see it through his children's eyes. The place looked less barren at least, more homely. He sat down in a chair. Not too bad. He stood up and went and lay down on the couch with a faint stirring of pleasure. He felt weary, felt like closing his eyes.

Long day. The seventh since he had last had a drink.

Seven days. Only a hundred and seventy-three to go.

He thought of the Fireman's Arms and his mind cajoling him: just one drink. He thought about Cliffy's family. The fucking thing was that he couldn't be sure his family would ever be like that again. Anna and himself and Carla and Fritz. How did you get that back? How did you build that sort of bond?

That made him remember the photo and he got up on impulse to find it. He found it in his briefcase and went and lay down again with the light on. He studied the photo. Benny, Anna, Carla and Fritz.

Eventually he got up, went up to the bedroom and put it on the windowsill above the bed. Then he took a shower. His cell phone rang when he was lathered with soap. He made a wet trail to the bed and answered it. It might be Anna.

'Griessel.'

'It's Cloete, Benny. The Sunday papers are driving me crazy,' the liaison officer said.

'Well, tell them to go to hell.'

'I can't. It's my job.'

'What do those vultures want?'

'They want to know if Laurens is Artemis.'

'If *she* is Artemis?'

'You know, whether it was Artemis that murdered her.'

'We don't know what the fucker's name is.'

Cloete was annoyed. 'Is it the same murder weapon, Benny?'

'Yes, it's the same murder weapon.'

'And the same MO?'

'Yes.'

'And I can tell them that?'

'It won't make any difference.'

'It will make a hell of a difference in *my* life,' said Cloete. 'Because then they will stop fucking phoning me.' He put the phone down.

27

At three minutes to ten he knocked on the door of his own house like some stranger. Anna opened up and then she asked, 'Are you sober, Benny?' and he said, 'Yes.'

'Are you sure?'

He looked in her eyes to let her know the first 'yes' was enough. She was looking pretty. She had done something with her hair. It was shorter. Her face was made up, lips red and shiny.

She took her time before reacting. 'I'll get the children.' When he lifted a foot to enter, she shut the door in his face. He stood there dumbstruck and then the humiliation descended on him. He lowered his head in case the neighbours were outside and saw him like this. Everyone would know he had been kicked out. This street was like a village.

The door opened and Carla charged at him, threw her arms around his neck and squeezed him saying, 'Daddy,' like she did when she was little. Her hair smelled of strawberries. He held her close and said, 'My child.'

He saw Fritz in the doorway with a rucksack in his hand.

'Hi, Dad.' Uneasy.

'Hello, Fritz.'

'Bring them back at six,' said Anna who stood behind her son.

'I will,' he said.

She closed the door.

Why was she looking so nice? What was she planning today?

Carla talked too much, too gaily, and Fritz, sitting in the back, said not a word. In the rear-view mirror, Griessel could see the boy gazing out of the car window expressionlessly. In Fritz's profile he saw echoes of Anna's features. He wondered what Fritz was thinking. About that last night his father had been at home and had hit his mother? How could he fix that? And Carla babbled on about the upcoming Matric Farewell and the intrigues of who had asked whom to go with them, as if she could make a success of the day single-handed.

'I thought we might eat at the Spur,' he said when Carla stopped for breath.

'Okay,' she said.

'We're not at prep school any more,' said Fritz.

'The Spur is a *family* restaurant, stupid,' said Carla.

'The Spur is for little kids,' said Fritz.

'Well, you choose, Fritz,' said Griessel. 'Anywhere.'

'It doesn't matter.'

As they walked up the stairs to his flat, he thought it would be awful for the children. This small bare space: Dad's penitentiary. He opened up and stood aside so they could enter. Carla disappeared up the stairs straight away. Fritz stood in the door and surveyed the place.

'Cool,' he said.

'Oh?'

'Bachelor pad,' said his son in answer and went in. 'Haven't you got a TV, Dad?'

'No, I . . .'

'You've got a *sweet* place, Dad,' said Carla from the top of the stairs. Then his cell phone rang, he unclipped it from his belt and said, 'Griessel,' and Jamie Keyter said, 'I thought I should come over to you and report. Where do you live?'

He would have to talk to Keyter even though he didn't want him here. He gave directions and said goodbye.

'I'll have to do a little work today,' he said to the children.

'What kind of work?'

'It's a case. My shift partner is coming round.'

'What case, Dad?' asked Carla.

'It's a guy who's stabbing people with an assegai.'

'Cool,' said Fritz.

'Artemis? You're working on the Artemis case?' asked Carla in excitement.

'Yes,' he said, and wondered if he had ever discussed his work with his children before. When he was sober.

Carla dived onto the new couch with the anonymous stains and said: 'But that's not a guy. The television says it's a woman. Artemis. She's taking revenge on everyone who messes with children.'

'It's a man,' said Griessel, and sat down on one of his new chairs, opposite his son. Fritz's legs hung over the armrest. He had taken a magazine out of his rucksack. *New Age Gaming*. He flipped through it.

'Oh,' said Carla deflated. 'Do you know who it is, Dad?'

'No.'

'So how do you know it's a man?'

'It's highly improbable that it's a woman. Serial killers are usually men. Women almost never use—'

'Charlize Theron was a serial murderer,' said Carla.

'Who?'

'She got an Oscar for it.'

'For the murders?'

'Dad doesn't know who Charlize Theron is,' said Fritz from behind his magazine.

'Dad knows,' said Carla, and they both looked at him to settle the argument and he knew the time had come to say what he must say, the words he had composed in his head while he drove to Brackenfell that morning.

'I am an alcoholic,' he said.

'Dad . . .'

'Wait, Carla. There are things we must talk about. Sooner or later. It's no use pretending.'

'We know you're an alky,' said Fritz. 'We know.'

'Shut up,' said Carla.

'What for? That's all we did and what use was that and now they're getting divorced and Dad drinks like a fish.'

'Who says we're getting divorced?'

'Dad, he's talking rubbish . . .'

'Did your mother say we're getting divorced?'

'She said you could come back when you stop drinking. And we know you can't stop drinking.' Fritz's face was hidden behind the magazine again, but he could hear the anger in his son's voice. And the helplessness.

'I have stopped.'

'It's eight days already,' said Carla.

Fritz sat motionless behind *NAG*.

'You don't think I can stop?'

Fritz clapped the magazine shut. 'If you wanted to stop, why didn't you do it long ago? Why?' The tears were close. 'Why did you do all those things, Dad? Why did you hit Mom? Swear at us. Do you think it's funny seeing your father like that?'

'Fritz!' But she couldn't shut him up.

'Putting you in bed every night when you pass out? Or finding you in a chair in the morning, stinking and you never even remembered what you did? We never had a father. Just some drunkard who lived with us. You don't know us, Dad. You don't know anything. You don't know we hide the liquor away. You don't know we take money out of your wallet so you can't buy brandy. You don't know we can't bring our friends home because we're ashamed of our father. We can't sleep over at our friends because we're scared you'll hit Mom when we're not there. You still think we like to go to the Spur, Dad. You think Charlize Theron is a criminal. You don't know anything, Dad, and you drink.'

He could no longer hold back the tears and he got up and rushed up the stairs. Griessel and Carla stayed behind and he could not meet her eyes. He sat in his chair and felt shame. He saw the fuck-up he had made of his life. The whole irrevocable fuck-up.

'You *have* stopped, Dad.'

He said nothing.

'I *know* you have.'

The unease had driven Thobela up Table Mountain early Sunday morning. He drove to Kirstenbosch and climbed the mountain from behind, up Skeleton Gorge, until he stood on the crest and looked over everything. But it didn't help.

He pulled and kneaded the emotion, looking for reasons, but none came.

It wasn't only the woman.

'Oh God,' she had said. He had come from the shrubs and the shadows and in the dark he grabbed the firearm in her hand and gave it a sharp twist, so that she lost her grip. The dogs were barking madly around them, the sheepdog biting at his heels with sharp teeth. He had to kick the animal and Laurens had formed her last word.

'No.'

She had shielded herself with her hands when he lifted the assegai. When the long blade went in, peace had come over her. Just like Colin Pretorius. Release. That was what they wanted. But inside him there was a cry, a shout that said he couldn't make war on women.

He heard it still, but there was something else. A pressure. Like walls. Like a narrow corridor. He had to get out. Into the open. He must move. Go on.

He walked over the mountain in the direction of Camp's Bay. He clambered over rocks until the Atlantic Ocean lay far beneath his feet.

Why did he feel this urge now? To fetch his motorbike and have a long, never-ending road stretching ahead. Because he was doing the right thing. He did not doubt any more. In the Spur with the street children he had found an answer that he hadn't looked for. It had come to him as if it were sent. The things people did to them. Because they were the easiest targets.

He walked again. The mountain stretched out to the south, making humps you don't expect. How far could you walk like this, on the crest? As far as Cape Point?

He was doing the right thing, but he wanted to get away.

He was feeling claustrophobic here.

Why? He hadn't made a mistake yet. He knew that. But some-thing was wrong. The place was too small. He stood still. This was instinct, he realised. To move on. To hit and then disappear. That was how it was, in the old days. Two, three weeks of preparation until you did your job and you got on a plane and were gone. Never two consecutive strikes in the same place: that would be looking for trouble. That left tracks, drew attention. That was poor strategy. But it was already too late, because he had drawn attention. Major attention.

That was why he had to get away. Get in his truck and drive.

28

He put the kettle on.

'I'll make the coffee, Dad,' said Carla.

'I want to do it,' he said. Then: 'I don't even know how you take your coffee.'

'I drink it with milk and without sugar and Fritz takes milk and three sugars.'

'Three?'

'Boys,' she said with a shrug.

'Do you have a boyfriend?'

'Kind of.'

'Oh?'

'There is a guy . . .'

'Is powdered milk okay?'

She nodded. 'His name is Sarel and I know he likes me. He's quite cute. But I don't want to get too involved now, with the exams and things.'

He could hear Anna's voice in hers, the intonation and the wisdom. 'That's smart,' he said.

'Because I want to study next year, Dad.'

'That's good.'

'Psychology.'

In order to analyse her father's mind?

'Maybe I can get a bursary if I do well, that's why I don't want to get involved now. But Mom says she's put a bit of money aside for our studies.'

He knew nothing about it. He poured the water into the mugs, then the powdered milk and the sugar for Fritz.

'I want to take him his coffee.'

'Don't worry about him, Dad. He's just a typical teenager.'

'He's struggling with his father's alcoholism,' he said, climbing the stairs. Fritz lay on Griessel's bed with the photo in his hands, the photo of them together as a family.

'Three sugars,' he said.

Fritz said nothing. Griessel sat on the foot of the bed. 'I'm sorry,' he said.

Fritz replaced the photo on the windowsill. 'It doesn't matter.' He sat up and took the coffee.

'I'm sorry about everything I did to you. And to your mother and Carla.'

Fritz looked at the steam rising from the coffee mug. 'Why, Dad? Why do you drink?'

'I'm working on that Fritz.'

'They say it's genetic,' said his son, and tested the temperature of the liquid with a cautious sip.

Jamie Keyter was wearing a sports shirt and tight khaki trousers. The short sleeves of the shirt were too narrow and had shifted up above the bulging biceps. He sat on one of the bar stools at the breakfast bar and drank coffee with two sugars and milk and he glanced periodically at Carla while he spoke. That annoyed Griessel.

'And I went up to the little house, like a little *kaia*, and you couldn't see anything, hear anything but the TV show inside, the one with the crazy kaffi . . . green fellow who gives away prizes in green language and I knocked but they didn't hear me. So I opened the door and there they sat drinking. All four, glass in the hand. Cheers! But when they saw me, you should have seen them jump and it was mister this and mister that. The house was dirty and it was empty. Typical greens: they have nothing, but there's this giant TV in the corner and there are four greens living in the *kaia*, two old and two young ones. I don't know how people can live like that. And they didn't want to talk; they just sat there and stared at me. And when they did talk, they lied. The girl works in the house and it was all: "Miss Laurens was a good missus, she was good to all of us." They're lying, Benny, I'm telling you.' He looked pointedly at Carla, who lay on the couch.

'Did you ask them about her fits of rage?'

'I asked and they said it wasn't so, she was a good missus and they kept turning back to the TV and looking sideways at the wine box. Bloody drunken lot, if you ask me.' He was still looking at Carla.

'And they didn't see anything?' He knew what the answer would be.

'Saw nothing, heard nothing.'

'The pathologist says it was the same weapon. The same assegai as the previous murders.'

'Okay,' said Keyter.

'Did you ask about Bothma? What she's like?'

'Oh, no. We already know.'

He let that go. He didn't want to say something in front of the children.

'So,' said Keyter to Carla. 'What do you do?'

'I'm writing matric.'

'Okay,' he said. 'I get it.'

'What?' she asked.

'If I give you a rand, will you phone me when you're finished.'

'In your dreams,' she said. 'And what is your problem anyway?'

'My problem?'

'Greens? Only racists say things like that.'

'I haven't got a racist hair on my head.'

'Yeah, right.'

Griessel had been busy with his thoughts. He missed this exchange. 'Do me a favour, Jamie.'

'Okay, Benny.'

'The file on Cheryl Bothma, the daughter. Find out who's handling that.'

'I thought you talked to them yesterday?'

'I only talked to the guys who dealt with the assegai murders. I'm talking about the case of the child. When they arrested Laurens.'

'I get it.'

'Please.'

'No, I mean I know which one you mean. But what's the use?'

'Something is not right with this thing. I don't know what. Yesterday Bothma . . .'

'But the pathologist said it's the same guy?'

'I'm not talking about the murder of Laurens. I'm talking about the murder of the child.'

'But that's not our case.'

'It's our job.'

'He's weird,' said Carla when they eventually got rid of Keyter.

'He's a *drol*,' Fritz called down the stairs.

'Fritz!' said Griessel.

'I could use a ruder word, Dad.'

'But where does he get the money?' asked Carla.

'What money?'

'Didn't you notice, Dad? The clothes. Polo shirt, Daniel Hechter trousers. Nikes.'

'Who's Daniel Hechter?'

'He's married to Charlize Theron, Dad!' yelled Fritz from upstairs. 'But he's not a murderer.'

For the first time Carla laughed and then Griessel laughed with her.

In the Ocean Basket in Kloof Street, while they waited for their food, Carla asked him about the Artemis case. He suspected that was her way of avoiding the silences. Out of the blue, in the middle of the discussion, she asked: 'Why did you become a policeman, Dad?'

He had no ready answer. He hesitated and saw Fritz look up from the magazine and knew he had to get this right. He said, 'Because that is who I am.'

His son raised an eyebrow.

Griessel rolled his shoulders. 'I just knew I was a policeman. Don't ask me why. Everyone has a vision of himself. That is how I saw myself.'

'I don't see myself,' said Fritz.

'You're still young.'

'I'm sixteen.'

'It will come.'

'I am not a policeman. And besides, I'm not going to drink. Policemen drink.'

'Everyone drinks.'

'Policemen drink more.'

And with that he went back to his magazine and took no further part in the conversation. Until they had eaten and Griessel asked Carla casually if she knew an Afrikaans song with the words: ''n Bokkie wat vanaand by my kom lê, sy kan maar lê, ek is 'n loslappie.' A babe who wants to lie with me tonight, can lie with me, I'm free and easy.

She was still pointing her thumb at her brother when Fritz, without looking up, asked: 'What recording?'

'I don't know, I just heard it the other night over the radio.'

'Was it a medley or a whole song?'

'A whole song.'

'Kurt Darren,' said Fritz.

Griessel had no idea who Kurt Darren was but he wasn't going to admit it. He didn't need another Charlize Theron quip.

'Kurt Darren needs to get himself a decent bass guitarist,' said Griessel.

Something changed in his son's face. It was as if the sun came up. 'Yeah right, that's right, his whole mix is wrong. It's an ancient song, but it has to rock. Theuns Jordaan does it better. He's the guy who does the medley with "*Loslappie*", but he's just as scared of proper bass. There is only one oke in Afrikaans who makes good use of bass, but he doesn't sing that song. It's a helluva pity.'

'Who's that?'

'Anton Goosen.'

'I know Anton Goosen,' said Griessel with relief. 'He's the guy who sang that thing about the donkey cart?'

'A donkey cart?'

'Yes, what was the name of the song? *Kruidjie-roer-my-nie*?'

'That's like, a hundred years ago, Dad,' said Fritz in amazement. 'The Goose doesn't sing stuff like that any more. He rocks now. He's got the Bushrock Band.'

'Unbelievable.'

'No, you know what's really unbelievable, Dad? The guy who plays bass for the Bushrock Band is the same guy who backed Theuns Jordaan with his "*Loslappie*" medley. And he had Anton L'Amour on lead, but Theuns is too middle-of-the-road. Not bad, but he doesn't want to rock. He doesn't want to badass. Diff-olie is badass. And . . .'

'Diff-olie?'

'Yes. And—'

'Diff oil is the name of a *band*?'

'With all due respect, how long were you drunk, Dad? There's Diff-olie and Kobus and Akkedis and Battery 9 and Beeskraal and Valiant Swart and they all kick butt. There's every type of rock in Afrikaans now, from heavy metal to Country. But you have to listen to Anton live in concert if you want to hear bass and genuine rock. Anton likes heavy bass, he turns it on. The only downside of that concert is the flippin' audience.'

'The flippin' audience?'

'Yup. That will teach the Goose to play in the State Theatre. They did this awesome rock and instead of the people going ape, they clapped. I ask you. It's not a flippin' school concert, it's rock, but they gave him these self-conscious ovations. Flippin' Pretoria.'

'Mister Boere Rock,' said Carla, and cast her eyes up to heaven.

'It's better than that Leonard Cohen crap that *you* listen to.'

Griessel was beginning to form a reproof when he began to laugh. He couldn't help himself and he knew why: he was in total agreement with his son.

When he had stopped laughing Fritz said, more to himself than to Griessel: 'That's the one way I see myself.'

'How?'

'Bass guitarist.'

'For Karen Zoid, I suppose,' said his sister.

He pulled up his nose at Carla. 'Only the uninformed think she's into rock only. You read too much *You* magazine. Zoid is closet ballad queen, not a rock chic. But she *is* awesome and that's a fact.'

'And you have an enormous crush on her.'

'No,' said Fritz with regret. 'Karen is spoken for.' Then he turned to his father. 'So you like bass too, Dad?'

'A little,' said Griessel. 'A little.'

Cloete phoned again when they were on their way to Brackenfell.

'I thought you had a thing about the media, Benny.'

'What?'

'Last night. Then it was "vultures" and "tell them to go to hell" and this morning I see you prefer to speak to them direct.'

'What are you talking about?'

'Front page of the *Rapport*, Benny. Front fucking page: "A source close to veteran Detective Inspector Benny Griessel of the Peninsula Unit for Serious and Violent Crimes (SVC) says that the team is still investigating the possibility that the vigilante was not responsible for the murder of Laurens." I know I didn't fucking say that.'

'I did not f . . .' He realised the children were in the car with him. 'It wasn't me.'

'Must have been the ghost girl of Uniondale.'

'I'm telling you, it wasn't me . . .' Then he fell silent because he knew who it was. Biceps Keyter. That's who.

'Doesn't matter. Thing is, the dailies want a follow-up, because everyone has an opinion now. Even the politicians. The DP says the ANC is to blame, the Death Penalty Party say it's the voice of the people and the *Sunday Times* ran an opinion poll and seventy-five per cent of the nation say the assegai man is a hero.'

'Jissis.'

'Now the dailies are phoning me like crazy. So I thought, while you're doing my job, you can handle the enquiries yourself.'

'I told you, Cloete, it wasn't me.'

Cloete was quiet for a moment, then asked, 'What's new?'

'Since yesterday?'

'Yes.'

'Nothing.'

'Benny, you have to give me something. The dailies want blood.'

'One thing, Cloete, but you have to clear it with Matt Joubert.'

Cloete said nothing.

'Do you hear?'

'I hear.'

'We were with the commissioner last night. The plan is to put together a task team tomorrow. We're bringing people in from the stations.'

'To do what?'

'I'm not telling the press that.'

'That's fuck-all, Benny. A task team. So what?'

'Talk to Joubert.'

'I prefer to talk to the source close to veteran Detective Inspector Benny Griessel,' said Cloete, and put the phone down in his ear.

'What was that all about?' asked Fritz from the back.

'The media,' said Benny and sighed.

'They're like a bunch of hyenas,' said Fritz.

'Vultures,' said Griessel.

'Yup,' said Fritz. 'When there's a carcass they start circling.'

He dropped them off at his wife's at three minutes to six. Fritz said: 'Hang on just a minute,' and jumped out of the car.

'It was a lovely day, Dad,' said Carla and hugged him.

'It was,' he said.

'Bye, Dad. See you next week.'

'Bye, my child.'

She got out and went into the house. Fritz came out of the door with an object in his hand. He came up to Griessel's window and held it out.

Griessel took it. It was a CD case. anton & vrinne & die bushrockband. Anton & friends & the bushrockband.

'Enjoy,' said Fritz.

His flat was silent. Suddenly empty. He sat down on the couch where Carla had sat. He turned the CD case over and over in his fingers. He had fuck-all to play it on.

He needed to do something. He couldn't just sit here and listen to the silence. There was too much trouble in his head.

Where had Anna been today? Why was she all dolled up? What for?

Why did Fritz think they were getting divorced? Had she said something? Made some remark? 'Your father won't stop drinking anyway.' Is that what his wife believed?

Of course she fucking believed that. What else, with his record? So, if she knew how it would end, what stopped her from filling the vacuum in the meantime? Why not allow some or other young, handsome and sober shit to take her out. And what else did she allow him? What else? How hungry was she? Anna, who always said, 'I like to be touched.' Who was doing the fucking touching now? God knows it wasn't veteran Detective Inspector Benny fucking Griessel.

He got up from the couch, his hands searching for something. What a day. His children. His wonderful children. That he barely knew. His son with his base guitar genes and accusing words. Carla, who tried so desperately to pretend everything was normal, everything would work out right. As if her sheer will-power would keep him sober, if only she believed strongly enough.

We never had a father. Just some drunkard who lived with us.

Shit. The damage he had done. It burned him inside, the extent of it, all the multiple implications. It gnawed at him and he looked up and realised he was searching for a bottle, his hands itching to pour, his soul needing medication for this pain. Just one drink to make it better, to make it manageable, and that was when he realised he didn't stand a chance. Here he was with all the shit of his life suffocating him, the shit his boozing had created – and he wanted a drink. He knew with absolute certainty that if there had been a bottle in the flat he would have opened it. He had already ticked off the possibilities in his mind – where he could go to get a drink, what places would still be open on a Sunday evening.

He made a noise in the back of his throat and kicked one of his new secondhand armchairs. What the fuck was it about him that had made him such an absolute shit? What?

He felt for the cell phone with trembling hands. He typed the number and when Barkhuizen answered he just said: 'Jissis, Doc. Jissis.'

29

At half-past six the next morning he walked to the reservoir and he knew the feeling he had was vaguely familiar, but he did not yet recognise it. First he looked at the mountain. And the sea. He listened to the birds and thought about one more day he had survived without alcohol. Even if yesterday had been touch and go.

'What is it about me, Doc?' he had asked Barkhuizen in despair. Because he needed to know the cause. The root of the evil.

The old man had talked about chemistry and genes and circumstance. Long, easy explanations, he could hear how Barkhuizen was trying to calm him down. The oppression and the gnawing anxiety slowly ebbed away. At the end of the discussion the doctor told him it didn't matter where it came from. What counted was how he went on from here, and that was the truth. But when Griessel lay in bed with a great weariness upon him, he still searched, because he could not fight a thing he could not understand.

He wanted to go back to the source, wanted to remember how things were when the drinking began. Sleep overcame him before he got there.

By five o'clock he was awake, fresh and rested, with the assegai affair occupying him and his mind full of ideas and plans. It drove him out of bed, here to the park in shorts and T-shirt and he felt that pleasure again. The morning and the view belonged only to him.

'My name is Benny Griessel and I am an alcoholic and this is my ninth day without alcohol,' he said out loud to the morning in general. But that was not the reason he felt a certain rush. Only once he was on the way to work did he realise what it was. He shook his head because it was like a voice from his past, a forgotten friend. Today the race was on. The search was about to begin. It was the first tingle of adrenaline, expectation, a last short silence before the storm. What surprised him most was how hungry he was for it.

Matt Joubert told the detectives on morning parade that Griessel would lead the assegai case and through the tepid applause he heard the jokesters calling, 'Klippies and Coke squad' and, 'So, we don't really want to catch him.'

Joubert held up a hand. 'The officers who will assist him are Bushy Bezuidenhout, Vaughn Cupido and Jamie Keyter.'

Fantastic, thought Griessel. Now he had the sloppy one and the braggart and the semi-useful detective. Where the fuck were all the stalwarts? He did an involuntary stocktaking. Only Matt Joubert and himself remained from the old days. And Joubert was at least the commanding officer, a senior superintendent. The rest were new. And young. He was the only inspector over forty.

'This morning the commissioner is pulling in four people from the Domestic Violence Unit and ten uniformed people from the Peninsula to help with research,' said Joubert. Here and there people whistled. The political pressure had to be intense because it was a big team. 'They will use the old lecture hall in B-block as a centre of operations. Some of you are storing stuff there – please remove it directly after parade. And give Benny and his team all the cooperation you can. Benny?'

Griessel stood up.

'Drunk, but standing,' someone said in an undertone. Some muffled laughs. There was an air of expectation in the room, as if they knew he was going to make a fool of himself.

Fuck them, he thought. He had been solving murders when they were investigating how to copy their Science homework without getting caught.

At first he just stood there, until there was complete silence. Then he spoke. 'The greatest single reason that we have case discussions at morning parade is because thirty heads are better than one. I want to tell you how we are going to approach this case. So that you can blow holes in my argument. And make better suggestions. Any ideas are welcome.'

He saw he had their attention. He wondered for an instant if it was astonishment that he could string five sentences together. 'The bad news is the similarity between the assegai vigilante murders and serial murders. The victims are, I believe, unknown to the murderer. The choice of victims is relatively unpredictable. The motive is unconventional and, although we can speculate about it, still reasonably unclear. I don't know how many of you remember the red ribbon murders about six years ago: eleven prostitutes murdered over a period of three years. Most were from Sea Point, the murder weapon was a knife, and all the bodies were found with mutilated breasts and genitalia and a red ribbon around the neck. We had the same problem then. The choice of victim was limited to a specific category, the motive was psychological, sexual and predictable and the murder weapon consistent. We could build a profile, but not one definite enough to identify a suspect.

In this case we know he has a hang-up about people who molest or murder children. That is our category, regardless of race or gender. From that we can more or less deduce the motive. And the weapon of choice is an assegai that is used in a single fatal stab. The psychologists will tell us that indicates a highly organised murderer, a man with a mission. But let us focus on the differences between the typical serial murderer and our assegai man. He does not mutilate the victims. There are no sexual undertones. The single wound is deep. One terrible penetration . . . There is anger, but where does it originate? The only reasonable conclusion is that we are dealing with revenge. Was he personally molested as a child? I think the possibility is very strong. It fits. If that is the motive we are in trouble. How do you track down such a suspect? However, there is another possibility. Perhaps he lost a child through some crime. Perhaps the system failed him. We will have to look at the baby that was raped by Enver Davids. Is there a father who wants revenge? The families of the children molested by Pretorius. But it's possible that he was not directly affected by any of these crimes.

As far as his race goes, we must not be blinded by the assegai. It could be a deliberate ploy to mislead us. Here is a man who found Davids in a coloured neighbourhood just as easily as he got into Pretorius's house in a white neighbourhood in the early evening. We must keep our options open. But I swear the assegai means something. Something important. Any comments?'

They sat and listened in absolute quiet.

'We can approach this thing from four perspectives. The first is to find out if we can identify any suspects close to the original child victims. The second is to look at all unsolved crimes against children. We must begin in the Western Cape, since that is where he's operating. If we find nothing, we must expand the search. A long process, I know. Needle in a haystack. But it must be done. The third thing is the murder weapon. We know it's a typical Zulu assegai. We know it was made by hand in the traditional way, most likely in the last year or so. That means we might determine *where* it was made. How it was distributed and sold. But why would someone choose an assegai? We will talk to the forensic psychologists too. Everyone with me so far?'

He saw Bushy Bezuidenhout and Matt Joubert nod. The rest just sat and stared at him.

'The problem with all three of these strategies is that they are speculative. We must go on with them and hope they produce results, but there are no guarantees. They will take time too – the one thing we don't have. The media is on fire and there are political aspects . . . That is why I want to try a fourth approach. And for that I need your help. The question I ask myself is how he selects a victim. I think there can only be two methods: he is part of the system, or he sees it in the media. All three victims were in the news. Davids when he was acquitted, Pretorius when he was in court, Laurens when she was arrested. So he is either part of the justice system, a policeman, prosecutor, court orderly or something – ' they shifted around for the first time since he had begun to speak '– or he's just a member of the public with time to read the

papers or watch the news on TV. That's more likely. But one or
the other – that is how we are going to catch him. I want to know of
every serious crime against children in the next week or so. We
want something we can blow up in the media. We want something
that will get everyone talking.'

Jamie Keyter's voice came from somewhere near the wall: 'You
want to set a trap for him, Benny?'

'That is correct. We want to catch him in a snare.'

'Sup,' said Bushy Bezuidenhout, 'there's something I want you all
to know from the start.'

Griessel, Keyter, Bezuidenhout and Cupido sat in Joubert's
office while they waited for the lecture hall to be cleared.

'Go on, Bushy,' said Joubert.

'I don't have a problem with this guy.'

'You mean the assegai man?'

'That's right.'

'I am not sure I understand you, Bushy?'

'Benny says he's like a serial killer. I don't see it like that. This
guy is doing what we should have done a long time ago. And that is
to take these evil fuckers who do things to children and hang them
by the neck. Christ, Sup, I worked on the original Davids case.
Lester Mtetwa and I stood and cried over that baby's body. When
we arrested Davids, I had to hold Lester back, because he wanted
to blow that fucking animal's head away, he was that upset.'

'I understand, Bushy. We all felt like that. But the big question
is: will it prevent you doing your work? From bringing him in?'

'I will do my best.'

'Benny?'

He could not afford to lose Bezuidenhout. 'Bushy, all I ask is: if
you feel there is something you can't do, just tell me.'

'Okay.'

'I don't know what your problem is,' said Keyter to Bezuidenhout.

'Jamie,' said Griessel.

'What? All I said was—'

'I agree,' said Cupido. 'He's a murderer, end of story.'

'Listen,' said Bezuidenhout. 'You're still wet behind the ears and you want to—'

'Bushy! Leave it.' Griessel turned to Cupido and Keyter. 'Everyone has the right to feel what he feels. As long as it doesn't affect the investigation, we respect each other. Do you understand? I don't need any trouble.'

They nodded, but without conviction.

'Talking of trouble,' said Joubert. Their heads turned to him. 'The trap, Benny . . .'

'I know. It's a risk.'

'I don't want another Woolworths episode, Benny. I don't want people in hospital. I won't have civilians in danger. If there is any chance it could turn into a fiasco, walk away. I want your word on that.'

'You have it.'

Keyter told him it was Inspector Tim Ngubane who had investigated the murder of Cheryl Bothma. Griessel found Ngubane in the tearoom.

'Tim, I need your help.'

'Impressive speech this morning, Benny.'

'Oh, I . . . er . . .'

'You've got all the angles on this one.'

'I hope so.'

'What can I do for you?'

'The Bothma child . . .'

'Yes.'

'You handled that.'

'Anwar and I did.'

'An easy one?'

'Open and shut. When we got there, Laurens was already waiting with her wrists together, ready for the cuffs. Crying a river, "I didn't mean to do it", that sort of thing.'

'She admitted it?'

'Full confession. Said she was drunk and the kid was going on and on, being disgusting, disobedient, a real little terror. Ignored her mother . . .'

'Bothma.'

'Yes, the mother. And then Laurens lost it. Grabbed the pool cue, actually wanted to hit the kid on the backside, but because she was drunk . . .'

'Fingerprints on the pool cue?'

'Yes.'

'Only *her* prints?'

'What are you saying, Benny?'

'I'm not saying anything.'

'It was open and shut, Benny. She confessed, for fuck's sake. What more do you want?'

'Tim, I don't want to interfere. I'm just curious. I thought Bothma—'

'You're not just curious. What do you have that I don't know about?'

'Did you test her blood?'

'What for?'

'For alcohol.'

'Why the fuck would I need to do that? I could smell the booze. She fucking confessed. And then the prints came back and they were hers on the pool cue. That's enough, for fuck's sake. What's your story?'

'I don't have a story, Tim.'

'You fucking whiteys,' said Ngubane. 'You think you're the only people who can do detective work.'

'Tim, it's nothing to do with that.'

'Fuck you, Benny. It has everything to do with it.' Ngubane turned and walked away. 'At least I was able to smell the booze on her breath,' he said. 'Not everyone in this building could have done that.'

He disappeared down the corridor.

By eleven the assegai task team were still waiting for computers and extra telephone lines, but Griessel couldn't wait any longer.

He called the team together and began to allocate work. The most senior officer of the Domestic Violence Unit was a coloured woman, Captain Helena Louw. He made her group leader of research into previous cases where minors were the victims. He gave Bezuidenhout five uniformed men to help with the reinvestigation of the first two assegai victims. He took Cupido aside and spoke to him seriously and at length about his responsibility to investigate the assegai background. 'Even if you have to fly to Durban, Vaughn, but I want to know where it comes from. Make yourself the greatest expert on assegais in the history of mankind. Do you understand?'

'I understand.'

'Well then. Get going.' Then he raised his voice so that everyone could hear him. 'I will move between teams and check out a lot of the stuff myself. My cell phone number is up on the board. Anything, day or night. Call me.'

He walked out, down the stairs. He heard steps behind him, knew who it was.

Keyter stopped him just outside the main entrance.

'Benny . . .'

Griessel stood.

'What about me, Benny?'

'What about you, Jamie?'

'I haven't got a group.'

'How do you mean?'

'You haven't given me anything to do.'

'But that's not necessary. You already are the unofficial media liaison officer, Jaaa-mie.'

'Uh . . . I don't get it.'

'You know what I mean, you little shit. You talked to the papers behind my back. That means I can't trust you, Jaaa-mie. If you have a problem with me, talk to the sup. Tell him why I haven't given you anything to do.'

'It's this chick at the *Burger*, Benny. I've known her since the car syndicate case. She phones me non-stop, Benny. The whole day. You don't know what it's like . . .'

'Don't tell me I don't know what it's like. How long have I been a policeman?'

'No, what I mean . . .'

'I don't give a fuck what you mean, Jaaa-mie. You only drop me once.' He turned on his heel and strode to his car. He thought about self-control. He could not afford to hit a colleague.

He drove through Durbanville and out along the Fisantekraal road. He could never understand why this piece of the Cape was so ugly and without vineyards. Rooikrans bushes and Port Jackson trees and advertising hoardings for new housing developments. How the hell would the Cape handle all the new people? The road system was already overloaded – nowadays it was rush hour from morning till night.

He turned right on the R312, crossed the railway bridge and stopped on the gravel road that turned off to the left. There was a small hand-painted sign that read *High Grove Riding School. 4 km.* Assegai man would have seen it in the dark and begun to look for a place to leave his car. How far was he prepared to walk?

He drove slowly, trying to imagine what a person would see in the night. Not much. There were no lights nearby. Plenty of cover, the rooikrans grew in dense ugly thickets. He stopped awhile, took out his cell phone and rang Keyter.

'Detective Sergeant Jamie Keyter, Serious and Violent Crimes Unit.'

'What's with all that, Jamie?'

'Er . . . hello, Benny,' in a cautious tone. 'It's just in case.'

'In case of what?'

'Oh . . . um . . . you know . . .'

He didn't, but he left it at that. 'Do you want to help, Jamie?'

'I do, Benny.' Keen.

'Phone the weather office at the airport. I want to know what the phase of the moon was on Friday night. Whether it was overcast or not. That night, specifically, let's say between twelve and four.'

'The phase of the moon?'

'Yes, Jamie. Full moon, half moon, understand?'

'Okay, okay, I get it, Benny. I'll call you just now.'

'Thanks, Jamie.'

Roads turned off to other smallholdings with ridiculous names. *Eagle's Nest*. But an eagle wouldn't be seen dead here. *Sussex Heights* but it was flat. *Schoongesicht*. More like a dirty view. *The Lucky Horseshoe Ranch*. And then *High Grove Riding School*. If it were him, he would have driven past the turnoff. Gone quite a bit further on, perhaps, to check out the area. Then turned around.

He did exactly that. Nearly a kilometre beyond High Grove the road ended at a gate. He stopped twenty metres in front of the gate and got out. The southeaster blew his hair up in the air. There was an old gravel pit beyond the gate, desolate, obviously long out of use. The gate was locked.

If it were him, he would have parked here. You wouldn't want to turn into the High Grove driveway. Not if you had never been there before. You wouldn't know what to expect, or who would see you.

His phone rang.

'Griessel.'

'It's Jamie, Benny. The guy at the weather office said it was half moon, Benny, and zero per cent cloudy.'

'Zero per cent.'

'That's right.'

'Thank you, Jamie.'

'Is there anything else I can do, Benny?' Sucking up.

'Just stand by, Jamie. Just stand by.'

A clear night, light of a half moon. Enough to see by. Enough to keep your headlights switched off. He would have parked here. Somewhere around here, since this section of road would have no traffic, a dead end. The road up to the gate was too hard to show tracks. But he would have to have turned around if he came this far. Griessel began to walk down the boundary fence on the High Grove side of the road, searching for tracks on the sandy verge. Where would he have parked? Perhaps over there, where the rooikrans bushes leaned far over the fence. Bleached white grass tufts and sandy soil beside the fence.

Then he spotted the tracks, two vague rows of tyre marks. And in one spot the unmistakeable hollow where a tyre had stood still for a while.

Got you, you bastard!

He walked with care, building the picture in his mind. Assegai man had driven to the gravel-pit gate and turned around. Then the car would be facing in the direction of the High Grove turnoff. He would see the rooikrans thicket in the moonlight even with his lights turned off. He left the road about here and pulled up close to the fence. Opened the door and put a foot on the ground. Griessel searched for the footprint.

Nothing. Too much grass.

He squatted on his haunches. Only one cigarette butt, that was all he needed. A little trace of saliva for DNA testing. But there was nothing to find, only a fat black insect that scurried through the faded grass.

Still squatting, he phoned Keyter.

'I have another job for you.'

30

He knew it would be an hour or two before Forensics turned up. He wanted to determine assegai man's route to the house. Had he climbed through the fence, here, without knowing where the homestead was? Possible, but unlikely. Along the road would be better. He could see headlights coming from far off and have enough time to duck into the shadows.

Griessel walked slowly along the road. The wind blew from diagonally in front. The sun shone on his back, his shoes crunched on the gravel. He scanned the ground for footprints. He became aware of a pleasurable feeling. Just him here. On the trail of the murderer. Alone. He never had been a team player. He had done his best detection work on his own.

Now he was a task team leader.

Joubert was hiding Benny's alcoholism from the Area and Provincial Commissioners. Maybe he was lying about that because, despite the recent appointments of the top structures, the Force was like a small village. Everyone knew everything about everybody.

But why? Did Joubert feel sorry for Anna? Or was it loyalty to an old colleague who had come through the wars with him? The last two old soldiers, who had survived the antics of the old regime and affirmative action of the new era. Who had survived without becoming entangled in politics or monkey business.

No. It was because there was no one else. This morning he had sat and watched them. There were good people, enthusiastic young detectives, clever ones and hard workers and those with ambition, but they didn't have the experience. They didn't have twenty years of hard-grind policing behind them. Task team leader because he was a drunk-but-standing veteran.

But it was neither here nor there. He had better make it work, because it was all he had. *Last stand at the High Grove corral.*

He walked as far as the smallholding's driveway. No footprints. He turned up the drive, the wind now at his back. He knew the house was four hundred metres north. The question was, how long was it before the dogs had heard assegai man in the quiet of the night? He would have stopped, moved off the road and into hiding, at a place where he could overlook the yard.

The stables were ahead, on his left. A coloured man was busy with a pitchfork. The man didn't notice him. He kept on walking and could see the house now, two hundred metres further on. The place where Laurens had fallen.

The dogs began to bark.

He stopped. The workman looked up.

'Afternoon, sir,' said the man warily.

'Good afternoon.'

'Can I help you, sir?'

'I'm from the police,' he said.

'Oh.'

'I just want to look around.'

'Okay, sir.'

The garden began here, shrubs and bushes in old overgrown beds. He would have jumped in behind the shrubbery when the dogs started barking in the night. Then made his way through the plants till he was closer to the house. Plenty of camouflage. He followed the imaginary route searching for tracks. He estimated the distance and built a picture. You could survey the whole yard from behind the garden plants. You could watch a woman in her nightclothes, with a firearm in her hand. You could see the dogs that barked nervously in the darkness. Now you were close to the house, close to her. You ignore her shouts. 'Who's there?' Or perhaps a more threatening, 'Come out or I'll shoot!' You wait until her back is turned and then you rush out of the shadows. Grab the firearm. Raise the assegai. The dog bites at your trousers. You kick.

Something like that.

He looked for footprints in the flowerbed.

Nothing.

How likely was that? Or was the fucker cool and calm enough to wipe them out?

The labourer was still standing and watching.

'What is your name?'

'Willem, sir.'

He walked over to the man and put out his hand. 'I'm Benny Griessel.'

'Pleased to meet you, sir.'

'Bad business this, Willem.'

'A very bad business, sir.'

'First the child and then Miss Laurens.'

'Ai, sir, what will happen to us?'

'What do you mean, Willem?'

'It was Miss Laurens's place. Now it will be sold.'

'Maybe the new owners will be good people.'

'Maybe, sir.'

'Because I hear Laurens could be quite difficult.'

'Sir, she wasn't so difficult. She was good to us.'

'Oh.'

'The people around here pay minimum wage, but Miss Laurens paid us a thousand clean and we didn't have to pay for the house.'

'I believe she drank, Willem.'

'Hai, sir! That's not true.'

'And had a terrible temper . . .'

'No, sir . . .'

'No?'

'She was just strict.'

'Never got angry?'

Willem shook his head and glanced at the house. Elise Bothma stood there in her dressing gown just outside the homestead door.

It was late afternoon by the time he got back to the SVC building. He found Matt Joubert in his office with a stack of files in front of him.

'Do you have ten minutes, boss?'

'As much time as you need.'

'We have a possible tyre print of the assegai man's car.'

'From the smallholding?'

'Just outside, along the fence. Forensics have made a plaster mould. They will let us know. If you could hurry things up, I would be glad.'

'I'll give Ferreira a ring.'

'Matt, the Bothma child . . .'

'I hear you have a problem with it.'

'You hear?'

'Tim was here, just after lunch. Upset. He says you're a racist.'

'Fuck.'

'Relax, Benny. I talked to him. What's the problem?'

'It wasn't Laurens, Sup.'

'Why do you say that?'

'When we questioned Bothma on Saturday . . . There was something – I knew she was lying about something. I thought at first it was about Laurens's death. But then I got to thinking. Keyter questioned the labourers. This morning I went myself. And I don't think it was Laurens.'

'You think it was Bothma?'

'Yes.'

'And Laurens took the blame to protect her? Hell, Benny . . .'

'I know. But it happens.'

'Do you have proof?'

'I know Bothma is the one with the temper.'

'That's all?'

'Matt, I know it's too thin for the courts . . .'

'Benny, Laurens made a statement. She admitted guilt. Her fingerprints are on the billiard cue. And she's dead. We don't have a snowball's chance.'

'Give me an hour with Bothma . . .'

Joubert sat back in his chair and tapped a ballpoint pen on the folder in front of him. 'No, Benny. It's Tim's case. The best I can do is ask him to look at it carefully again. You have the assegai case.'

'It's the same thing. If Laurens was innocent, it means the vigilante punished the wrong one. It changes everything.'

'How so?'

Griessel waved his arm. 'The whole fucking world out there is on his side – the guy who reinstated the death penalty. The noble knight who is doing the pathetic police force's work. Even Bushy says we should leave him; let him get on with it . . . Say there is a witness somewhere. Someone who saw him. Or knows something. He could have a wife or a girlfriend, people who support him because they think he is doing the right thing.'

Joubert tapped his pen again. 'I hear what you're saying.'

'I hate that expression.'

'Benny, let me talk to Tim. That's the best I can do. But they will kill us in court.'

'We don't need the court. Not yet, in any case. All I want is for the media to know we suspect Bothma. And that Laurens might have been innocent.'

'I'll talk to Tim.'

'Thanks, Matt.' He turned to go.

'Margaret and I want to ask you to dinner,' said Joubert before he reached the door.

He stopped. 'Tonight?'

'Yes. Or tomorrow, if that suits you. She'll be cooking anyway.'

He realised that he had only had a tearoom sandwich since that morning. 'That would be . . .' But he envisioned himself at Joubert's family table surrounded by Matt's wife and children. He, alone. 'I . . . I can't, Matt.'

'I know things are crazy here.'

'It's not that.' He sat down on the chair opposite the commanding officer. 'It's just . . . I miss my family.'

'I understand.'

He suddenly needed to talk about it. 'The children . . . I had them yesterday.' He felt the emotion well up. He didn't want that now. He raised a hand to his eyes and dropped his head. He didn't want Joubert to see him like this.

'Benny . . .' He could hear the awkwardness.

'No, Matt, it's just . . . shit, I fucked up so much.'

'I understand, Benny.' Joubert got to his feet and came around the desk.

'No, fuck. Jissis. I mean . . . I don't know them, Matt.'

There was nothing Joubert could say, just put a hand on Griessel's shoulder.

'It's like I was away for fucking ten years. Jissis, Matt, and they are good children. Lovely.' He dragged a sleeve under his nose and sniffed. Joubert patted his shoulder rhythmically.

'I'm sorry, I didn't mean to bloody cry.'

'It's okay, Benny.'

'It's the withdrawal. Fucking emotional.'

'I'm proud of you. It's already, what, a week?'

'Nine days. That's fuck-all. What's that against ten years of damage?'

'It's going to be okay, Benny.'

'No, Matt. I don't know if it will ever be okay.'

He walked into the task group office in the old lecture hall. They were all sitting waiting for him. He was tired. It was as if the tears he had shed with Joubert had drained him. Captain Helena Louw motioned him closer. He went to her. 'How's it going, Captain?'

'Slowly, Inspector. We have—'

'My name is Benny.'

She nodded and pointed at the computer in front of her. 'We have started a database of all the unsolved cases where children were the victims. There are a lot . . .' She had a peaceful manner, a slow way of speaking. 'We start with the most serious. Murder. Rape. Sexual abuse. So far one hundred and sixty.'

Griessel whistled softly through his teeth.

'Yes, Inspector, it's bad. This is only the Peninsula. Lord knows how many in the whole country. We put in the names of the children, the next of kin and the suspects. We include the nature of the crime and the location. If it's gang-related, we mark it "B" because those are a bit different. We indicate the weapon, if there is one. And the dates of the offences. That's about it. Then we can start cross-referencing. As new information comes in, we can plot it against what we have.'

'Sounds good.'

'But will it help?'

'You never know what will help. But we can't afford not to do something.'

He didn't know if he had convinced her. 'Captain, we need two more items.'

'Call me Helena.'

'I want another field in the database. For vehicles. We have a tyre print. Maybe we'll get something from it.'

'That's good.'

'I'm not sure how we will handle the last thing. I wonder how he makes his choices. The murderer. How does he decide who the next victim will be?'

She nodded.

'There are two possibilities. One is that he is part of the system – policeman or prosecutor or something. But if you say there are more than a hundred and sixty . . . and the victims are too disparate regarding their location and their offences. I have a feeling he is using the media. Radio, or newspapers. Maybe TV. My trouble is I don't read the papers and I don't listen to the radio much. But I want to know when the victims were in the news. I want to know the date of the reports compared to the date of the assegai murders. Am I being clear?'

'Yes. Is it okay if we draw up a table on this blackboard?' She pointed at the front wall of the old lecture hall.

'That would work,' he said. 'Thanks.'

Griessel stood up. Jamie Keyter sat in the corner at the back and watched him in expectation. Cupido and Bezuidenhout sat beside each other, each at his own desk. He drew up a chair and sat down opposite them.

'The assegai is a stuff-up,' said Cupido. He leaned back and from behind him picked up a wrapped parcel, long and thin. He unrolled the brown paper and let the assegai drop onto the desktop. The shiny blade gleamed in the fluorescent light.

'Wallah!' he said. He pronounced the 'W' like 'Willy'.

'Voilà,' Bezuidenhout corrected him with a fake accent. 'It's a fucking French word. It means "check me out".'

'Since when are you the great language expert?'

'I'm just helping you not make a fool of yourself.'

Griessel sighed. 'The assegai . . .' he said.

'On loan from Pearson's African Art. In Long Street. Six hundred rand, VAT included. Imported from Zulu Dawn, a distributor in Pinetown. I talked to Mr Vijay Kumar, the sales manager at Zulu Dawn. He says they have agents who drive around and buy them up, there must be at least thirty places in KwaZulu that make them.'

'That's not *art*,' said Bezuidenhout.

'Bushy . . .' said Griessel.

'I'm just saying. Nowadays everything is art. I wouldn't pay fifty rand for that thing.'

'But you're not a German tourist with euros, pappa,' said Cupido. 'The fact of the matter is, our suspect could have bought it on any street corner. Pearson's say there are five or six chaps in the city alone who peddle them. And then there's another place or two on the Waterfront, two in Stellenbosch and one in the southern suburbs. The whiteys from Europe like them and the African masks like nobody's business. And ostrich eggs. They sell ostrich eggs for two hundred rand apiece. And they're empty . . .'

'I want Forensics to look at the thing, Vaughn . . .'

'Sorted. They're busy already. I took two on loan; I wanted to bring one in for you to see, Benny. Forensics will compare it with the chemical results of the three stab wounds.'

'Thanks, Vaughn. Good work.'

'You said it. But it doesn't look like I'm going to score a trip to Durbs.'

'You'll let me know what Forensics say?'

'Absolutely. Tomorrow I'm going to all the places that sell

assegais. See if they have sales records we can trace. Credit-card slips, tax invoices, anything. See what I can find.'

'I want those names in the database, please. They must be compared with the names Captain Louw has.'

'You got it, chief.'

Griessel turned to Bezuidenhout. 'Anything, Bushy?'

Bezuidenhout pulled a pile of files closer with an air of getting to the important stuff at last. 'I don't know.' He pulled them one by one off the pile. 'The Enver Davids rape,' he said. 'Strongest possibility so far. The baby's parents live in the informal settlement on the corner of Vanguard and Ridgeway. Residents call it Biko City; municipality doesn't call it anything. Father is unemployed, one of those men who stand on Durban Road in the morning and raise their hands if the builders come to pick up cheap labour. The mother works at a paper recycling plant in Stikland. They buy old cardboard boxes and turn them into toilet paper. Dawn soft. What the "dawn" has to do with "soft" who the fuck knows, but then I'm just a policeman. Anyway, they say they were together in their shack in Biko City the night of Davids' murder. But the father says, and I quote, "good riddance" about Davids' death. He says if he had known where to find the bastard, he would have stabbed him himself. But he says it wasn't him and he doesn't own an assegai. Their neighbours say they know nothing about that night. Saw nothing, heard nothing.'

'Hmm,' said Griessel.

Bezuidenhout took another file off the heap. 'Here's a list of all the children that were molested by Pretorius. Eleven. Can you believe it! Eleven that we know of. I have started phoning. Most of the parents are in the Bellville area. I'll start with them tomorrow. It will be a long day. I'll get the names onto the database too.'

'Use the uniform guys, Bushy.'

'Benny, I don't want to be funny, but I prefer to talk to them myself. The uniforms are very green.'

'Let them talk to neighbours or something. We have to use them.'

'What about Jamie?'

'What about him?'

'He's doing fuck-all.'

'Do you want him?'

'I could use him.'

'Bushy . . .' Then he changed his mind. 'Jamie,' he called in Keyter's direction.

'Yes, Benny?' Keyter responded eagerly. He leapt up, almost knocking his chair over.

'Tomorrow you go with Bushy.'

He had reached them. 'Okay, Benny.'

'Do the first few interviews with him. Is that understood?'

'Okay.'

'I want you to learn, Jamie. Then Bushy will let you know which you can do on your own.'

'I get it.'

'Jamie . . .'

'Yes, Benny.'

'Don't say that.'

'Don't say what?'

'Don't say "I get it". It irritates the hell out of me.'

'Okay, Benny.'

'It's Amerikaans anyway,' said Bezuidenhout.

'Amerikaans?' asked Cupido.

'Yes, you know. The way they say it in America.'

'An Americanism,' said Griessel wearily.

'That's what I said.'

Griessel said nothing.

'You said "Amerikaans" you clot. You're not a language expert's backside,' said Vaughn Cupido, getting up to leave.

31

He wanted to go home. Not to the flat, but to his *home*. Where his wife and children were. He had a pounding headache and a sluggishness as if his fuel had run out. But he steered the car towards the city. He wondered what the children were doing. And Anna.

Then he remembered. He wanted to phone her. About the thing that had been bothering him since yesterday. He took out his phone while driving and looked up her number on the list. He pressed the button and it rang.

'Hello, Benny.'

'Hello, Anna.'

'The children say you are still sober.'

'Anna . . . I want to know. Our agreement . . .'

'What agreement?'

'You said if I could stop drinking for six months . . .'

'That's right.'

'Then you'll take me back?'

She said nothing.

'Anna . . .'

'Benny, it's been barely a week.'

'It's been nine fucking days already.'

'You know I don't like it when you swear.'

'All I'm asking is if you are serious about the agreement?'

The line was quiet. Just as he was about to say something, he heard her. 'Stay off the booze for six months, Benny. Then we can talk.'

'Anna . . .' but she had disconnected him.

He didn't have the energy to lose his temper. Why was he

putting himself through this? Why was he fighting the drink? For a promise that was suddenly no longer a promise?

She had someone else. He knew it. He was a bloody detective; he could put two and two together.

It was her way of getting rid of him. And he wasn't going to fall for that. He wasn't going through this hell for fuck-all. No, damnit, not the way he felt now. One glass and the headache would be gone. Just one. Saliva flooded his mouth and he could already taste the alcohol. Two glasses for energy, for gas in the tank, for running the assegai task force. Three, and she could have as many toy boys as she liked.

He knew it would help. It would make everything better. Nobody need ever know. Just him and that sweet savour in his flat and then a decent night's rest. To deal with this thing with Anna. And the case. And the loneliness. He looked at his watch. The bottle stores would still be open.

When he arrived at his door with the bottles of Klipdrift and Coke in a plastic bag, there was a parcel on the threshold wrapped in aluminium foil. He unlocked the door first and put the bottles down before picking up the package. There was a note stuck to it. He unpeeled the sticky tape.

For the hard-working policeman. Enjoy. From Charmaine – 106.

Charmaine? What was the woman's case? He unwrapped the foil. It was a Pyrex dish with a lid. He lifted the lid. The fragrance of curry and rice steamed up to his nostrils. Boy, it smelt good. His hunger overcame him. Light-headed, he grabbed a spoon and sat down at the counter. He dug in the spoon and filled his mouth. Mutton curry. The meat was tender under his teeth; the flavour seeped through his body. Charmaine, Charmaine, whoever you are, you can cook, that's for sure. He took another spoonful, picked out a bay leaf with his finger, licked it off and put it aside. He took another mouthful. Delicious. Another. The curry was hot and fine beads of perspiration sprang out on his face. The spoon fell into a rhythm. Damn, he was hungry. He must make a plan about eating. He must take a sandwich to work.

He looked at the bottle of Klippies on the counter beside him. Soon. He would relax in his armchair with a full belly and take his drink as it should be: slowly, with savour.

He ate like a machine down to the last spoonful of curry, carefully scraped up a morsel of meat and a last bit of sauce and brought it to his mouth.

Damn. That was good. He pushed the dish away.

Now he would have to take it back to Charmaine at 106. He had a mental picture of a plump young woman. Why was that? Because her food was so good? Somewhat lonely? He got up to rinse the dish in the sink, then the lid and his spoon. He dried it off, found the foil, folded it neatly and placed it inside the dish. He fetched his keys, locked the door behind him and walked down the passage.

She knew he was a policeman. The caretaker must have told her. He would have to tell her he was a married man. And then he would have to explain why he was living here alone . . . He stopped in his tracks. Did he really need to go through all that shit? He could just leave the dish at her door.

No. He must thank her.

Perhaps she wouldn't be in, he hoped. Or asleep or something. He knocked as softly as possible, thought he could hear the sound of a television inside. Then the door opened.

She was small and she was old. The wrong side of seventy, he judged.

'You must be the policeman,' she said, and she smiled with a snow-white set of false teeth. 'I'm Charmaine Watson-Smith. Please come in.' Her accent was very British and her eyes were large behind the thick lenses of her spectacles.

'I'm Benny Griessel,' he said and his intonation sounded too Afrikaans to him.

'Pleased to meet you, Benny,' she said and took the dish from him. 'Did you enjoy it?'

'Very much.' The inside of the flat was identical to his, just full. Crammed with furniture, lots of portraits on the walls, full of bric-a-brac in display cabinets, on bookshelves and small coffee tables:

porcelain figurines and dolls and framed photographs. Crocheted cloths and books. A giant television set with some or other soapie on the go.

'Please take a seat, Benny,' she said and turned the sound of the television completely off.

'I don't want to interrupt your programme. I've actually just come to say thank you very much. It was very nice of you.' He sat down on the edge of a chair. He didn't want to stay long. His bottle awaited him. 'And the curry was fantastic.'

'Oh, it was a pleasure. You not having a wife . . .'

'I, uh, do. But we are – ' he searched for the word – '. . . separated.'

'I'm sorry to hear that. I sort of assumed, seeing your children yesterday . . .'

She didn't miss much. 'Yes,' he said.

She sat down opposite him. She seemed to be settling in for a long discussion. He didn't want . . .

'And what sort of policeman are you?'

'I'm with the Serious and Violent Crimes Unit. Detective Inspector.'

'Oh, I'm delighted to hear that. Just the right man for the job.'

'Oh? What job is that?'

She leaned forward and stage-whispered conspiratorially: 'There's a thief in this building.'

'Oh?'

'You see, I get the *Cape Times* every morning,' she said, still in that exaggerated whisper.

'Yes?' A light began to go on for him. There is no such thing as a free curry and rice.

'Delivered to my postbox at the entry hall. And somebody is stealing it. Not every morning, mind you. But often. I've tried everything. I've even watched the inner door from the garden. I believe you detectives would call it a stakeout, am I right?'

'That's right.'

'But the perpetrator is very elusive. I have made no headway.'

'My goodness,' he said. He had no idea what else to say.

'But now we have a real detective in the building,' she said with immense satisfaction and sat back in her chair.

Griessel's phone rang in his shirt pocket.

'I'm sorry,' he said. 'I have to take this.'

'Of course you do, my dear.'

He took the phone out. 'Griessel.'

'Benny, it's Anwar,' said Inspector Anwar Mohammed. 'We've got her.'

'Who?'

'Your assegai woman. Artemis.'

'Assegai woman?'

'Yup. She's made a complete statement.'

'Where are you?'

'Twenty-three Petunia Street in Bishop Lavis.'

He got up. 'You'll have to direct me. I'll phone you when I'm nearby.'

'Okay, Benny.'

He switched off the connection. 'I'm really sorry, but I have to go.'

'Of course. Duty calls, it seems.'

'Yes, it's this case I'm working on.'

'Well, Benny, it was wonderful meeting you.'

'And you too,' he said on the way to the door.

'Do you like roast lamb?'

'Oh, yes, but you mustn't go to any trouble.'

'No trouble,' she said with a big white smile. 'Now that you're working on my case.'

Petunia Street was in uproar. Under the streetlights stood a couple of hundred spectators, so that he had to drive slowly and wait for them to open a path for him. In front of number 23 rotated the blue lights of three police vans and the red ones of an ambulance. Forensics and the video team's two Toyota minibuses were parked halfway up the pavement. In front of the house next door were two minibuses from the SABC and e.tv.

He got out and had to push his way through the bystanders. On the lawn a coloured constable in uniform tried to stop him. He showed his plastic ID card and instructed him to call in more people for crowd control.

'There aren't any more, the entire station is here already,' was the reply.

Griessel walked through the open front door. Two uniformed members sat in the sitting room watching television.

'No, damnit,' Griessel said to them. 'The crowd is about to come in the door and you sit here watching TV?'

'Don't worry,' one answered. 'This is Bishop Lavis. The people are curious, but decent.'

Anwar Mohammed heard his voice and came out of an inner room.

'Get these people outside, Anwar, this is a fucking crime scene.'

'You heard the inspector, hey?'

The men stood up reluctantly. 'But it's *Frasier*,' said one, pointing at the screen.

'I don't care what it is. Go and do your work,' said Mohammed. Then, to Griessel: 'The victim is here, Benny.' He led the way to the kitchen.

Griessel saw the blood first – a thick gay arc of red starting on the kitchen cupboard door and sweeping up, all the way to the ceiling. To the right against the fridge and stove was more blood in the distinctive spatters of a severed artery. A man lay in a foetal position in the corner of the smallish room. The two members of the video team were setting up lights to film the scene. The light made the reddish-brown blood on the victim's shirt glisten. There were a few rips in the material. Beside him lay an assegai. The wooden shaft was about a metre long, the bloodied blade about thirty centimetres long and three or four centimetres wide.

'This is not the assegai man,' said Griessel.

'How can you know?'

'Whole MO is different, Anwar. And this blade is too small.'

'You better come talk to the girl.'

'The girl?'

'Nineteen. And pretty.' Mohammed gestured with his head to the door. He walked ahead.

She was sitting in the dining room with her head in her hands. There was blood on her arms. Griessel walked around the table and pulled out the chair beside her and sat down. Mohammed stood behind him.

'Miss Ravens,' said Mohammed softly.

She raised her head from her hands and looked at Griessel. He could see she was pretty, a delicate face with deep, dark, nearly black eyes.

'Good evening,' he said.

She just nodded.

'My name is Benny Griessel.'

No reaction.

'Miss Ravens, this inspector has been working on the assegai case. Tell him about the others,' said Mohammed.

'It was me,' she said. Griessel saw her eyes were unfocused. Her hands trembled slightly.

'Who is the man in there?' he asked.

'That's my dada.'

'You did that?'

She nodded. 'I did.'

'Why?'

She slowly blinked her big eyes.

'What did he do?'

She was looking at Griessel but he wasn't sure she was seeing him. When she spoke there was surprising strength in her voice, as if it belonged to someone else. 'He would come and sleep with me. For twelve years. And I wasn't allowed to tell anyone.'

Griessel could hear the anger.

'And then you read about the man with the assegai?'

'It's not a man. It's a woman. It's me.'

'I told you,' said Mohammed.

'Where did you get this assegai?'

'At the station.'

'Which station?'

'The station in Cape Town.'

'At the station flea market?'

She nodded.

'When did you buy it?'

'Yesterday.'

'Yesterday?' queried Mohammed.

'And then you waited for him to come home tonight?'

'He wouldn't stop. I asked him to stop. I asked him nicely.'

'Did you two live here alone?'

'My mother died. Twelve years ago.'

'Miss Ravens, if you only bought the assegai yesterday, how could you have killed the other people?'

Her black eyes moved over Griessel's face. Then she looked away. 'I saw it on TV. Then I knew. It's me.'

He put out a hand and rested it on her shoulder. She jerked away and in her eyes he saw momentary fear. Or hate, he couldn't differentiate. He dropped his hand.

'I called SS,' said Mohammed quietly behind him.

'That's good, Anwar,' he said. Social Services could handle her better. He rose and led Mohammed out by the elbow. In the kitchen, beside the body, he said: 'Watch her. Don't leave her alone.'

Before Mohammed could reply, they heard Pagel's voice in the door. 'Evening, Nikita, evening, Anwar.'

'Evening, Prof.'

The pathologist was in evening wear with his case in his hand. He shuffled past the video team and squatted down beside the man on the floor.

'This is not our assegai, Nikita,' he said as he opened his case.

'I know, Prof.'

'Benny,' a voice called from the sitting room.

'Here,' he said.

Cloete, the officer from Public Relations, walked in. 'Hell, but it's busy here.' He looked at the victim. 'He's copped it.'

'Oh, so now you're a pathologist too?' asked one of the video men.

'Look out, Prof, Cloete's after your job,' said the other.

'That's because Benny's sober now. One less job opportunity for Cloete.'

'But Benny doesn't *look* better.'

'Shit, but you're funny tonight,' said Griessel. To Cloete: 'Come, we'll talk in there.' He saw Mohammed following them. 'Anwar, get someone to watch the girl before you come.'

'Will she try to escape?' asked Cloete.

'That's not what I'm afraid of,' said Griessel, and sat down on a chair in the sitting room. The television was still showing a situation comedy. Laughter sounded. Griessel leaned forward and turned it off.

'Did you see the television people outside?'

Griessel nodded. Before he could say more the cell phone in his pocket rang. 'Excuse me,' he said to Cloete as he took the call: 'Griessel.'

'It's Tim Ngubane. Joubert says you're looking for bait. For the assegai thing . . .'

'Yes.' A little surprised at the friendly tone.

'How does a Colombian drug lord who's got a thing for little girls grab you?'

'It sounds good, Tim.'

'Good? It's perfect. And I've got it for you.'

'Where are you?'

'Camps Bay, home to the rich and famous.'

'I'll come as soon as I can.'

Before he could put the phone away, Cloete forged ahead. He pointed outside: 'Someone told them it was Artemis. The papers are here too. I had to hear it from them.' Accusing.

'I just got here myself.'

'I didn't say it was you, but the fuck knows . . .'

'Cloete, I'm sorry about yesterday. It was one of my team members that talked to the media. It won't happen again.'

'What do you want, Benny?'

'What do you mean?'

'The day you apologise is the day you want something. What's going on here?'

'This is a difficult one. Nineteen-year-old girl stabbed her father with an assegai because he molested her. But she didn't commit the other murders.'

'Are you sure?'

'Absolutely.'

'How do you want me to handle this?'

'Cloete, there are politics involved with the assegai thing. Between you and me, the girl in there was partly inspired by our murderer, if you know what I mean. But if you tell the media that, the commissioner will have a stroke, because he's under pressure from above.'

'The minister?'

'Parliamentary Commission.'

'Fuck.'

'You must talk to Anwar, too, so we all have the same story. I feel we should only mention a domestic fight and a sharp instrument. Don't let on about the weapon for now.'

'That's not the thing you want from me, Benny, is it?'

'No, you're right. I need another favour.'

Cloete shook his head in disbelief. 'The fuck knows, I am nothing but a whore. A police prostitute, that's what I am.'

32

The town was too small.

He couldn't reconnoitre. This afternoon when he drove down the long curve of the main street there were eyes on him. The eyes of coloured people in front of a few cafés, the eyes of black petrol attendants at the filling station, which consisted of a couple of pumps and a dilapidated caravan. The eyes of Uniondale's few white residents watering their dry gardens with hosepipes.

Thobela knew he had only one chance to find the house. He wouldn't be able to look around; he wouldn't be able to drive up and down. Because here everyone knew about the Scholtz scandal and they would remember a black man driving a pick-up – a strange black man in a place where everyone knew everybody.

He had to be content with a signboard in the main street indicating the road. It was enough. He took the R339 out of the town, the one running east towards the mountain. As the road curved around the town, he saw there was a place to park with pepper trees and clefts in the ridges beside the road where he could leave the vehicle in the dark. He drove on, through the pass, along the Kamannasie River, and at twelve kilometres he filled up with petrol beside the cooperative at Avontuur.

Where was he going? asked the Xhosa petrol attendant.

Port Elizabeth.

So why are you taking *this* road?

Because it is quiet.

Safe journey, my brother.

The petrol attendant would remember him. And that forced him to drive back to the main road and turn right. Towards the

Langkloof, because the man's eyes could follow him. If he deviated from that route, the man would wonder why and remember him even better.

In any case he had to pass the time until dark. He made a long detour. Gravel roads, past game farms and eventually back via the pass. To this spot above Uniondale where he stood beside the pick-up in the moonlight and watched the town lights below. He would have to walk through the veld and over the ridge. Sneak. Between the houses. He would have to avoid dogs. He must find the right house. He must go in and do what he had to do. And then come back and drive away.

It would be hard. He had too little information about the lay of the land and the position of the house. He didn't even know if they would be home.

Leave. Now. The risk was too great. The town was too small.

He took the assegai from behind the seat. He stood on a rock and looked over the town. His fingertips stroked the smooth wooden shaft.

He had all night.

Between Bishop Lavis and Camps Bay his cell phone rang twice.

First it was Greyling from Forensics: 'Benny, your man drives a pick-up.'

'Oh, yes?'

'And if we are not mistaken, it's a four-by-two with diff lock. Probably a double cab. Because the imprint is from a RTSA Wrangler. A Goodyear 215/14.'

'What make is the pick-up?'

'Hell, no, it's impossible to say, the whole lot come out of the factory with the Wrangler – Ford and Mazda, Izuzu, Toyota, you name it.'

'How do you know it's not an ordinary pick-up?'

'Your ordinary one comes out with the CV 2000 from Good-year, which is a 195/14, the G 22, they call it. Trouble is, nearly every minibus-taxi comes out with the same tyre, so it's chaos. And your four-by-four is a 215/15. But this print is definitely a

215/14, which is put on the four-by-twos. And eighty per cent of your four-by-twos are double cabs or these other things with only two doors, the Club Cabs. Which also means our suspect is not a poor man, because a double cab costs the price of a farm these days.'

'Unless it's stolen.'

'Unless it's stolen, yes.'

'Thanks, Arrie.'

'Pleasure, Benny.'

Before he had time to ponder the new evidence, the phone rang again.

'Hi, Dad.' It was Fritz.

'Hi, Fritz.'

'What're you doing, Dad?' His son wanted to chat?

'Working. It's a circus today. Everything is happening at once.'

'With the vigilante? Has he nailed someone else?'

'No, not him. Someone else who thinks they are the assegai man.'

'Cool!'

Griessel laughed. 'You think it's cool?'

'Definitely. But I actually wanted to know if you listened to the CD, Dad.'

Damn. He had completely forgotten about the music. 'I only realised last night that I didn't have a CD player. And there wasn't time today to get one. It was a madhouse . . .'

'It's okay.' But he detected disappointment. 'If you want it, I've got a portable CD player. The bass isn't too great.'

'Thanks, Fritz, but I must get something for the flat. I'll make a plan tomorrow, I promise.'

'Great. And then let me know.'

'The minute I have listened to it.'

'Dad, don't work too hard. And Carla sends her love and says yesterday was cool.'

'Thanks, Fritz. Give her my love too.'

'Okay, Dad. Bye.'

'Sleep well.'

He sat behind the wheel and stared into the dark. Emotion welled up in him. Maybe Anna didn't want him any more, but the children did. Despite all the harm he had done.

The dramatic difference between the crime scenes at Bishop Lavis and Camps Bay was immediately apparent. In the wealthy neighbourhood there were practically no onlookers, but at least twice as many police vehicles. The uniformed officers huddled on the sidewalk as if they expected a riot.

He had to drive down the street a bit to find parking and walk back up the slope. All the houses were three storeys high to see the now invisible view of the Atlantic Ocean. They were all in the same style of concrete and glass – modern palaces that stood empty most of the year while their owners were in London or Zurich or Munich busy raking in the euros.

At the steps a uniform stopped him. 'Sorry, Inspector Ngubane only wants key personnel inside,' the constable said.

He took out his identity card from his wallet and showed it. 'Why are there so many people here?'

'Because of the drugs, Inspector. We have to help move them when they are finished.'

He walked up to the front door and looked in. It was as big as a theatre. Two or three sitting areas on different levels, a dining area and, to the right, on the balcony side, a sparkling blue indoor swimming pool. Two teams of Forensics were busy searching for bloodstains with ultraviolet lights. On the uppermost level, on a long leather couch, four men sat in a neat row, handcuffed and heads bowed as if they felt remorse already. Beside them stood uniformed policemen, each with a gun on his arm. Griessel went up.

'Where is Inspector Ngubane?' he asked one of the uniforms.

'Top floor,' one indicated.

'Which one of these fuckers messed with the girl?'

'These are just the gofers,' said the uniform. 'The inspector is busy with the big chief. And it's not just about *messing* with the kid.'

'Oh?'

'The child has disappeared . . .'

'How do I get up there?'

'The stairs are there,' pointed the constable with the stock of his shotgun.

In the first-floor passage, Timothy Ngubane stood and argued with a large white detective. Griessel recognised him from the faded blue and white cloth hat sporting a red disa flower emblem and the word *WP Rugby*: Senior Superintendent Wilhelm 'Boef' Beukes, a former member of the old Murder and Robbery and Narcotics branches and now a specialist in organised crime.

'Why not? The girl is not in there.'

'There might be evidence in there, Sup, and I can't risk . . .' He spotted Griessel. 'Benny,' he said with a degree of relief.

'Hi, Tim. Boef, how are you?'

'Crap, thanks. Drugs haul of the decade and I have to stand in line.'

'Finding the child has priority, Sup,' said Ngubane.

'But she's not here. You already know that.'

'But there might be evidence down there. All I'm asking is that you wait.'

'Get your butts moving,' said Beukes and stalked off down the passage.

Ngubane sighed deeply and at length. 'It's been an amazing night,' he said to Griessel. 'Absolutely amazing. I've got everybody down there—'

'Down where?'

'There's this storeroom in the basement with more drugs than anyone's ever seen, and the entire SAPS is here – the commercial branch and organised crime and the drugs guy from Forensics, and they all have their own video teams and photographers, and I can't let them in, because there might be leads to where the girl is.'

'And the suspect?'

'He's in here.' Ngubane pointed at the door behind him. 'And he's not talking.'

'Can I go in?'

Ngubane opened the door. Griessel looked in. It was not a big room. Untidy. A man sat on a cardboard box. Thick black hair, drooping black moustache, white shirt unbuttoned, the breast pocket seemed torn. A red bruise on the cheekbone.

'*Sy naam is Carlos*,' began Ngubane deliberately in Afrikaans so that Sangrenegra would not understand and took a small notebook from his trouser pocket. 'Carlos San . . . gre . . . ne . . . gra,' he carefully enunciated the syllables.

'Fuck you,' said Sangrenegra with venom.

'Did someone beat him up?' Griessel spoke Afrikaans.

'The mother. Of the little girl. He's a Colombian. His visa . . . expired long ago.'

'What happened, Tim?'

'Come in. I don't want to leave the cunt alone.'

'You curse very prettily in Afrikaans.'

Ngubane moved into the room ahead of Griessel. 'I'm well coached.' He closed the door behind him. It looked as if it was meant to be a study. Shelves against the wall, dark glowing wood, but empty. Boxes on the floor.

'What's in the boxes?' Griessel asked.

'Look,' said Ngubane and sat down on the single chair, an expensive piece of office furniture with a high back and brown leather.

Griessel opened one of the boxes. There were books in it. He took one out. *A Tale of Two Cities* was printed in gold lettering on the spine of the book.

'Look inside.'

He opened it. There were no pages – just a plastic filler with sides that looked like paper.

'Not a great reader are you, Carlos?' said Griessel.

'Fuck you.'

'A woman phoned Caledon Square about eight o'clock.' Ngubane continued in Afrikaans. 'She was crying. She said her child had been abducted and she knew who it was. They sent a team to the flat in Belle Ombre Street and found the lady. She was confused and bleeding from the head and she said a man had assaulted her and taken her child. She was . . .' he searched for the Afrikaans word.

'Unconscious.'

Ngubane nodded. 'She gave the man's name and this address and she said he had raped her too. She said she knew him and he liked children . . . you know? And then she told us he's a drug lord.'

Griessel nodded and turned to look at Sangrenegra. The brown eyes smouldered. He was a lean man, veins prominent on his forearms, dressed in blue denim and trainers. His hands were cuffed behind his back.

'The uniforms phoned the station commander and the SC phoned us and I was on call and talked to Joubert and got the task force. Then we were all here and the task force arrived by helicopter and the works. We found five men here. Carlos and those four downstairs. They found the drugs in the basement and the girl's clothes in this one's room. Then they found blood in his BMW and a dog, one of those stuffed toys, but no child and this cunt won't talk. He says he knows nothing.'

'The child. It's a little girl?'

'Three years old. Three.'

Griessel felt a red flood of revulsion. 'Where is she?' he asked Carlos.

'Fuck you.'

He jumped up and grabbed the man by the hair, jerked his head back and kept pulling the dark locks. He shoved his face close up to Sangrenegra. 'Where is she, you piece of shit?'

'I don't know!'

Griessel jerked his hair. Sangrenegra winced. 'She lie. The whore, she lie. I know nothing.'

'How did the girl's clothes get in your room, you cunt?' He jerked again as hard as he could as frustration gnawed at him.

'She put it there. She is a whore. She was *my* whore.'

'Jissis,' said Griessel with disgust and gave the hair one last pull before he left him. His hand felt greasy. He wiped it off on Sangrenegra's shirt. 'You lie. You cunt.'

'I've been through that process,' said Ngubane behind him in a calm voice, as if nothing had happened.

'Ask my men,' said Sangrenegra.

Griessel laughed without humour. 'Who gave you this?' he asked and shoved a finger hard onto the bruise on Carlos's cheek.

The Colombian spat at him. Griessel drew his hand back to slap him.

'He said he visited the complainant today,' Ngubane said. 'He says she is a prostitute. She invited him to her flat. The child wasn't there. Then she hit him for no reason. So he hit her back.'

'That's his story?'

'That's his story?'

'And the mother?'

'Social Services are with her. She's . . . traumatised.'

'What do you think, Tim?' Griessel realised he was out of breath. He sat down on a box.

'The child was in his car, Benny. The blood. And the dog. She *was* there. He drove somewhere with her. We have two hours from the assault on the complainant until we got here. He took the child somewhere. He thought because the mother is a call girl, he could do what he wanted. But something happened in the car. The child got scared, or something. So he cut her. That's what the blood looks like. It's against the armrest of the back seat. Looks like an –' he searched for the Afrikaans word again – '. . . artery. Then he knew he was in trouble. He must have got rid of the kid.'

'Jissis.'

'Yes,' said Ngubane.

Griessel looked at Sangrenegra. Carlos stared back, with disdain.

'I don't think we should be optimistic about the child. If she was alive, this cunt would want to bargain.'

'Can I try something?' Griessel asked.

'Please,' said Ngubane.

'Carlos,' said Griessel, 'have you heard of Artemis?'

'Fuck you.'

'Let me tell you a story, Carlos. There is this guy out there. He has a big assegai. Do you know what an assegai is, Carlos? It's a spear. A Zulu weapon. With a long blade, very sharp. Now, this guy is a real problem for us, because he is killing people. And do you know who he kills, Carlos? He is killing people who fuck with children. Sure you haven't heard about this, Carlos?'

'Fuck you.'

'We are trying to catch this guy. Because he is breaking the law. But with you we can make an exception. So this is what I'm going to do. I'm going to tell all the newspapers and the television that you have abducted this beautiful little girl, Carlos. I will give them your address. And we will publish a photograph of you. And I'm going to see to it that you make bail. And I'm going to keep all your friends in jail, and leave you here, in this big house, all alone. We will sit outside to make sure you don't go back to Colombia. And we will wait for the guy with the spear to find you.'

'Fuck you.'

'No, Carlos. You are the one who is fucked. Think about it. Because when he comes, we will look the other way.'

Sangrenegra said nothing, just stared at Griessel.

'This assegai guy, he has killed three people. One stab, right through the heart. With that long blade.'

No reaction.

'Tell me where the girl is. And it can be different.'

Carlos just stared at him.

'You want to die, Carlos? Just tell me where the girl is.'

For a moment Sangrenegra hesitated. Then he shouted, in a shrill voice: 'Carlos don't know! Carlos don't fucking know!'

33

When they shoved Sangrenegra into the back of a police van and clanged the door shut, Ngubane said: 'I owe you an apology, Benny.'

'Oh?'

'About this morning.' Griessel realised he had already forgotten the incident; it had been a long day.

'We get a little paranoid, I suppose,' said Ngubane. 'Some of the white cops . . . they think we're shit.'

Griessel said nothing.

'I went to visit Cliffy Mketsu. In hospital. He says you're not like that.'

Griessel wanted to add that no, he wasn't like that. His problem was that he thought *everyone* was crap. 'How's Cliffy doing?'

'Good. He says you have more experience than the rest of us combined. So I want to ask you, Benny, what more can I do here? How do I find this kid?'

He looked at Ngubane, at the neat suit, the white shirt and red tie, at the man's ease with himself. In the back of his mind a light began to shine.

'Are there other properties, Tim? These drug guys, they have more than one place. They have contingency plans.'

'Right.'

'Talk to Beukes. They must have known about Sangrenegra. They will know about other places.'

'Right.'

'Has Forensics been to the mother's place?'

He nodded. 'They got his prints there. And they drew the mother's blood. For DNA comparison with the blood in the car. They say that way they can tell if it belongs to the kid.'

'I don't think she's alive, Tim.'

'I know.'

They stood in silence a moment. 'Can I go and see the mother?'

'Sure. Are you going to use this guy as bait?'

'He's perfect. But I have to talk to the mother. And then we'll have to talk to the sup, because Organised Crime is involved, and I can tell you now, they won't like it.'

'Fuck them.'

Griessel chuckled. 'That's what I was thinking too.'

When he drove through the city towards Tamboerskloof, his thoughts jumped between Boef Beukes and Timothy Ngubane and the children he saw in Long Street. At half-past eleven at night there were children everywhere he looked. Teenagers on a fucking Monday night at the top end of Long Street, at the clubs and restaurants and cafés. They stood on the pavements with glasses and cigarettes in their hands, small groups huddled beside parked cars. He wondered where their parents were. Whether they knew where their children were. He realised he did not know where his own children were. But surely Anna knew. If she were at home.

Beukes. Who had worked with him in the old days. Who had been a drinking partner. When his children were small and he was still whole. What the hell had happened? How had he progressed from drinks with the boys to a full-blown alcoholic?

He had started drinking when Murder and Robbery was still located in Bellville South. The President in Parow had been the watering hole, not because it was anything like a presidential hotel, but there would always be a policeman leaning on the long mahogany bar, no matter what time of the day you turned up there. Or that other place beyond Sanlam in Stikland that made those delicious pizzas, the Glockenberg or something, Lord, that was a lifetime ago. The Glocken*burg*. There was a Spur Steak Ranch there now, but in those days it had been a colossal tavern. One night, thoroughly drunk, he had climbed on the stage and told the band they must cut the crap and play real rock 'n' roll and give me that bass, do you know 'Blue Suede Shoes'? His colleagues at the big table had shouted and kicked up a row and clapped and the four-piece band had nervously said yes, they knew it, young Afrikaner fuckers with soft beards and long hair who played 'Smokie' and he put the bass around his neck and got behind the mike and sang 'One for the money . . .' and they were off and rocking, between the commotion from the floor and the orchestra's relief that he was not hopeless. They were cooking; they thrashed that fuckin' song and people came in from the bar and from outside. And that Benny Griessel had run his fingers up and down the neck of the bass guitar and he laid down a fucking carpet of bass for the rock 'n' roll and when they had finished everybody screamed for more, more, more. So he let rip. Elvis songs. And he sweated and played and sang till who knows what time, and Anna came looking for him, he saw her at the back of the Glock. At first angry with arms folded tight, where was her husband, look at the time. But the music melted her too, she loosened up and her hips began to sway and she clapped too and screamed: 'Go, Benny, go!' because that was *her* Benny up there on the fucking stage, *her* Benny.

Lord, that was a lifetime ago. He hadn't been an alky then, just a hard-drinking detective. Like the rest of them. Just like Matt Joubert and Boef Beukes and fat Sergeant Tony O'Grady, the whole damn lot of them. They drank hard because, hell, they worked hard, back then in the late eighties. Worked like slaves while the whole world shat on them. Necklace murders, old people murdered, gays murdered, gangs, armed robbery wherever you turned. It never stopped. And if you said you were a policeman, the room would fall silent and everyone looked at you as if you were lower than lobster crap, and that, they always said, was as low as you could go.

Then he had been as Tim Ngubane was now. At ease with himself. Lord, and he *could* work. Hard, yes. But clever. He nailed them, murderers and bank robbers and kidnappers. He was ruthless and enthusiastic. He was light of foot. That was the thing – he had danced when the others plodded. He was different. And he thought he would be like that always. But then all the shit had a way of overwhelming you.

Maybe that was the problem. Maybe the booze only got the dancers; look at Beukes and Joubert, they don't drink like fish, they plod along still. And he? He was fucked. But there in the back of his mind the germ of an idea remained that he was better than them all, that he was the best fucking detective in the country, end of story.

Then he laughed at himself there behind the steering wheel, at the top end of Long Street near the swimming baths, because he was a wreck, a drunkard, a guy who had bought a bottle of Klippies an hour ago after nine days of sobriety and only half an hour ago had lost control with the Colombian because he was carrying so much shit around with him and here he was, thinking he was the be-all and end-all.

So what had happened? Between Boef Beukes and the Glockenburg and now? What the fuck happened? He had reached Belle Ombre Street and there was no parking so he pulled half onto the pavement.

Before he opened the door, he thought about the body tonight in Bishop Lavis. There had been no death screams in his head. No dreadful voices.

Why not? Where had they gone? Was it part of his drinking; was it the alcohol?

He paused a few moments longer and then pushed open the door, because he had no answers. The building had ten or twelve floors so he took the lift. There were two black policemen in civilian clothes at the door, each with a shotgun. Griessel asked who they were. One said they were from Organised Crime and that Boef Beukes had sent them, since she would be a target now.

'Did you know about Sangrenegra before this happened?'

'You should talk to Beukes.'

He nodded and opened the door. A young woman jumped up in the sitting room and came over to him. 'Did you find her?' she asked, and he could hear the hysteria just below the surface. Behind her on the couch sat two police officers of the gentler sort, smaller and thinner, with caring hands folded sympathetically on their laps. Social Services. The members of the Force who appear on the scene when all the shit is already cleared away. A man and a woman.

'Not yet,' he said.

She stood in the middle of the room and uttered a sound. He could see her face was swollen and there was a cut that someone had treated. Her eyes were red with weeping. She balled her fists and her shoulders drooped. The coloured woman from SS got up and came over to her and said: 'Come and sit down, it's better if you sit.'

'My name is Benny Griessel,' he said and held out his hand.

She shook it and said, 'Christine van Rooyen.' He thought that she didn't look like your usual whore. But then he smelt her, a mixture of perfume and sweat; they all smelt like that, it didn't wash out.

But she looked different from the ones he knew. He searched for the reason. She was tall, as tall as he was. Not scrawny, strongly built. Her skin was smooth. But that wasn't it.

He said he worked with Ngubane and he knew it was a difficult time for her. But perhaps there was something she knew that could help. She said he must come through and she went over to a sliding door and pushed it wider. It led onto a balcony and she sat on one of the white plastic chairs. He got the idea that she wanted to get away from the SS people and that said something. He joined her on another of the chairs and asked her how well she knew Sangrenegra.

'He was my client.' He noticed the unusual shape of her eyes. They reminded him of almonds.

'A regular client?'

In the light from the sitting room he could only see her right hand. It was on the arm of the chair, finger folded into the palm, the nails pressing into the flesh.

'At first he was like the rest,' she said. 'Nothing funny. Then he told me about the drugs. And when he found out I had a child . . .'

'Do you know what we found at his house?'

She nodded. 'The black man phoned.'

'Did Carlos ever take you to other places? Other houses?'

'No.'

'Have you any idea where he would have taken . . . er . . . your daughter?'

'Sonia,' she said. 'My daughter's name is Sonia.'

The fingers moved in her palm, the nails dug deeper. He wanted to reach out to her. 'Where would he have taken Sonia?'

She shook her head back and forth. She did not know. Then she said: 'I won't see her again.' With the calm that only absolute despair can bring.

In the early hours it was only five minutes' drive from Belle Ombre to his flat. The first thing he saw when he switched on the light was the brandy bottle. It stood on the breakfast counter like a sentry watching over the room.

He locked the door behind him and picked up the bottle and turned it in his hands. He examined the clock on the label and the golden brown liquid within. He imagined the effect of the alcohol in his fibres, light-headedness, and effervescence just under his skull.

He put down the bottle as if it were sacred.

He should open the bottle and pour the brandy down the sink. But then he would smell it and he wouldn't be able to resist it.

Get control first. He rested his palms on the counter and took deep breaths.

Lord, it had been close, earlier that evening.

Only his hunger had stopped him getting drunk.

He took another deep breath.

Fritz was going to phone him to find out if he had listened to the CD and he would have been drunk and his son would have known. That would have been bad. He considered his son's voice. It wasn't so much the boy's interest in his opinion about the music. Something else. A craving. A longing. A desire to make contact with his father. To have a bond with him. *We never had a father.* His son wanted a father now. So badly. He had been so close to fucking it up. So close.

He drew another deep breath and opened a kitchen cupboard. It was empty inside. He quickly picked up the bottle and put it inside and shut the door. He went upstairs. He didn't feel so tired any more. Second wind, when your brain gets so busy you just keep on going, when your thoughts jump from one thing to another.

He showered and got into bed and shut his eyes. He could see the prostitute and he felt a physical reaction, tumescence and he thought, hello, hello, hello? He felt guilty, as she had just lost her child and this was his reaction. But it was odd because whores had never done it for him. He knew enough of them. They were in a profession that was a magnet for trouble; they worked in a world that was just one small step away from serious crime. And they were all more or less the same – regardless of the fee they charged.

There was something about Christine van Rooyen that set her apart from the others he knew. But what? Then when he lined her up against the rest he identified it. Prostitutes, from the Sea Point streetwalkers to the few who serviced the tourists for big money in the Radisson, had two things in common. That distinctive bitter-sweet smell. And the damage. They had an atmosphere of depression. Like a house, a neglected house, where someone still lives, but you can see from the decay that they don't really care any more.

This one was not like that. Or less so. There was a light still burning.

But that wasn't what was giving him an erection. It was something else. The body? The eyes?

Hell, he had never once been unfaithful to Anna. Except by boozing. Maybe Anna reasoned like that: he was unfaithful to her because he loved alcohol with an all-encompassing passion. So she was justified in looking elsewhere. His head said she had the right, but the green monster sprang to life, made him writhe in the bed. He would pulp the fucker. If he caught them. If he should walk into his house and bedroom and they were busy . . . He saw the scene too clearly. He turned over violently; pulled up the sheet, thrust his head under the pillow. He did not want to see. Some or other handsome young shit pumping his wife and he could see Anna's face, her ecstasy, that small private sublime smile that told him she

was in her own little world of pleasure and her voice, he remembered her voice, the whispering. Yes, Benny, yes, Benny, yes,
Benny. But now she would be saying someone else's name and he
leapt up and stood beside the bed and he knew: he would shoot the
fucker. He had to phone her. *Now*. He had to drink. He must get
the bottle out of the kitchen cupboard. He took a step toward the
wardrobe. He clenched his fist and stopped himself.

Get a hold of yourself, he said out loud.

He felt the absence below. His erection was gone.

No fucking wonder.

It was an old stone house with a corrugated iron roof. He climbed a
sagging wire boundary fence and had to deviate around the carcass
of a Ford single cab pick-up on blocks before he could make out
the number on one of the pillars of the veranda. The seven hung
askew.

It was dark inside. Thobela retraced his steps to the back door.
He turned the knob. It was open. He went in, closing the door
quietly behind him, assegai in his left hand. He was in the kitchen.
There was an odour in the house. Musty, like fish paste. He
allowed his eyes to grow accustomed to the deeper dark inside.
Then he heard a sound from the next room.

Once the two from the police force's Social Services had gone, she
took a big flask of coffee and two mugs to the armed men on guard
outside her door. Then she locked the door and went out onto the
balcony.

The city lay before her, a creature with a thousand glittering
eyes that breathed more slowly and deeply in the depths of
night. She gripped the white railing feeling the cold metal in her
hands. She thought about her child. Sonia's eyes pleading with
her.

It was her fault. She was responsible for her child's fear.

From the sitting room he heard a snore like the grunt of a boar:
short, crude and powerful.

Thobela peered around the doorframe and saw the man on the couch under a blanket.

Where was the woman?

The Scholtzes. Their two-year-old son had died in hospital in Oudtshoorn two weeks ago from a brain haemorrhage.

The district surgeon had found lesions on the tiny organs and thin fragile ribs and ulna, cheekbones and skull. From them he had reconstructed a jigsaw of abuse. 'The worst I have seen in fifteen years as coroner,' the Sunday paper had quoted his testimony.

He walked closer to Scholtz over the bare floor. In the dark the silver half-moons of rings gleamed in the visible ear. Across the bulky arm was a spider web of black tattoo, the pattern unclear without light. The mouth was open and at the peak of every breath he made that animal noise.

Where was the woman? Thobela smoothed the cushion of his thumb over the wooden shaft of the assegai as he slipped past, deeper into the house. There were two bedrooms. The first one was empty, on the wall hung a child's drawings, now without colour.

He felt revulsion. How did these people's minds work? How could they display the child's art on his bedroom wall and moments later smash his head against it? Or batter him until the ribs splintered.

Animals.

He saw the woman in the double bed of the other room, her shape outlined under the sheet. She turned over. Muttered something inaudible.

He stood still. Here was a dilemma. No, two.

Christine let go of the railing and went back inside. She closed the sliding door behind her. In the top drawer in the kitchen she found the vegetable knife. It had a long narrow blade, slightly curved with a small, sharp point. It was what she wanted now.

He didn't want to execute the woman. That was his first problem.

A war against women was not a war. Not *his* war, not a Struggle he wanted to be involved in. He knew that now, after Laurens. Let the courts, imperfect as they were, take responsibility for the women.

But if he spared her, how would he deal with the man? That was his second problem. He needed to wake him. He wanted to give him a weapon and say: 'Fight for your right to crack a two-year-old skull, and see where justice lies.' But the woman would wake up. She would see him. She would turn on lights. She would get in the way.

Christine sat on the edge of the bath after closing the bathroom door. She took the cap off the bottle of Dettol and dipped the blade of the little knife into the brown fluid. Then she lifted her left foot onto her right knee and chose the spot, between her heel and the ball of her foot. She pressed the sharp point of the blade gently against the soft white skin.

Sonia's eyes.

He walked around the door of the bedroom where the woman lay, right up close. That's when he saw the key in the lock and knew what he must do.

He pulled the key out of the lock. It made a scraping sound and he heard her breathing become shallow. Quickly he closed the door. It creaked. He pushed the key in from the outside. In haste he struggled to get it in.

He heard her say something in the room, a bleary, unrecognisable word.

At last the key went in and he turned it.

'Chappie?' called the woman.

The man on the couch stopped snoring. Thobela turned towards him.

'Chappie!' she shouted, louder now. 'What are you doing?'

The man sat up on the couch and threw the blanket aside.

'I am here about the child,' said Thobela.

He noted Scholtz's shoulders. A strong man. It was good.

'There's a kaffir in the house!' the man shouted to his wife.

*　　*　　*

She jabbed the blade into her foot, as hard as she could. She could not help the cry that fell from her lips.

But the pain was intense. It burned the hurt away; it covered over everything, just as she had hoped.

34

He dreamed wild, mixed-up dreams that drove him from his sleep and made him get up twice before he finally dropped off again at three in the morning. He was busy talking to Anna, a conversation of no use or direction, when the cell phone woke him. He grabbed it, missed, the handset fell from the windowsill and landed somewhere on the bed. He found it by the light of the screen.

'Yes?' He couldn't disguise his confusion.

'Inspector Griessel?'

'Yes.'

'Sorry to wake you. Tshabalala here, from Oudtshoorn detective branch. It's about your assegai murderer.'

'Yes?' He felt for his watch on the windowsill.

'It seems he was in Uniondale last night.'

'Uniondale?' He found his watch and checked it. 04:21.

'We have a child batterer here, Frederik Johannes Scholtz, out on bail with his wife. Stabbed to death in his house last night.'

'Uniondale,' he repeated. 'Where is Uniondale?'

'It's about a hundred and twenty kilos east of here.'

It made no sense. Too far from the Cape. 'How do you know it's my assegai man?'

'The wife of the deceased. The suspect locked her in the bedroom. But she could hear what was going on . . .'

'Did she see him?'

'No, he locked the door while she was asleep. She heard Scholtz shout from inside the house. And he said the guy had an assegai.'

'Wait, wait,' said Griessel. 'He locked her in the bedroom? How did he get the man out of the bedroom?'

'The woman says they don't share a bed any more, since the

child died. He slept in the sitting room. She woke up when Scholtz began shouting. She heard him say: "He's got an assegai." But there's something else . . .'

'Yes?'

'She said he shouted it was a black man.'

'A black man?'

'She said he shouted: "There's a kaffir in the house."'

It didn't fit. A black man? That's not how he had pictured the assegai man in his head.

'How reliable that is, I'm not sure. It seems they were fighting in the dark.'

'What does the wound look like?'

'The fatal wound is in the chest, but it looks like he was trying to fend it off with his hands. There are some cuts. And there is furniture overturned and broken. They obviously fought a round or two.'

'The chest wound – is there an exit wound in the back?'

'Looks like it. The district surgeon is still busy.'

'Listen,' said Griessel. 'I am going to ask our pathologist to phone him. There are a lot of forensic details they must see to. It's important—'

'Relax,' said Tshabalala. 'We have it under control.'

He showered and dressed before he phoned Pagel, who took the early call with grace. He passed on the numbers to call. Then he drove to the Quickshop at the Engen garage in Annandale Road. He bought a pile of pre-packed sandwiches and a large take-away coffee and drove to work. The streets were quiet, the office quieter still.

He sat down behind his desk and tried to think, pen in hand.

Union-fucking-dale. He opened a sandwich. Bacon and egg. He took the lid off the coffee. The steam drifted lazily upwards. He inhaled the aroma and sipped.

It would be a day or two before they knew whether it was the same assegai, regardless of how much pressure the commissioner exerted. He bit into the sandwich. It was reasonably fresh.

A black man. Scholtz wrestling with an attacker in the dark, frightened, he sees the long blade of the assegai. Had he made an assumption? Could he really see?

A black man with a pick-up. In Uniondale. Big surprises. Too big. The sudden detour to a place five hundred kilos from the Cape.

They didn't need a copycat, God knows. And this thing could easily spawn a lot of copycats. Because of the children.

He began to jot down notes in the crime report file in front of him.

'No, damnit,' said Matt Joubert and shook his head with finality.

Griessel and Ngubane were in the senior superintendent's office at seven in the morning. All three were too frenetic to sit.

'I've—' said Ngubane.

'Matt, just a few days. Two or three,' said Griessel.

'Lord, Benny, can you see the trouble if he gets away? Flees the country? These fuckers have false passports like confetti. There's no way . . .'

'I—' said Ngubane.

'We have the manpower, Matt. We can shut the whole place down. He won't be able to move.'

Joubert still shook his head. 'What do you think Boef Beukes will do? He has the biggest drug bust of his career and you want to let his big fish out on bail? He'll squeal like a skinny pig.'

'Matt, last night I—' said Ngubane.

'Fuck Beukes. Let him squeal. We won't get bait like this again.'

'No, damnit.'

'Listen to me,' barked Ngubane in frustration, and they looked at him. 'Last night I talked to one of the people from Investigative Psychology at head office. She's here in Cape Town. She's helping Anwar with a serial rapist in Khayelitsha. She says if he gets the chance, Sangrenegra will go to the child. Whether she is alive or not. She says the chances are good that he will lead us to her.'

Joubert sat down heavily on his chair.

'That makes our case very strong,' said Griessel.

'Think about the child,' said Ngubane.

'Let the commissioner decide, Matt. Please.'

Joubert looked up at the pair of them leaning shoulder to shoulder over his desk. 'Here comes trouble,' he said. 'I can see it a mile away.'

Pagel phoned him before eight to say indications were that the Uniondale assegai was the same blade, but he would have to wait for the tissue samples being brought by car from Oudtshoorn. Griessel thanked the prof and called his team together in the task team room.

'There have been a few interesting developments,' he told them.

'Uniondale?' asked Vaughn Cupido with a know-it-all smirk.

'It was on Kfm news,' said Bushy Bezuidenhout, just to spoil Cupido's moment.

'What did they say?'

'It's all Artemis, Artemis, Artemis,' said Cupido. 'Why must the media always give them a name?'

'It sells newspapers,' said Bezuidenhout.

'But this is radio . . .'

'What did they say?' asked Griessel louder.

'They said there is a suspicion that it is Artemis but that it can't be confirmed,' said Keyter piously.

'Our assegai man is black,' said Griessel. That shut them up. He described what they knew of the sitting-room battle in the small town. 'Then there is the question of the tyre tracks from yesterday. Forensics says he drives a pick-up, probably a two-by-four. Not yet a breakthrough, but it helps. It can help us focus . . .' He saw Helena Louw shaking her head. 'Captain, you don't agree?'

'I don't know, Inspector.' She got up and crossed over to the notice board on the wall. There were newspaper clippings in tidy rows, separated into sections by pinned strands of different coloured knitting wool.

'We researched the publicity surrounding each of the victims,' she said and pointed at the board. 'The first three were in all the papers, and probably on the local radio too. But when we heard about Uniondale this morning we had a look.'

She tapped a finger on the single report in a red-wool section. 'It was only in *Rapport*.'

'So what's your point, sister?' asked Cupido.

'Afrikaans, genius,' said Bushy Bezuidenhout. '*Rapport* is Afrikaans. Blacks don't read that paper.'

'I get it,' said Jamie Keyter, followed by: 'Sorry, Benny.'

'Coloured,' said Griessel. 'Maybe he's coloured.'

'We coloured chaps are always handy with a blade,' said Cupido proudly.

'Or it could just have been very dark in that house,' said Griessel.

Joubert appeared at the door with a sombre face and beckoned Griessel to come out. 'Excuse me,' he said and left. He shut the door behind him.

'You've got four days, Benny,' said the senior superintendent.

'The commissioner?'

Joubert nodded. 'It's just the political pressure. He sees the same dangers I do. But you have till Friday.'

'Right.'

'Jesus, Benny, I don't like it. The risks are too high. If it goes bad . . . If you want to get the assegai man you will have to use the media. Organised Crime is highly pissed. The child is still missing. There's just too much—'

'Matt, I will *make* it work.'

They looked each other in the eyes.

'I will make it work.'

He took ten of the uniformed members of the task team along with Bezuidenhout, Cupido and Keyter and they drove in four cars to the house in Shanklin Crescent, Camps Bay to investigate the lay of the land.

He knew the problem was the rear of the castle-like dwelling. It was built against the mountain, with a plastered wall to keep trespassers out, but it was less than two metres tall – and it was a large area.

'If he comes here and spots us, he'll disappear – we won't find him in the bushes. So the men lying here must not be seen, but must be able to see everything. If you see him, you must allow him to get over the wall. Everyone understand?'

They nodded solemnly.

'If I were him, I would come down the mountain. That's where the cover is. The street is too problematic, too open. Only two entry points and it's practically impossible to get into the house from that side. So we will deploy most of our people on the mountain.'

He checked his street map. 'Kloof Nek runs up above, on the way to Clifton. If he doesn't park there, he will at least drive up and down a few times. Which of you can handle a camera?'

Keyter raised his hand like a keen prep-school boy.

'Only Jamie?'

'I can try,' said a black constable with alert eyes.

'What's your name?'

'Johnson Madaka, Inspector.'

'Johnson, you and Jamie must find a spot where you can watch the road. I want photos of every pick-up that passes. Jamie, talk to the photography guys about cameras. If you have trouble, phone me.'

'Okay, Benny,' said Keyter, pleased with his task.

He divided them into two teams – one for day and one for night. He determined every point on the street and against the mountain that would be manned. He asked Bezuidenhout to find out if any house in the street was empty, and whether they could use it. 'I'm going to talk to Cloete. The media should start humming by tonight. All of you go home and rest, but at six I want the night shift in place.

He walked into Joubert's office and found Cloete and the senior superintendent wearing graveyard faces. Cloete said: 'I want you to know that I had nothing to do with this, Benny.'

'With what?' he asked and Cloete handed him the *Argus*.

COP SCRAP
OVER ARTEMIS

Front page.

'They haven't got news, that's the fucking problem,' said Cloete. He read the article.

Senior police officials are up in arms over the appointment of a confirmed alcoholic as leader of the task team investigating the Artemis vigilante murders in the Peninsula. A source within the senior ranks of the SAPS called it 'a huge blunder' and 'a mess-up just waiting to happen'.

The top cop in the firing line is veteran Serious and Violent Crimes Unit Detective Inspector Bennie Griessel, who was reportedly admitted to Tygerberg Hospital just a fortnight ago after an alleged drinking binge. A hospital spokesperson confirmed that Griessel had been admitted, but declined to comment on his illness.

'Fuck,' said Griessel, and all he could think about were his children.

'Benny . . .' said Joubert and Griessel knew what was coming and said: 'You're not taking me off this case, Sup.'

'Benny . . .'

'Not a fock, Matt. Not a fock, you won't take me off.'

'Just give me a chance . . .'

'Who are these cunts?' he asked Cloete. 'Who gave them this?'

'Benny, I swear I don't know.'

'Benny,' said Joubert. 'This is not my call. You know I wouldn't take you off if it was my call.'

'Then I'm coming along to the commissioner.'

'No. You have enough to do. You have to get the media sorted. Go. Let me talk to the commissioner.'

'Don't take me off, Matt. I'm telling you.'

'I will do my best.' But Griessel could read his body language.

★　　★　　★

He struggled to concentrate on his strategy with Cloete. He wanted to know who the shits were who had sold him out to the press. His eyes strayed back to the copy of the *Argus* lying on Cloete's desk.

Jamie Keyter, the well-known newspaper informant? He would kill him, the little shit. But he had his doubts: it was too political for Keyter, too sophisticated. It was interdepartmental. Organised Crime must have got wind of his plans. That was what he suspected. He had four people from Domestic Violence in his task team. And Domestic Violence fell under OC in the new structure, God knows why. Was Captain Helena Louw the tattle-tale? Perhaps not her. One of the other three?

When he had finished with Cloete, he drove into the city. He bought a newspaper at a streetlight and parked in a loading zone in Caledon Street. The SAPS Unit for Organised Crime was located in an old office building just around the corner from Caledon Square. He had to take the lift up to the third floor and he could feel the pressure of rage inside him and he knew he must slow down or he would stuff up everything. But what did it matter, they were going to pull him anyway.

He walked in and asked the black woman at reception where he could find Boef Beukes and she asked, 'Is he expecting you?'

'For sure,' he said with emphasis, newspaper in hand.

'I'll find out if he can see you.' She reached out for the telephone and he thought what shit this was, policemen hiding behind secretaries like bank managers, and he slapped his ID card down in front of her and said, 'Just show me where his office is.'

With wide-open eyes that clearly showed her disapproval, she said, 'Second door on the left,' and he walked out down the corridor. The door was open. Beukes sat there with his fucking ridiculous little Western Province hat. There was another detective present, seated, collar-and-fucking-tied, and Griessel threw the newspaper down in front of him and said: 'Was it your people, Boef?'

Beukes looked up at Griessel and then down at the paper. Griessel stood with his hands on the desk. Beukes read. The detective in the suit just sat and looked at Griessel.

'Ouch,' said Beukes after the second paragraph. But not terribly surprised.

'Fuck ouch, Boef. I want to know.'

Beukes pushed the newspaper calmly back to him and said: 'Why don't you sit down a moment, Benny?'

'I don't want to sit.'

'Was I ever a backstabber?'

'Boef, just tell me – do you guys have anything to do with this?'

'Benny, you insult me. There are only ten or twelve of us left from the old days. Why would I nail you? You should look for traitors at Violent Crimes. I hear you are one big happy family there after all the affirmative action.'

'You are pissed, Boef, about Sangrenegra. You have the motive.' He glanced at the other detective sitting there with a taut face.

'Motive?' Beukes queried. 'Do you think we really care if you keep Sangrenegra busy for a few days? Do you think it makes a difference to us . . . ?'

'Look me in the eyes, Boef. Look me in the eyes and tell me it wasn't you.'

'I understand that you're upset. I would have been too. But just calm down so you can think straight; was I ever a backstabber?'

Griessel examined him. He saw the mileage on Beukes's face. Police miles. He had them too. They had been together in the dark days of the eighties. Copped the same deal, ate the same shit. And Beukes had never been a backstabber.

Griessel sat in the back of the courtroom and waited for the moment when the state prosecutor said, 'The state does not oppose bail *per se*, your honour.' He watched Sangrenegra and saw his surprise, how he stiffened beside his lawyer.

'But we do ask that it be set at the highest possible figure, at least two million rand. And that the defendant's passport be held. We also ask the court to rule that the defendant reports to the Camps Bay Police Station every day before twelve noon. That is all, Your Honour.'

The magistrate shuffled papers around, made some notes, and

then he set bail at two million rand. Lawyer and client conferred under their breath and he wished he knew what was said. Just before Sangrenegra left the court, his eyes searched the public benches. Griessel waited until the Colombian spotted him. And then he grinned at him.

Sangrenegra's shoulders sagged, as if a great burden had come to rest on them.

He was on the way to Faizal's pawnshop in Maitland when Tim Ngubane phoned him.

'The blood in Sangrenegra's BMW belongs to the kid. The DNA matches,' he said.

'Fuck,' said Griessel.

'So you'll have to watch him very carefully, Benny.'

'We will,' he said and he wanted to add: if I am still on the case by tonight. He thought better of it.

'Tim, I have a suspicion Organised Crime have been after Sangrenegra longer than they let on. Just a feeling. I have just come from Beukes. He knows something. He's hiding something.'

'What are you saying, Benny?'

'I wonder more and more whether they were following Sangrenegra before he abducted the child.'

Ngubane paused before he answered. 'Are you saying they know something? About the kid?'

'I'm not saying anything. I'm just wondering. Perhaps you can try and find out. Talk to Captain Louw. She's from Domestic Violence, but she's working on my task team. Maybe her loyalty will be to the child. Maybe she can find out.'

'Benny, if they do know something . . . I can't believe it.'

'I know. I'm also having trouble with it. But see it from their point of view. They are messing about with Nigerian syndicates distributing crack in Sea Point when suddenly they come across something a hundred times bigger. Something that makes them look like real policemen. Colombia. The Holy Grail. There was a shithouse full of drugs in that storeroom. If it were me, I would have gone to the national commissioner and made a stink about jurisdiction. But they just sit there. Why? They know something. They're busy with something. And I think they have been busy with it for quite some time.'

'Geeeeez,' said Ngubane.

'But we'll have to see.'

'I'll go talk to the captain.'

'Tim, the number of that shrink . . . do you still have it?' asked Griessel.

'The one who was down here from Pretoria? The profiler?'

'Yes.'

'I'll text it.'

35

Faizal said the base guitar was not in the market; the rapper from Blackheath had paid up and collected it. Griessel said what he was looking for now was a CD player, nothing fancy, just something for listening to music at home.

'Car, portable, or hi-fi component?' asked Faizal.

Griessel thought about it and said portable, but with good bass.

'Portable with speakers or portable with headphones?'

Headphones would be better in the flat. Faizal took a Sony Walkman out and said: 'This is the D-NE seven-ten, it can also play MP threes, sixty-four-track programmable, but the most important thing is, it has an equaliser and bass boost, the sound quality is awesome, Sarge. Great headphones. And just in case you are chilling in the bath and it falls off the soap dish, it's waterproof too.'

'How much?'

'Four hundred, Sarge.'

'Jissis, L.L., that's robbery. Forget it.'

'Sarge, this is brand new, slightly shop-soiled, no previous owner. Three fifty.'

Griessel took out his wallet and held two hundred-rand notes out to Faizal.

'Think of my children, Sarge,' groaned the shopkeeper. 'They must eat too.'

He stood in the street beside his car with his new CD player in his hand and felt like going home, locking the door and listening to the music his son had lent him.

Because they *were* going to pull him off the case. He knew it. It was too political to keep an alky in charge. Too much pressure. The image of the Service. Even though he and the other dinosaurs like Matt Joubert talked about the Force, it was the Service now. The politically correct, criminal-procedures-regulated, emasculated and disempowered Service, where an alcoholic could not be the leader of a task team. Don't even talk about the fucking constitutional protection of criminals' rights. So let them pull him, let them give the whole fucking caboodle to someone else, one of the Young Turks, and he would watch from the sidelines as chaos descended.

He unlocked his car and got in. He opened the box of the CD player, shifted the plastic flap and pushed in the batteries. He leaned across and took the CD out of the cubbyhole. He scanned the titles on the back of the jewel case. Various artists performing Anton Goosen's songs. He knew almost none of them. '*Water-blommetjies*'. Lord, that took you back. Twenty years? No. Thirty! Thirty years ago, Sonja Herholdt sang '*Waterblommetjies*' and the whole country sang along. He had a crush on her, then. A vague teenage desire. I will cherish-and-protect-and-regularly-service-you. She was so . . . pure. And innocent. Darling of the people, the Princess Di of the Afrikaners before the world knew Princess Di. With those big eyes and that sweet voice and the blonde hair that was so . . . he didn't know what the style was called, but it was seventies cool, if anything could be 'cool' back then.

He had been sixteen. Puberty in Parow. All he could think about in those days was sex. Not always about the deed itself, but how to get some. With the girls in Parow in the seventies it was well nigh impossible. Middle-class Afrikaners, the iron grip of the Dutch Reformed Church and girls who didn't want to make the same mistakes as their mothers, so that the best a guy could do was perhaps some heavy petting in the back of the bioscope. If you were lucky. If you could draw the attention of one. So he began to play bass guitar to get their attention, since he was no athlete or academic giant, he was just another little fucker with a sprinkling of pimples and an ongoing battle with school rules to grow his hair long.

In Standard Nine at a garage party there was this four-man band, guys of his age from Rondebosch. English speaking *Souties*, not very good, the drummer was so-so and the rhythm guitarist knew only six chords. But the girls didn't care. He saw how they looked at the band members. And he wanted to be looked at like that. So he talked to the leader when the band took a break. He told him he played a bit of acoustic and a bit of piano by ear, but the guy said get a bass guitar, china, because everyone played six-string and drums, but bass guitarists were hard to find.

So he began to look into it and he bought a bass for a knockdown price from an army guy in Goodwood whose Ford Cortina needed new rings. He taught himself in his room, with the help of a book that he bought in Bothners in Voortrekker Road. He dreamed dreams and he kept his ear to the ground until he heard of a band in Bellville that was looking for a bass. Five-piece: lead, rhythm, drums, organ and bass. Before he knew what happened he was on the stage of an English-medium primary-school hall laying down a foundation of Uriah Heep's 'Stealin'' and he sang the fucking song – he, Benny fucking Griessel, stood in front of the teen girls in an undersized T-shirt and his Afrikaans haircut and he sang, 'Take me across the water, 'cause I got no place to hide, I done the rancher's daughter and it sure did hurt his pride', and they all looked at him, the girls looked at him with those eyes.

It only brought him one sexual experience while he was at school. What he hadn't known was that while the band played, the guys who were dancing had the advantage. By the time the party broke up, all the girls had to go home. But it had given him the music. The deep notes he picked off the strings and via the amplifier, resonating through his whole body. The knowledge that his bass was the basis of every song, the substructure, the defining foundation from which the lead guitarist could deviate or the organist could drift away, always to return to the steadfast form that Benny laid down. Even though he knew he would never be good enough to go pro.

Unlike the police work. He knew from the start that was his

thing. That was the place where all the connections came together, that was how his brain was wired.

Now they were going to pull him off the assegai case and he put the CD down and took out his phone, because he wanted to talk to the psychologist before they posted him. He wanted to test a few of his theories before they took him off.

She met him at the Newport Deli in Mouille Point, because she was 'mad about the place'. They sat outside on the pavement at a high, round table.

Captain Ilse Brody, Investigative Psychology Unit, Serious and Violent Crime, Head Office, he read on the card she passed across the little table. She was a smoker, a woman in her thirties with a wedding ring and short black hair. 'You're lucky,' she said, 'I fly back tonight.' Relaxed, self-assured. Accustomed to the man's world she worked in.

He remembered her. He had been on a course she presented two or three years ago. He didn't mention it, as he couldn't remember how sober he had been.

They ordered coffee. She ordered a flat biscuit with chocolate on top and nuts underneath with some Italian-sounding name that he didn't quite catch.

'Do you know about the assegai murders?' he asked.

'Everyone down here is talking about them, but I don't have the details. I hear the media first speculated that it was a woman.'

'Couldn't be a woman. The weapon, the MO, everything . . .'

'There's another reason too.'

'Oh?'

'I'll get to that. Tell me everything first.'

He told her. He liked the intense way she listened. He began with Davids and finished with Uniondale. He knew she wanted details of the crime scene. He gave her everything he knew. But two things he withheld: the pick-up and the fact that the suspect might be black.

'Mmm,' she said, and turned her cigarette lighter over and over in her right hand. Her hands were tiny. They made him think of an old person's hands. There were fine grey hairs between the black at her temples.

'The fact that he confronts them in their own homes is interesting. The first deduction is that he is intelligent. Above average. And determined. Orderly, organised. He has guts.'

Griessel nodded. He agreed with the guts part, but the intelligence was a surprise.

'It will be difficult to determine a vocational group. Not a labourer, he's too clever for that. Something that allows him to be alone so he doesn't have to explain how he spends his time. He can drive to Uniondale without anyone asking questions. Sales? His own business? He must be quite fit. Reasonably strong.'

She took a cigarette from a white packet with a red square on it and put it in her mouth. Griessel liked her mouth. He wondered what effect her work had on her. To use the gruesomeness of death to paint a mental picture of the suspect, until she could see him, vocation and all.

'He's white. Three white victims in white neighbourhoods. It would be difficult if he wasn't white.' She lit the cigarette.

Exactly, he thought.

'In his thirties, I would say.' She drew on the cigarette and blew a long white plume into the air. It was windless here where the mountain blocked the southeaster. 'But what you really want to know is why he is using an assegai. And why he is killing people.'

He wondered why he was so conscious of her mouth. He shifted his eyes to a point on her forehead, so that he could concentrate.

'I think the assegai is one of two things. Either he is trying to convince you he is not white, to put you off the trail. Or he is looking for media sensation. Is there any indication that he has made contact with the media yet?'

Griessel shook his head.

'Then I would go with the first option. But I'm guessing.'

'Why doesn't he just shoot them? That's what I'm wondering.'

'I think it must be connected to the why,' she said, and drew again on the cigarette. There was a masculine manner to her smoking, probably because she always smoked with men. 'It definitely isn't because he was molested or abused himself. In that case the victims and the MO would have been very different. That's another reason it has to be a man. When men are damaged, if they are abused or molested, they want to do the same to others. Women are different. If there is damage from a young age, they don't do it to others. They do it to themselves. Therefore not a woman. If it had been a man who was damaged, his target would have been children. But this one is going for the ones who are doing the damage. And he is psychologically strong. What makes more sense to me is that a child of his has been a victim. Or at least a close member of his family. A younger sister or brother perhaps. A personal vendetta. A pure vigilante. They are rare. In our country it is usually a group with a very specific dynamic.'

'And the assegai?'

'I have to admit the assegai bothers me. Let's think about stabbing versus shooting. Stabbing is much more personal. Intimate and direct. That fits a personal loss. It makes him feel that he himself is exacting retribution. There's no distance between him and the victim, he isn't acting on behalf of a group, he represents only himself. But he could have done that with a knife. Because he is smart, he knows a knife can be messy. Also less effective. He wants to get it over quickly. There is no pathology of hanging about at the scene. He leaves no messages. But maybe he wants to intimidate them with the assegai; maybe it's a tool to gain immediate control, so that he can do his work and be done with it. Now I'm speculating freely, because I can't be sure.' She stubbed out the cigarette in the small glass ashtray.

He told her he also thought the suspect was white. And he still thought so, but there was evidence to the contrary. He told her about Uniondale and the fact that the child abuse report only appeared in *Rapport*. She pressed the tip of a finger on the biscuit crumbs in her plate and licked them off. She did it again. He wondered if she knew it made him think of sex, and then he was faintly surprised that he was thinking of sex at all and eventually he said: 'If he is black, you have much bigger problems.'

A third time the finger went to the plate and then to her mouth and he looked at her mouth again. An eyetooth, just the one, was canted to the inside.

'I would also put more check marks against intelligence and motivation. And that puts another light on the assegai. Now we start to talk of symbolism, of traditional values and traditional justice. He's sophisticated, at home in a city environment. He's not a country boy – it takes too much skill to execute three white victims in white neighbourhoods without being seen. He reads Afrikaans newspapers. He is aware of the police investigation. That's possibly why he went to Uniondale. To divide attention. You should not underestimate him.'

'If he's black.'

She nodded. 'Improbable but not impossible.' She looked at her watch. 'I will have to finish up,' she said and opened her handbag.

Quickly he told her about Sangrenegra and asked if she thought the ambush would work.

She held her purse in her hand. 'It would have been better if you could have set your trap outside Cape Town. He feels the pressure here.'

'I'm paying,' he said. 'But will he come?'

She took out a ten-rand note. 'I'll pay half,' she said and put the money under the saucer with the bill. 'He will come. If you play your cards right with the media, he will come.'

He drove along the coast, because he wanted to go to Camps Bay again. He saw the new developments on the sea front in Green Point. Big blocks of flats under construction, with advertising boards romantically depicting the finished product. *From R1.4 million.* He wondered if it would revive this part of the city. What would they do with the *bergie* hobos that lived on the commonage behind? And the old, dilapidated buildings in between, with paint peeling off in long strips and the rooms rented out by the hour?

That made him think of Christine van Rooyen and that he should tell her what they were planning, but he would have to pick his words carefully.

Along Coast Road through Sea Point. It looked a lot better here by the sea. But he knew it was a false front – further inland was erosion and decay, dark corners and dirty alleys. He stopped at a traffic light and saw the scaffolding on a sea-front building. He wondered who would win this battle. It was Europe against Africa – rich Britons and Germans against Nigerian and Somalian drug networks, the South Africans marginalised as spectators. It depended on how much money poured in. If it was enough, the money would win and crime would find another place, southern suburbs, he thought. Or the Cape Flats.

The money ought to win, because the view was stunningly beautiful. That's what money did. Reserved the most beautiful for the rich. And shunted policemen off to Brackenfell.

At the traffic circle he turned left in Queens, then right in Victoria, all along the sea, through Bantry Bay. A Maserati, a Porsche and a BMW X5 stood side by side in front of a block of flats. He had never felt at home here. It was another country.

Clifton. A woman and two young children walked over the road. She was carrying a big beach bag and a folded umbrella. She was wearing a bikini and a piece of material around her hips, but it blew open. She was tall and pretty, long brown hair down the length of her back. She looked down the road, past him. He was invisible to her in his middle-class police car.

He drove on to where Lower Kloof Street turned up left and then took the road round the back, to Round House. He drove up and down three times and tried to assess it as the assegai man would. He couldn't park here, it was too open. He would have to walk a long way, above maybe, from the Signal Hill Road side. Or below. So that, when he had finished with Sangrenegra, he could flee downhill.

Or would he choose not to come through the bushes? Would he chance the street?

He has guts, Ilse Brody had said. He has guts *and* he's clever.

He phoned Bushy Bezuidenhout and asked him where he was. Bezuidenhout said they had found a house diagonally opposite Sangrenegra's. Belonged to an Italian who lived overseas. They had got the keys from the estate agent. They were not allowed to smoke in the house. Griessel said he was on his way.

His cell phone rang almost immediately. 'Griessel.'

'Benny, it's John Afrika.'

The commissioner.

Fuck, he thought.

36

He wanted to shower, eat and sleep.

Thobela was driving down York Street in George when he spotted the Protea Forester's Lodge. It was nameless enough for him. He parked in front of the building and had already put a hand on his bag when the newsreader began to talk about the Colombian and the child over the radio.

He listened with one hand still on the carry straps of his bag, the other on the door latch and his eyes on the front door of the hotel.

He sat like this for three or four minutes after he had heard everything. Then he let go of the bag, started the pick-up and put it in reverse. He made a U-turn and drove down York Street, turned right into C.J. Langenhoven Street. He headed for the Outeniqua Pass.

The policemen who should have been guarding Christine van Rooyen's door were not there. Griessel knocked and assumed they would be inside.

'Who's that?' her voice sounded faint from the other side of the door. He gave his name. The guards were not inside, or she would not have answered. As the door opened he saw her face first. It didn't look good. She was pale and her eyes were swollen.

'Come in.' She was wearing a jersey, although it wasn't cold. Her shoulders were hunched. He suspected she knew she would not see her child again. She sat down on the couch. He saw the television was showing a soapie, the sound muted. Is that how she got time to pass?

'Do you know he was granted bail?'
She nodded.

'Do you know we arranged it?'

'They told me.' Her voice was toneless, as if she was beyond caring.

'We think he will lead us to Sonia.'

Christine just stared at the television, where a man and woman stood facing each other. They were arguing.

He said: 'It's a possibility. We have forensic psychologists helping us. They say the chances are good he will go to her.'

She turned her eyes back on him. She knows, he thought. She knows now.

'Would you like coffee?' she asked.

He considered a moment. He was hungry. He hadn't eaten since breakfast. 'Can I go and buy food? Take aways?'

'I'm not hungry.'

'When did you last eat?'

She didn't answer.

'You have to eat. What can I get you? Even if it's something small.'

'Whatever.'

He stood. 'Pizza?'

'Wait,' she said and went into the kitchen. A Mr Delivery booklet was stuck to the door of the big two-door fridge with a magnet. 'They can deliver,' she said and brought the booklet to him. She sat down again. 'I don't want you to leave now.'

'Where are the two policemen that were at the door?'

'I don't know.'

He flipped through the booklet. 'What do you like?'

'Anything. Just not garlic or onion.' Then she reconsidered. 'It doesn't matter. Anything.'

He took out his cell phone, phoned and placed an order. He hesitated when asked for the address and she provided it. He said he had an official call to make and asked if he could go out on the balcony. She nodded. He slid the door open and went out. The wind was blowing. He closed the door behind him and found Ngubane's number on the cell phone.

'Tim, are you aware that Organised Crime's people aren't guarding the mother any more?'

'No. I haven't been there today. I called, but she didn't say anything.'

'Jissis, they're idiots.'

'Maybe they think she isn't in danger any more.'

'Maybe they think it's not their problem now.'

'What can we do?'

'I haven't any spare people. My entire team is busy in Camps Bay.'

'I'll talk to the sup.'

'Thanks, Tim.'

He gazed out over the city. The last rays of the sun reflected off the windows of the hotels in the Strand area. Was she in danger? His SVC team was watching Sangrenegra. His four henchmen were still in the cells.

Boef Beukes would know. He would know how big Sangrenegra's contingent was. How many there were who did not live at the Camps Bay place. There had to be more. Local hangers-on, assistants, people involved: you don't run such a big drug operation with only five people. He called SVC and asked if Captain Helena Louw was still there. They put him through and he asked her if she had Boef Beukes's cell phone number.

'Just a minute,' she said. He waited until she came back and gave it to him.

'Thanks, Captain.' Could he trust her? With Domestic Violence part of the Organised Crime structure? Where did her loyalties lie?

He called Beukes. 'It's Benny, Boef. I want to know why you withdrew Christine van Rooyen's protection.'

'It's your show now.'

'Jissis, Boef, don't you think you might have told us?'

'Did you tell us anything? When you decided to hang Carlos up for bait. Did you have the decency to consult with us?'

'You feel fuck-all for her safety?'

'It's a question of manpower.' But there was something in his voice. He was lying.

'Fuck,' said Griessel. He ended the call and stood with his handset in his hand thinking, that's the problem with the fucking

Service, the jealousy, the competition, everyone had to fucking PEP, everyone was measured by Performance Enhancement Procedure and everyone's balls were on the block. Now they were stabbing each other in the back.

Commissioner John Afrika had phoned him while he was on his way to Christine van Rooyen. Benny, are you sober? he had asked. He had said yes, Commissioner, and John Afrika had asked him, Are you going to stay sober and he said yes, Commissioner. Afrika said, I will get the people who ran to the papers, Benny. Matt Joubert tells me you are the best he has. He says you are on the wagon and that's good enough for me, Benny, you hear? I will stand by you and I'm going to tell the papers that. But, fuck, Benny, if you drop me . . .

Because if he dropped the commissioner, then the commissioner's PEP was blown to hell.

But he appreciated it that the man was standing by him. A coloured man. He was thrown on the mercy of a coloured man who had to swallow so much crap from the whites in the old days. How much mercy had John Afrika received, then?

He had said: 'I won't drop you, Commissioner.'

'Then we understand each other, Benny.' There were a few beats of silence over the air, then John Afrika sighed and said, 'This backstabbing gets me down. I can't get a grip on it.'

Griessel thought over his conversation with Beukes. Organised Crime were on to something. He knew it. That's why they went to the papers. That's why they withdrew the guard detail.

What?

He opened the sliding door; he couldn't hang around out there for ever.

Before he came in, while he was putting his phone away, he tried to think like Boef Beukes. Then he understood and he froze. Christine van Rooyen was OC's bait. They were using *her* as an ambush. But for whom? For Sangrenegra?

His visit to Beukes's office. The other detective there, the one in the suit and tie. Nobody dressed like that any more. Who the fuck was that? The Scorpions, the special unit for the public prosecutor?

Never. Beukes and Co. would rather slit their wrists in the lavvy than work with the Scorpions.

He became aware that Christine had got up and was standing watching him.

'Are you okay?'

'Yes,' he said. But would *she* be okay?

In the sultry late afternoon of a Highveld summer, at the New Road filling station between the old Pretoria Road and Sixteenth Avenue in Midrand, the stolen BMW 320d stopped in front of the Quickshop. John Khoza and Andrew Ramphele got out and walked through the automatic glass doors. They walked casually up to the fast-food counter in the back of the shop.

While Ramphele ordered two chicken burgers, Khoza inspected the four corners of the large room. There was only one security camera. It was against the eastern wall opposite the cash register.

He murmured something to Ramphele, who nodded.

Griessel's phone rang while they waited for the pizzas.

'Benny, the boss says we can give her Witness Protection, but it's going to take time,' said Ngubane.

'How much time?'

'Probably only tomorrow. That's the best we can do.'

'Okay, Tim. Thanks.'

'What are you going to do? For tonight?'

'I'll make a plan,' he said.

Khoza waited until the last of the four clients in the shop had paid and left. Then he walked up to the woman behind the cash register, shoved his hand in the back of his denim jacket and drew out a pistol. He shoved it against her face and said, 'Just open it up, sister, and give us the cash. Nobody will get hurt.'

'I'll have to sleep on your couch tonight,' said Griessel.

Christine looked up at him and nodded.

'We will place you in Witness Protection tomorrow. They are organising it now, but it takes a little time.'

'What does that mean?' she asked.

'It depends.'

There was a knock on the door. Griessel got up and took out his Z88 service pistol. 'That must be our pizzas,' he said.

The Toyota Microbus of the South African Police Services Task Force Unit stopped at the filling station for petrol. The nine policemen were stiff from hours of sitting and thirsty. They had last stretched their legs at Louis Trichardt. They all got out. The young black constable, the sharpshooter of the team, knew it was his duty as the youngest to take the orders for cool drinks.

'What do you want to drink?' he asked.

That was when two men came out of the Quickshop, each carrying a pistol in one hand and a green, purple and red plastic bag in the other.

'Hey,' said the sharpshooter and dropped a hand to the firearm on his hip holster. The other eight members of the Task Force team looked instinctively at what the constable had seen. For a moment they could hardly believe their eyes. For a very short moment.

'Just now, you said you did not want me to leave. Why?' asked Griessel, but her mouth was full of pizza and she had to finish chewing before she answered.

'You are the first person I have seen today,' she said and left it at that. He could see she was struggling not to cry.

He understood. He visualised her day. Her child was missing, probably dead. The awful worry and doubt. Fear perhaps, because the guards were gone. Alone, between these four walls. 'I'm sorry,' he said.

'You needn't be sorry. It's my fault. Only mine.'

'How can you say that?'

She closed her eyes. 'If I wasn't a whore, I would never have met him.'

The first thing that popped into his head was to ask her why she had become a whore. 'It doesn't work like that,' he said. She just shook her head, keeping her eyes closed. He wanted to get up and go over and put his arm around her shoulders.

He stayed where he was. 'It's a psychological thing,' he said. 'We see it often. Victims or their families blame themselves. You can't be responsible for someone else's behaviour.'

She didn't react. He looked down at the pizza on the plate in front of him and pushed it away and wiped his hands on a paper serviette. He looked at her. She was wearing jeans. She sat on the chair with her bare feet folded under her. Her long blonde hair was half covering her face. What could he say to her? What could anyone say to him if it had been his child?

'I actually came to tell you about something else.'

She opened her eyes. 'I don't want to hear bad news.'

'I don't think it is bad news. It's just that I think you have the right to know. You know about the Artemis affair the papers are writing about?'

With a sudden movement of her head she tossed her hair back and said, 'Yes. And I wish he would come and kill Carlos.' She said it with hate he could understand.

'It's my case. The assegai man. I want to use Carlos to catch him.'

'How?'

'We know he picks his victims when the media writes about them. About their crimes. Today we gave the media a lot of information about Carlos. About how he . . . abducted Sonia. About his drug-dealing background. We think it will lure the assegai man.'

'And then?'

'That's another reason we're watching Carlos so carefully.'

It was some time before she answered. He saw the process in her face, the eyes narrowing, the lips thinning. 'So it's not about Sonia,' she said.

'It *is* about her. All the indications are that he will lead us to her.' He tried hard to be convincing, but he felt guilty. He had told

Sangrenegra what they were going to do. This morning in court he had looked Carlos in the eyes and reinforced the message: you are bait. He knew Carlos was going nowhere, because Carlos knew the police were watching him. The chances that the Colombian was going to lead them anywhere were nil.

'I don't believe you.'

Could she hear from the tone of his voice that he was lying? 'My black colleague talked to the psychologist this morning. She said people like Carlos go back to their victims. I give you my word. It's true. It's a chance. It's possible. I can't swear it will happen, but it's possible.'

Her face altered, the venom dissolved and he saw she was about to cry. He said: 'It's possible,' again, but to no avail.

She put her face in her hands and said: 'Leave him. Let him kill Carlos.' Then her shoulders heaved. He couldn't take it any more. Guilt and pity drove him to her. He put a hand on her shoulder. 'I understand,' he said.

She shook her head.

'I have children too,' he said, and inhaled her smell, perfume and the faint scent of perspiration.

He sat on the arm of the chair. He put his hand behind her neck onto her far shoulder. His fingers patted her comfortingly. He felt a bit of an idiot because she was unyielding under his touch. 'I understand,' he repeated.

Then she moved and he felt her soften and she pressed her head against him. With her arm around his hip she wept.

37

He thought many thoughts while she leaned against him, shrunken under his arm. For the first time since Anna had kicked him out, some sort of calm came over him. A kind of peace.

He looked around the flat. The sitting room and kitchen were one big room separated by a white melamine counter. A passage led off to the right behind him. To the bedrooms? He noted the large fridge and big flat-screen television. New stuff. A child's drawings of multicoloured animals were stuck up on the fridge with magnets. A crocodile and a rhinoceros and a lion. He noted the coffee machine in the kitchen, shiny chrome, with spouts and knobs. But the chairs at the counter were scuffed; one sitting-room chair was old and worn. Two worlds in one.

Leaning against the wall to the left of him was a painting. Large and original. A rural landscape, a blue mountain in the distance and a green valley, the grass in the veld growing high and verdant. A young girl was running through the grass. She was a tiny figure on the left, dwarfed by the landscape, but he could distinguish the blonde hair bouncing up behind. Four or five steps ahead of her there was a red balloon, with a string hanging down, a thin, barely visible black stripe against the blue of the mountain. The girl's hand was stretched out to it. The grass bent away from her. It must be the wind, he thought. Blowing the balloon away from her. He wondered if she were running fast enough to catch it.

He had a partial erection.

She wouldn't be able to feel it, as she wasn't in contact there. Her breathing was quieter now, but he couldn't see her face.

He crossed his legs to hide his state. He couldn't help it; there were a lot of things affecting him here. Knowing that sex was her job. She was attractive. And vulnerable. Hurt. Something in him that responded to that. Something that somewhere in his brain did surveys and sent out primitive orders: take your chance, the time is right. He knew that was how his head worked. He – and the other members of his sex. Also the mentally ill, those for whom it was more than just an opportunity for sexual victory. Like serial murderers. They searched out the weak, soft targets for their dark deeds. Often prostitutes. Not always deliberately, with preconceived reasoning and planned strategy. Instinct. Somewhere, in the pre-alcoholic period a memory stirred, something he had worked out for himself. He was a good policeman because he understood others through self-knowledge. He could use his own weaknesses, his own fears and instincts, because he knew them. He could magnify them, amplify them like turning up an imaginary volume control to the level where they made other people commit murder or rape, lie or steal. As he sat there he realised it was one of the things that had made him start drinking. The slow realisation that he was like them and they were like him, that he was not a better man. As he had felt last night or the previous, he couldn't remember which, when he had seen Anna and her young, imaginary lover in his mind and the jealousy had turned on the switches with an evil hand and he had wanted to shoot. If he were to find them like that and he had his service pistol on his hip, he would shoot the fucker, between the eyes, no fucking doubt about that.

But that was not the main reason he drank. No. It was not the only reason. There were others. Large and small. He began to realise it all now. He was a rough stone and he was cut with a thousand facets and it was his bad luck that this shape fitted so well into the crooked hole of alcoholism.

The thing that he was had consequences. The way in which the fine wiring of his brain made connections, had implications. It enabled him to view a crime scene and *see* things; it also wakened an urge in him to hunt. It made the search sweet; inside his skull he experienced an addictive pleasure. But the selfsame wiring made him drink. If you wanted to hunt and search, you had to look death in the eye. And what if death frightened you? Then you drank, because it was part of you. And if you drank long enough, then the alcohol created its own wiring, its own thoughts, its own justification. Its own thick glasses through which you saw yourself and the world.

What do you do about it? What do you do about the consequences, the opposite sides of the coin, if it fucked up your life? Leave the police and go and drive a white Toyota Tazz for Chubb Security around Brackenfell's streets at night and leave notes under people's doors? *You left your window open. Your alarm went off.* Or do you sit behind the small black-and-white screens of a shopping centre's closed-circuit television and watch the dolled-up mommies spending the daddies' money?

And you never hunt again and you die here inside.

He experienced a sudden feeling of despair, like someone trapped in a labyrinth. He needed to think of other things – of the woman leaning against him and the fact that it satisfied a need. The need to be held. That he needed to be touched. Ever since he had been thrown out of his house, he had an increasing need for it.

He wondered about her.

Why had she found it necessary to become a whore? An *Afrikaner* girl. Not as beautiful as a model. Attractive rather, sexy.

Did all women have this potential? Did it lie hidden until circumstances arose? Or was it, like his own polished facets, connected to a specific combination of angles and surfaces?

It hadn't been necessary for him to come around here tonight. But it had been in the back of his mind all day: he wanted to look in.

Was it coincidence that he had recalled his first experience of sex with such clarity on his way here? At the same time he had been wondering how alcohol and memory interacted. He had a mental image of synapses submerged in brandy; while he stayed sober the level kept dropping and, like a dam drying up, exposed old, rusty objects.

Not all the memories were pleasant, but he focused on those from long ago: the one of the girl with the gold chain around her neck and her name in gold letters against her throat. YVETTE.

She was wearing jeans and a T-shirt with blue-and-white horizontal stripes and she had used too much perfume. But it smelt heavenly.

There were odd details that he had remembered this afternoon. They had a gig in Welgemoed against the Tygerberg at the sixteenth birthday party of some or other rich man's son. They set up beside the swimming pool on imported ceramic tiles. The rich wanker had kept hanging around and asking, 'Have you got rubbers for the feet of the drums?' When he was a distance away, the drummer said, 'I have rubbers for your daughter,' and they all laughed. The rich wanker, one of those men who dress as if they were still sixteen too, stopped and asked, 'What did you say?' The drummer said: 'I said I have rubbers,' but with a smirk. The rich man stood there knowing he was making a fool of himself, but there was not a lot he could do about it.

When they played, the girl was there. She moved at the edge of the big group, half in the twilight. She wasn't truly part of it. Or didn't want to be. Sometimes she danced on her own. She looked at him and he noticed her eyes first, big brown eyes that looked sad. Long straight brown hair. Then he noticed her neat little breasts and pretty round bottom and he saw a potential opportunity and began to play to her.

The prospect was nearly too much for him. He was afraid his hopes were unrealistic. He waited until late that night, until their very last break. He went over to her and said 'Hi' and she said 'Hi' and looked at him with that lost smile as if to say I know what you're thinking. Then the strangest thing happened. She took his hand and led him past the house into the shadows. She opened a door low down at the side of the house. It was a storeroom of sorts. She closed the door and it was pitch-dark. He could see fuck-all. Then she was against him, hands around his neck and kissing him. He tasted alcohol on her tongue and Spearmint Beechies and smelt her perfume. Lust took hold of them in the dark, they kissed and undressed each other with searching hands and he felt her body – he ran his palms over her face and neck and breasts and hips and bottom. They bumped into invisible garden tools and somehow or other found a place to lie, a canvas tarpaulin over some sacks – not soft, but not as hard as the floor. He remembered the smell of turpentine and old paint, but above all, her perfume. The only sounds were their breathing and urgency. She took his dick and put it in her mouth. Lord, he would never forget that. For a moment she was nowhere to be found and then her hand was around his thing and then there was something warm and wet around it and it hit him like a sledgehammer, his dick was in her mouth. The realisation of every masturbatory dream. He wanted to see it. He wanted terribly to capture it in his mind, so that he could know what it looked like and remember, but there was no light, absolutely none. He groaned partly from frustration and partly from ecstasy and he stretched out his hand until he found her bush, slid his finger in and felt her heat like glowing coals inside.

Afterwards she opened the door for light so they could find their clothes and dress. He watched her silhouette faintly etched against the little light from outside. That was the last he saw of her. He went back, self-conscious and worried he hadn't dressed properly in the storeroom. He hadn't been missed. He looked around for her, but she was gone.

Yvette. That was all he knew. That night he had lain in bed with a strange melancholy. Her smell was on his fingers and on his body. But the next morning it was gone. Just like her.

While she was in the bathroom, he walked quickly out to his car and fetched the music and the CD player.

When she came out her hair was clean and wet. She made up a bed on the couch for him. She put out a big blue towel for him and said he was welcome to use the bathroom. He said he would like to shower. He was aware of the awkwardness between them. Or was it just him?

Tonight he was going to share a house with a whore. He couldn't look at her and forced a polite smile.

'Well, I'll say goodnight, then.'

'Sleep well,' he said.

'You too.' She went down the passage and shut her door. He went to the bathroom. It was still steamy from her shower and filled with her fragrances, soap and shampoo and lotion. It smelt different from Anna's bathroom. Fuller. Richer.

He undressed and neatly folded his clothes and put them on the toilet lid, on top of his service pistol. He looked down at his body. Naked in a whore's bathroom. He looked at the chest hairs already turning grey and the middle age slackening of his belly. His penis was in that no-man's land between indifference and desire, a half-smoked cigar. Not exactly your Greek God. Not exactly seductive in Christine van Rooyen's eyes. He smiled wryly at himself in the steamy mirror.

He showered using her semi-transparent soap that was the colour of red wine, and shampoo from a white bottle. He rinsed off and towelled. Put only his trousers on and carried the rest of his clothes and his firearm to the sitting room. He stacked them in a neat pile beside the couch and sat. He examined his bed. It was a big, wide couch. Long enough. He took out the Anton Goosen jewel case and had another look at it. He took out the second disc of the double set and put it in the player. Earphones on. He switched off the standard lamp beside the couch, swung his feet up and placed the player on his stomach. Pressed Play.

Only once the nine members of the Task Force had grown tired of laughing and jesting and gone on their way did the detective in Midrand get a chance to take the fingerprints of the two suspects. Then he had them locked up in the cells again.

He sat down at his desk and began to go through the evidence systematically. In one of the transparent plastic evidence bags he saw the identity documents that the Task Force men had found in the BMW. He took them out and looked at the names.

Let's see, he thought, and picked up the phone. The number he keyed was that of the SAPS Criminal Records Centre in Pretoria.

As the applause after the last cut faded, he lay with closed eyes and a light heart. He wondered what he had lost in the past few years.

He was the drinking equivalent of Rip van Winkel with this huge hole in his life, a black hole of unconsciousness. Everything had grown up. His children, the music of his culture . . . his fucking country. Everything except him. In his mind he was being exposed to the alternatives, how different things might have been. He didn't want to see that now. He took the earphones off.

City sounds penetrated faintly from outside. His eyes were adjusted to the dark now. Streetlights illuminated the room sufficiently through the gauzy curtains. The outlines of the furniture, the dark shape of the painting against the wall. Small red and green lights shone from the fridge and the TV.

He wanted to tell Fritz. Reaching over the little table he found his cell phone and scrolled through the menu to text messages. He struggled a bit with the tiny pads of the keyboard. CD IS BASS HEAVEN. THANKS. DAD.

He sent the SMS and put the CD player and phone on his pile of clothes. He must sleep. He didn't want to think, enough thinking for one day. He shifted around on the couch, struggling to be comfortable. It was best with his back against the backrest. Too hot for the blanket. Sleep.

He thought once of Christine lying in the bedroom, but he put her out of his mind and tried to think of Anna. That brought no peace so he thought about the music and he did what he used to do when he was seventeen: he visualised himself on stage. At the State Theatre. With Anton & friends. He was playing bass guitar. Playing without effort, going with the flow of the music, letting his fingers run where they would and he heard the bedroom door open and soft footfalls on the carpet. She must be going to the bathroom. But here she was beside him. She lay down on the couch. Her back was against him. She shifted up close to him so they lay like two spoons. He hardly dared breathe. He must pretend to be asleep. Keep his breathing even and calm. He could smell her, her shoulder right by his nose.

She wanted comfort. She just needed a person. She didn't want to be alone, she missed her child, she was raw and hurting. He knew all that.

He made a sound that he hoped would sound like a person asleep and put a hand on her hip. A comforting gesture. Half on thin material and half on bare flesh.

He felt the heat of her body. Now he was getting a fucking erection, it blossomed irreverently and there was no way to stop it. He had to think of something. He made another vague noise and shifted his hips back. Lord, she mustn't know. He should have put his underpants on, that would have kept it reined in. Perhaps she wasn't fully awake. He tried to listen to her breathing, but all his senses returned to him were her heat and her scent.

She shifted back against him. Right against him. Up here. Down there.

He wanted to apologise. He wanted to mumble 'I'm sorry' or something, but he was too scared. She was half asleep and that would make it all worse. He lay very still. Thought about the music. Played bass guitar along with '*gee die harlekyn nog wyn, skoebiedoewaa, skoebiedoewaa, rooiwyn vir sy lag en traan en pyn, skoebiedoewaa, skoebiedoewaa . . .*' Give the harlequin more wine, scoobydoowaa, scoobydoowaa, red wine for his laughter and tears and pain . . .

She moved her arm, her hand, put it over his. She held it on her hip a moment and then drew it up under her nightie, oh fuck, up to her breast, her palm on the back of his hand and he felt her, felt the softness and she sighed deeply and pressed his hand tightly and roughly against her. Moved again, her hips away from his pelvis and her hand came down there, behind her back and undid the clip of his trousers, how he had no idea. Unzipped his trousers. Slipped in her hand and grasped him. Lust was one high perfect note in his head, a lead guitar that took flight to the rhythm of his heart's bass and then she pushed him into her from behind.

Long after his orgasm they lay still like that, belly to back, still inside her, though spent and flaccid now. The first words she spoke, barely aloud, were: 'You are broken too.'

He thought for a long time before answering. He wondered how she knew. How she could see it. Or feel it. Why had she come to him? Her need? Or her gift to him? A comfort?

So he told her. About Anna. About his children. The drinking. Without plan or structure, he let it flow as it came into his head, his arm tight around her now, and his hand softly on the fullness of her breast. Her face against his, the fine hairs against his stubble.

He told her how he had been, in the days before the booze. He had been an optimist, an extrovert. A joker. He was the one who could make everyone laugh, at the funniest moments. In the parade room, when tensions ran high and tempers were stretched, he could spot the silly side of the matter and cut through all the crap with a phrase and leave them helpless with laughter. He was the one everyone phoned first when they wanted to throw some meat on the griddle for a *braai*. Two or three times a month he would join Murder and Robbery for an impromptu barbecue, a *braai*. Three o'clock on a Friday afternoon, just to relieve the never-ending pressure, at Blouberg or Silvermine or even at the office itself in Bellville South. Beer and meat and bread, laughter, chat and drink, he would be first on the list, because he was Sergeant Benny Griessel, instinctive investigator and unofficial, cynical chief clown who could ridicule the job and the bureaucracy and affirmative action but with compassion. So that they could all face up to it again.

Now, this side of the booze, they still had their *braais*. But no one called him. No one wanted him there, the sot who staggered and couldn't string two coherent words together. The oaf who bumped into others, swore and fought and had to be taken home to a wife who opened the door reluctantly. Because she didn't want that drunkard or the humiliation.

He told Christine he had been sober for eleven days now and he didn't know the man this side of the booze.

Everything had changed around him. His children, his wife, his colleagues. Jissis, he was an old has-been amongst all the *Sturm und Drang* of the young policemen in the Service.

But the main thing was, he believed he *had* changed. He wasn't sure how. Or how much. A strange fellow in his forties with a gaping hole in his life.

He told her all this and somewhere in the telling she asked: 'Why do you want your wife back?' He wondered about that before he answered. He said the thing was, he had been happy then. They had. She was the woman he had begun his life with. They had nothing, just each other. Set up house together, suffered together. Laughed together. Shared the same wonder at the magic of Carla and Fritz's births. Celebrated together when he was promoted. They had history, the sort of history that mattered. They were friends and lovers and he wanted that back. He wanted the bond and the camaraderie and the trust. Because that was a great part of who he had been, what made him what he had been.

And he wanted to be that again.

If he couldn't get Anna back, he had fuck-all. That was it.

She said: 'A person can never be like that again,' and before he could react, she asked, 'Do you still love her?' It made no difference how long he thought about that one, he could not answer her. He wanted to talk shit about 'what is love', but he kept quiet and suddenly felt weary of himself, so he asked, 'What about you?'

'What about me?'

'Why was it necessary . . . to become a prostitute?'

'A sex worker,' she said, but in quiet self-mockery.

She moved slowly and he slipped out of her. A small moment of loss. She turned over so her face was towards him and his hand was off her breast.

'Would you have asked me that if I was selling flowers?' There was no confrontation in her voice. Her words were flat and without emotion. She didn't wait for an answer. 'It's just a job.'

He drew a breath to answer, but she went on: 'People think it's this dreadful thing. Bad. Damaging. Your work brings you damage too. That's what you just said. But it's okay to be a policeman. Just don't be a whore.'

He thought if she hadn't been a sex worker, Sonia would have been safe at home, but he knew he could never say it.

'When I began, I also wondered what was different about me. All my clients ask the same thing. "Why did you become an escort?" It makes you think there's something wrong with you.

Then you think, but why should it be something *wrong*? Why can't it be something *right*? Why can't it just be that I think further than most people? What is sex? Is it so bad? What makes it such a bad thing?'

She got up and walked away from him and he was sorry he had asked her. He didn't mean to upset her. He should have thought. He wanted to say he was sorry, but she had disappeared down the passage. He became aware of his trousers still unfastened so he zipped them up.

She came back. He saw her shadowy figure moving and here she was, but this time she sat at his feet.

'Do you want a cigarette?'

'Please.'

She put two cigarettes in her mouth and clicked the lighter. In the light of the flame he could see her breasts and face and bare shoulders.

She passed one to him. He drew deeply.

'I was always different,' she said and blew a plume of smoke that cast a ghostly shadow on the opposite wall. 'It's hard to explain. When you are small, you understand nothing. You think there's something wrong with you. My parents . . . I come from a good home. My father was in the army and my mother was mostly at home and they were okay with that. With their little world. With that kind of life. The older I got the harder it was for me to understand. How could that be all? How could that be enough? You go to school, you find a husband or a wife, you raise kids, you retire by the sea and then you die. You never upset anyone, you do the right thing. Those are my father's words. "My child, you do the right thing." Whose right thing? The people's? Who are they to decide what the right thing is? You pay your parking money and you never drive too fast and don't make a noise after ten at night. And you do your duty. That's another of my father's classics. "People must do their duty, my child." To your family, to your town, to your country. What for? What did they get for doing their duty? My father did his duty to the army and he was dead before he took his pension. My mother did her duty to us and she has never been to Cape Town or Europe or anywhere. After all the duty, there was never money for anything. Not for clothes or cars or furniture or holidays. But it was okay for them, because people mustn't be flashy, that's not the right thing to do.

'Everyone wants you to be ordinary. Everything everyone teaches you, is just so you won't be different. But I was different. I couldn't help it. It's the way I am. If my parents or the school or whoever said that is what you should do, then I wondered what it felt like to do the opposite. I wanted to see what it looked like from the other side. So I did. I smoked a bit and I drank a bit. But when you are fifteen or sixteen, almost all the rules are about sex. You mustn't do this and you mustn't do that, because you must be a decent girl. I wanted to know why you had to be a decent girl. What for? So you could get a decent man? And a decent life, with decent children? And a decent funeral with lots of people? So I did things. And the more things I did, the more I realised the other side is the interesting one. Most people don't want to be decent, they've all got this stuff inside that wants to be different, but they don't have the guts. They are all too scared someone will say something. They are afraid they will lose all the boring things in their lives. There was this teacher, he was so dutiful. I worked on him. And I slept with him on the Students Christian Association camp at The Island. He said, God, Christine, I've wanted you so long. So I asked him why he hadn't done something about it. He couldn't answer me. And this friend of my father. When he came to our house he would look at me sideways but then go and sit next to his wife and hold her hand. I knew what he wanted. I worked on him and he said he liked young girls but that it was his first time.'

She stubbed the cigarette out and half turned to him.

'He was as old as you,' she said, and for a second he thought he heard scorn in her voice.

She leaned her back against his feet. She folded her arms below her breasts.

'Do you know why my parents sent me to university? To find a husband. One with education. And a good job. So I could have a good life. A good life. What does a good life help? What use is it when you die and you can say to yourself I had a good life? Boring, but good.

'At varsity this guy was visiting me, third-year medical student. His parents lived in Heuwelsig and they had money. I saw how they lived. I saw if you have money you don't have to be dutiful and ordinary and good. Having money means more than being able to buy things. You can be different and no one says anything. Then I knew what I wanted. But how to get it? You could marry a rich man, but it's still not your money. I got a job working weekends for a catering business. One night at a golf course I stood having a smoke and this man comes up to me. He had a car business in Zastron Street, and he asked me, "How much do you earn?" When I told him he said, "Wouldn't you rather make a thousand rand a night?" and I asked, "How would I do that?" and he said, "With your body, love." He gave me his card and he said "Think about it." I phoned him that Monday. And I did it. In a flat, they were seven guys who had a flat in Hilton, and sometimes at lunchtime or sometimes in the evening they would phone me at the hostel and I would go.

'But then, just before final exams, I got pregnant,' she said. 'I was on the pill, but it didn't work. When I told them they said they would pay for the abortion, but I said no. So they gave me money and I came to Cape Town.'

38

Orlando Arendse had a fixed routine every morning. In his large, pretty house in West Beach, Milnerton, he got up at six without the help of an alarm clock. He put on slippers and a burgundy dressing gown. He picked up his reading glasses from the kitchen table, left his wife sleeping and went to the kitchen. He put the spectacles on the kitchen table and ground a 50/50 mix of Italian and Mocca Java coffee beans – enough for four large mugs. He filled the coffee machine with water and carefully poured in the ground coffee. Then he pressed the switch.

He walked to the front door, opened it and went out. He looked up to see what the weather was doing today, then crossed the paved driveway to the big, automatic security gate. He walked briskly erect, despite his 66 years, most of them lived on the Cape Flats. To the right of the gate was the postbox. He opened it and took out *Die Burger*.

Without unfolding the newspaper he glanced at the headlines. He had to hold the paper at arm's length, as he was not wearing his glasses.

He walked back to the house and just before he went through the door he looked left and right. It was instinctive behaviour, no longer functional.

He spread the paper open neatly on the Oregon pine table in the kitchen. He put on his reading glasses. His right hand drifted down to the dressing gown pocket. It was empty and he clicked his tongue in exasperation. He no longer smoked. His wife and doctor were conspiring against him.

He only read the front page. By now the coffee machine ended its burbling with a final sigh. Orlando Arendse sighed with it as he did every morning. He got up and fetched two mugs from the cupboard above the machine and placed them on the counter. First he filled one cup and inhaled the aroma with pleasure. No milk or sugar. Just as it was. He poured the rest of the coffee into a flask so it would stay fresh. Mug in hand, he sat down at the paper again. He turned the page and inspected the small photo of the page-three editor, a lovely woman. Then he shifted his gaze to page two and began to read in earnest.

Usually at seven he would pour coffee from the flask into the other mug and take it to his wife. But at ten to seven, while he was reading the cricket report on the sports page, the electronic box in the entrance hall made its irritating noise.

Orlando stood up and crossed to the hall. He pressed a button and held his mouth close to the microphone. 'Yes?'

'Orlando?'

He knew that deep voice, but couldn't place it at the moment. 'Yes?'

'It's Thobela.'

'Who?'

'Tiny. Tiny Mpayipheli.'

He ran down a green valley through knee-high grass, chasing a red balloon. He stretched out a hand to the string but stumbled and fell and it shot up into the air. He woke in Christine van Rooyen's sitting room and smelt the sex on his body. *What the fuck have I done?*

He swung his legs off the couch and rubbed his eyes. He knew he hadn't slept enough, could feel the lethargy in his mind and body, but that was not what lay so heavily. He didn't want to think about it. He stood up a little unsteadily. He pushed his Z88 pistol and cell phone under the couch and took the little pile of clothes and shoes with him to the bathroom. He would have liked to brush his teeth, but that would have to wait. He got under the shower and opened the taps.

Jissis. Drunkard and adulterer. Whore-fucker. Fucking weakling who couldn't control himself, telling her his entire life story. What the fuck was wrong with him? He wasn't a fucking teenager any more.

He scrubbed himself with the soap, washing his genitals two, three, four times. What was he going to do with her now? How far was Witness Protection? He would have to call them. How had the night gone for Bushy Bezuidenhout and company out at Camp's Bay? While he lay in the embrace of a prostitute. With premeditation, that was the fucking thing – he had come here looking for it. Wanting her to touch him because he needed someone to touch him so fucking much. Because he thought a whore would find it easier to touch him. Because he couldn't wait six fucking months for his wife, just maybe, to touch him.

He got out of the shower and towelled himself aggressively. Jissis, if only he could brush his teeth, his mouth tasted as if a mongoose had shat in it. He smelt his trousers. They still smelt of sex, he couldn't go to work like that. Better phone Tim Ngubane and find out if Witness Protection could come and collect her.

Why did she have to come and lie with him? And then to tell him her story as if it was *his* fucking fault?

He was still standing like that holding his trousers up to his nose, when she opened the bathroom door and said in a frightened voice: 'I think there is someone at the door.'

Arendse had last seen Tiny Mpayipheli five years ago. Sitting together at the Oregon table, he could see that the Xhosa had changed. Still a very big man with a voice like a cello. Still the pitch-black eyes that made him shiver the first time he looked into them. But the lines in the face were a bit deeper and the short-cropped hair had acquired a little grey at the temples.

'Tell me about Carlos Sangrenegra,' said his visitor, taking a swallow of his coffee.

Arendse looked down at the front page of the newspaper before him and then up at the big man. He saw absolute intent. He was on the point of saying something, asking a lot of questions, while the tumblers dropped slowly but surely. He looked down at the newspaper again, back at Tiny and it all became clear. Everything.

'Jesus, Tiny.'

The Xhosa said nothing, just looked back with that eagle's eye.

'What happened?' asked Arendse.

Thobela looked at him for a long time, then shook his head, left and right, once only.

'I am retired,' said Arendse.

'You know people.'

'It's all different now, Tiny. It's not like the old days. They've marginalised us coloured people. Even in the drug trade.'

No reaction.

'I owe you. That's true.' Arendse stood and crossed over to the coffee machine. 'Let me just take my wife her coffee or I'll never hear the end of it. Then I'll make a few calls.'

Griessel tried to pull his trousers on, but he was in too much of a hurry. He lost his balance while he was standing on one leg. In the fall he knocked his head against the edge of the washbasin with a dull thud. He swore, jumped up and got the trousers on and fastened the clip only and strode out of the bathroom to the couch under which his weapon lay.

As he bent to retrieve the Z88 he felt dizzy. He got a hand on the pistol and went to the door.

'Who's there?' He pressed down the safety clip of the pistol.

At first he heard nothing and then only the sound of the footsteps of more than one person. Footsteps receding down the passage. He turned the key with his left hand, jerked the door open and swung the barrel of his pistol into the passage. To the right he saw a figure disappearing into the lift. He ran that way. His head was still not clear.

The door to the lift had closed. He hesitated just a fraction then ran for the stairs and down, two steps at a time.

Six bloody storeys. With his left hand on the rail, firearm in the right, just his trousers on, down, down. On the third floor his legs couldn't keep up and he slipped and it was only his hand on the stair rail that prevented a headlong fall. He saw a pair of legs in front of him and looked up. A very fat woman in a bright purple tracksuit stood staring with a mouth like an 'O', her face glowing with perspiration.

'Excuse me,' he said and dragged himself upright, squeezing past her and taking the next set of stairs.

'You're bleeding,' he heard the fat woman say. Instinctively he touched a hand to his forehead to check and it came away wet, warm and red. Run. What was he going to do when he reached the bottom if there were more than one? His breath laboured, chest burned, legs complained.

Second storey, first storey, ground.

He went in pistol first, but the entrance hall was empty. He jerked the glass door open and sprinted out into the morning sun just as below at the corner of Belle Ombre and Kloof Nek Road a white Opel turned the corner with screeching tyres.

When the call came from Midrand, the detective had to find the file in a forgotten pile against the wall.

Then he began to remember the two who had shot the boy at the garage. And the father who had bought the contents of the file.

He tapped a middle finger on the cover of the file. He wondered if he would still be interested. Whether there might be another opportunity here.

He looked up the father's details in the documents. He found a number with a Cathcart code. Pulling the phone nearer he keyed them in. It rang for a long time. Eventually he put the phone down.

He would try again later.

She had heard someone trying to open the door, she said as she cleaned the wound on his forehead with a warm, damp facecloth. His nose was full of the smell of Dettol. She stood up against him where he sat on the couch. She was wearing a thin dressing gown. He didn't want her this close.

At first she hadn't been certain. She had gone to put the kettle on in the kitchen while he was showering when she heard it. She saw the door latch move. That was when she went to the door and called: 'Is anyone there?' It had been quiet a second and then someone had rattled the door. She had run to him in the bathroom.

'You have a bump and a cut.' She stepped back to view her handiwork.

She was gentler this morning, but he didn't want to think about it.

'Witness Protection will be here soon,' he said. He had called them before she had started on the cut.

'I'll get ready.'

'They will take you to a safe house. You must pack clothes.'

He looked up at her face. She was watching him with an unreadable expression. She stretched out a hand to his face, touched her fingertips to his chin. Softly. She stroked up across his cheekbone to the plaster she had put over his wound.

There was a foil-wrapped parcel at his door. He picked it up, unlocked the door and went inside. The room felt dead, as if no one lived there. He put the food on the counter and went up the stairs. His legs were stiff from the earlier exercise. He brushed his teeth long and thoroughly. Washed his face. He found clean clothes, dressed in a hurry and jogged down the stairs. He was out of the door when he remembered the food parcel. He went back. Charmaine had left a note again. It read:

> *Care of your food and living; and believe it,*
> *My most honour'd lord,*
> *For any benefit that points to me,*
> *Either in hope or present, I'd exchange*
> *For this one wish, that you had power and wealth*
> *To requite me, by making rich yourself.*
>
> Timon of Athens.

He hadn't the faintest idea who that Greek was.

Bushy Bezuidenhout looked pointedly at his watch as Griessel entered the house opposite Sangrenegra's.

'Sorry, Bushy. It's been a rough morning.'

'Very rough, I see. What happened to your head?'

'It's a long story,' he said and he could read the drunkenness question in his colleague's bloodshot eyes.

'How's it going here?'

'The other night-shift people have already gone. I've been waiting for you.'

He felt extremely guilty and for a moment considered telling him where he had been. But he had already given one version of his night over the phone to Matt Joubert. He didn't want to go through it again. 'Thanks, Bushy.'

'Nothing happened here. No suspicious vehicles, no pedestrians except an old girl taking her dogs for a walk this morning. Carlos's last lights went off at a quarter-past twelve.'

'Any sign of him this morning?'

'Nothing. But he has to report to the police station before twelve, so he will probably start moving around soon.' Then, as an afterthought. 'We should have bugged his phone.'

Griessel thought it over. The chances that the assegai man would phone him were slim. 'Maybe.'

'I'll be off then.'

'I'll stay until eight tonight, Bushy.'

'No, it's okay. I won't be able to sleep that long anyway.'

Vaughn Cupido was on the third floor with a large pair of binoculars.

'*My moer*, Benny, what happened to your head?'

'It's a long story.'

'I'm not going anywhere.'

Griessel put his dish of food on a chest of drawers and went to stand next to Cupido. He held out his hand for the binoculars. Cupido handed them over and Griessel aimed them at Sangrenegra's house.

'There's not much to see,' said Cupido.

That was true. Most of the windows had reflective glass. 'He has to go to the police station.'

'Fielies will follow him in a car.' Cupido tapped the radio on his hip. 'He'll keep us informed.'

Griessel handed the binoculars back. 'I don't think he'll come in daytime.'

'The assegai man?'

Griessel nodded.

Cupido sat in an armchair that had a view outside. 'You never know. I try putting myself in his shoes, but I can't. What's in the package?'

Griessel leaned back against the wall. He would have preferred to lie down on the double bed behind them. 'Lunch.'

'Are you back with the missus, Benny?'

'No.'

'Made it yourself?'

'Do I question you about your fucking eating arrangements, Vaughn?'

'Okay, okay, I'm just making conversation. Stakeout was never my idea of high excitement. So, tell me about the knob. Or is that also off limits?'

'I bumped my head on a washbasin.'

'Sure.'

'Jissis, Vaughn, what do you think? That I was pissed? Do you want to smell my fucking breath? So you can run to the papers and tell the fucking journalists what a fuck-up I am? Here, use my cell phone. Call them. Go on, take it. Do you think I care? Do you think it still bothers me?'

'Jeez, Benny, take it easy. I'm on *your* side.'

Griessel folded his arms. The radio on Cupido's hip beeped. 'Vaughn, its Fielies, come in.'

'I'm standing by.'

'Do we have someone in number forty-eight?'

'Not that I'm aware of.'

'There's a man with a huge pair of binoculars on the second floor. I don't think he knows I can see him.'

'Is he watching Carlos?'

'Yep.'

'Tell him I'll check it out,' said Griessel.

'Wait,' said Cupido. 'Here comes King Carlos.'

Griessel looked at Sangrenegra's house. The door of the double garage was slowly opening. 'Fuck,' he said, 'give me the radio.' He took it from Cupido. 'Fielies, this is Benny. Does the guy have *only* binoculars?'

'That is all that I can see.'

'Carlos is on his way. Look carefully at the window . . .'

'Only the binoculars. There, they've gone now . . .'

Please not a sniper, thought Griessel. 'Is everyone on this frequency?' he asked Cupido, who nodded.

'Everyone, stand by.'

'The binoculars are back,' said Fielies.

'Follow Carlos, Fielies.' To Cupido: 'Who is his back-up?'

'He's on his own. You know we don't have enough manpower for back-up.'

'Fielies . . .'

'Standing by.'

'Don't lose him.'

When Carlos's BMW disappeared down the road, Griessel left the house and crossed the street. It was hot outside and windless in the lee of the mountain. The heat reflected up from the ground and perspiration sprang out on his skin. He worried that the smells of last night would come out again. Number 48 was another rich man's house, white-painted concrete filling the entire plot. Nowhere for children to play. A playground for adults only. He looked up at the windows of the second floor. There was a room overlooking the street and Sangrenegra's house and the curtains were parted. There was no one there now.

He approached the front door and rang the bell. He couldn't hear it ring. He never could understand why people didn't make their doorbells audible. How were you supposed to know if it was working or not? You stand there pressing like crazy, and most of the time it's out of order and you wait like a fool at the door, but no one knows you're there.

Irritably he pressed again. Once, twice, three times.

Nothing happened. Not a sound.

Fielies had clearly seen something. The binoculars. Appearing and disappearing.

He hammered on the door with the base of his fist. Boom, boom, boom, boom, the sound echoed inside. Open up, fuckers.

No reaction, no sound of footsteps.

He took out his phone and looked up Boef Beukes's number that he had called last night. Pressed the green key. It rang unanswered. Boef knew who was calling. And he probably knew why, because the chump with the binoculars up there had probably phoned his boss and said the SVC people were at the door.

He banged one last time on the door, more out of frustration than expectation.

Then he turned and left.

39

He had fetched himself a chair from the luxurious sitting room, carried it up the stairs and positioned it next to Cupido's. They watched Sangrenegra return and listened while Fielies reported. The Colombian had been to the police and directly home again.

They sat and waited and had meaningless chats. They tried to keep the attention of the team, the detectives down the street, and the others hidden in the veld behind the house.

It was 15:34 now and the sleepiness felt like lead inside him. He must have been asleep with his eyes open, because when Cupido said with an edge, 'Benny . . .,' he jumped in fright. Looking down at the street he saw a panel van parked at Carlos's door. There was a big blue cross on the side. *First Aid for Pools. Intensive Care Unit.*

A black man got out. Big. Blue overalls.

Griessel picked up the radio. 'Stand by, everyone.'

The man walked around to the back of the panel van and took out pipes, nets and other paraphernalia.

'That's their sign on the wall,' said Cupido, binoculars to eyes. 'What?'

'On the wall of Carlos's house. There, beside the garage door. "Swimming pool care by First Aid for Pools". And a number.'

The swimming-pool man approached the front door. He pressed the intercom and waited.

'The number is four eight seven double-o, double-o.'

Griessel called it and waited.

The door across the street opened. They could see Carlos. He held the door open. The black man picked up all his things and went in.

'The number you have dialled does not exist,' said the woman's voice in his ear. 'Fuck,' he said. 'Are you sure of that number?'

'Four eight seven double-o, double-o.'

'That's what I . . .' He realised he hadn't added the Cape Town code and he swore and pressed 021 and then the number again. At the fourth ring a woman answered.

'First Aid for Pools, good afternoon. This is Ruby speaking. How may I help you?'

'This is Detective Inspector Benny Griessel here from Serious and Violent Crimes. Can you tell me whether you have a San-grenegra on your books? Forty-five Shanklin Crescent in Camps Bay.' He tried to communicate urgency in his voice so she wouldn't fuck around.

'I'm sorry, sir, we cannot give you that information over the telephone . . .'

He stayed calm with effort and said: 'Ruby, this is a police emergency and I do not have the time to . . .' He wanted to say 'fuck around' and had to think of other words. '. . . Please, Ruby, I'm asking you really nicely here.'

She was quiet at the other end and perhaps it was the despera-tion in his voice, because eventually she said: 'What was that name again?'

'Sangrenegra.' He spelt it out for her. Across the street the front door was still shut.

He faintly heard Ruby tapping her keyboard. 'We have no Sangrenegra on our records, sir.'

'Are you sure?'

'Yes, sir, I am. Our computer doesn't lie.' Sharply.

'Okay. Now we have to be sure here. Do you have a forty-five Shanklin Crescent in Camps Bay?'

'One moment.'

'Postman,' said Cupido, pointing down the street. A man in uniform was riding a bicycle from postbox to postbox. At Carlos's house all was quiet.

'Sir?'

'I'm here,' said Griessel.

'We do have a forty-five Shanklin Crescent, Camps Bay on our books . . .'

He felt extremely relieved.

'The client is a company, it seems.'

'Yes.'

'The Colombian Coffee Company.'

'Okay,' said Griessel. The tension began to ebb.

'Here he comes,' said Cupido. The big black man exited the front door. He was holding only a white plastic pipe.

'They seem to be good clients. All paid up,' said Ruby.

'He must be fetching something from the van,' said Cupido.

Griessel's eyes followed the black man in the blue overalls. The clothes looked a bit tight on him. The man opened the driver's side door.

'We service them . . .'

The man tossed the swimming-pool pipe into the front of the van.

'. . . on Fridays,' said Ruby.

The man got into the van.

'What?' said Griessel.

'Something's not right,' said Cupido. 'He's leaving . . .'

'We service them on Fridays.'

'. . . and his tools are still inside.'

Griessel grabbed his radio: 'Stop him! Stop the swimming-pool man, everybody!' He rushed down the stairs, phone in one hand and radio in the other. Ruby said 'Excuse me?' faintly over the phone as he screamed into the radio: 'Fielies, turn your car around and stop the swimming-pool man!'

'Are you there, sir?'

'I'm on my way, Benny.'

He nearly fell as he turned the corner on the last set of stairs and the thought crossed his mind that the world was a fucking funny place. For years you don't climb stairs and then all of a sudden you are faced with more stairs than your fucking legs can manage. 'Hello?' said Ruby over the cell phone. 'He's around the corner!" shouted Fielies over the radio.

'Go, Fielies, drive, man!'

Griessel sprinted across the street to Carlos's house. He heard feet slapping behind him, and half turning he saw Cupido and two constables running across the tar.

'Sir, are you there?'

The postman on his bicycle was in front of him, wide-eyed and mouth agape. Griessel sidestepped and for a second he thought they were going to collide.

'Hello?'

His knee bumped the rear tyre of the bicycle and he thought if he fell now the cell phone and the radio would be buggered. He regained his balance. He shoved the door open and ran in and saw the Colombian lying by the swimming pool, blood everywhere. He reached him, he lay on his face and Benny turned him over and saw he was stone dead, a huge hole in his chest. He said: 'Fuck, fuck, fuck,' and Ruby said: 'That's it!' and the cell phone made three beeps and the three policemen behind him skidded to a halt and then everything went quiet.

On the corner of Shanklin and Eldon, Detective Constable Malcolm Fielies wondered whether the swimming-pool man had turned left or right. He turned left, guessing, and ahead saw the panel van turning right and he put his foot flat on the accelerator and the tyres screeched.

He turned right down Cranberry after the man and he saw on the sign that it was a crescent and he thought, got you, motherfucker, let's see you get out of this one! But the road ran straight as an arrow and he saw the brake lights go on ahead and the van turned left and Fielies cursed and shouted into the radio: 'I'm after him!' but he knew they only worked over short distances and he didn't know whether they heard him.

He threw the radio down on the seat beside him and turned left. Geneva Drive. He suspected it was the street leading up to Camps Bay Drive, the one leading into the city, and he changed the Golf down to a lower gear and listened to the engine scream as he drove.

He was catching up, slowly but surely he was catching the
motherfucker, although this motherfucker could drive.

He grabbed the microphone of the police radio off its hook and
called Control and said he needed back-up, but then Geneva
curved sharply to the right, so fucking unexpectedly, and he felt
the back of the Golf go and he grabbed the steering wheel with
both hands. The tyres screeched and he saw he was going to hit
the kerb. Look *through* the turn, that was what they were taught.
He looked *through* the fucking turn. Too fast. There went the
back end and he spun, 360 degrees, and the engine stalled on
him. He said 'motherfucker' very loudly. He turned the key and
it whined and whined and then it took and the Golf and
Detective Constable Malcolm Fielies pulled away with screaming
tyres. At the T-junction with Camps Bay Drive he stopped and
looked left and right and left again, but there was no sign of the
panel van.

The swimming-pool floor of the house was filled with policemen
and forensic people. Griessel sat to one side with his cell phone in
his hands. He felt he had robbed Christine van Rooyen of her last
chance to know her daughter's fate. He thought, if the child was
still alive somewhere, they would never find her now.

He knew that Senior Superintendent Esau Mtimkulu and Matt
Joubert, first and second in command of SVC, and Commissioner
John Afrika, the provincial head of Investigation, were arguing
about his future down there beside the pool. If they sent him down
the tubes, it was only right, because he had continued to believe the
assegai man was white, even after he had had good evidence to the
contrary. That was why he had been so slow to react to the
swimming-pool van. That was why he had phoned first.

His fault. Too much fucking faith in his instinct, too cocky, too
self-assured – and now he would pay for it.

The phone rang.

'Griessel.'

'Inspector, the helicopter has found the swimming-pool company's van on Signal Hill Road. We are sending a patrol vehicle.'

'And the suspect?'

'He's gone. It's just the vehicle.'

'Explain to me where it is.'

'It's the road that turns off Kloof Nek Road to the lookout points on Signal Hill, Inspector. About half a kilometre in there is a clump of trees on the right-hand side.'

'No one goes near the vehicle, please. They must just secure the area.' He was on his feet and walking over to Cupido. 'Vaughn, they found the van on Signal Hill. I want you to think carefully – was he wearing gloves?'

'No fucking way. I checked him out thoroughly.'

'So you're sure?'

'I'm sure.'

Griessel crossed over to the three senior officers. They stopped arguing when he approached. 'Superintendent,' he said to Joubert, 'the helicopter has found the van on Signal Hill. We think we have a good chance of getting fingerprints. He wasn't wearing gloves. I want to take Forensics immediately . . .'

He could see from the three faces that it was coming now.

'Benny,' said John Afrika, quietly so that only the four of them could hear. 'You will understand if Superintendent Joubert takes over now?'

He fucking well deserved it, but it hurt and he didn't want to show that. He said: 'I understand, Commissioner.'

'You are still part of the team, Benny,' said Matt.

'I . . .' he began, but didn't know what to say.

'Take Forensics, Benny. Call if you find something.'

They found nothing.

The assegai man had wiped the steering wheel and gear lever and the door catch with a cloth or something. Then Griessel recalled he had taken stuff out of the back and the forensic examiner sprayed his spray and dusted with his brush and said: 'We have something here.'

Griessel came around to look. Against the outer panel of the rear door a fingerprint showed up clearly against the white paint.

'It's not necessarily his,' said the man from Forensics.

Griessel said nothing.

He sat at the breakfast counter of his flat and ate some of the thinly carved roast leg of lamb from Charmaine Watson-Smith's dish. But his mind was on the bottle of Klipdrift in the cupboard above.

Why not? He couldn't think of a single good answer to his question.

He had no appetite, but ate because he knew he must.

Last night he had had big theories about why he drank. Griessel the philosopher. It was *this* and it was *that* and everything but the truth. And the truth was: he was a fuck-up. That's all. Whore-fucking wife-beating drunken sot fuck-up.

Where was that jovial fellow who used to play the bass guitar? That's where he had been last night and now he knew. That guy was already a fuck-up, he just didn't know it. You can fool some of the people some of the time . . . But you can't fool life, pappa. Life will fucking catch you out.

He stood up. So weary. He scraped the last of the food into the bin. He washed and dried the dish. He didn't feel like taking it to the old girl now. He would leave it at her door in the morning with a note.

You can't fool life.

His cell phone rang in his pocket.

Let the fucking thing ring.

He took it out and checked the screen.

ANNA.

What did she want? Can you fetch the kids on Sunday? Are you sober? Did she really care whether he was sober or not? Really? She didn't believe he had it in him in any case. And she was right. She knew him better than anyone. She had watched the whole process, lived through it. She was witness number one. Life had caught him out and she had had a ringside seat. She knew in six months' time she would phone an attorney and say let us put an end to this marriage with my alcoholic husband who still drinks. The six months were just to show the children she wasn't heartless.

Let her call. Let her go to hell.
1 MISSED CALL.
1 MISSED LIFE.
The phone rang again. It was the number from work. What did they want?

'Griessel.'

'We've got him, Benny,' said Matt Joubert.

40

They were all in the task team room at SVC when he walked in. He could feel the excitement, saw it in their faces, heard it in their voices.

Joubert sat beside Helena Louw where she was working on the computer. Bezuidenhout and his night team were there too. Keyter stood talking to a constable; the fucking camera he had borrowed was still hanging from his neck, zoom lens protruding.

Griessel sat down at one of the small tables.

Joubert looked up and saw him, beckoned him closer. He got up and went over. 'Sit here with me, Benny.'

He sat. Joubert stood up. 'May I have your attention, please?'

The room quietened.

'We have identified a suspect, thanks to fingerprints that Inspector Griessel and his team recovered from the vehicle of the swimming-pool company. His name is Thobela Mpayipheli. He is a Xhosa man in his forties from the Eastern Cape. His registered address is Cata, a farm in the Cathcart district. That is in the Eastern Cape. Earlier this year Mpayipheli lost his son during an armed robbery at a filling station. Two suspects were arrested, but escaped from detention during the trial. It seems as if that is where it all began. By the way, he owns an Izuzu KB pick-up, which fits with the tyre print that Inspector Griessel found, and we must assume that that is the vehicle with which he travelled to Cape Town and Uniondale. That is all the information we have at this time.'

Griessel's cell phone rang again and he took it out of his pocket. ANNA.

He switched it off.

'So,' said Joubert. 'Since I am going to ask Griessel to go to the Eastern Cape, I will hold the fort at this end.'

He didn't want to go anywhere.

'We are going to search the Cape with a fine-tooth comb for Mpayipheli. He must be staying somewhere. Benny will find out if he has any family or friends here, but in the meantime we will have to visit or contact every establishment that offers accommodation. We are waiting . . .'

Joubert's eyes turned to the door and everyone followed suit. Boef Beukes had come in. Behind him was the man in the suit that Griessel had seen in Beukes's office. Joubert nodded in their direction.

'We are waiting for good photos from Home Affairs and you will each get one, along with the best description we can compile. There already is a bulletin out for the pick-up and we are putting up roadblocks on the N-one, N-two, N-seven, R-twenty-seven, R-forty-four and four places on the R-three hundred around Mitchells Plain and Khayelitsha. We will also provide details to the media and ask the public to cooperate. In an hour or so we should have a timetable drawn up, so that you can begin phoning places of accommodation. Stand by until we are ready for you.'

Joubert came to sit beside Griessel directly. 'Sorry about that, Benny. There was no time to warn you.'

Griessel shrugged. It made no difference.

'Are you okay?'

He wanted to ask what that meant, but he just nodded instead.

'We've booked you onto the nine o'clock flight to Port Elizabeth. It's the last one today.'

'I'll go and pack.'

'I need you there, Benny.'

He nodded again. Then Boef Beukes and Mr Red Tie came up to them. The unknown man was holding a big brown envelope.

'Matt, can we have a word?' Beukes said, and Griessel wondered why he was speaking English.

'Things are a bit mad here,' said Joubert.

'We have some information . . .' said Beukes.

'We're listening.'

'Can we talk in your office?'

'What's with the English, Boef? Or are you practising for when the *Argus* phones?' Griessel asked.

'Let me introduce you to Special Agent Chris Lombardi of the DEA,' said Beukes and turned to Red Tie.

'I work for the United States Drug Enforcement Agency, and I've been in your country now for three months,' said Chris Lombardi. With his bald pate and long fleshy ears, Griessel thought he looked like an accountant.

'Superintendent Beukes and I have been part of an inter-agency operation to investigate the flow of drugs between Asia and South America, in which South Africa, and Cape Town in particular, seems to play a prominent part.' Lombardi's accent was strongly American, like a film star's.

Three months, thought Griessel. The fuckers had been watching Carlos for three months.

Lombardi took an A4-size sheet of paper from his brown envelope and placed it on Joubert's desk. It was a black-and-white portrait photograph of a clean-shaven man with dark curly hair. 'This is César Sangrenegra. Also known as *El Muerte*. He is the second in command of the Guajira Cartel, one of the biggest Colombian drug-smuggling operations in South America. He is one of the three infamous Sangrenegra brothers, and we believe he arrived in Cape Town early this morning.'

'Carlos's brother,' said Griessel.

'Yes, he is the brother of the late Carlos. And that's part of the problem. But let me start at the beginning.' Lombardi took another photograph from the envelope. 'This is Miguel Sangrenegra, a.k.a. *La Rubia*, or *La Rubia de la Santa Marta*. "Rubia" means "blond", and as you can see, the man isn't blond at all. He is the patriarch of the family, seventy-two years old, and has been retired since nineteen ninety-five. But it all started with him. In the nineteen-fifties Miguel was a coffee smuggler in the Caribbean and was perfectly positioned to graduate to marijuana in the sixties and seventies. He hails from the town of Santa Marta in the Guajira province of Colombia. Now, the Guajira is not the most fertile of the Colombian districts, but it has one strange advantage. Due to soil quality and chemistry, it produces a very popular variant of marijuana, called Santa Marta Gold. It is much sought-after in the US, and the street price is considerably higher than any other form of weed. In the Guajira, they refer to Santa Marta Gold as *La Rubia*. And that is what Miguel started smuggling, hence his nickname.'

Lombardi took a map out of the envelope and unfolded it on the desk.

'This is Colombia, and this area, on the Caribbean coast, is the Guajira. As you can see, what the province lacked in soil fertility, it made up for in geographic location. Just look at this length of coastline. If you wanted to smuggle marijuana to the US, you either sent a boat to the Guajira coast, or you sent a cargo plane. Miguel knew the farmers who grew the stuff in the mountains, and he knew the coast like the back of his hand. So he became a *marimbero*. A smuggler of marijuana. The Colombians refer to it as *marimba*. Anyway, he made a killing in the seventies. But then, in the late seventies and eighties, cocaine became the drug of preference internationally. And the balance of drug power, the money, and the focus of law enforcement, moved to central Colombia. To people like Pablo Escobar and the Medellín Cartel. Carlos Lehder, the Ochoa brothers, José Rodríguez-Gacha . . .

'Miguel did not like cocaine, and he didn't have the natural contacts for it, so he stuck to *marimba*, made good money, but he never reached the dizzy heights of wealth and power like Escobar or Lehder. However, in the long run, this was to his great advantage. Because when we started hunting the big cartels, Miguel was quietly going about his business. And in the nineties, his family stepped into the vacuum after the removal of the big guns.'

Another photograph came out of the brown envelope.

'This is Miguel Sangrenegra's eldest son, Javier. He is short and stocky, like his mother. And we think he has the old lady's brains and ambition too. He was the one who put pressure on his father to expand the family business into cocaine. Miguel resisted, and Javier sidelined the old man. Not immediately, but slowly and quietly retired him in a way that meant everybody's respect remained intact.

'Now let's talk about Carlos.' Another photograph, this time of the youngest brother. Grainy black and white. In a sunny street in a South American town, a younger Carlos was getting out of a Land Rover Discovery.

Griessel checked his watch. He still had to pack. He wondered what the point of this story was.

'Carlos was the runt of the litter. The least intelligent of the brothers, bit of a playboy, with a taste for young girls. He managed to get a fourteen-year-old girl from the neighbouring town of Barranquilla pregnant and Javier shipped him off to Cape Town to avoid trouble. He needed someone here he could trust. To oversee his operations. Because, by 2001, the Guajira Cartel, as they are now known, had gone truly international. And they had branched out into the whole spectrum of drugs.

'Carlos was doing okay. He kept out of trouble, managed his side of the business reasonably well with the help of a team very loyal to Javier – the four guys we have in custody. And then he got into the mess with the prostitute's daughter. And now, as you know, Carlos is dead.

'Enter César Sangrenegra. *El Muerte*. The Death, they call him. If Javier is the brains of the cartel, César is its strong arm. He is a killer. Rumour has it that he has executed more than three hundred people in the last ten years. And we're not talking about ordering the death of opponents. We're talking about personally twisting the knife.'

The last photographs came out of the envelope. Lombardi spread them over the desk. Men with amputated genitals pushed into their mouths. The bodies of women with breasts removed.

'And this is the necktie method. See how the tongue is pulled through the slit throat. *El Muerte* is one sick puppy. He is big and strong and very, very fit. He is totally ruthless. Some say he is a sociopath. When his name is whispered in Guajira, people tremble.'

'So what's he doing in Cape Town?' Matt Joubert asked.

'That's why we're here,' said Boef Beukes.

'You see, there is a simple code in the Guajira,' said Lombardi. 'When someone takes from you – money, possessions, or whatever – it is said that he walks with *culebras* on his back. It means "snakes". He walks with a snake on his back, a poisonous thing that can strike at any time, which keeps him looking over his shoulder in fear. The *guajiro* unconditionally believe in *justicia*. Justice. Revenge.'

'So what are you saying?' asked Griessel.

'I am saying that you, Inspector Griessel, will be held responsible for Carlos's death. You, the spearman and the prostitute. You are all walking with *culebras* on your backs.'

The detective inspector with the snake on his back was going to be late. He packed his suitcase in too much of a hurry and when he reached the kitchen he grabbed the brandy bottle from the cupboard and put it in as well.

He tore a sheet of paper from his notebook and wrote a thankyou note to Charmaine Watson-Smith in an untidy scrawl. For a moment he thought that the only rhyme he knew began with, 'There was a young man from Australia . . .' He couldn't remember the rest, but it didn't matter, as it wasn't exactly relevant.

He put the clean dish down at her door and hurried to the entrance of the block of flats. As he walked he realised what was happening to Charmaine's newspaper to make it disappear. He stopped in his tracks, turned and jogged back to her door and knocked. He picked up the dish.

It was a while before she opened.

'Why, Inspector . . .'

'Madam, I'm sorry, I have to catch a flight. I just wanted to say thank you. And I know what happens to your newspaper.'

'Oh?' she said and took the dish.

'Someone takes it when they are going out. They take it with them. In the morning.'

'My goodness . . .'

'I have to run. I will look into it when I get back.'

'Thank you, Inspector.'

'No, madam, thank you. That . . .' and for a moment he couldn't think what the English word was. He wanted to say 'sheep's meat' although he knew it was incorrect. '. . . Lamb, that lamb was wonderful.' He jogged back to the front entrance and thought he had better hurry, because now he *was* late.

When the second brandy and Coke flooded through him like a heavenly heat wave, he leaned back in the seat of the plane and sighed deeply in pleasure. He was a fuck-up, a drunk, but that was that – he was born to drink, made for drink. That was what he did best, that was when he felt whole and right and one with the universe. Then the rhyme came back to him.

> *There was a young man from Australia*
> *Who painted his arse like a dahlia.*
> *The colours were bright,*
> *And the look·was all right*
> *But the smell was a hell of a failure.*

He grinned and wondered how many others he could remember, now that his brain was working again. He could rattle them off in his jokester days. *There was a young man from Brazil, who swallowed a dynamite pill* . . . Perhaps he should compose one about himself. *A detective inspector who drank. . . .*

He took another swallow from the bloody small plastic airline cup with its two blocks of ice and thought, no,

> *There was a dumb cop from the Cape,*
> *Who let a black spearman escape.*

The stewardess approached from the front and he held his glass up and tapped an index finger on it. She nodded, but didn't seem extremely friendly. Probably afraid he would get paralytically drunk on her plane. She with her hair combed back and little red mouth, she could relax; he might be a wife-beating, whore-fucking fuck-up of a policeman, but he could hold his drink, daddio. That was one thing he could do with great, well-oiled skill.

> *He thought he was white,*
> *And that's not all right.*

But what the fuck rhymed with 'Cape' and 'Escape'? All he could think of was 'rape'. Maybe he should start over; here came the stewardess with his next drink.

> *On his back's not a snake, but an ape.*

'Sir, are you all right?' asked the woman at Budget Rent-a-Car with a slight frown and he said: 'As right as rain,' and he signed flamboyantly next to every fucking cross she made on the document. She gave him the keys and he walked out into the windy evening in Port Elizabeth. He thought he ought to turn on his bloody cell phone, but, first, find the car. Then again, why turn on the phone? He was relieved of his responsibilities, wasn't he?

They had given him a Nissan Almera, that's what it said on the tag on the keys. He couldn't find the fucking car. Suitcase in hand he walked down the rows of cars. The whole lot were white, almost. He couldn't recall what an Almera looked like. He used to have a Sentra, a demonstration model he had bought at Schus in Bellville for a helluva bargain, never had any shit with that car. Jissis, it was a lifetime ago. Here was the fucking Almera, right here under his nose. He pressed the button on the key and the car said 'beep' and the lights flashed. He unlocked the boot and put his suitcase away. Maybe turn on the phone, they might have caught the guy by now.

He had to lean against the car. He had to admit he was a bit tipsy.

YOU HAVE THREE MESSAGES. PLEASE CALL 121.

He pressed the tabs. A woman's voice. 'You have three new voice messages. First message . . .'

'Benny, it's Anna. Where are you? Carla isn't home yet. We don't know where she is. If you are sober, phone me.'

What time had Anna phoned? It was sometime in the afternoon that he had switched the phone off. Why did she sound so panicky?

'This is Tim Ngubane. The time is now twenty forty-nine. Just wanted to let you know Christine van Rooyen is missing, Benny. Witness Protection called me. She walked out on them, apparently. They kept her in a house in Boston, and she's just gone. Will keep you posted. Bye.'

She walked out on them? Now why would she do that? He pressed seven to delete the message.

'Benny, it's Anna. I talked to Matt Joubert. He says you have gone to PE. Call me, please. Carla is still not home. We have phoned everyone. I am very worried. Call me when you get this message. Please!'

There was despair in Anna's voice that penetrated through his alcoholic haze, that made him realise this was trouble. He pressed nine and cut the connection. He leaned against the Almera. He couldn't phone her, because he was drunk.

Where was Carla? Jissis, he had to get some coffee or something, he had to sober up fast. He got in the car. The driver's seat was shifted right up to the steering wheel, he had to feel around for the lever underneath before he could get in. At last he got the car going.

Not so very drunk, he just had to concentrate. He pulled away, must get to the hotel. Drink some coffee. And walk, keep walking until the haze lifted, then he could phone Anna; she mustn't hear he had been drinking. She would know. Seventeen fucking years' experience – she would catch him out at the speed of white light. He should never have had those drinks. He had even packed the bottle. He was ready to start drinking full bore again and now Carla was missing and a suspicion began to grow in him and he didn't want to think of it.

Cell phone rang.

He checked. It wasn't Anna.

Who was phoning him at eleven at night?

He would have to pull over. He wasn't sober enough to drive and talk.

'Griessel.'

'Is that Detective Inspector Benny Griessel?' The 'g' was spoken softly and in a vaguely familiar accent.

'Yes.'

'Okay. Detective Inspector Griessel, you will have to listen very carefully now, because this is very important. Are you listening very carefully?'

'Who is this?'

'I will ask again: are you listening very carefully?'

'Yes.'

'I understand you are hunting the killer of Carlos Sangrenegra. This is so?'

'Yes.' His heart was racing.

'Okay. This is good. Because you must bring him to me. You understand?'

'Who are you?'

'I am the man who has your daughter, Detective Inspector. I have her here with me. Now, you must listen very, very carefully. I have people who work with you. I know everything. I know if you do a stupid thing, you understand? When you do a stupid thing, I will cut off a finger of Carla, you understand? If you tell other police I have your daughter, I will cut her, you understand?'

'Yes.' He forced out the words with great effort; thoughts were scrabbling through his brain.

'Okay. I will call you. Every day. In the morning and in the afternoon, I will call you, for three days. You must find this man who kill Carlos, and you must bring him to me.'

'I don't know where you are . . .' Panic overflowed into his voice, he couldn't stop it.

'You are scared. That is good. But you must be calm. When I call you and you tell me you have this man, I will tell you where to go, you understand?'

'Yes.'

'Three days. You have three days to get this man. Then I will kill her. Okay, now I have to do something, because I know people. Tomorrow, you think you are more clever than this phone man. So I have to do something to let you remember tomorrow, okay?'

'Okay.'

'Carla is here with me. We take her clothes. Your daughter has a good body. I like her tits. Now, I will put this knife in her tit. It will hurt, and it will bleed. But I want you to listen. This is the thing I want you to remember. This sound.'

PART THREE
Thobela

41

'I will leave you to it,' said Sangrenegra and walked away from him.

Thobela said his name. 'Carlos.' The lone word echoed around the interior of the large room. The Colombian turned.

Thobela swiftly and deftly drew the assegai by the shaft out of the white swimming-pool pipe. 'I am here about the girl,' he said.

'No,' said Carlos.

He said nothing, just stepped closer to where the man stood beside the pool.

'She lie,' said Carlos walking backwards.

He adjusted his grip on the assegai.

'Please,' said Carlos. 'I did not touch the girl.' He raised empty hands in front of him. Terror distorted his face. 'Please. She lie. The whore, she lie.'

Fury washed over him. At the man's cowardice, his denial, everything he represented. He moved fast, raised the assegai high.

'The police . . .' said Carlos, and the long blade descended.

Christine saw the minister's eyes were red-rimmed and tired, but she knew she still held his attention.

She rose from her chair and leaned over the desk. When she stood like that, slightly bent over, arms stretched out to the cardboard carton, her breasts were prominent. She was aware of it, but also that it didn't matter any more. She pulled the box to her side of the desk and folded the flaps open.

'I have to explain this now,' she said and reached into the carton. She took out two newspaper clippings. She unfolded one. She glanced briefly at the photograph and article on it, specifically at the young girl emerging from a helicopter with a man. She put the clipping down on the desk and smoothed it with her hand.

'This is my fault,' she said, and rotated the article so that the minister could see better. She tapped a fingertip on the photo. 'Her name is Carla Griessel,' said Christine.

While the minister looked she reached for the second clipping.

He came out of Sangrenegra's front door and in the corner of his eye he spotted a movement. Opposite, in the big house, behind a window. The discomfort of Carlos's reaction, the Colombian's choice of words and the overwhelming feeling of being watched unfolded in his belly.

Something wasn't right.

Five objects lay on the desk in an uneven row. The two newspaper clippings were on the far right. Then the brown and white dog, a stuffed toy with big, soft eyes and a little red tongue hanging out of the smiling mouth. Next the small white plastic container with medicinal contents. And last on the left, a large syringe.

Christine shifted the box to the left again. It was not yet empty.

'The next morning, after Carlos had seen Sonia for the first time, I phoned Vanessa.'

He braked with screeching tyres next to his pick-up, grabbed the white pipe holding his assegai and leapt out.

Slowly, his head told him. Slowly. Do the right thing.

He unlocked his pick-up, tilted the backrest forward and put the pipe behind it. He unzipped his sports bag, looking for an item of clothing. He took out a blue and white T-shirt. He had bought it at the motorbike training centre at Amersfoort. One each for himself and Pakamile. He walked back to the swimming-pool van.

A siren approached, he wasn't sure from which side, not sure how close. Adrenaline made his heart jump.

Slowly. He wiped the panel van's steering wheel with the T-shirt. The gear lever.

The siren was closer.

The inside door handle. The window winder.

What else?

Another siren, from somewhere in the city.

What else had he touched? Rear-view mirror? He wiped but he was in a hurry, didn't do it properly.

Slowly. He wiped it again, back and front of the mirror.

His eye caught the speck of the helicopter in the blue sky where it came around Devil's Peak.

They were after him.

When he raced away from Sangrenegra's house, just before he turned the corner at the bottom of the street, he had seen something in the rear-view mirror. Or had he?

They were on to him.

He cursed in Xhosa, a single syllable. A walker came around the bend, down the slope from the Signal Hill side.

He took four long strides to get to his pick-up.

'I didn't know how the whole thing would end,' she said to the minister, to try and justify what she was yet to tell him. She listened to the lack of intonation in her voice. She was aware of her fatigue, as if she didn't have the strength for the final straight. It was because she had gone through it so many times in her head, she told herself.

The first time she had seen the clipping, the eyes of Carla Griessel and the terrible knowledge that it was all her fault and also the relief that she still had the ability to feel guilt and remorse. After everything. After all the lies. After all the deception. All the years. She could still feel someone else's pain. Still feel compassion. Still feel pity for someone besides herself. And the guilt that she felt that relief.

She took a deep breath to gather her strength, because this explanation was the one that mattered.

'I was afraid,' she said. 'You have to understand that. I was terrified. The way Carlos looked at Sonia . . . I thought I knew him. That was one of the problems. I know men. I *had* to know them. And Carlos was the naughty child. Sort of harmless. He was nagging and possessive and jealous, but he wanted so much to please. He had my clients beaten up, but he never did the hitting himself. Up to that moment I still thought I could control him. That's the main thing. With all the men. To be in control without them knowing it. But then I saw his face. And I knew, everything I had thought was wrong. I didn't know him. I had no control over him. And I panicked. Totally.

'I . . . It wasn't like I worked out a plan or anything. There was just all this stuff in my head. The Artemis guy and the stuff in Carlos's house, the drugs and all, and the panic over the way he looked at Sonia. I think if a person is really scared, like terrified, then a part of your brain starts working that you don't know about, it takes over. I don't know if you understand that, because you have to *be* there.

'I phoned Carlos and said I wanted to talk to him.'

He drove with the radio on. He deliberately chose alternate routes and drove instinctively east, towards Wellington and through Bains Kloof, over Mitchells Pass to Ceres and via gravel roads to Sutherland.

At first he rejected the possibility that Sangrenegra might be innocent.

It was the other elements that came together first – the movement in the house opposite, the man he thought he saw running across the road in his rear-view mirror. The newspaper reports that taunted him. Carlos's words, 'The police . . .' He wanted to say something, something he knew.

They were waiting for him. They had set up an ambush and he had walked into it like a fool, like an amateur – unconcerned, overconfident.

He wondered how much they knew. Did they have a camera in that house across the street? Was his photograph on its way to the newspapers and television right now? Could he risk going home?

But he kept coming back to the possibility that Carlos was innocent.

His protestations. His face.

The big difference between Carlos and the rest, who welcomed the blade as an escape. Or justice.

Lord. If the Colombian was innocent, Thobela Mpayipheli was a murderer rather than an executioner.

Thirty kilometres west of Fraserburg, over a radio signal that came and went, he heard the news bulletin for the first time.

'A task team of the police's Serious and Violent Crime Unit was just too late to apprehend the so-called Artemis vigilante . . . set up various roadblocks in the Cape Peninsula and Boland in an apparent attempt . . . a two-thousand-and-one model Isuzu KB two-sixty with registration number . . .'

That was the moment when self-recrimination evaporated, when he knew they knew and the old battle fever revived. He had been here before. The prey. He had been hunted across the length and breadth of strange and familiar continents. He knew this, he had been trained for it by the best; they could do nothing he hadn't experienced before, *handled* before.

That was the moment he knew he was wholly back in the Struggle. Like in the old, old days when there was something worth protecting to the death. You see furthest from the moral high ground. It brought a great calm over him, so that he knew precisely what to do.

She met Carlos at the Mugg & Bean at the Waterfront. She watched him coming towards her with his self-satisfied strut, arms swinging gaily, head half cocked. Like an overgrown boy that has got his own way. Fuck you Carlos; you have no idea.

'So how's your daughter, conchita?' he said with a smirk as he sat down.

She had to light a cigarette to hide her fear.

'She's fine.' Curtly.

'Ah, conchita, don't be angry. It is your fault. You hide things from Carlos. All Carlos wants to do is to know you, to care for you.'

She said nothing, just looked at him.

'She is very beautiful. Like her mother. She have your eyes.' And he thought that would make her feel better?

'Carlos, I will give you what you want.'

'What I want?'

'You don't want me to see other clients. You don't want me to hide things from you. Is that right?'

'*Sí*. That is right.'

'I will do that, but there are certain rules.'

'Carlos will take good care of you and the leetle conchita. You know that.'

'It's not the money, Carlos.'

'Anything, conchita. What you want?'

He drove from Merweville across the arid expanses of the Great Karoo to Prince Albert as the sun set in spectacular colours.

According to the radio they thought he was still in the Cape.

In the dark of night he crossed the Swartberg Pass and cautiously descended to Oudtshoorn. On the odd one-lane tarred road between Willowmore and Steytlerville he recognised that fatigue had the better of him and he looked out for a place to turn off and sleep. He shifted into a more comfortable position on the front seat and closed his eyes. At half-past three in the morning he slept, only to wake at first light, stiff-limbed, scratchy-eyed, his face needing a wash.

At Kirkwood, in the grimy toilets of a garage, he brushed his teeth and splashed cold water on his face. This was Xhosa country and no one looked twice at him. He bought take-away chicken portions at Chicken Licken and drove. Towards home.

At half-past ten he crossed the Hogsback Pass and thirty-five minutes later he turned in at the farm entrance and saw the tracks on the reddish-brown dirt of the road.

He got out.

Only one vehicle. Narrow tyres of a small sedan. In. Not yet out. Someone was waiting for him.

'My daughter's name is Sonia.'

'That is very beautiful.' Like he really meant it.

'But I will not bring her to your house, Carlos. We can go somewhere together. Picnic, or the movies, but not to your house.'

'But, conchita, I have this pool . . .'

'And you have these bodyguards with guns and baseball bats. I will not allow my daughter to see that.'

'They are not bodyguards. They are my crew.'

'I don't care.'

'Hokay, hokay, Carlos will send them away when you come.'

'You won't.'

'No? Why not?'

'Because they are with you all the time.'

'No, conchita, I swear,' he said, and made the sign of the cross over his upper body.

'When my daughter is with me, I don't sleep with you and we don't sleep over. That is final.'

'Carlos unnerstand,' he said, but couldn't hide his disappointment.

'And we will take it slowly. I have to talk to her about you first. She must get used to you slowly.'

'Hokay.'

'So, tomorrow night, we will see if you are serious. I will come to your house and it will only be you and me. No bodyguards.'

'*Sí.* Of course.'

'I will stay with you. I will cook for you and we will talk.'

'Where will Sonia be?'

'She will be safe.'

'At the nanny's place?' Pleased with himself, because he knew.

'Yes.'

'And maybe the weekend, we can go somewhere? You and me and Sonia?'

'If I see I can trust you, Carlos.' But she knew she had him. She knew the process had begun.

42

Thobela left his pick-up behind the ridges at the Waterval Plantation and walked along the bank of the Cata River towards his house, assegai in his left hand.

A kilometre before the homestead came into view he turned northeast, so he could approach from the high ground. They would be expecting him from the road end.

He sat watching for twenty minutes, but saw only the car parked in front of the house. No antennae, nothing to identify it as a police vehicle. Silence.

It made no sense.

He kept the shed between him and the house, checking that the doors were still locked. Crouching, he approached the house, below window level, to where the car was parked.

There was one set of footprints in the dust. They began at the driver's door and led directly to the steps of the front veranda.

One man.

He ran through alternatives in his head while he squatted on his haunches with his back to the veranda wall. Something occurred to him. The detective from Umtata. Must have heard the news. Knew him, knew everything, from the start.

The detective had come for more money.

He stood, relieved and purposeful, and strode up his veranda steps and in at the front door, assegai now in his right hand.

The man was sitting there on the chair, pistol on his lap.

'I thought you would come,' said the white man.

'Who are you?'

'My name is Benny Griessel,' he said and raised the Z88 so that it pointed straight at Thobela's chest.

Christine took the stuffed toy dog from the desk and held it in her hands. 'I had a battle to get the right dog,' she said. 'Every year there are different toys in the shops.'

Her fingers stroked the long brown ears. 'I bought her one when she was three years old. It's her favourite, she won't go anywhere without it. So I had to get another and switch them, because the one she played with had her genetics on it. The police computers can test anything. So I had to take the right one along.'

He stood in front of the white man weighing up his chances, measuring the distance between the assegai and the pistol, and then he allowed himself to relax, because now was not the moment to do anything.

'This is my house,' he said.

'I know.'

'What do you want?'

'I want you to sit there and be quiet.' The white man motioned with the barrel of the Z88 towards the two-seater couch opposite him. There was something about his eyes and voice: intensity, a determination.

Thobela hesitated, shrugged and sat down. He looked at Griessel. Who was he? The bloodshot eyes, a hint of capillaries on the nose that betrayed excessive drinking. Hair long and untidy – either he was trying to keep the look of his youth in the seventies alive, or he didn't care. The latter seemed more likely, since his clothes were rumpled, the comfortable brown shoes dull. He had the faint scent of law enforcement about him and the Z88 confirmed it, but policemen usually came in groups, at least in pairs. Police waited with handcuffs and commands, they didn't ask you to sit down in your own house.

'I'm sitting,' he said, and placed the assegai on the floor beside the couch.

'Now you just have to be quiet.'

'Is that what we are going to do? Sit and stare at each other?'

The white man did not answer.

'Will you shoot me if I talk?'

No response.

'The pills were easy,' said Christine. She indicated the white medicinal container on the desk. 'And the dress. I don't have it; it's with the police. But the blood . . . I couldn't do it at first. I didn't know how to tell my child I had to push a needle into her arm and that it would hurt and the blood would run into the syringe and I had to spray it on the seat of a man's car. That was the hardest thing. And I was worried. I didn't know whether the blood would clot. I didn't know if it would be enough. I didn't know if the police would be able to tell it wasn't fresh blood. I didn't know how they did all those genetics. Would the computer be able to tell the blood had been in the fridge for a day?'

She held the dog against her chest. She didn't look at the minister. She looked at her fingers entangled in the toy's ears.

'When Sonia was in the bath, I went in and I lied to her. I said we had to do it, because I had to take a little bit of her blood to the doctor. When she asked, "Why?" I didn't know what to say. I asked her if she remembered the vaccination she had at play school so she wouldn't get those bad diseases. She said, "Mamma, it was sore", and I said, "But the sore went away quickly – this sore will also go away quickly, it's the same thing, so you can be well." So she said, "Okay, Mamma" and she squeezed her eyes shut and held out her arm. I have never drawn blood from someone before, but if you are a whore, you have your AIDS test every month, so I know what they do. But if your child says, "Ow, Mamma, ow", then you get the shakes and it's hard and you get a fright if you can't get the blood . . .'

'What are we waiting for? What do you want?' he asked. But the man just sat and looked at him, with his pistol hand resting on his lap, and said nothing. Just the eyes blinking now and again, or drifting off to the window.

He wondered whether the man was right in the head. Or on drugs, because of that terrible intensity, something eating him. The eyes were never completely still. Sometimes a knee would jerk as if it were a wound spring. The pistol had its own fine vibration, an almost unnoticeable movement.

Unstable. Therefore dangerous. Would he make it, if he could pull himself up by the armrest and launch himself over the little more than two metres between them? If he picked a moment when the eyes flicked to the window? If he could deflect the Z88?

He measured the distance. He looked into the brown eyes.

No.

But what were they sitting here and waiting for? In such tension?

He had partial answers later when the cell phone rang twice. Each time the white man started, a subtle tautening of the body. He lifted the phone from his lap and then just sat dead still, and let it ring. Until it stopped. Fifteen, twenty seconds later it beeped twice to show a message had been left. But Griessel did nothing about it. He didn't listen to his messages.

They were waiting for instructions; that much Thobela gathered. Which would be delivered via the cell phone. The intensity was stress. Anxiety. But why? What did it have to do with him?

'Are you in trouble?'

Griessel just stared at him.

'Can I help you in some way?'

The man glanced at the window, and back again.

'Do you mind if I sleep a bit?' asked Thobela. Because that was all he could do. And he needed it.

No reaction.

He made himself comfortable, stretched his long legs out, rested his head on the cushion of the couch and closed his eyes.

But the cell phone rang again and this time the white man pressed the answer button and said; 'Griessel' and, 'Yes, I have him.' He listened. He said: 'Yes.'

And again: 'Yes.' Listened. 'And then?'

Thobela could hear a man's voice faintly over the phone, but couldn't make out any words, just the grain of a voice.

Griessel took the cell phone away from his ear and stood, keeping a safe distance.

'Come,' he said. 'Let's go.'

'I'm very comfortable, thank you.'

A shot thundered through the quiet of the room and the bullet ripped a hole beside him in the couch. Stuffing and dust exploded from it, falling back to the floor in slow motion. Thobela looked at the white man, who said nothing. Then he got up, keeping his hands away from his body.

'Easy now,' he said to Griessel.

'To the car.'

He went.

'Wait.'

He looked back. Griessel stood beside the assegai. He looked at it, looked at him, as if he had to make a decision. Then he bent and picked it up.

Thobela drew his own conclusions. The man didn't want to leave any evidence. And that was not good news.

He was supposed to pick her up at half-past four, but at a quarter past there was a knock on the door; when she opened up, there stood Carlos with a big smile and a bunch of flowers.

He came inside and said, 'So, conchita, this is where you live. This is your place. It is nice. Very nice.'

She had to remain calm and friendly, but the tension was overwhelming. Because the toy dog was lying in sight and the syringe of blood was still in the fridge.

She wanted to hide it in the shopping bags along with the ingredients for the meal she was going to cook. Sonia's dress was folded up in her handbag. Carlos wanted to see where she slept, where her daughter's room was. He was impressed with the big television screen (Carlos will get you one like this, conchita. For you and Sonia.') He wandered over to her fridge. 'Now dees ees a freedge,' he said in awe, and as he reached for the handle and pulled, she said, 'Carlos,' sharply, so that the sound of her voice gave her a fright and he looked around like a child who had been naughty.

'Will you help me to get the groceries to the car, please?' She could send him down to the car with a few of the plastic bags.

'*Sí*. Of course. What are you going to cook for us?'

'It's a surprise, so don't open the fridge.'

'But I want to see how big it is.'

'Another time.' There wouldn't be one.

The white man sat in the left back seat of the car and let Thobela drive.

'Go.'

'Where?'

'Just drive.'

Thobela took the farm road out. He couldn't see in the rear-view mirror what was happening on the back seat. He turned his head, as if he had seen something outside the car. At the edge of his vision he saw Griessel with a roadmap on his lap.

He added up what he knew. He was reasonably certain Griessel was a policeman. The Z88, the attitude. The white man had known where the farm was and that Thobela would be on his way there. More important: no other policemen had shown up. The law considered the farm covered.

Griessel had waited for the right call to come over the cell phone. *Yes. I have him.* But that was not police procedure. Couldn't be.

Who else was after him? To whom else did he have value?

'Go to George,' said Griessel. Thobela looked around, saw the roadmap was folded now.

'George?'

'You know where it is.'

'It's nearly six hundred kilometres.'

'You drove more than a thousand yesterday.'

The policeman knew he had left the Cape yesterday. He had access to official information, but he wasn't official. It didn't make sense. He would have to try something. He could do something with the car on the gravel road because he was wearing a seatbelt and Griessel was not. He could brake suddenly and grab the man when he was thrown forward. Try and get the pistol.

Not without risks.

Was the risk necessary? George? What was at George? If the policeman had been official they would have been on the way to Cathcart or Seymour or Alice or Port Elizabeth. Or Grahamstown. To the nearest place with reinforcements and cells and state prosecutors.

He was a high-profile suspect; he knew that. If you were SAPS and you caught the Artemis vigilante, then you called the guys with guns and helicopters, you didn't get off your cell phone until you had your detainee in ten sets of handcuffs.

Unless you were working for someone else. Unless you were supplementing your income . . .

He considered the alternatives and there was only one logical conclusion.

'How long have you been working for Sangrenegra?' He turned the mirror with his left hand. Bloodshot eyes stared back. He got no response.

'That's the problem with this country. Money means more than justice,' he said.

'Is that how you justify your murders?' said the policeman from behind.

'Murder? There was only one murder. I didn't know Sangrenegra was innocent. It was you people who used him for an ambush.'

'Sangrenegra? How do you know he was innocent?'

'I saw it in his eyes.'

'And Bernadette Laurens? What did her eyes tell you?'

'Laurens?'

The policeman said nothing.

'But she confessed.'

'That's what they all keep telling me.'

'But it wasn't her?'

'I don't think it was. I think she was protecting the child's mother. Like others would protect their children.'

The unexpectedness of it left Thobela dumb.

'That's why we have a justice system. A process. That is why we can't take the law into our own hands,' said Griessel.

Thobela wrestled with the possibility, with rationalising and acceptance of guilt. But he couldn't tip the scales either way.

'So why did she confess then?' he asked himself, but aloud.

There was no response from the back seat.

43

While they carried the shopping bags into Carlos's kitchen, she could think of nothing but the syringe of blood.

The house was unnaturally quiet and empty without the body-guards; the large spaces echoed footsteps and phrases. He embraced her in the kitchen after they had put the groceries down. He pressed her to him with surprising tenderness and said: 'This is right, conchita.'

She made her body soft. She let her hips flow against his. 'Yes,' she said.

'We will be happy.'

In answer she kissed him on the mouth, with great skill, until she could feel his erection developing. She put her hand on it and traced the shape. Carlos's hands were behind her back. He pulled her dress up inch by inch until her bottom was exposed and slipped his fingers under the elastic of her panties. His breathing quickened.

She moved her lips over his cheek, down his neck, over the cross that hung in his chest hair. Her tongue left a damp trail. She freed herself and dropped to her knees, fingers busy with his zipper. With one hand she pulled his underpants down and with the other she pulled his penis out. Long, thin and hairy, it stood up like a lean soldier with an outsized shiny helmet.

'Conchita.' His voice was a whispering urgency, as she had never done this without a condom before.

She stroked with both hands, from the pubic hairs to the tip.

'We will be happy,' she said and softly put it in her mouth.

Thobela Mpayipheli and his white passenger, sitting in the back like a colonial property baron, drove past Mwangala and Dyamala, where fat cattle grazed in the sweet green grass. They turned right onto the R63. Fort Hare was quiet over the summer holidays. Five minutes later they were in busy Alice. Fruit vendors on the pavements, women with baskets on their heads and children on their backs who walked stately and unhurried across the road and down the street. Four men were gathered around a board game on a street corner. Thobela wondered if the policeman saw all this. If he could hear the Xhosa calls that were exchanged across the broad street. This was ownership. The people owned this place.

Thirty kilometres on was Fort Beaufort and he turned south. Four or five times he spotted the Kat River on the left where it meandered away between the hills. It had been one of his plans to bring Pakamile here: just the two of them with rucksacks, hiking boots and a two-man tent. To show his boy where he had grown up.

Thobela knew every bend of the Kat. He knew the deep pools at Nkqantosi where you could jump off the cliff and open your eyes deep under the greenish-brown water and see the sunbeams fighting against the darkness. The little sandy beach below Komkulu. Where he had discovered the warrior inside him thirty years before. Mtetwa, the young buffalo who was a bully, an injustice he had to correct. The first.

And far over that way, out of sight, his favourite place. Four kilometres from the place where it flowed into the Great Fish River, the Kat made a flamboyant curve, as if it wanted to dally one last time before losing its identity – a meander that swept back so far that it almost made an island. It was about ten kilometres from the Mission Church manse where he lived, but he could run there in an hour down the secret game paths around the hills and through the valleys. All so he could sit between the reeds where the chattering weaverbirds in brilliant colour lured females to their hanging nests. To listen to the wind. To watch the fat iguana warming itself in the sun on the black rocky point. In the late afternoon the bushbuck came out of the thickets like phantoms to dip their heads to the water. First the grace of the does in their red glowing coats. Later the rams would come two by two, dark brown in the dusk, sturdy, short, needle-sharp horns that rose and dipped, rose and dipped.

He had wondered if they were still there. Whether he and his son would see the descendants of the animals he had waited for with bated breath as a child. Did they still follow the same paths through the reeds and bulrushes?

Would he still know the paths? Should he stop here, take off his shoes and disappear between the thorn trees? Search out the same paths at a jogtrot; find that rhythm when you felt you could run for ever, as long as there was a hill on the horizon for you to climb?

While Carlos was seated in front of the TV with a glass and a bottle of red wine, she took the syringe of blood out of her handbag and hid it deep in a cupboard where pots and pans were stacked, bright, new and unused.

She looked for a hiding place for the toy dog before she took it out from under packs of vegetables in the shopping bags.

Her hands shook because she would not hear Carlos coming before he was in the room.

They drove in silence for two hours. Beyond Grahamstown, in the dark of early evening, he said: 'Did you ever hear of Nxele?' His tongue clicked sharply pronouncing the name.

He did not expect an answer. If he did get one he knew what it would be. White people didn't know this history.

'Nxele. They say he was a big man. Two metres tall. And he could talk. Once he talked himself off a Xhosa execution pyre. And then he became chief, without having the blood of kings.'

He didn't care if the white man was listening or not. He kept his eyes on the road. He wanted to shake off his lassitude, say what this landscape awakened in him. He wanted to relieve the tension somehow.

'Exceptional in that time, nearly two hundred years ago. He lived in a time when the people fought against each other – and the English too. Then Nxele came and said they must stop kneeling to the white God. They must listen to the voice of Mdalidiphu, the

God of the Xhosa, who said you must not kneel before Him in the dust. You must live. You must dance. You must lift your head and grab hold of life. You must sleep with your wife so we can increase, so we can fill the earth and drive the white man out. So we can take back our land.

'You could say he was the father of the first Struggle. Then he gathered ten thousand warriors together. Did you see where we travelled today, Griessel? Did you see? Can you imagine what ten thousand warriors would look like coming over these hills? They smeared themselves red with ochre. Each had six or seven long throwing spears in his hand and a shield. They ran here like that. Nxele told them to be silent, no singing or shouting. They wanted to surprise the English here at Grahamstown. Ten thousand warriors in step, their footsteps the only sound. Through the valleys and over the rivers and hills like a long red snake. Imagine you are an Englishman in Grahamstown waking up one morning in April and looking up to the hills. One moment things look as they do every day, and the next moment this army materialises on the hilltops and you see the glint of seventy thousand spears, but there is no sound. Like death.

'Nxele moved through them. He told them to break one of their long spears over their knees. He said Mdalidiphu would turn the British bullets to water. They must charge the cannons and guns together and throw the long spears when they got close enough. And they could throw, those men. At a range of sixty metres they could launch a spear through the air and find the heart of an Englishman. When the last long spear had been thrown, they must hold the spear with the broken shaft. Nxele knew you couldn't use a long spear when you could see the whites of your enemy's eyes. Then you needed a weapon to stab open a path in front of you.

'They say it was a clear day. They said the English couldn't believe the way the Xhosa moved up there on the crest. Deathly quiet. But each knew exactly where his place in line was.

'Down below, the Redcoats erected their barriers. Up there, the red men waited for the signal. And when the whites sat down at their tables laid for midday dinner, they came down.

'From the time I first heard that story from my uncle I wanted to be with them, Griessel. They said that when the warriors charged, a terrible cry went up. They say that cry is in every soldier. When you are at war, when your blood is high in battle, then it comes out. It explodes from your throat and gives you the strength of an elephant and the speed of an antelope. They say every man is afraid until that moment, and then there is no more fear. Then you are pure fighter and nothing can stop you.

'All my life I wanted to be a part of them. I wanted to be there at the front. I wanted to throw my spears and keep the short assegai for last. I wanted to smell the gunpowder and the blood. They said the stream in town ran red with blood that day. I wanted to look an Englishman in the eyes and he must lift his bayonet and we must oppose each other as soldiers, each fighting for his cause. I wanted to make war with honour. If his blade was faster than mine, if his strength was greater, then so be it. Then I would die like a man. Like a warrior.'

He was quiet for a long time. A distance past the turnoff to Bushmans River Mouth he said: 'There is no honour any more. It makes no difference what Struggle you choose.'

Again silence descended on the car, but it felt to Thobela as if the character of the silence had changed.

'What happened, that day?' Griessel's voice came from the back.

Thobela smiled in the darkness. For many reasons.

'It was a tremendous battle. The English had cannon and guns. Shrapnel shells. A thousand Xhosa fell. Some of them they found days later, miles away, with bunches of grass pushed into their gaping wounds to stem the bleeding. But it was a close thing. There was time in the battle when the balance began to swing in favour of the Xhosa. The ranks of Nxele were too fast and too many, the English could not reload quickly enough. Time stood still. The battle was on a knife edge. Then the Redcoats got their miracle. His name was Boesak, can you believe it? He was a Khoi big-game hunter turned soldier. He was out on patrol with a hundred and thirty men and they came back, on that day. At just the right time for the English, when the British captain was ready to sound the retreat. Boesak and a hundred and thirty of the best marksmen in the country. And they aimed for the biggest warriors, the Xhosa who fought up front, who ran between the men and urged them on. The heart of the assault. They were shot down one by one, like bulls from the herd. And then it was all over.'

She tried to grind the pills in a flour sifter, but they were too hard.

She took the breadboard and a teaspoon and crushed the pills – some pieces shot over the floor and she began to panic. She used more pills, pressed. The teaspoon banged on the breadboard.

Would Carlos hear?

She wiped the yellow powder off the breadboard into a small dish she had set on one side. Was it fine enough?

She set the table. She couldn't find candles or candlesticks so she just put the place mats and cutlery on the table. She called Carlos to come to the table and then she brought out the food: fillet of beef stuffed with smoked oysters, baked potatoes and *petit pois*.

Carlos couldn't compliment her enough, although she knew the food wasn't that special. He was still buttering her up. 'You see, conchita, no crew. Just me and you. No problem.'

She said he must save room for dessert, pears in wine and cinnamon. And she was going to make him real Irish coffee and it was very important to her that he drink it because she had made it the way she had been taught, long ago when she worked for a caterer in Bloemfontein.

He said he would drink every drop and then they were going to make love, right here on the table.

Somewhere on the N2, fifty kilometres before Port Elizabeth, Griessel made him stop.

'Do you need a piss?'

'Yes.'

'Now's the time.'

When they had finished, standing four metres apart, the white man holding his organ in one hand and the pistol in the other, they went on their way.

At the outskirts of the city they stopped for petrol without getting out of the car.

When they passed the turnoff to Hankey and the road began to descend down to the Gamtoos Valley, Griessel spoke again: 'When I was young I played bass guitar. In a band.'

Thobela didn't know if he should respond.

'I thought that was what I wanted to do.

'Yesterday night I listened to music my son gave me. When it was finished I lay in the dark and I remembered something. I remembered the day I realised I would never be more than an average bass guitarist.

'I had finished school, it was December holidays and there was a battle of the bands at Green Point. We went to listen, the guys from my band and me. There was this bassist, short with snow-white hair in one or other of the rock bands that played other people's songs. Jissis, he was a magician. Standing stock-still, not moving his body in the slightest. He didn't even look at the neck, just stood there with closed eyes and his fingers flew and the sounds came out like a river. Then I realised where my place was. I saw someone who had been born for bass guitar. Fuck, I could tell we felt the same. The music did the same inside; it opened you up. But feeling and doing are not the same thing. That is the tragedy. You want to be like *that*, so fucking casually brilliant, but you don't have it in you.

'So I knew I would never be a real bass guitarist, but I wanted to be like that in something. That good. So . . . skilful. In something. I began to wonder how you found it. How did you start to search for the thing you were made for? What if there wasn't one? What if you were just an average fucker in everything? Born average and living your average life and then you fucking die and no one knows the difference.

'While I was searching I joined the police, because what I didn't know is that you know without knowing. Something deep in your head directs you to what you *can* do. But it took me a while.

Because I didn't think being a policeman was something you could feel, like music.

'Also, it doesn't happen just like that. You have to pay your dues, you have to learn, make your own mistakes. But one day you sit with a case file that makes no sense to any other fucker, and you read the statements and the notes and the reports and it all comes together. And you feel this thing inside. You hear the music of it, you pick up its rhythm deep inside you and you know this is what you were made for.'

Thobela heard the white man sigh. He wanted to tell him he understood.

'And then nothing can stop you,' said Griessel. 'Nobody. Except yourself.

'Everyone thinks you're good. They tell you. "Fuck it, Benny, you're the best. Jissis, pal, you're red hot." And you want to believe it, because you can see they are right, but there is this little voice inside you that says you are just a Parow Arrow who was never really good at anything. An average little guy. And sooner or later they will catch you out. One day they will expose you and the world will laugh because you thought you were something.

'So, before it happens, you have to expose yourself. Destroy yourself. Because if you do it yourself, then you at least have a sort of control over it.'

There was a noise behind, almost a laugh. 'Fucking tragic.'

44

He fell asleep at the table. She saw it coming. Carlos's tongue began to drag more and more. He switched over to Spanish, as if she understood every word.

He leaned heavily on his place mat, eyes struggling to focus on her.

The scene played out as if she had no part in it, as if it were happening in another space and time. He had a stupid smile on his face. He mumbled.

He lowered his head interminably slowly to the tabletop. He put his palms flat on the surface. He said one last, incomprehensible word and then his breath came deep and easy. She knew she couldn't leave him like that. If his body relaxed he would fall.

She rose and came around behind him. She put her hands under his arms, entwining the fingers of her hands with his. Lifted him. He was as heavy as lead, dead weight. He made a sound and gave her a fright, not knowing if he was deeply enough asleep. She stood like that, feeling she couldn't hold him. Then she dragged him, step by step, over to the big couch. She fell back into a sitting position with Carlos on top of her.

He spoke, clear as crystal. Her body jerked. She sat still a moment, realising he was not conscious. She rolled him over her with great effort, so that he lay skew on the couch. She squirmed out from under him and stood beside the couch, breath racing, perspiration sprung out on her skin, needing badly to sit to give her legs time to recover from their trembling.

She forced herself to continue. First she called a taxi, so they could arrive sooner; she didn't know how much time she would have.

She made sure the plastic container of pills was in her handbag. She took the dog and the syringe and went down the stairs to the garage.

The BMW was locked. She swore. Went up again. She couldn't find the keys. Panic overcame her and she was conscious of how her hands shook while she searched. Until she thought to look in Carlos's trouser pocket and there they were.

Back to the garage. She pressed the button on the key and the electronic beep was sudden and shrill in the bare space. She opened the door. She shoved the toy dog under the passenger seat. Taking the syringe, she put her thumb on the depressor and aimed the point at the backrest of the rear seat. Her hand shook badly. She made a noise of frustration and put her left hand on her right wrist to stabilise it. She must get this part right. She squeezed the syringe quickly and jerked it from right to left. The dark red jet hit the material. Fine drops spattered back onto her arms and face.

She inspected her handiwork. It didn't look right. It didn't look real.

Her heart thumped. There was nothing she could do. She climbed out looking back one last time. She had forgotten nothing. Shut the door.

There were still a couple of drops in the syringe. She must get them on the dress. And put the garment somewhere in his cupboard.

He weighed up the policeman's words. He assumed the man was trying to explain why he had become corrupt. Why he was doing what he was doing.

'How did they find you?' he asked later, beyond the turnoff to Humansdrop.

'Who?'

'Sangrenegra. How did you come to work for them?'

'I don't work for Sangrenegra.'

'Who do you work for, then?'

'I work for the SAPS.'

'Not at the moment.'

It took a while for Griessel to grasp what he had said. He repeated that ironic laugh. 'You think I'm crooked. You think that's what I meant when I said . . .'

'What else?'

'I drink, that's what I do. I booze my fucking life away. My wife and children and my job and myself. I never took a cent from anyone. I never needed to. Alcohol is efficient enough if you want to fuck yourself up.'

'Then why are we driving this way – why am I not in a cell in Port Elizabeth?'

It burst out and he heard the rage and the fear in the man's voice: 'Because they've got my daughter. The brother of Carlos Sangrenegra took my daughter. And if I don't deliver you to them, they will . . .'

Griessel said no more.

Thobela had all the pieces of the jigsaw now and he didn't like the picture they made.

'What is her name?'

'Carla.'

'How old is she?'

Griessel took a long time answering, as if he wanted to ponder the meaning of the conversation. 'Eighteen.'

He realised the white man had hope, and he knew he would have, too, if he were in the same position. Because there was nothing else you could do.

'I will help you,' he said.

'I don't need your help.'

'You do.'

Griessel did not respond.

'Do you really believe they will say, "Thank you very much, here is your daughter, you may leave"?'

Silence.

'It's your decision, policeman. I can help you. But it's your decision.'

*   *   *

Eleven minutes past seven in the morning he hammered on her door, as she knew he would. She opened up and he rushed in and grabbed her arm and shook her.

'Why you do that? Why?' The pressure of his fingers hurt her and she slapped him against the head with her left hand, as hard as she could.

'Bitch!' Carlos screamed and let go of her arm and hit her over the eye with his fist. She nearly fell, but regained her balance.

'You cunt,' she screamed as loud as she could and hit out at him with her fist. He jerked his head out of the way and smacked her on the ear with an open hand. It sounded like a cannon shot in her head. She hit back, this time striking his cheekbone with her fist.

'Bitch!' he shouted again in a shrill voice. He grabbed her hands and pulled her off her feet. The back of her head hit the carpet and for a moment she was dizzy. She blinked her eyes; he was on top of her now. 'Fucking bitch.' He slapped her against the head again. She got a hand loose and scratched at him.

He grabbed her wrist and glared at her. 'You like, bitch, Carlos see you like this.'

He pinned her down with both hands above her head. 'Now you will like even more,' he said and grabbed her nightie at the bosom and jerked. The garment tore.

'Are you going to fuck me good?' she said. 'Because it will be the first time, you cunt.'

He slapped her again and she tasted blood in her mouth.

'You can't fuck. You are the world's worst fuck!'

'Shut up, bitch!'

She spat at him, spat blood and saliva on his face and shirt. He grabbed her breast and squeezed until she shrieked in pain. 'You like that, whore? You like that?'

'Yes. At least I can feel you now.'

Squeezed again. She screamed.

'Why you drug me? Why? You steal my moneys! Why?'

'I drugged you because you are such a shit lover. That's why.'

'First, I will fuck you. Then we will find the moneys.'

'Help me!' she shouted.

He pressed a hand over her mouth.

'Shut the fuck-up.'

She bit the soft part of his palm. He yelled and hit out at her again. She jerked her head away, screaming with all her might. 'Help me, please, help me!'

One of her hands came free; she struggled and punched, scratched and screamed. A man's voice came from somewhere outside, or down the corridor, she couldn't be sure. 'What's going on?'

Carlos heard. He bumped her with both hands on her chest. He stood up. He was out of breath. There was a swelling on his cheek.

'I will come back,' he said.

'Promise me you will fuck me good, Carlos. Just promise me that, you shitless cunt.' She lay on the ground, naked, bleeding and gasping. 'Just once.'

'I will kill you,' he said and stumbled towards the door. Opened it. 'You take my moneys. I will kill you.' Then he was gone.

Beyond Plettenberg Bay he asked Griessel: 'Where must you take me?'

'I will know when we get to George. They will phone again.'

She examined herself in the mirror before calling the police. She was bleeding. The left side of her face was red. It had begun to swell. There was a cut over her eyes. There were dark red finger marks on her breasts.

It looked perfect.

She took her cell phone and sat down on the couch. She looked up the number she had saved in the phone yesterday. Her fingers worked precisely. She looked down at the phone. She was rock steady.

She dropped her head, trying to feel the pain, the humiliation, the anger, hate and fear. She took a deep breath and let it out tremulously. Only a single tear at first, then another and another. Until she was crying properly. Then she pressed the call button.

It rang seven times. 'South African Police Services, Caledon Square. How can we help you?'

The policeman's phone rang while they were stopped at yet another traffic light in Knysna.

Griessel spoke quietly, swallowing his words, and Thobela could not hear what he said. The conversation lasted less than a minute.

'They want us to keep driving,' he said at last.

'Where to?'

'Swellendam.'

'Is that where they are?'

'I don't know.'

'I need to stretch my legs.'

'Get out of town first.'

'Do you think I want to escape, Griessel? Do you think I will run away from this situation?'

'I think nothing.'

'They have your daughter because I killed Sangrenegra. It's my responsibility to fix it.'

'How can you do that?'

'We'll see.'

Griessel ruminated on that, then said, 'Stop when you like.'

Seventy kilometres on, on the long sweeping curves the N2 makes between George and Mossel Bay, something dropped onto the front seat beside Thobela. When he looked down, the assegai lay there. The blade was dull in the lights of the instrument panel.

45

First came police in uniform and she was hysterically crying and screaming: 'He's got my child, he's got my child!' They got the information out of her and tried to calm her down.

More policemen arrived. They sent for an ambulance for her. Suddenly her flat was full of people. She wept uncontrollably. A first-aid man was cleaning her face while a black detective questioned her. He introduced himself as Timothy Ngubane. He sat beside her and she told her story between sobs while he wrote in his notebook and said earnestly: 'We will find her, ma'am.' Then he called out orders and then there were fewer people around.

Later the two from Social Services arrived, and then a large man with a Western Province cap. He showed no sympathy. He asked her to repeat her story. He did not take notes. There came a moment in the conversation when she realised he didn't believe her. He had a way of looking at her with a faint smile that only lasted a moment. Her heart went cold. Why wouldn't he believe her?

When she had finished he stood up and said: 'I am going to leave two men here with you. Outside your door.'

She looked at him in inquiry.

'We don't want anything to happen to you, do we?'

'But didn't you arrest Carlos?'

'We did.' The faint smile again, like someone sharing a secret.

She wanted to phone Vanessa to hear how Sonia was and she wanted to get away from here. Away from all the people and the fuss, away from the gnawing tension, because it was not over yet.

Another detective. His hair was too long and ruffled. 'My name is Benny Griessel,' he said, and he held out his hand and she took it and looked into his eyes and looked away again because of the intensity in them. As if he saw everything. He took her out onto the balcony, and asked her questions in a gentle voice, with a compassion she wanted to embrace. But she couldn't look him in the eye.

They turned off the N2 and drove into Swellendam. There was a filling station deep in the town, past a museum and guesthouses and restaurants with small-town Afrikaans names, deserted at this late hour.

When Griessel got out Thobela saw the Z88 was not in his hand. He got out too. His legs were stiff and there were cramps in the muscles of his shoulders. He stretched his limbs, feeling the depth of his fatigue, his red, burning eyes.

Griessel had the Nissan filled up. Then he came to stand next to Thobela, not speaking, just looking at him. The white man looked rough. Shadows around the eyes, deep lines in his face.

'The night is too long,' he said to Griessel.

The detective nodded. 'It's nearly over.'

Thobela nodded back.

'I want you to know we got Khoza and Ramphele,' said Griessel.

'Where?'

'They were arrested yesterday evening in Midrand.'

'Why are you telling me this?'

'Because no matter what happens tonight, I will make sure they don't get away again.'

She lay on her bed and told herself she must suppress the urge to go and lie with the detective who was asleep on her couch, because it would be for all the wrong reasons.

Griessel's cell phone rang and he answered and said, 'Yes' and 'Yes' and 'Six kilometres' and 'Yes' and 'Okay'.

Then Thobela heard him say: 'I want to hear her voice.'

Silence on the street in Swellendam. 'Carla,' said Griessel. Thobela felt a hand squeeze his heart because of the awful emotion in the white man's voice when he said: 'Daddy is coming to fetch you, you hear? Daddy is coming.'

She needed to be held. She wanted him to hold her because she was afraid. Afraid of Carlos and of the detective in the rugby cap and afraid that the whole scheme was going to collapse in on her. Afraid that Griessel would see through her with those eyes of his, that he would expose her with that energy of his. It wasn't right, because she wanted to lie with him to make him blind.

She must not do that.

She got up.

'Infanta,' said Griessel. 'Six kilometres outside town the road to Infanta turns off. There will be a car there. They will drive behind us from there.'

They got back into the Nissan, Thobela in front and Griessel behind.

'Infanta,' he heard the man say, as if the name made no sense to him.

On the instrument panel the numbers of the LCD display of the clock glowed yellow. 03:41.

He drove out of town, back to the N2.

'Turn right. Towards Cape Town.'

Over a bridge. *Breede River*, the signboard read. Then he spotted the road sign. *Malgas. Infanta.*

'This one,' said Griessel.

He put the left indicator on. Gravel road. He saw the vehicle parked there, chunky in the lights of the Nissan. A Mitsubishi Pajero. Two men stood beside it. Each with a firearm, shading eyes from the headlights with their free hands. He stopped.

Only one man approached. Thobela wound his window down. The man did not look at him, but at Griessel. 'Is this the killer?'

'Yes.'

The man was clean-shaven, including his head. There was just a small tassel of hair below his lip. He looked at Thobela. 'You die tonight.'

Thobela looked back, into his eyes.

'You the father?' Shaven Head asked Griessel and he said: 'Yes.'
The man smirked. 'Your daughter has a nice little cunt.'

Griessel made a noise behind him and Thobela thought: not
now, don't do anything now.

Shaven Head laughed. Then he said: 'Hokay. You ride straight.
We will be somewhere behind you. First, we will look if you
brought some friends. Now go.'

They were in control, he realised. Didn't even look for weapons,
because they knew they held the trump card.

Thobela pulled away. He wondered what was going on in
Griessel's head.

The two detectives from Witness Protection were carrying shot-
guns when they came to collect her.

She packed a suitcase. They accompanied her down in the lift
and they all got in the car and drove away.

The house was in Boston, old and quite shabby, but the
windows had burglar proofing and there was a security gate at
the front door.

They showed her around the house. The master bedroom was
where she could 'make herself at home', there were groceries in the
kitchen, the bathroom had towels. There was television in the
sitting room and piles of magazines on the coffee table, old issues
of *Sports Illustrated*, *FHM* and a few copies of *Huisgenoot*.

'That's how they bring in the drugs,' said Griessel when they had
been on the gravel road for half an hour.

Thobela said nothing. His mind was on their destination. He
had seen the weapons of the two in the Pajero. New stuff, hand
carbines, he guessed they were Heckler & Koch, family of the G36.
Costly. Efficient.

'Infanta and Witsand. Every fucker with a ski boat goes there to
fish,' said Griessel. 'They are bringing the stuff in small boats.
Probably off ships . . .'

So that was how the detective was keeping his mind occupied.

He didn't want to think of his child. He didn't want to imagine what they had done to his daughter.

'Do you know how many there are?' asked Thobela.

'No.'

'You will want to reload your Z88.'

'I only fired one shot. In your house.'

'Every round will count, Griessel.'

She was in the sitting room when there was a knock on the door. The two detectives first looked through the peephole and then opened the series of locks on the front door.

She heard heavy steps and then the big man with the Western Province rugby cap stood there and he said: 'You and I must talk.'

He came to sit on the chair closest to her and the two Witness Protection detectives hung around in the doorway.

'Let's not make her nervous, chaps,' said Beukes.

Reluctantly, they retreated down the passage. She heard the back door open and close.

'Where is the money?' he asked when the house was quiet.

'*What* money?' Her pulse beat in her throat.

'You know what I'm talking about.'

'I don't.'

'Where is your daughter?'

'Ask Carlos.'

'Carlos is dead, you slut. And he never had your daughter. *You* know it and *I* know it.'

'How can you *say* that?' She began to weep.

'Save the fucking tears. They won't work on me. You should just be fucking grateful I was following him yesterday morning. If it had been one of the others . . .'

'I don't know what you're talking about . . .'

'Let me tell you what I'm talking about. The team that was on duty day before yesterday said you went to his house in his BMW. And in the middle of the fucking night you take a taxi from the front of his house and you have all these Pick and Pay bags and you're in a helluva hurry. What was in the bags?'

'I cooked dinner for him.'

'And took everything home again?'

'Just what I didn't use.'

'You're lying.'

'I swear.' She wept and the tears were genuine, because the fear was back.

'What I don't know is where you went with the fucking taxi. Because my fucking so-called colleagues didn't think to send someone after you. Because their job was to watch *him*. That's what you get when you work with the policeman of today. Fucking black rubbish. But yesterday was another story, because I was in the saddle, my dear. And Carlos drove out of there as if the devil was on his tail, straight to your little flat. Ten minutes later he comes out with this big red mark on his face, but there's no child anywhere. But the next minute the whole fucking radio is full of Sangrenegra and before I could do anything the Task Force was there and SVC and who knows what. But one thing I do know: your child was not with him. Not the night before last, and not yesterday morning. Of all the money in that strong room of his, there is a shithouse full of rands missing. Only rands. Now why, I ask myself, why of all the dollars and euros and pounds would someone only take South African rands? I guess it was an amateur. Someone who doesn't want to bother with foreign exchange. Someone who had time to think about what she wanted to steal. What she could use. That she could carry in Pick and Pay shopping bags.'

She realised something and without further thought she asked: 'How do you know there are rands missing?'

'Fuck you, whore. I'm telling you now; this thing is not over yet. Not for *you*, anyway.'

Griessel's cell phone rang. He answered and told Thobela: 'They say we must drive slower.'

He reduced speed. The Nissan rattled on the dirt road. Behind them the Pajero's headlights shone dim through the cloud of dust. The lights of Witsand twinkled on the Breede River off to the left.

'He says we must turn left at the road sign.'

He slowed even more, spotted the sign that said *Kabeljoubank*. He put on his indicator and turned. The road narrowed between two boundary fences. It ran down to the river. In the rear-view mirror he saw the Pajero was behind them.

'Are you calm?' Thobela asked the detective.

'Yes.'

He felt the fizz inside him, now that they were close.

In the headlights he saw three, four boats on trailers. And two vehicles. A minibus and a pick-up. Figures moving. He stopped a hundred metres away from the vehicles. He turned the key and the Nissan's engine fell silent. He deliberately kept the lights on.

'Get out and hide that pistol of yours,' he said, and picked up the assegai, pushed it down behind his neck, under his shirt. There was barely enough room in the car, the angle was too tight. He heard the blade tear the material of his shirt, felt the chill of the blade against his back. It would have to do. He opened the door and got out. Griessel stood on the other side of the Nissan.

Four men approached from the minibus – one was tall and broad, considerably bigger than the others. The Pajero pulled up behind them. Thobela stood beside the car, aware of the four in front, the two behind. He heard their footsteps on the gravel, smelt the dust and the river and the fish from the boats, heard the waves in the sea beyond. He felt the stiffness throughout his body, but the weariness was gone, his arteries were full of adrenaline. The world seemed to slow down, as if there were more time for thinking and doing.

The quartet came right up to him. The big one looked him up and down.

'You are the spearman,' he said as if he recognised him. He was as tall as Thobela, with long straight black hair down to his massive shoulders. He wasn't carrying a firearm. The others had machine pistols.

'Where is my daughter?' asked Griessel.

'I am the spearman,' said Thobela. He wanted to keep the attention; he didn't know how stable Griessel was.

'My name is César Sangrenegra. You killed my brother.'

'Yes. I killed your brother. You can have me. Let the girl and the policeman go.'

'No. We will have *justicia*.'

'No, you can—'

'Shut the fuck up, black man.' Spit sprayed from César's lips, the drops making shiny arcs in the light from the Nissan. '*Justicia*. You know what it means? He made the trap for Carlos, this policeman. Now I have to go back to my father and say I didn't kill him? That will not happen. I want you to know, policeman, before you die. I want you to know we fucked your daughter. We fucked her good. She is young. It was a sweet fuck. And after you are dead, we will fuck her again. And again. We will fuck her so long as she can be alive. You hear me?'

'I will kill you,' said Griessel, and Thobela could hear his breaking point was close.

He laughed at Griessel, shaking his head. 'You can do nothing. We have your kid. And we will find the white whore too. The one who tells lies about Carlos. The one who steals our money.'

'You are a coward,' Thobela said to César Sangrenegra. 'You are not a man.'

César laughed in his face. 'You want me to attack you? You want me to lose my temper?'

'I want you to lose your life.'

'You think I did not see the spear you put behind your back? You think I am stupid, like my brother?' He turned around, to one of his henchmen. '*Déme el cuchillo*.'

The man drew a knife from a long sheath on his hip. César took it from him.

'I will kill you slowly,' he said to Thobela. 'Now take out that spear.'

46

When Superintendent Boef Beukes had gone, she went to the bedroom where her things were.

She opened her handbag, took out her identity document and put it on the bed. She took out her purse, cigarettes and a lighter. She clipped the bag shut and lifted up her dress. She pushed the ID book and the purse down the front of her panties. She carried the cigarettes in her hand.

She walked to the front of the house and said: 'I'm going outside for a smoke.'

'At the back,' gestured the one with the moustache. 'We don't want you to go out the front.'

She nodded, went through the kitchen and out the back door. She closed it behind her.

There were fruit trees in the backyard. The grass was long. A concrete wall surrounded the property. She walked straight to the wall. She put her cigarettes on the ground and looked up at the wall. She drew a deep breath and jumped. Her hands gripped the top of the wall. She pulled herself up, swung one leg over. The top of the wall felt sharp against her knee.

She dragged her whole body up onto the wall. Beyond was another garden. Vegetables in tidy rows. She jumped, landing in the mud of a wet vegetable bed. She got up. One of her sandals stayed behind in the mud. She pulled it out and put it on again. She walked around the house to the front.

She heard the animal's paws on the cement path before it appeared around the corner. A big brown dog. The animal barked deeply and feinted back a little, as much in fright as she was. She kept her hands protectively in front of her. The dog stood square, growling, exposing big sharp teeth.

'Hello, doggy, hello,' she said.

They stood facing each other, the dog blocking her way around the house.

Don't look scared, she knew, she remembered that from some-where. She let her hands drop and stood up straight.

'Okay, doggy.' She tried to keep her tone caressing, while her heartbeat rocked her.

The animal growled again.

'Easy, boy, good dog.'

The dog shook his head and sneezed.

'I just want to come past, doggy, just want to come past.'

The hairs on the dog's neck dropped. The teeth disappeared. The tail gave one uncertain wag.

She took one step forward. The dog came closer, but didn't growl. She put out her hand to his head.

The tail wagged more vigorously. He pressed his head against her hand. The dog sneezed again.

She began to walk slowly, the dog following. She could see the front garden gate. She walked faster.

'Hey,' came a voice from the front veranda.

An old man stood there. 'Can I help you?' he asked.

'I'm just walking through,' she said, one hand on the gate. 'I'm just passing through.'

He reached for the assegai behind his neck and César Sangre-negra's movement was subtle and rapid and the long knife cut through Thobela's shirt and across his ribs, a sharp, red-hot pain. He felt the blood run down his belly.

He took a step back and saw the grin on the Colombian's face. He held the assegai in his right hand and bent his knees for better balance. He moved to the right, watching César's eyes; never watch the blade, there are no warnings there. César stabbed. Thobela jumped back and the knife flashed past in front. He stabbed with the assegai. César was no longer there. The knife came again. He jerked back his arm, the blade sliced over his forearm. Another step back. The man was fast. Light on his feet, ten kilograms lighter than he was. Moved again, this time to the left, César feinted right, moved left. Thobela dodged, up against the front of the Nissan, he must not be trapped against the car, three, four short steps to the right, the knife flashed so fast, it missed him by millimetres.

Thobela knew he was in trouble; the big man with the long hair was skilled. Faster than him. Lighter, younger. And he had another great advantage – he could kill, Thobela could not. Carla Griessel's life depended on him not killing César.

He must use the length of the assegai. He adjusted his grip, held it by the end of the shaft and swung it with a whooshing noise through the night, back and forth, back and forth. He felt the wound in his arm; saw an arc of blood spray as he swung. César moved back, but calmly. The henchman widened the circle. One made a remark in Spanish and the other four laughed.

The opponents looked into each other's eyes. The Colombian darted forward, the knife flashed, then he was back.

The man was toying with him. César was aware of his superior speed. Thobela would have to neutralise that. He would have to use his power, his weight, but against a knife that was impossible.

The Colombian's eyes betrayed his attack. Thobela pretended to move back, but came forward, he must keep the knife away, forward again, within the sweep of the knife arm, stabbed with the assegai. César grabbed at it, grasping the blade in his left hand and unexpectedly jerked it towards him, Thobela lost his balance. Saw the blood on César's hand where the assegai had cut deeply, here came the knife, jerked his own left hand up to block it, got hold of Cesar's arm, forced it back. César adjusted his grip on the assegai, getting his hand on the shaft.

They stood locked in that grip. The knife bowed down, the point entered Thobela's biceps, deep. The pain was intense. He would have to move his grip close to the wrist. Would have to do it swiftly and efficiently. He shifted suddenly; the knife cutting through his biceps saved him, because it kept the hand static for a split second.

He knew the injury was serious. He had César's wrist, all his strength behind it. His forearm shrieked. Brought up his knees, kicked César as hard as he could in the belly. Saw in his eyes it was a good contact.

Would have to finish now, in this moment of slight advantage. Pushed the knife hand back. His left arm would not last; the muscle was deeply cut. Shifted his point of balance, jerked the assegai free from the grasp, let it drop in the dust. Both hands on the knife-arm, bent it behind César's back. Lord, he was strong. Straining, he kicked him at the back of the knee and César began to fall; he twisted the arm the last centimetres and César made a sound. The henchmen called out. Swinging weapons from their shoulders, they moved too late. He twisted the arm until something popped and the knife came free from the fingers.

His right hand pressed César's arm against his back, the left hand had the knife, arm around the throat, pressing the point into the hollow of the neck. Deep. César screamed and jerked and struggled. Strong. Would have to neutralise that. Turned the arm another bit, until ligaments tore. César's knees buckled. He kept the man upright, as a shield in front of him.

He pressed the point of the knife deeper into the neck. Felt the blood run over his hand. He felt his own pain shrill in his arm. He didn't know how much blood he was losing. His entire left side was soaking, warm.

'You are very close to death,' he said softly into César's ear. The henchmen had carbines and machine pistols aimed at them.

The Colombian was frozen against him.

'If I move the knife, I will cut an artery,' he said. 'Do you hear me?'

A noise.

'Your men have to put down their weapons.'

No reaction. Was it going to work? He thought he understood the hierarchy of the drug industry. The autocracy.

'I will count to three. Then I cut.' He tightened the muscles of his arm as if in readiness but it didn't work so well. He knew there were sinews cut.

'One.'

César jerked again, but the arm was bent too far back, the pain must be dreadful.

'Two.'

'*Coloque sus armas*.' Practically inaudible.

'Louder.'

'*Coloque sus armas*.'

The henchmen did nothing, just stood there. Thobela began to move the knife point slowly, deeper into the throat.

'*¡Ahora!*'

The first one moved slowly, putting his weapon carefully down on the ground. Another one.

'No,' said one of the Pajero men, the one with the shaven head.

He stood beside Griessel, the Heckler & Koch against the detective's temple. 'I will shoot this one,' said Shaven Head.

'Shoot,' said Thobela.

'Let César go.'

'No.'

'Then I shoot this one.'

'Do I care? He is a policeman. I am a murderer.' He turned the knife in César's throat.

'*¡Ahora!*' The cry was hoarse and high and desperate and he knew the blade had scraped against something.

Shaven Head looked at César, back at Griessel and spat out a word. He threw the carbine in the dust.

'*Now*,' said Thobela in Afrikaans. 'Now you must get your daughter.'

At a stop sign in Eleventh Avenue she knocked on the window of a woman's Audi and said: 'Please, ma'am, I need your help.'

The woman looked her up and down, saw the mud on her legs and drove off.

'Fuck you!' Christine yelled after her.

She walked in the direction of Frans Conradie Avenue, looking back often. By now they must know she was gone. They must be looking for her.

At the traffic lights she looked left and right. There were shops across the street. If she could just get there. Unseen. She ran. A car braked and hooted at her. She kept on running. Oncoming traffic. She stood on the traffic island waiting. Then it was clear. Jogged across. The sandals were not made for this sort of thing.

Turned left, up the hill. Not far now. She was going to make it. She must phone Vanessa. No taxis. They would follow those up; know where she was dropped off. Vanessa would have to fetch her. Vanessa and Sonia. Take them to a station. Catch a train, anywhere. Get away. She could buy a car, in Beaufort West or George or wherever. She must just get away. Disappear.

Griessel crossed in front of him where he held César in an embrace. The policeman walked slowly, with empty hands. Thobela wondered where the pistol was. Wondered what the expression in the white man's eyes meant.

Griessel walked to the minibus.

He opened it. Thobela saw movement inside. He heard Griessel speak. Lean inwards. Saw two arms encircle Griessel's neck.

He looked at the henchmen. They stood still. Uneasy. Ready, their eyes on César.

He made sure of his grip on the Colombian. He didn't know whose blood was running over him. Looked back at the minibus. Griessel stood half in the minibus, his daughter's arms around him. He thought he heard the detective's voice.

'Griessel,' he said, because he didn't know how long he could hold out.

A henchman shuffled his feet.

'You must be quiet. I will cut this man's throat.'

The man looked at him with an unreadable expression.

'Shoot them,' said César, but the words came out with blood, unclear.

'Shut up, or I will kill you.'

'Shoot them.' More audible.

The henchmen inched closer. Shaven Head stepped towards his firearm.

'I will kill César *now*.' The pain in his upper arm reached new heights. There was a buzzing in his head. Where was the policeman? He looked quickly. Griessel stood there, with the Z88, and his daughter, hand in hand.

They all looked at Griessel. He shuffled up to the first henchman.

'Did he?' he asked his daughter.

She nodded. Griessel raised the pistol and fired. The man flew over backwards.

Father and daughter approached the next one. 'And he?'

She nodded. He aimed at the man's head and pulled the trigger. The second shot thundered through the night and the man fell. Shaven Head dived for his weapon. Thobela knew it would all happen now and he pulled the knife across César's throat and let him fall. He knew where the nearest machine pistol lay, threw his body that way, heard another shot. He kept his eyes on the firearm. Hit the gravel, stretched out, heard another shot. Got his finger on the steel. Dizzy, a lot of blood lost. His left arm wouldn't work. Rolled over. Couldn't see well in the lights of the Nissan. Tried to get up, but had no balance.

Got onto one knee.

Shaven Head was down. César lay. Three others as well. Griessel had the Z88 trained on the last one. Carla was close to Thobela now. He saw her face. He knew in that moment he would never forget it.

Her father turned to the last one.

'And this one?'

His daughter looked at the man and nodded her head.

PART FOUR
Carla

47

Beyond Calvinia he saw the clouds damming up against the mountains, the snow-white cumulus towers in late morning sun, the straight line they formed over the dry earth. He wanted to show Carla. He wanted to explain his theory of how the contours of the landscape created this weather.

She was asleep in the passenger seat.

He looked at her. He wondered if it was a dreamless sleep.

A huge plain opened up ahead of them. The road was as straight as an arrow, to Brandvlei – a pitch-black ribbon stretching to the point of invisibility.

He wondered when she would wake up, because she was missing everything.

The minister looked at the newspaper clipping. There was a photo of two people getting out of a helicopter. A man and a young woman. The man's hair was dark and untidy, with a hint of grey at the temples. A somewhat Slavic face, with a severe expression. His head was turned towards the young woman in concern.

There was a resemblance between them, a vague connection between brow and the line of the chin. Father and daughter, perhaps.

She was pretty, with an evenness of feature below her black hair. But there was something about the way she held her head, how she looked down. As if she were old and unattractive. Maybe the minister got the impression because the jacket over her shoulders was too big for her. Maybe he was influenced by the headline of the report.

ABDUCTION DRAMA ENDS IN BLOODBATH

John Afrika, Matt Joubert and Benny Griessel were sitting in the spacious office at Serious and Violent Crimes. Keyter came in and greeted them. They did not reciprocate.

'I am only going to ask you once, Jamie,' said Griessel, and his voice was quiet but it carried across the room. 'Was it you?'

Keyter looked back at them, nervously from one to the next.

'Uh . . . um . . . What are you talking about, Benny?'

'Did you give Sangrenegra the information?'

'Jesus, Benny . . .'

'Did you?'

'No. Never.'

'Where do you get the money, Jamie? For the clothes. And that expensive cell phone of yours? Where does the money come from?' Griessel had risen halfway from his chair.

'Benny,' said John Afrika, his voice soothing.

'I . . .' said Jamie Keyter.

'Jamie,' said Joubert. 'It's better if you talk.'

'It's not what you think,' he said and his voice shook.

'What is it?' asked Griessel, forcing himself to sit.

'I moonlight, Benny.'

'You moonlight?'

'Modelling.'

'Modelling?' said John Afrika.

'For TV ads.'

No one said a word.

'For the French. And the Germans. But I swear, I'm finished with that.'

'Can you prove it, Jamie?'

'Yes, Sup. I have the videos. Ads for coffee and cheese spread. And clothes. I did one for the Swedes for milk, I had to take my shirt off, but that's all, Sup, I swear . . .'

'TV ads,' said John Afrika.

'Jissis,' said Griessel.

'Was this about my clothes, Benny? Did you suspect me just because of my *clothes*?'

'There was a fax, Jamie. It was sent from here. From SVC's fax machine. With Mpayipheli's photo.'

'It could have been anyone.'

'You were the dresser, Jamie.'

'But it wasn't me.'

Silence settled over the room.

'You may go, Jamie,' said Joubert.

The detective constable dallied. 'I thought, Benny . . .'

They looked at him impatiently.

'I thought about how they got your daughter's address. And your cell phone number. All that stuff . . .'

'What are you trying to say?'

'They must have phoned him. Carlos's brother. Not just sent faxes.'

'Yes?'

'He must have had a cell phone, Commissioner. The brother. And you get missed calls and received calls and dialled numbers.'

It took them a while to grasp what he meant.

'Fuck,' said Griessel and got up.

'Sorry, Benny,' said Keyter and ducked, but Griessel was already past him, heading for the door.

By 12:30 they had reached Brandvlei and he decided to stop at a café with a concrete table under a thatched roof. Coloured children played barefoot in the dust.

Carla woke up and asked him where they were. Griessel told her. She looked at the café.

'Do you want to eat something?'

'Not really.'

'Let's have something to drink.'

'Okay.'

He got out and waited for her. It was boiling hot outside the car. She put on trainers before getting out, stretched and came around the car. She was wearing a short-sleeved blouse and bleached jeans. His lovely daughter. They sat at one of the concrete tables. It was slightly cooler under the thatch.

He saw her watching the coloured children with their wire cars. He wondered what she was thinking.

'How far is it to Upington still?'

'About a hundred and fifty to Kenhardt, another seventy to Keimoes and then maybe fifty to Upington. Just under three hundred,' he quickly added up.

A coloured woman brought them single-page menus. At the top of the white laminated page was printed *Oasis Café*. There was an amateurish palm tree alongside the words. Carla ordered a white Grapetiser. Griessel said: 'Make that two.'

As the woman walked away he said, 'I've never had Grapetiser before.'

'Never?'

'If it didn't go with brandy, I wasn't interested.'

She smiled, but it didn't extend further than the corners of her mouth.

'This is another universe, here,' she said and looked up the main street.

'It is.'

'Do you think you will find something in Upington?'

'Perhaps.'

'But why, Dad? What's the use?'

He made a gesture with his hand that said he didn't know himself. 'I don't know, Carla. It's the way I am. That's why I am a detective. I want to know the reasons. And the facts. I want to understand. Even if it won't necessarily make a difference. Loose ends . . . I don't like them.'

'Weird,' she said. She put out her hand to him and wiggled her fingers under his. 'But wonderful.'

He called the numbers on César Sangrenegra's received calls list on the speakerphone in Joubert's office. With the first three he got voice mailboxes in Spanish. The fourth rang and rang and rang. Eventually it switched over to a cell phone messaging service.

'Hello, this is Bushy. When I've caught the crooks, I will phone you back.'

'I won't go to hell for Carlos,' said Christine. 'Because I saw the look in his eyes when he saw Sonia. And I know God will forgive me for being a sex worker. And I know he will understand that I had to draw the blood. And take the money.' She looked at the minister. He didn't want to assent to that.

'But He punished everyone for Carla Griessel.' She opened the second newspaper clipping. The headline read: MASSIVE COP CORRUPTION SCANDAL.

'Carlos's brother and his bodyguards. The Artemis man. All dead. And these policemen are going to jail,' she said, and tapped the two photos with the report. 'But what about me?'

'I didn't even know them,' said Bushy Bezuidenhout.

'But you gave them the information,' said Joubert.

'For money, you piece of shit,' said Griessel.

Joubert put his big hand soothingly on the inspector's arm.

Bezuidenhout wiped the perspiration from his forehead and shook his head. 'I'm not going down alone for this.'

'Give us the others, Bushy. You know, if you cooperate . . .'

'Jissis, Sup.'

'Give me five minutes alone with this cunt,' said Griessel.

'Jissis, Benny, I didn't know what they were going to do. I didn't know. Do you think I would—?'

Griessel shouted him down. 'Who, Bushy? Tell me who!'

'Beukes, fuck it. Beukes with his bloody cap brought me this shitload of money in a fucking brown envelope . . .'

Matt Joubert's voice was sharp in the room. 'Benny, no. Sit. I will not let you go.'

Fourteen kilometres beyond Keimoes he saw the sign and turned right to Kanoneiland. They crossed the river that flowed peaceful and brown under the bridge, and between green vineyards heavy with giant bunches of grapes.

'Amazing,' said Carla, and he knew what she meant. This fertility here, the surprise of it. But he was also aware that she was observing, that she was less turned in on herself, and it gave him hope again.

They drove up the long avenue of pines to the guesthouse and Carla said, 'Look,' and pointed a finger at his side of the road. Between the trees he could see the horses: big Arabians, three bays and a magnificent grey.

When Christine van Rooyen walked down the street in Reddersburg, the sun came up over the Free State horizon, a giant balloon breaking loose from the hills and sweeping over the grassland.

She turned off the main street, down an unpaved street, past houses that were still dark and silent.

She looked intently at one of them. The babysitter said a writer lived here, a man hiding away from the world.

It was a good place for it.

The secretary at the high school shook her head and said she had only worked here for three years. But he could ask Mr Losper. Mr Losper had been at the school for years. He taught Biology. But it was holidays now; Mr Losper would be at home. She gave him precise directions and he drove there and knocked on the door.

Losper was somewhere in his fifties, a man with smoker's wrinkles and rough voice who invited him in, since it was cooler in the dining room. Would he like a beer? He said no thanks, he was fine.

When they were seated at the dining-room table and he asked his question, the man shut his eyes for a moment, as if sending up a quick prayer to heaven, and then he said, 'Christine van Rooyen.' Solemnly, he put his arms on the table and folded his hands together.

'Christine van Rooyen,' he repeated, as if the repetition of the name would open up his memory.

Then he told Griessel the story, regularly inserting admissions of guilt and rationalisation. Of Martie van Rooyen who lost her soldier husband in Angola. Martie van Rooyen, the blonde woman with the big bosom and the small blonde daughter. A woman the community gossiped about even when her husband was still alive. Rumours of visits when Rooies was away on training courses, or on the Border.

And after Rooies' death there was very soon a replacement. And another. And another. She lured them home from the ladies' bar at the River Hotel with red lipstick and a low neckline. While the child wandered around the yard with a stuffed dog in her arms, an object that later became so filthy it was scandalous.

The gossipmongers said the substitute for Rooies used to hit Martie. And sometimes played around with more than just the mother. But in Upington, many watch but few act. Social Welfare tried to step in, but the mother sent them packing and Christine van Rooyen grew up like that. Sad and wild. Earned a reputation of her own. Loose. Easy. There was talk when the girl was a teenager. About an old friend of her father's who . . . you know. And an Afrikaans teacher. There were goings-on at the school. The child was difficult. Smoking and drinking with the rough crowd, the school had always had one, it was a funny town, this, with the Army and all.

Losper had heard the story that when Christine had finished school she walked out of the house with a suitcase while her mother was in bed with a substitute. Went to Bloemfontein, apparently, but he didn't know what became of her.

'And the mother?'

She had also left, he had heard. With a man in a pick-up. Cape Town. Or the West Coast: there were so many stories.

She walked past. Three houses down she turned in at a garden gate that creaked on opening. It needed oiling.

The garden was overgrown with weeds. She took the box and put it down on the veranda. It was light now.

In the minister's study she had pulled it towards her one last time and taken out the cash. Four hundred thousand rand in one-hundred-rand notes.

'This is a tenth,' she said.

'You can't buy the Lord's forgiveness,' he had answered wearily, but couldn't keep his eyes off the money.

'I don't want to buy anything. I just want to give. It's for the Church.'

She had waited for his response and then he walked her to the door and she could smell the odour of his body behind her, the smell of a man after a long day.

She came back off the veranda and stooped to pull out a weed. The roots came free of the reddish soil and she thought it looked fertile here.

She went over to the steps. She reached for the sign to the right of them, the one that said *Te Koop/For Sale*. She pulled. It had been hammered in deep and had been there a long time. She had to wiggle it back and forth before it slowly began to shift and eventually came out.

She carried it up, put it down on the veranda. Then she took her keys out and quietly unlocked the door. On the new couch the large black babysitter was reclining. She was fast asleep.

Christine went down the passage to the master bedroom. Sonia lay there in a foetal position, her whole body curled around the toy dog. She lay down gently beside her daughter. Later, when they had finished breakfast, she would ask Sonia if she would like to exchange the stuffed animal for a real one.

Griessel thought about Senior Superintendent Beukes as he drove back to the guesthouse. Three weeks ago, they confronted him.

They would not allow him to be present at the interrogation – Joubert had put his foot down. He had to sit with the disillusioned American, Lombardi. Tried to explain to him that not *all* the police in Africa were corrupt. But afterwards Joubert came to tell him. Beukes would admit nothing. Right till the end when they got his bank statements through a court order and spread them out in front of him. And Beukes had said, 'Why don't you try and find the whore? She's the one who stole money. And lied about her daughter.'

He didn't know whether it was true or not. But now, after Losper's story, he hoped it was. Because he recalled the words of the forensic psychologist. *Women are different. When there is damage at a young age, they don't do to others. They do to themselves.*

He only hoped she used the money well. For herself and her daughter.

His cell phone rang while he was driving up the avenue of pine trees. He pulled over.

'Griessel.'

'This is Inspector Johnson Mtetwa. I am phoning from Alice. I wonder if you could help me?'

'Yes, Inspector.'

'It's about the death of Thobela Mpayipheli . . .'

'Yes?'

'The trouble is, I had some people here. The missionary priest from the Knott Memorial between us and Peddie.'

'Yes?'

'He told me the strangest thing, Inspector Griessel. He said he saw Mpayipheli, yesterday morning.'

'How strange.'

'He said he saw a man walking, from the Kat River hills to near the manse. He went out to see who it might be. When he came close, the man turned away. But he could swear it was Mpayipheli, because he knew him. In the old days. You see, Mpayipheli's father was also a missionary.'

'I see.'

'I went out with the people from Cathcart station to Mpayipheli's farm. They have to deal with things there. And now they tell me there is a motorbike missing. A . . . Hang on. . . . A BMW R eleven-fifty GS.'

'Oh?'

'But the people in the Cape say you were a witness to his death.'

'You must request the file, Inspector. They did search the river for his body . . .'

'Strange,' said Mtetwa, 'that someone would steal only the motorbike.'

'That's life,' said Griessel. 'Strange.'

'That's true. Thank you, Inspector. And good luck there in the Cape.'

'Thank you.'

'Thank *you*.'

Benny Griessel put the cell phone back in his breast pocket. He put his hand out to the ignition key but, before starting the car, he saw something that made him wait.

Between the trees, there in the horse paddock, Carla stood by a large grey. She was leaning against the magnificent beast, her face in the horse's mane, her hand gently stroking the long muzzle.

He got out of the car and went over to the fence rail. He had eyes only for her, and a tenderness that might just overwhelm him.

His child.

ACKNOWLEDGEMENTS

More than any of my previous books, *Devil's Peak* is to a great extent the product of the astounding goodwill, unselfishness, readiness to share knowledge – and unconditional support of a large number of people.

I wish to thank them:

Even now I don't know her real name, but as a sex worker she went by the name of 'Vanessa'. In two long morning interviews she talked intelligently, openly and honestly about her work and life. When I had finished the book, I tried to contact her to thank her. The message on her cell phone said 'I am no longer in the business . . .' May all her dreams be realised.

The three other nameless sex workers who made time to talk to me in coffee shops and tell me their stories.

The personnel of Sex Worker Education and Advocacy Taskforce (SWEAT) in Cape Town, and specifically the director, Ms Jayne Arnott.

Ms Ilse Pauw, a clinical psychologist, who shared hours of her knowledge of and insight into sex workers.

Captain Elmarie Myburgh of the South African Police Service's Psychological Investigation Unit in Pretoria. Her incredible insight, experience and knowledge of the psychology of people in general and specifically crime and criminals, her enthusiasm for the project and many hours of patience left me deeply in her debt. She is any author's research dream and a wonderful ambassador for her unit and the SAPS.

Inspector Riaan Pool, SAPS Liaison Officer in Cape Town.

Superintendent Mike Barkhuizen of the SAPS Serious and Violent Crimes Unit in Cape Town.

Gerhard Groenewald of Klipbokkop, for his knowledge of tyres.

Dr Julie Wells of Rhodes University History Department, for the background of the Xhosa stabbing assegai.

All the wonderful curio-shop people of Cape Town city centre who provided information on assegais so freely, even when they knew I did not wish to buy.

Professor Marlene van Niekerk of the Department Afrikaans and Nederlands of the University of Stellenbosch, for her compassion, understanding, patience, great knowledge, intellect and creativity. She is a national treasure, in every sense of the word.

All the members (the veterans and the young ones!) of the US MA class in Creative Writing. That dinner is coming . . .

My editor, Dr Etienne Bloemhof, for his eagle eye, his enthusiasm, support and depth of knowledge.

My agent Isobel Dixon, to whom I owe so much – and all her colleagues at Blake Friedmann, especially David Eddy and Julian Friedmann.

My wife, Anita, who gets up and has coffee with me before dawn and never stops supporting and believing and reading and loving. And the children who wait so patiently for the writing door to open.

The ATKV, for the financial support that made so much of the research possible.

One of the great joys of researching a manuscript is finding and reading relevant books – and hunting down relevant information on the Internet. I am grateful for the following:

Smokescreen by Robert Sabbag, Canongate, London, 2002.

Killing Pablo by Mark Bowden, Atlantic Books, London, 2002.

With Criminal Intent, Rob Marsh, Ampersand Press, Cape Town, 1999.

Frontiers by Noel Mostert, Pimlico, London, 1992.

www.alcoholicsanonymous.org.au

www.alcoholics-anonymous.org.uk

www.fda.gov

www.digitalnaturopath.com
www.heckler-koch.de
www.dieburger.com
www.iol.com

Translated by K. L. Seegers, October 2005